TEX

MW01114549

# Mark Twain's Best Short Stories

By
Mark Twain
(Samuel L. Clemens)

Piccadilly Books, Ltd.
Colorado Springs, CO

**Piccadilly Books, Ltd.**
**P.O. Box 25203**
**Colorado Springs, CO 80936, USA**
**info@piccadillybooks.com**
**www.piccadillybooks.com**

ISBN 10: 1-936709-22-8
ISBN 13: 978-1-936709-22-9

Published in the USA

# CONTENTS

Mark Twain

# HOW TO TELL A STORY

*The Humorous Story an American Development.—Its Difference from*
*Comic and Witty Stories.*

I do not claim that I can tell a story as it ought to be told. I only claim to know how a story ought to be told, for I have been almost daily in the company of the most expert story-tellers for many years.

There are several kinds of stories, but only one difficult kind—the humorous. I will talk mainly about that one. The humorous story is American, the comic story is English, the witty story is French. The humorous story depends for its effect upon the manner of the telling; the comic story and the witty story upon the matter.

The humorous story may be spun out to great length, and may wander around as much as it pleases, and arrive nowhere in particular; but the comic and witty stories must be brief and end with a point. The humorous story bubbles gently along, the others burst.

The humorous story is strictly a work of art—high and delicate art—and only an artist can tell it; but no art is necessary in telling the comic and the witty story; anybody can do it. The art of telling a humorous story—understand, I mean by word of mouth, not print—was created in America, and has remained at home.

The humorous story is told gravely; the teller does his best to conceal the fact that he even dimly suspects that there is anything funny about it; but the teller of the comic story tells you beforehand that it is one of the funniest things he has ever heard, then tells it with eager delight, and is the first person to laugh when he gets through. And sometimes, if he has had good success, he is so glad and happy that he will repeat the "nub" of it and glance around from face to face, collecting applause, and then repeat it again. It is a pathetic thing to see.

Very often, of course, the rambling and disjointed humorous story finishes with a nub, point, snapper, or whatever you like to call it. Then the listener must be alert, for in many cases the teller will divert attention from that nub by dropping it in a carefully casual and indifferent way, with the pretence that he does not know it is a nub.

Artemus Ward used that trick a good deal; then when the belated audience presently caught the joke he would look up with innocent surprise, as if wondering what they had found to laugh at. Dan Setchell used it before him, Nye and Riley and others use it to-day.

But the teller of the comic story does not slur the nub; he shouts it at you—every time. And when he prints it, in England, France, Germany, and Italy, he italicizes it, puts some whooping exclamation-points after it, and sometimes explains it in a parenthesis. All of which is very depressing, and makes one want to renounce joking and lead a better life.

Let me set down an instance of the comic method, using an anecdote which has been popular all over the world for twelve or fifteen hundred years. The teller tells it in this way:

### THE WOUNDED SOLDIER

In the course of a certain battle a soldier whose leg had been shot off appealed to another soldier who was hurrying by to carry him to the rear, informing him at the same time of the loss which he had sustained; whereupon the generous son of Mars, shouldering the unfortunate, proceeded to carry out his desire. The bullets and cannon-balls were flying in all directions, and presently one of the latter took the wounded man's head off—without, however, his deliverer being aware of it. In no-long time he was hailed by an officer, who said:

"Where are you going with that carcass?"

"To the rear, sir—he's lost his leg!"

"His leg, forsooth?" responded the astonished officer; "you mean his head, you booby."

Whereupon the soldier dispossessed himself of his burden, and stood looking down upon it in great perplexity. At length he said:

"It is true, sir, just as you have said." Then after a pause he added, "But he TOLD me IT WAS HIS LEG—"

Here the narrator bursts into explosion after explosion of thunderous horse-laughter, repeating that nub from time to time through his gaspings and shriekings and suffocatings.

It takes only a minute and a half to tell that in its comic-story form; and isn't worth the telling, after all. Put into the humorous-story form it takes ten minutes, and is about the funniest thing I have ever listened to—as James Whitcomb Riley tells it.

He tells it in the character of a dull-witted old farmer who has just heard it for the first time, thinks it is unspeakably funny, and is trying to repeat it to a neighbor. But he can't remember it; so he gets all mixed up and wanders helplessly round and round, putting in tedious details that don't belong in the tale and only retard it; taking them out conscientiously and putting in others that are just as useless; making minor mistakes now and then and stopping to correct them and explain how he came to make them; remembering things which he forgot to put in in their proper place and going back to put them in there; stopping his narrative a good while in order to try to recall the name of the soldier that was hurt, and finally remembering that the soldier's name was not mentioned, and remarking placidly that the name is of no real importance, anyway—better, of course, if one knew it, but not essential, after all—and so on, and so on, and so on.

The teller is innocent and happy and pleased with himself, and has to stop every little while to hold himself in and keep from laughing outright; and does hold in, but his body quakes in a jelly-like way with interior chuckles; and at the end of the ten minutes the audience have laughed until they are exhausted, and the tears are running down their faces.

The simplicity and innocence and sincerity and unconsciousness of the old farmer are perfectly simulated, and the result is a performance which is thoroughly charming and delicious. This is art and fine and beautiful, and only a master can compass it; but a machine could tell the other story.

To string incongruities and absurdities together in a wandering and sometimes purposeless way, and seem innocently unaware that they are absurdities, is the basis of the American art, if my position is correct. Another feature is the slurring of the point. A third is the dropping of a studied remark apparently without knowing it, as if one were thinking aloud. The fourth and last is the pause.

Artemus Ward dealt in numbers three and four a good deal. He would begin to tell with great animation something which he seemed to think was wonderful; then lose confidence, and after an apparently absent-minded pause add an incongruous remark in a soliloquizing way; and that was the remark intended to explode the mine—and it did.

For instance, he would say eagerly, excitedly, "I once knew a man in New Zealand who hadn't a tooth in his head"—here his animation would die out; a silent, reflective pause would follow, then he would say dreamily, and as if to himself, "and yet that man could beat a drum better than any man I ever saw."

The pause is an exceedingly important feature in any kind of story, and a frequently recurring feature, too. It is a dainty thing, and delicate, and also uncertain and treacherous; for it must be exactly the right length—no more and no less—or it fails of its purpose and makes trouble. If the pause is too short the impressive point is passed, and [and if too long] the audience have had time to divine that a surprise is intended—and then you can't surprise them, of course.

On the platform I used to tell a negro ghost story that had a pause in front of the snapper on the end, and that pause was the most important thing in the whole story. If I got it the right length precisely, I could spring the finishing ejaculation with effect enough to make some impressible girl deliver a startled little yelp and jump out of her seat—and that was what I was after. This story was called "The Golden Arm," and was told in this fashion. You can practise with it yourself—and mind you look out for the pause and get it right.

## THE GOLDEN ARM

Once 'pon a time dey wuz a monsus mean man, en he live 'way out in de prairie all 'lone by hisself, 'cep'n he had a wife. En bimeby she died, en he tuck en toted her way out dah in de prairie en buried her. Well, she had a golden arm—all solid gold, fum de shoulder down. He wuz pow'ful mean—pow'ful; en dat night he couldn't sleep, Gaze he want dat golden arm so bad.

When it come midnight he couldn't stan' it no mo'; so he git up, he did, en tuck his lantern en shoved out thoo de storm en dug her up en got de golden arm; en he bent his head down 'gin de win', en plowed en plowed en plowed thoo de snow. Den all on a sudden he stop (make a considerable pause here, and look startled, and take a listening attitude) en say: "My LAN', what's dat!"

En he listen—en listen—en de win' say (set your teeth together and imitate the wailing and wheezing singsong of the wind), "Bzzz-z-zzz"—en den, way back yonder whah de grave is, he hear a voice! he hear a voice all mix' up in de win' can't hardly tell 'em 'part— "Bzzz-zzz—W-h-o—g-o-t—m-y—g-o-l-d-e-n arm?—zzz—zzz—W-h-o g-o-t m-y g-o-l-d-e-n arm!" (You must begin to shiver violently now.)

En he begin to shiver en shake, en say, "Oh, my! OH, my lan'!" en de win' blow de lantern out, en de snow en sleet blow in his face en mos' choke him, en he start a-plowin' knee-deep towards home mos' dead, he so sk'yerd—en pooty soon he hear de voice agin, en (pause) it 'us comin' after him! "Bzzz—zzz—zzz—W-h-o—g-o-t m-y—g-o-l-d-e-n—arm?"

When he git to de pasture he hear it agin closter now, en a-comin'!—a-comin' back dah in de dark en de storm—(repeat the wind and the voice). When he git to de house he rush up-stairs en jump in de bed en kiver up, head and years, en lay dah shiverin' en shakin'—en den way out dah he hear it agin!—en a-comin'! En bimeby he hear (pause—awed, listening attitude)—pat—pat—pat—hit's acomin' up-stairs! Den he hear de latch, en he know it's in de room!

Den pooty soon he know it's a-stannin' by de bed! (Pause.) Den—he know it's a-bendin' down over him—en he cain't skasely git his breath! Den—den—he seem to feel someth'n c-o-l-d, right down 'most agin his head! (Pause.)

Den de voice say, right at his year— "W-h-o g-o-t—m-y—g-o-l-d-e-n arm?" (You must wail it out very plaintively and accusingly; then you stare steadily and impressively into the face of the farthest-gone auditor—a girl, preferably—and let that awe-inspiring pause begin to build itself in the deep hush. When it has reached exactly the right length, jump suddenly at that girl and yell, "You've got it!")

If you've got the pause right, she'll fetch a dear little yelp and spring right out of her shoes. But you must get the pause right; and you will find it the most troublesome and aggravating and uncertain thing you ever undertook.

# THE INVALID'S STORY

I seem sixty and married, but these effects are due to my condition and sufferings, for I am a bachelor, and only forty-one. It will be hard for you to believe that I, who am now but a shadow, was a hale, hearty man two short years ago, a man of iron, a very athlete!—yet such is the simple truth. But stranger still than this fact is the way in which I lost my health. I lost it through helping to take care of a box of guns on a two-hundred-mile railway journey one winter's night. It is the actual truth, and I will tell you about it.

I belong in Cleveland, Ohio. One winter's night, two years ago, I reached home just after dark, in a driving snow-storm, and the first thing I heard when I entered the house was that my dearest boyhood friend and schoolmate, John B. Hackett, had died the day before, and that his last utterance had been a desire that I would take his remains home to his poor old father and mother in Wisconsin. I was greatly shocked and grieved, but there was no time to waste in emotions; I must start at once. I took the card, marked "Deacon Levi Hackett, Bethlehem, Wisconsin," and hurried off through the whistling storm to the railway station. Arrived there I found the long white-pine box which had been described to me; I fastened the card to it with some tacks, saw it put safely aboard the express car, and then ran into the eating-room to provide myself with a sandwich and some cigars. When I returned, presently, there was my coffin-box back again, apparently, and a young fellow examining around it, with a card in his hands, and some tacks and a hammer! I was astonished and puzzled. He began to nail on his card, and I rushed out to the express car, in a good deal of a state of mind, to ask for an explanation. But no—there was my box, all right, in the express car; it hadn't been disturbed. [The fact is that without my suspecting it a prodigious mistake had been made. I was carrying off a box of guns which that young fellow had come to the station to ship to a rifle company in Peoria, Illinois, and he had got my corpse!] Just then the conductor sung out "All aboard," and I jumped into the express car and got a comfortable seat on a bale of buckets. The expressman was there, hard at work—a plain man of fifty, with a simple, honest, good-natured face, and a breezy, practical heartiness in his general style. As the train moved off a stranger skipped into the car and set a package of peculiarly mature and capable Limburger cheese on one end of my coffin-box—I mean my box of guns. That is to say, I know now that it was Limburger cheese, but at that time I never had heard of the article in my life, and of course was wholly ignorant of its character. Well, we sped through the wild night, the bitter storm raged on, a cheerless misery stole over me, my heart went down, down, down! The old expressman made a brisk remark or two about the tempest and the arctic weather, slammed his sliding doors to, and bolted them, closed his window down tight, and then went bustling around, here and there and yonder, setting things to rights, and all the time contentedly humming "Sweet By and By," in a low tone, and flatting a good deal. Presently I began to detect a most evil and searching odor stealing about on the frozen air. This depressed my spirits still more, because of course I attributed it to my poor departed friend. There was something infinitely saddening about his calling himself to my remembrance in this dumb pathetic way, so it was hard to keep the tears back. Moreover, it distressed me on account of the old expressman, who, I was afraid, might notice it. However, he went humming tranquilly on, and gave no sign; and for this I was grateful. Grateful, yes, but still uneasy; and soon I began to feel more and more uneasy every minute, for every minute that went by that odor thickened up the more, and got to be more and more gamey and hard to stand. Presently, having got things arranged to his satisfaction, the expressman got some wood and made up a tremendous fire in his stove.

This distressed me more than I can tell, for I could not but feel that it was a mistake. I was sure that the effect would be deleterious upon my poor departed friend. Thompson—the expressman's name was Thompson, as I found out in the course of the night—now went poking around his car, stopping up whatever stray cracks he could find, remarking that it didn't make any difference what kind of a night it was outside, he calculated to make us comfortable, anyway. I said nothing, but I believed he was not choosing the right way. Meantime he was humming to himself just as before; and meantime, too, the stove was getting hotter and hotter, and the place closer and closer. I felt myself growing pale and qualmish, but grieved in silence and said nothing.

Soon I noticed that the "Sweet By and By" was gradually fading out; next it ceased altogether, and there was an ominous stillness. After a few moments Thompson said,

"Pfew! I reckon it ain't no cinnamon 't I've loaded up thish-yer stove with!"

He gasped once or twice, then moved toward the cof—gun-box, stood over that Limburger cheese part of a moment, then came back and sat down near me, looking a good deal impressed. After a contemplative pause, he said, indicating the box with a gesture,

"Friend of yourn?"

"Yes," I said with a sigh.

"He's pretty ripe, ain't he!"

Nothing further was said for perhaps a couple of minutes, each being busy with his own thoughts; then Thompson said, in a low, awed voice,

"Sometimes it's uncertain whether they're really gone or not—seem gone, you know—body warm, joints limber—and so, although you think they're gone, you don't really know. I've had cases in my car. It's perfectly awful, becuz you don't know what minute they'll rise up and look at you!" Then, after a pause, and slightly lifting his elbow toward the box— "But he ain't in no trance! No, sir, I go bail for him!"

We sat some time, in meditative silence, listening to the wind and the roar of the train; then Thompson said, with a good deal of feeling,

"Well-a-well, we've all got to go, they ain't no getting around it. Man that is born of woman is of few days and far between, as Scriptur' says. Yes, you look at it any way you want to, it's awful solemn and cur'us: they ain't nobody can get around it; all's got to go—just everybody, as you may say. One day you're hearty and strong"—here he scrambled to his feet and broke a pane and stretched his nose out at it a moment or two, then sat down again while I struggled up and thrust my nose out at the same place, and this we kept on doing every now and then—" and next day he's cut down like the grass, and the places which knowed him then knows him no more forever, as Scriptur' says. Yes'ndeedy, it's awful solemn and cur'us; but we've all got to go, one time or another; they ain't no getting around it."

There was another long pause; then—

"What did he die of?"

I said I didn't know.

"How long has he ben dead?"

It seemed judicious to enlarge the facts to fit the probabilities; so I said, "Two or three days."

But it did no good; for Thompson received it with an injured look which plainly said, "Two or three years, you mean." Then he went right along, placidly ignoring my statement, and gave his views at considerable length upon the unwisdom of putting off burials too long. Then he lounged off toward the box, stood a moment, then came back on a sharp trot and visited the broken pane, observing,

"'Twould 'a' ben a dum sight better, all around, if they'd started him along last summer."

Thompson sat down and buried his face in his red silk handkerchief, and began to slowly sway and rock his body like one who is doing his best to endure the almost unendurable. By this time the fragrance—if you may call it fragrance— was just about suffocating, as near as you can come at it. Thompson's face was turning gray; I knew mine hadn't any color left in it. By and by Thompson rested his forehead in his left hand, with his elbow on his knee, and sort of waved his red handkerchief towards the box with his other hand, and said—

"I've carried a many a one of 'em—some of 'em considerable overdue, too—but, lordy, he just lays over 'em all!—and does it easy Cap., they was heliotrope to HIM!"

This recognition of my poor friend gratified me, in spite of the sad circumstances, because it had so much the sound of a compliment.

Pretty soon it was plain that something had got to be done. I suggested cigars. Thompson thought it was a good idea. He said,

"Likely it'll modify him some."

We puffed gingerly along for a while, and tried hard to imagine that things were improved. But it wasn't any use. Before very long, and without any consultation, both cigars were quietly dropped from our nerveless fingers at the same moment. Thompson said, with a sigh,

"No, Cap., it don't modify him worth a cent. Fact is, it makes him worse, becuz it appears to stir up his ambition. What do you reckon we better do, now?"

I was not able to suggest anything; indeed, I had to be swallowing and swallowing, all the time, and did not like to trust myself to speak. Thompson fell to maundering, in a desultory and low-spirited way, about the miserable experiences of this night; and he got to referring to my poor friend by various titles—sometimes military ones, sometimes civil ones; and I noticed that as fast as my poor friend's effectiveness grew, Thompson promoted him accordingly— gave him a bigger title. Finally he said:

"I've got an idea. Suppos'n we buckle down to it and give the Colonel a bit of a shove towards t'other end of the car?—about ten foot, say. He wouldn't have so much influence, then, don't you reckon?"

I said it was a good scheme. So we took in a good fresh breath at the broken pane, calculating to hold it till we got through; then we went there and bent over that deadly cheese and took a grip on the box. Thompson nodded "All ready," and then we threw ourselves forward with all our might; but Thompson slipped, and slumped down with his nose on the cheese, and his breath got loose. He gagged and gasped, and floundered up and made a break for the door, pawing the air and saying hoarsely, "Don't hender me!—gimme the road! I'm a-dying; gimme the road!" Out on the cold platform I sat down and held his head a while, and he revived. Presently he said,

"Do you reckon we started the Gen'rul any?"

I said no; we hadn't budged him.

"Well, then, that idea's up the flume. We got to think up something else. He's suited wher' he is, I reckon; and if that's the way he feels about it, and has made up his mind that he don't wish to be disturbed, you bet he's a-going to have his own way in the business. Yes, better leave him right wher' he is, long as he wants it so; becuz he holds all the trumps, don't you know, and so it stands to reason that the man that lays out to alter his plans for him is going to get left."

But we couldn't stay out there in that mad storm; we should have frozen to death. So we went in again and shut the door, and began to suffer once more and take turns at the break in the window. By and by, as we were starting away from a station where we had stopped a moment, Thompson pranced in cheerily and exclaimed,

"We're all right, now! I reckon we've got the Commodore this time. I judge I've got the stuff here that'll take the tuck out of him."

It was carbolic acid. He had a carboy of it. He sprinkled it all around everywhere; in fact he drenched everything with it, rifle-box, cheese and all. Then we sat down, feeling pretty hopeful. But it wasn't for long. You see the two perfumes began to mix, and then—well, pretty soon we made a break for the door; and out there Thompson swabbed his face with his bandanna and said in a kind of disheartened way,

"It ain't no use. We can't buck agin him. He just utilizes everything we put up to modify him with, and gives it his own flavor and plays it back on us. Why, Cap., don't you know, it's as much as a hundred times worse in there now than it was when he first got a-going. I never did see one of 'em warm up to his work so, and take such a dumnation interest in it. No, Sir, I never did, as long as I've ben on the road; and I've carried a many a one of 'em, as I was telling you."

We went in again after we were frozen pretty stiff; but my, we couldn't stay in, now. So we just waltzed back and forth, freezing, and thawing, and stifling, by turns. In about an hour we stopped at another station; and as we left it Thompson came in with a bag, and said—

"Cap., I'm a-going to chance him once more—just this once; and if we don't fetch him this time, the thing for us to do, is to just throw up the sponge and withdraw from the canvass. That's the way I put it up." He had brought a lot of chicken feathers, and dried apples, and leaf tobacco, and rags, and old shoes, and sulphur, and asafoetida, and one thing or another; and he piled them on a breadth of sheet iron in the middle of the floor, and set fire to them.

When they got well started, I couldn't see, myself, how even the corpse could stand it. All that went before was just simply poetry to that smell—but mind you, the original smell stood up out of it just as sublime as ever—fact is, these other smells just seemed to give it a better hold; and my, how rich it was! I didn't make these reflections there—there wasn't time—made them on the platform. And breaking for the platform, Thompson got suffocated and fell; and before I got him dragged out, which I did by the collar, I was mighty near gone myself. When we revived, Thompson said dejectedly—

"We got to stay out here, Cap. We got to do it. They ain't no other way. The Governor wants to travel alone, and he's fixed so he can outvote us."

And presently he added,

"And don't you know, we're pisoned. It's our last trip, you can make up your mind to it. Typhoid fever is what's going to come of this. I feel it acoming right now. Yes, sir, we're elected, just as sure as you're born."

We were taken from the platform an hour later, frozen and insensible, at the next station, and I went straight off into a virulent fever, and never knew anything again for three weeks. I found out, then, that I had spent that awful night with a harmless box of rifles and a lot of innocent cheese; but the news was too late to save me; imagination had done its work, and my health was permanently shattered; neither Bermuda nor any other land can ever bring it back tome. This is my last trip; I am on my way home to die.

# THE STOLEN WHITE ELEPHANT

### CHAPTER 1

The following curious history was related to me by a chance railway acquaintance. He was a gentleman more than seventy years of age, and his thoroughly good and gentle face and earnest and sincere manner imprinted the unmistakable stamp of truth upon every statement which fell from his lips. He said:

You know in what reverence the royal white elephant of Siam is held by the people of that country. You know it is sacred to kings, only kings may possess it, and that it is, indeed, in a measure even superior to kings, since it receives not merely honor but worship. Very well; five years ago, when the troubles concerning the frontier line arose between Great Britain and Siam, it was presently manifest that Siam had been in the wrong. Therefore every reparation was quickly made, and the British representative stated that he was satisfied and the past should be forgotten. This greatly relieved the King of Siam, and partly as a token of gratitude, partly also, perhaps, to wipe out any little remaining vestige of unpleasantness which England might feel toward him, he wished to send the Queen a present—the sole sure way of propitiating an enemy, according to Oriental ideas. This present ought not only to be a royal one, but transcendently royal. Wherefore, what offering could be so meet as that of a white elephant? My position in the Indian civil service was such that I was deemed peculiarly worthy of the honor of conveying the present to her Majesty. A ship was fitted out for me and my servants and the officers and attendants of the elephant, and in due time I arrived in New York harbor and placed my royal charge in admirable quarters in Jersey City. It was necessary to remain awhile in order to recruit the animal's health before resuming the voyage.

All went well during a fortnight—then my calamities began. The white elephant was stolen! I was called up at dead of night and informed of this fearful misfortune. For some moments I was beside myself with terror and anxiety; I was helpless. Then I grew calmer and collected my faculties. I soon saw my course—for, indeed, there was but the one course for an intelligent man to pursue. Late as it was, I flew to New York and got a policeman to conduct me to the headquarters of the detective force. Fortunately I arrived in time, though the chief of the force, the celebrated Inspector Blunt was just on the point of leaving for his home. He was a man of middle size and compact frame, and when he was thinking deeply he had a way of knitting his brows and tapping his forehead reflectively with his finger, which impressed you at once with the conviction that you stood in the presence of a person of no common order. The very sight of him gave me confidence and made me hopeful. I stated my errand. It did not flurry him in the least; it had no more visible effect upon his iron self-possession than if I had told him somebody had stolen my dog. He motioned me to a seat, and said, calmly:

"Allow me to think a moment, please."

So saying, he sat down at his office table and leaned his head upon his hand. Several clerks were at work at the other end of the room; the scratching of their pens was all the sound I heard during the next six or seven minutes. Meantime the inspector sat there, buried in thought. Finally he raised his head, and there was that in the firm lines of his face which showed me that his brain had done its work and his plan was made. Said he—and his voice was low and impressive:

"This is no ordinary case. Every step must be warily taken; each step must be made sure before the next is ventured. And secrecy must be observed—secrecy profound and absolute. Speak to no one about the matter, not even the reporters. I will take care of them; I will see that they get only what it may suit my ends to let them know." He touched a bell; a youth appeared. "Alaric, tell the reporters to remain for the present." The boy retired. "Now let us proceed to business—and systematically. Nothing can be accomplished in this trade of mine without strict and minute method."

He took a pen and some paper. "Now—name of the elephant?"

"Hassan Ben Ali Ben Selim Abdallah Mohammed Moist Alhammal Jamsetjejeebhoy Dhuleep Sultan Ebu Bhudpoor."

"Very well. Given name?"

"Jumbo."

"Very well. Place of birth?"

"The capital city of Siam."

"Parents living?"

"No—dead."

"Had they any other issue besides this one?"

"None. He was an only child."

"Very well. These matters are sufficient under that head. Now please describe the elephant, and leave out no particular, however insignificant—that is, insignificant from your point of view. To me in my profession there are no insignificant particulars; they do not exist."

I described, he wrote. When I was done, he said:

"Now listen. If I have made any mistakes, correct me."

He read as follows:

"Height, 19 feet; length from apex of forehead insertion of tail, 26 feet; length of trunk, 16 feet; length of tail, 6 feet; total length, including trunk, and tail, 48 feet; length of tusks, 9 feet; ears keeping with these dimensions; footprint resembles the mark left when one up-ends a barrel in the snow; the color of the elephant, a dull white; has a hole the size of a plate in each ear for the insertion of jewelry and possesses the habit in a remarkable degree of squirting water upon spectators and of maltreating with his trunk not only such persons as he is acquainted with, but even entire strangers; limps slightly with his right hind leg, and has a small scar in his left armpit caused by a former boil; had on, when stolen, a castle containing seats for fifteen persons, and a gold-cloth saddle-blanket the size of an ordinary carpet."

There were no mistakes. The inspector touched the bell, handed the description to Alaric, and said:

"Have fifty thousand copies of this printed at once and mailed to every detective office and pawnbroker's shop on the continent." Alaric retired. "There—so far, so good. Next, I must have a photograph of the property."

I gave him one. He examined it critically, and said:

"It must do, since we can do no better; but he has his trunk curled up and tucked into his mouth. That is unfortunate, and is calculated to mislead, for of course he does not usually have it in that position." He touched his bell.

"Alaric, have fifty thousand copies of this photograph made the first thing in the morning, and mail them with the descriptive circulars."

Alaric retired to execute his orders. The inspector said:

"It will be necessary to offer a reward, of course. Now as to the amount?"

"What sum would you suggest?"

"To begin with, I should say—well, twenty-five thousand dollars. It is an intricate and difficult business; there are a thousand avenues of escape and opportunities of concealment. These thieves have friends and pals every-          where—"

"Bless me, do you know who they are?"

The wary face, practised in concealing the thoughts and feelings within, gave me no token, nor yet the replying words, so quietly uttered:

"Never mind about that. I may, and I may not. We generally gather a pretty shrewd inkling of who our man is by the manner of his work and the size of the game he goes after. We are not dealing with a pickpocket or a hall thief now, make up your mind to that. This property was not 'lifted' by a novice. But, as I was saying, considering the amount of travel which will have to be done, and the diligence with which the thieves will cover up their traces as they move along, twenty-five thousand may be too small a sum to offer, yet I think it worth while to start with that."

So we determined upon that figure as a beginning. Then this man, whom nothing escaped which could by any possibility be made to serve as a clue, said:

"There are cases in detective history to show that criminals have been detected through peculiarities, in their appetites. Now, what does this elephant eat, and how much?"

"Well, as to what he eats—he will eat anything. He will eat a man, he will eat a Bible—he will eat anything between a man and a Bible."

"Good very good, indeed, but too general. Details are necessary—details are the only valuable things in our trade. Very well—as to men. At one meal—or, if you prefer, during one day—how man men will he eat, if fresh?"

"He would not care whether they were fresh or not; at a single meal he would eat five ordinary men.

"Very good; five men; we will put that down. What nationalities would he prefer?"

"He is indifferent about nationalities. He prefers acquaintances, but is not prejudiced against strangers."

"Very good. Now, as to Bibles. How many Bibles would he eat at a meal?"

"He would eat an entire edition."

"It is hardly succinct enough. Do you mean the ordinary octavo, or the family illustrated?"

"I think he would be indifferent to illustrations that is, I think he would not value illustrations above simple letterpress."

"No, you do not get my idea. I refer to bulk. The ordinary octavo Bible weighs about two pound; and a half, while the great quarto with the illustrations weighs ten or twelve. How many Dore Bibles would he eat at a meal?"

"If you knew this elephant, you could not ask. He would take what they had."

"Well, put it in dollars and cents, then. We must get at it somehow. The Dore costs a hundred dollars a copy, Russia leather, beveled."

"He would require about fifty thousand dollars worth—say an edition of five hundred copies."

"Now that is more exact. I will put that down. Very well; he likes men and Bibles; so far, so good. What else will he eat? I want particulars."

"He will leave Bibles to eat bricks, he will leave bricks to eat bottles, he will leave bottles to eat clothing, he will leave clothing to eat cats, he will leave cats to eat oysters, he will leave oysters to eat ham, he will leave ham to eat sugar, he will leave sugar to eat pie, he will leave pie to eat potatoes, he will leave potatoes to eat bran; he will leave bran to eat hay, he will leave hay to eat oats, he will leave oats to eat rice, for he was mainly raised on it. There is nothing whatever that he will not eat but European butter, and he would eat that if he could taste it."

"Very good. General quantity at a meal—say about—"

"Well, anywhere from a quarter to half a ton."

"And he drinks—"

"Everything that is fluid. Milk, water, whisky, molasses, castor oil, camphene, carbolic acid—it is no use to go into particulars; whatever fluid occurs to you set it down. He will drink anything that is fluid, except European coffee."

"Very good. As to quantity?"

"Put it down five to fifteen barrels—his thirst varies; his other appetites do not."

"These things are unusual. They ought to furnish quite good clues toward tracing him."

He touched the bell.

"Alaric; summon Captain Burns."

Burns appeared. Inspector Blunt unfolded the whole matter to him, detail by detail. Then he said in the clear, decisive tones of a man whose plans are clearly defined in his head and who is accustomed to command:

"Captain Burns, detail Detectives Jones, Davis, Halsey, Bates, and Hackett to shadow the elephant."

"Yes, sir."

"Detail Detectives Moses, Dakin, Murphy, Rogers, Tupper, Higgins, and Bartholomew to shadow the thieves."

"Yes, sir."

"Place a strong guard—A guard of thirty picked men, with a relief of thirty—over the place from whence the elephant was stolen, to keep strict watch there night and day, and allow none to approach—except reporters—without written authority from me."

"Yes, sir."

"Place detectives in plain clothes in the railway; steamship, and ferry depots, and upon all roadways leading out of Jersey City, with orders to search all suspicious persons."

"Yes, sir."

"Furnish all these men with photograph and accompanying description of the elephant, and instruct them to search all trains and outgoing ferryboats and other vessels."

"Yes, sir."

"If the elephant should be found, let him be seized, and the information forwarded to me by telegraph."

"Yes, sir."

"Let me be informed at once if any clues should be found footprints of the animal, or anything of that kind."

"Yes, sir."

"Get an order commanding the harbor police to patrol the frontages vigilantly."

"Yes, sir."

"Despatch detectives in plain clothes over all the railways, north as far as Canada, west as far as Ohio, south as far as Washington."

"Yes, sir."

"Place experts in all the telegraph offices to listen in to all messages; and let them require that all cipher despatches be interpreted to them."

"Yes, sir."

"Let all these things be done with the utmost's secrecy—mind, the most impenetrable secrecy."

"Yes, sir."

"Report to me promptly at the usual hour."

"Yes, Sir."

"Go!"

"Yes, sir."

He was gone.

Inspector Blunt was silent and thoughtful a moment, while the fire in his eye cooled down and faded out. Then he turned to me and said in a placid voice:

"I am not given to boasting, it is not my habit; but—we shall find the elephant."

I shook him warmly by the hand and thanked him; and I felt my thanks, too. The more I had seen of the man the more I liked him and the more I admired him and marveled over the mysterious wonders of his profession. Then we parted for the night, and I went home with a far happier heart than I had carried with me to his office.

## CHAPTER 2

Next morning it was all in the newspapers, in the minutest detail. It even had additions—consisting of Detective This, Detective That, and Detective The Other's "Theory" as to how the robbery was done, who the robbers were, and whither they had flown with their booty. There were eleven of these theories, and they covered all the possibilities; and this single fact shows what independent thinkers detectives are. No two theories were alike, or even much resembled each other, save in one striking particular, and in that one all the other eleven theories were absolutely agreed. That was, that although the rear of my building was torn out and the only door remained locked, the elephant had not been removed through the rent, but by some other (undiscovered) outlet. All agreed that the robbers had made that rent only to mislead the detectives. That never would have occurred to me or to any other layman, perhaps, but it had not deceived the detectives for a moment. Thus, what I had supposed was the only thing that had no mystery about it was in fact the very thing I had gone furthest astray in. The eleven theories all named the supposed robbers, but no two named the same robbers; the total number of suspected persons was thirty-seven. The various newspaper accounts all closed with the most important opinion of all—that of Chief Inspector Blunt. A portion of this statement read as follows:

*The chief knows who the two principals are, namely, "Brick" Daffy and "Red" McFadden. Ten days before the robbery was achieved he was already aware that it was to be attempted, and had quietly proceeded to shadow these two noted villains; but unfortunately on the night in question their track was lost, and before it could be found again the bird was flown—that is, the elephant.*

*Daffy and McFadden are the boldest scoundrels in the profession;*
*the chief has reasons for believing that they are the men who stole*
*the stove out of the detective headquarters on a bitter night last*
*winter—in consequence of which the chief and every detective*
*present were in the hands of the physicians before morning, some*
*with frozen feet, others with frozen fingers, ears, and other members.*

When I read the first half of that I was more astonished than ever at the wonderful sagacity of this strange man. He not only saw everything in the present with a clear eye, but even the future could not be hidden from him. I was soon at his office, and said I could not help wishing he had had those men arrested, and so prevented the trouble and loss; but his reply was simple and unanswerable:

"It is not our province to prevent crime, but to punish it. We cannot punish it until it is committed."

I remarked that the secrecy with which we had begun had been marred by the newspapers; not only all our facts but all our plans and purposes had been revealed; even all the suspected persons had been named; these would doubtless disguise themselves now, or go into hiding.

"Let them. They will find that when I am ready for them my hand will descend upon them, in their secret places, as unerringly as the hand of fate. As to the newspapers, we must keep in with them. Fame, reputation, constant public mention—these are the detective's bread and butter. He must publish his facts, else he will be supposed to have none; he must publish his theory, for nothing is so strange or striking as a detective's theory, or brings him so much wonderful respect; we must publish our plans, for these the journals insist upon having, and we could not deny them without offending. We must constantly show the public what we are doing, or they will believe we are doing nothing. It is much pleasanter to have a newspaper say, 'Inspector Blunt's ingenious and extraordinary theory is as follows,' than to have it say some harsh thing, or, worse still, some sarcastic one."

"I see the force of what you say. But I noticed that in one part of your remarks in the papers this morning you refused to reveal your opinion upon a certain minor point."

"Yes, we always do that; it has a good effect. Besides, I had not formed any opinion on that point, anyway."

I deposited a considerable sum of money with the inspector, to meet current expenses, and sat down to wait for news. We were expecting the telegrams to begin to arrive at any moment now. Meantime I reread the newspapers and also our descriptive circular, and observed that our twenty-five thousand dollars reward seemed to be offered only to detectives. I said I thought it ought to be offered to anybody who would catch the elephant. The inspector said:

"It is the detectives who will find the elephant; hence the reward will go to the right place. If other people found the animal, it would only be by watching the detectives and taking advantage of clues and indications stolen from them, and that would entitle the detectives to the reward, after all. The proper office of a reward is to stimulate the men who deliver up their time and their trained sagacities to this sort of work, and not to confer benefits upon chance citizens who stumble upon a capture without having earned the benefits by their own merits and labors."

This was reasonable enough, certainly. Now the telegraphic machine in the corner began to click, and the following despatch was the result:

*FLOWER STATION, N. Y., 7.30 A.M.*
*Have got a clue. Found a succession of deep tracks across a farm*
*near here. Followed them two miles east without result; think*
*elephant went west. Shall now shadow him in that direction.*
*DARLEY, Detective.*

"Darley's one of the best men on the force," said the inspector. "We shall hear from him again before long."
Telegram No. 2 came:

*BARKER'S, N. J., 7.40 A.M.*
*Just arrived. Glass factory broken open here during night, and*
*eight hundred bottles taken. Only water in large quantity near here*
*is five miles distant. Shall strike for there. Elephant will be*
*thirsty. Bottles were empty.*
*DARLEY, Detective.*

"That promises well, too," said the inspector.
"I told you the creature's appetites would not be bad clues."
Telegram No. 3:

*TAYLORVILLE, L. I. 8.15 A.M.*
*A haystack near here disappeared during night. Probably eaten.*
*Have got a clue, and am off.*
*HUBBARD, Detective.*

"How he does move around!" said the inspector "I knew we had a difficult job on hand, but we shall catch him yet."

*FLOWER STATION, N. Y., 9 A.M.*
*Shadowed the tracks three miles westward. Large, deep, and ragged.*
*Have just met a farmer who says they are not elephant-tracks. Says*
*they are holes where he dug up saplings for shade-trees when ground*
*was frozen last winter. Give me orders how to proceed.*
*DARLEY, Detective.*

"Aha! a confederate of the thieves! The thing, grows warm," said the inspector. He dictated the following telegram to Darley:

*Arrest the man and force him to name his pals. Continue to follow the tracks to the Pacific, if necessary.*
*Chief BLUNT.*

Next telegram:

*CONEY POINT, PA., 8.45 A.M.*
*Gas office broken open here during night and three month; unpaid gas bills taken. Have got a clue and am away.*
*MURPHY, Detective.*

"Heavens!" said the inspector; "would he eat gas bills?"
"Through ignorance—yes; but they cannot support life. At least, unassisted."
Now came this exciting telegram:

*IRONVILLE, N. Y., 9.30 A.M.*
*Just arrived. This village in consternation. Elephant passed through here at five this morning. Some say he went east some say west, some north, some south—but all say they did not wait to notice, particularly. He killed a horse; have secure a piece of it for a clue. Killed it with his trunk; from style of blow, think he struck it left-handed. From position in which horse lies, think elephant traveled northward along line Berkley Railway. Has four and a half hours' start, but I move on his track at once.*
*HAWES, Detective*

I uttered exclamations of joy. The inspector was as self-contained as a graven image. He calmly touched his bell.
"Alaric, send Captain Burns here."
Burns appeared.
"How many men are ready for instant orders?"
"Ninety-six, sir."
"Send them north at once. Let them concentrate along the line of the Berkley road north of Ironville."
"Yes, sir."
"Let them conduct their movements with the utmost secrecy. As fast as others are at liberty, hold them for orders."
"Yes, sir."
"Go!"
"Yes, sir."
Presently came another telegram:

*SAGE CORNERS, N. Y., 10.30.*
*Just arrived. Elephant passed through here at 8.15. All escaped from the town but a policeman. Apparently elephant did not strike*

21

*at policeman, but at the lamp-post. Got both. I have secured a*
*portion of the policeman as clue.*

*STUMM, Detective.*

"So the elephant has turned westward," said the inspector. "However, he will not escape, for my men are scattered all over that region."

The next telegram said:

*GLOVER'S, 11.15*

*Just arrived. Village deserted, except sick and aged. Elephant passed through three-quarters of an hour ago. The anti-temperance mass-meeting was in session; he put his trunk in at a window and washed it out with water from cistern. Some swallowed it—since dead; several drowned. Detectives Cross and O'Shaughnessy were passing through town, but going south—so missed elephant. Whole region for many miles around in terror—people flying from their homes. Wherever they turn they meet elephant, and many are killed*

*BRANT, Detective.*

I could have shed tears, this havoc so distressed me. But the inspector only said:

"You see—we are closing in on him. He feels our presence; he has turned eastward again."

Yet further troublous news was in store for us. The telegraph brought this:

*HOGANSPORT, 12.19.*

*Just arrived. Elephant passed through half an hour ago, creating wildest fright and excitement. Elephant raged around streets; two plumbers going by, killed one—other escaped. Regret general.*

*O'FLAHERTY, Detective.*

"Now he is right in the midst of my men," said the inspector. "Nothing can save him."

A succession of telegrams came from detectives who were scattered through New Jersey and Pennsylvania, and who were following clues consisting of ravaged barns, factories, and Sunday-school libraries, with high hopes-hopes amounting to certainties, indeed. The inspector said:

"I wish I could communicate with them and order them north, but that is impossible. A detective only visits a telegraph office to send his report; then he is off again, and you don't know where to put your hand on him."

Now came this despatch:

*BRIDGEPORT, CT., 12.15.*

*Barnum offers rate of $4,000 a year for exclusive privilege of using elephant as traveling advertising medium from now till detectives* *find him. Wants to paste circus-posters on him. Desires immediate answer.*

*BOGGS, Detective.*

"That is perfectly absurd!" I exclaimed.

"Of course it is," said the inspector. "Evidently Mr. Barnum, who thinks he is so sharp, does not know me—but I know him."

Then he dictated this answer to the despatch:

*Mr. Barnum's offer declined.   Make it $7,000 or nothing.*

*Chief BLUNT.*

"There. We shall not have to wait long for an answer. Mr. Barnum is not at home; he is in the telegraph office—it is his way when he has business on hand. Inside of three—"

*Done.—P. T. BARNUM.*

So interrupted the clicking telegraphic instrument. Before I could make a comment upon this extraordinary episode, the following despatch carried my thoughts into another and very distressing channel:

*BOLIVIA, N. Y., 12.50.*

*Elephant arrived here from the south and passed through toward the forest at 11.50, dispersing a funeral on the way, and diminishing the mourners by two. Citizens fired some small cannon-balls into him, and they fled. Detective Burke and I arrived ten minutes later, from the north, but mistook some excavations for footprints, and so lost a good deal of time; but at last we struck the right trail and followed it to the woods. We then got down on our hands and knees and continued to keep a sharp eye on the track, and so shadowed it into the brush. Burke was in advance. Unfortunately the animal had stopped to rest; therefore, Burke having his head down, intent upon the track, butted up against the elephant's hind legs before he was aware of his vicinity. Burke instantly arose to his feet, seized the tail, and exclaimed joyfully, "I claim the re—" but got no further, for a single blow of the huge trunk laid the brave fellow's fragments low in death. I fled rearward, and the elephant turned and shadowed me to the edge of the wood, making tremendous speed, and I should inevitably have been lost, but that the remains of the funeral providentially intervened again and diverted his attention. I have just learned that nothing of that funeral is now left; but this is no loss, for there is abundance of material for another. Meantime, the elephant has disappeared again.*

*MULROONEY, Detective.*

We heard no news except from the diligent and confident detectives scattered about New Jersey, Pennsylvania, Delaware, and Virginia—who were all following fresh and encouraging clues—until shortly after 2 P.M., when this telegram came:

*BAXTER CENTER, 2.15.*

*Elephant been here, plastered over with circus-bills, any broke up a revival, striking down and damaging many who were on the point of entering upon a better life. Citizens penned him up and established a guard. When Detective Brown and I arrived, some time after, we entered inclosure and proceeded to identify elephant by photograph and description. All masks tallied exactly except one, which we could not see—the boil-scar under armpit. To make sure, Brown crept under to look, and was immediately brained—that is, head crushed and destroyed, though nothing issued from debris. All fled so did elephant, striking right and left with much effect. He escaped, but left bold blood-track from cannon-wounds. Rediscovery certain. He broke southward, through a dense forest.*

*BRENT, Detective.*

That was the last telegram. At nightfall a fog shut down which was so dense that objects but three feet away could not be discerned. This lasted all night. The ferry-boats and even the omnibuses had to stop running.

## CHAPTER 3

Next morning the papers were as full of detective theories as before; they had all our tragic facts in detail also, and a great many more which they had received from their telegraphic correspondents. Column after column was occupied, a third of its way down, with glaring head-lines, which it made my heart sick to read. Their general tone was like this:

*THE WHITE ELEPHANT AT LARGE! HE MOVES UPON HIS FATAL MARCH WHOLE VILLAGES DESERTED BY THEIR FRIGHT-STRICKEN OCCUPANTS! PALE TERROR GOES BEFORE HIM, DEATH AND DEVASTATION FOLLOW AFTER! AFTER THESE, THE DETECTIVES! BARNS DESTROYED, FACTORIES GUTTED, HARVESTS DEVOURED, PUBLIC ASSEMBLAGES DISPERSED, ACCOMPANIED BY SCENES OF CARNAGE IMPOSSIBLE TO DESCRIBE! THEORIES OF THIRTY-FOUR OF THE MOST DISTINGUISHED DETECTIVES ON THE FORCES! THEORY OF CHIEF BLUNT!*

"There!" said Inspector Blunt, almost betrayed into excitement, "this is magnificent! This is the greatest windfall that any detective organization ever had. The fame of it will travel to the ends of the earth, and endure to the end of time, and my name with it."

But there was no joy for me. I felt as if I had committed all those red crimes, and that the elephant was only my irresponsible agent. And how the list had grown! In one place he had "interfered with an election and killed five repeaters." He had followed this act with the destruction of two pool fellows, named O'Donohue and McFlannigan, who had "found a refuge in the home of the oppressed of all lands only the day before, and were in the act of exercising for the first time the noble right of American citizens at the polls, when stricken down by the relentless hand of the Scourge of Siam." In another, he had "found a crazy sensation-preacher preparing his next season's heroic attacks on the dance, the theater, and other things which can't strike back, and had stepped on him." And in still another place he had "killed a lightning-rod agent." And so the list went on, growing redder and redder, and more and more heartbreaking. Sixty persons had been killed, and two hundred and forty wounded. All the accounts bore just testimony to the activity and devotion of the detectives, and all closed with the remark that "three hundred thousand citizen; and four detectives saw the dread creature, and two of the latter he destroyed."

I dreaded to hear the telegraphic instrument begin to click again. By and by the messages began to pour in, but I was happily disappointed in they nature. It was soon apparent that all trace of the elephant was lost. The fog had enabled him to search out a good hiding-place unobserved. Telegrams from the most absurdly distant points reported that a dim vast mass had been glimpsed there through the fog at such and such an hour, and was "undoubtedly the elephant." This dim vast mass had been glimpsed in New Haven, in New Jersey, in Pennsylvania, in interior New York, in Brooklyn, and even in the city of New York itself! But in all cases the dim vast mass had vanished quickly and left no trace. Every detective of the large force scattered over this huge extent of country sent his hourly report, and each and every one of them had a clue, and was shadowing something, and was hot upon the heels of it.

But the day passed without other result.

The next day the same.

The next just the same.

The newspaper reports began to grow monotonous with facts that amounted to nothing, clues which led to nothing, and theories which had nearly exhausted the elements which surprise and delight and dazzle.

By advice of the inspector I doubled the reward.

Four more dull days followed. Then came a bitter blow to the poor, hard-working detectives—the journalists declined to print their theories, and coldly said, "Give us a rest."

Two weeks after the elephant's disappearance I raised the reward to seventy-five thousand dollars by the inspector's advice. It was a great sum, but I felt that I would rather sacrifice my whole private fortune than lose my credit with my government. Now that the detectives were in adversity, the newspapers turned upon them, and began to fling the most stinging sarcasms at them. This gave the minstrels an idea, and they dressed themselves as detectives and hunted the elephant on the stage in the most extravagant way. The caricaturists made pictures of detectives scanning the country with spy-glasses, while the elephant, at their backs, stole apples out of their pockets. And they made all sorts of ridiculous pictures of the detective badge—you have seen that badge printed in gold on the back of detective novels, no doubt it is a wide-staring eye, with the legend, "WE NEVER SLEEP." When detectives called for a drink, the would-be facetious barkeeper resurrected an obsolete form of expression and said, "Will you have an eye-opener?" All the air was thick with sarcasms.

But there was one man who moved calm, untouched, unaffected, through it all. It was that heart of oak, the chief inspector. His brave eye never drooped, his serene confidence never wavered. He always said:

"Let them rail on; he laughs best who laughs last."

My admiration for the man grew into a species of worship. I was at his side always. His office had become an unpleasant place to me, and now became daily more and more so. Yet if he could endure it I meant to do so also—at least, as long as I could. So I came regularly, and stayed—the only outsider who seemed to be capable of it. Everybody wondered how I could; and often it seemed to me that I must desert, but at such times I looked into that calm and apparently unconscious face, and held my ground.

About three weeks after the elephant's disappearance I was about to say, one morning, that I should have to strike my colors and retire, when the great detective arrested the thought by proposing one more superb and masterly move.

This was to compromise with the robbers. The fertility of this man's invention exceeded anything I have ever seen, and I have had a wide intercourse with the world's finest minds. He said he was confident he could compromise for one hundred thousand dollars and recover the elephant. I said I believed I could scrape the amount together, but what would become of the poor detectives who had worked so faithfully? He said:

"In compromises they always get half."

This removed my only objection. So the inspector wrote two notes, in this form:

*DEAR MADAM,—Your husband can make a large sum of money (and be entirely protected from the law) by making an immediate, appointment with me.*
*Chief BLUNT.*

He sent one of these by his confidential messenger to the "reputed wife" of Brick Duffy, and the other to the reputed wife of Red McFadden.

Within the hour these offensive answers came:

*YE OWLD FOOL: brick Duffys bin ded 2 yere.*
*BRIDGET MAHONEY.*

*CHIEF BAT,—Red McFadden is hung and in heving 18 month. Any Ass but a detective know that.*
*MARY O'HOOLIGAN.*

"I had long suspected these facts," said the inspector; "this testimony proves the unerring accuracy of my instinct."

The moment one resource failed him he was ready with another. He immediately wrote an advertisement for the morning papers, and I kept a copy of it:

*A.—xWhlv.   242  ht.   Tjnd—fz328wmlg.   Ozpo,—2  m!   2m!.   M!  ogw.*

He said that if the thief was alive this would bring him to the usual rendezvous. He further explained that the usual rendezvous was a glare where all business affairs between detectives and criminals were conducted. This meeting would take place at twelve the next night.

We could do nothing till then, and I lost no time in getting out of the office, and was grateful indeed for the privilege.

At eleven the next night I brought one hundred thousand dollars in bank-notes and put them into the chief's hands, and shortly afterward he took his leave, with the brave old undimmed confidence in his eye. An almost intolerable hour dragged to a close; then I heard his welcome tread, and rose gasping and tottered to meet him. How his fine eyes flamed with triumph! He said:

"We've compromised! The jokers will sing a different tune to-morrow! Follow me!"

He took a lighted candle and strode down into the vast vaulted basement where sixty detectives always slept, and where a score were now playing cards to while the time. I followed close after him. He walked swiftly down to the dim and remote end of the place, and just as I succumbed to the pangs of suffocation and was swooning away he stumbled and fell over the outlying members of a mighty object, and I heard him exclaim as he went down:

"Our noble profession is vindicated. Here is your elephant!"

I was carried to the office above and restored with carbolic acid. The whole detective force swarmed in, and such another season of triumphant rejoicing ensued as I had never witnessed before. The reporters were called, baskets of champagne were opened, toasts were drunk, the handshakings and congratulations were continuous and enthusiastic. Naturally the chief was the hero of the hour, and his happiness was so complete and had been so patiently and worthily and bravely won that it made me happy to see it, though I stood there a homeless beggar, my priceless charge dead, and my position in my country's service lost to me through what would always seem my fatally careless execution of a great trust. Many an eloquent eye testified its deep admiration for the chief, and many a detective's voice murmured, "Look at him—just the king of the profession; only give him a clue, it's all he wants, and there ain't anything hid that he can't find." The dividing of the fifty thousand dollars made great pleasure; when it was finished the chief made a little speech while he put his share in his pocket, in which he said, "Enjoy it, boys, for you've earned it; and, more than that, you've earned for the detective profession undying fame."

A telegram arrived, which read:

*MONROE, MICH., 10 P.M.*

*First time I've struck a telegraph office in over three weeks. Have followed those footprints, horseback, through the woods, a thousand miles to here, and they get stronger and bigger and fresher every day. Don't worry-inside of another week I'll have the elephant. This is dead sure.*

*DARLEY, Detective.*

The chief ordered three cheers for "Darley, one of the finest minds on the force," and then commanded that he be telegraphed to come home and receive his share of the reward.

So ended that marvelous episode of the stolen elephant. The newspapers were pleasant with praises once more, the next day, with one contemptible exception. This sheet said, "Great is the detective! He may be a little slow in finding a little thing like a mislaid elephant he may hunt him all day and sleep with his rotting carcass all night for three weeks, but he will find him at last if he can get the man who mislaid him to show him the place!"

Poor Hassan was lost to me forever. The cannonshots had wounded him fatally, he had crept to that unfriendly place in the fog, and there, surrounded by his enemies and in constant danger of detection, he had wasted away with hunger and suffering till death gave him peace.

The compromise cost me one hundred thousand dollars; my detective expenses were forty-two thousand dollars more; I never applied for a place again under my government; I am a ruined man and a wanderer on the earth but my admiration for that man, whom I believe to be the greatest detective the world has ever produced, remains undimmed to this day, and will so remain unto the end.

*[This story was originally included in "A Tramp Abroad", but was left out because it was feared that some of the particulars had been exaggerated, and that others were not true. Before these suspicions had been proven groundless, the book had gone to press. —M.T.]*

# THE NOTORIOUS JUMPING FROG OF CALAVERAS COUNTY

In compliance with the request of a friend of mine, who wrote me from the East, I called on good-natured, garrulous old Simon Wheeler, and inquired after my friend's friend, Leonidas W. Smiley, as requested to do, and I hereunto append the result. I have a lurking suspicion that *Leonidas* W. Smiley is a myth; that my friend never knew such a personage; and that he only conjectured that if I asked

old Wheeler about him, it would remind him of his infamous *Jim* Smiley, and he would go to work and bore me to death with some exasperating reminiscence of him as long and as tedious as it should be useless to me. If that was the design, it succeeded.

I found Simon Wheeler dozing comfortably by the bar-room stove of the dilapidated tavern in the decayed mining camp of Angel's, and I noticed that he was fat and bald-headed, and had an expression of winning gentleness and simplicity upon his tranquil countenance. He roused up, and gave me good-day. I told him a friend of mine had commissioned me to make some inquiries about a cherished companion of his boyhood named *Leonidas* W. Smiley—*Rev. Leonidas* W. Smiley, a young minister of the Gospel, who he had heard was at one time a resident of Angel's Camp. I added that if Mr. Wheeler could tell me anything about this Rev. Leonidas W. Smiley, I would feel under many obligations to him.

Simon Wheeler backed me into a corner and blockaded me there with his chair, and then sat down and reeled off the monotonous narrative which follows this paragraph. He never smiled, he never frowned, he never changed his voice from the gentle-flowing key to which he tuned his initial sentence, he never betrayed the slightest suspicion of enthusiasm; but all through the interminable narrative there ran a vein of impressive earnestness and sincerity, which showed me plainly that, so far from his imagining that there was anything ridiculous or funny about his story, he regarded it as a really important matter, and admired its two heroes as men of transcendent genius in *finesse*. I let him go on in his own way, and never interrupted him once.

"Rev. Leonidas W. H'm, Reverend Le—well, there was a feller here once by the name of *Jim* Smiley, in the winter of '49—or maybe it was the spring of '50—I don't recollect exactly, somehow, though what makes me think it was one or the other is because I remember the big flume warn't finished when he first come to the camp; but any way, he was the curiosest man about always betting on anything that turned up you ever see, if he could get anybody to bet on the other side; and if he couldn't he'd change sides. Any way that suited the other man would suit *him*—any way just so's he got a bet, *he* was satisfied. But still he was lucky, uncommon lucky; he most always come out winner. He was always ready and laying for a chance; there couldn't be no solit'ry thing mentioned but that feller'd offer to bet on it, and take ary side you please, as I was just telling you. If there was a horse-race, you'd find him flush or you'd find him busted at the end of it; if there was a dog-fight, he'd bet on it; if there was a cat-fight, he'd bet on it; if there was a chicken-fight, he'd bet on it; why, if there was two birds setting on a fence, he would bet you which one would fly first; or if there was a camp-meeting, he would be there reg'lar to bet on Parson Walker, which he judged to be the best exhorter about here, and so he was too, and a good man. If he even see a straddle-bug start to go anywheres, he would bet you how long it would take him to get to—to wherever he was going to, and if you took him up, he would foller that straddle-bug to Mexico but what he would find out where he was bound for and how long he was on the road. Lots of the boys here has seen that Smiley, and can tell you about him. Why, it never made no difference to *him*—he'd bet on *any* thing—the dangdest feller. Parson Walker's wife laid very sick once, for a good while, and it seemed as if they warn't going to save her; but one morning he come in, and Smiley up and asked him how she was, and he said she was considable better—thank the Lord for his inf'nit mercy—and coming on so smart that with the blessing of Prov'dence she'd get well yet; and Smiley, before he thought says, 'Well, I'll risk two-and-a-half she don't anyway.'

"Thish-yer Smiley had a mare—the boys called her the fifteen-minute nag, but that was only in fun, you know, because of course she was faster than that—and he used to win money on that horse, for all she was so slow and always had the asthma, or the distemper, or the consumption, or something of that kind. They used to give her two or three hundred yards' start, and then pass her under way; but always at the fag-end of the race she'd get excited and desperate-like, and come cavorting and straddling up, and scattering her legs around limber, sometimes in the air, and sometimes out to one side amongst the fences, and kicking up m-o-r-e dust and raising m-o-r-e racket with her coughing and sneezing and blowing her nose—and *always* fetch up at the stand just about a neck ahead, as near as you could cipher it down.

"And he had a little small bull-pup, that to look at him you'd think he warn't worth a cent but to set around and look ornery and lay for a chance to steal something. But as soon as money was up on him he was a different dog; his under-jaw'd begin to stick out like the fo'castle of a steamboat, and his teeth would uncover and shine like the furnaces. And a dog might tackle him and bully-rag him, and bite him, and throw him over his shoulder two or three times, and Andrew Jackson—which was the name of the pup—Andrew Jackson would never let on but what *he* was satisfied, and hadn't expected nothing else—and the bets being doubled and doubled on the other side all the time, till the money was all up; and then all of a sudden he would grab that other dog just by the j'int of his hind leg and freeze to it—not chaw, you understand, but only just grip and hang on till they throwed up the sponge, if it was a year. Smiley always come out winner on that pup, till he harnessed a dog once that didn't have no hind legs, because they'd been sawed off in a circular saw, and when the thing had gone along far enough, and the money was all up, and he come to make a snatch for his pet holt, he see in a minute how he's been imposed on, and how the other dog had him in the door, so to speak, and he 'peared surprised, and then he looked sorter discouraged-like, and didn't try no more to win the fight, and so he got shucked out bad. He give Smiley a look, as much as to say his heart was broke, and it was *his* fault, for putting up a dog that hadn't no hind legs for him to take holt of, which was his main dependence in a fight, and then he limped off a piece and laid down and died. It was a good pup, was that Andrew Jackson, and would have made a name for hisself if he'd lived, for the stuff was in him and he had genius—I know it, because he hadn't no opportunities to speak of, and it don't stand to reason that a dog could make such a fight as he could under them circumstances if he hadn't no talent. It always makes me feel sorry when I think of that last fight of his'n, and the way it turned out.

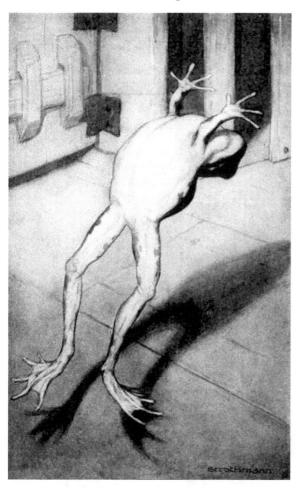

Dan'l Webster performing a backwards somerset (somersault).

"Well, thish-yer Smiley had rat-tarriers, and chicken cocks, and tomcats and all them kind of things, till you couldn't rest, and you couldn't fetch nothing for him to bet on but he'd match you. He ketched a frog one day, and took him home, and said he cal'lated to educate him; and so he never done nothing for three months but set in his back yard and learn that frog to jump. And you bet you he *did* learn him, too. He'd give him a little punch behind, and the next minute you'd see that frog whirling in the air like a doughnut—see him turn one summerset, or may be a couple, if he got a good start, and come down flat-footed and all right, like a cat. He got him up so in the matter of ketching flies, and kep' him in practice so constant, that he'd nail a fly every time as fur as he could see him. Smiley said all a frog wanted was education, and he could do 'most anything—and I believe him. Why, I've seen him set Dan'l Webster down here on

31

this floor—Dan'l Webster was the name of the frog—and sing out, "Flies, Dan'l, flies!'" and quicker'n you could wink he'd spring straight up and snake a fly off'n the counter there, and flop down on the floor ag'in as solid as a gob of mud, and fall to scratching the side of his head with his hind foot as indifferent as if he hadn't no idea he'd been doin' any more'n any frog might do. You never see a frog so modest and straightfor'ard as he was, for all he was so gifted. And when it come to fair and square jumping on a dead level, he could get over more ground at one straddle than any animal of his breed you ever see. Jumping on a dead level was his strong suit, you understand; and when it come to that, Smiley would ante up money on him as long as he had a red. Smiley was monstrous proud of his frog, and well he might be, for fellers that had traveled and been everywheres, all said he laid over any frog that ever *they* see.

"Well, Smiley kep't the beast in a little lattice box, and he used to fetch him down town sometimes and lay for a bet. One day a feller—a stranger in the camp, he was—come acrost him with his box, and says:

"'What might it be that you've got in the box?'

"And Smiley says, sorter indifferent-like, 'It might be a parrot, or it might be a canary, maybe, but it ain't—it's only just a frog.'

"And the feller took it, and looked at it careful, and turned it round this way and that, and says, 'H'm—so 'tis. Well, what's *he* good for?'

"'Well,' Smiley says, easy and careless, 'he's good enough for *one* thing, I should judge—he can outjump any frog in Calaveras county.'

"The feller took the box again, and took another long, particular look, and give it back to Smiley, and says, very deliberate, 'Well,' he says, 'I don't see no p'ints about that frog that's any better'n any other frog.'

"'Maybe you don't,' Smiley says. 'Maybe you understand frogs and maybe you don't understand 'em; maybe you've had experience, and maybe you ain't only a amature, as it were. Anyways, I've got *my* opinion and I'll risk forty dollars that he can outjump any frog in Calaveras county.'

"And the feller studied a minute, and then says, kinder sad like, 'Well, I'm only a stranger here, and I ain't got no frog; but if I had a frog, I'd bet you.'

He filled him full of quail shot.

"And then Smiley says, 'That's all right—that's all right—if you'll hold my box a minute, I'll go and get you a frog.' And so the feller took the box, and put up his forty dollars along with Smiley's, and set down to wait.

"So he set there a good while thinking and thinking to hisself, and then he got the frog out and prized his mouth open and took a teaspoon and filled him full of quail shot—filled him pretty near up to his chin—and set him on the floor. Smiley he went to the swamp and slopped around in the mud for a long time, and finally he ketched a frog, and fetched him in, and give him to this feller, and says:

"'Now, if you're ready, set him alongside of Dan'l, with his forepaws just even with Dan'l's, and I'll give the word.' Then he says, 'One—two—three—*git!*' and him and the feller touched up the frogs from behind, and the new frog hopped off lively, but Dan'l give a heave, and hysted up his shoulders—so— like a Frenchman, but it warn't no use—he couldn't budge; he was planted as solid as a church, and he couldn't no more stir than if he was anchored out. Smiley was a good deal surprised, and he was disgusted too, but he didn't have no idea what the matter was, of course.

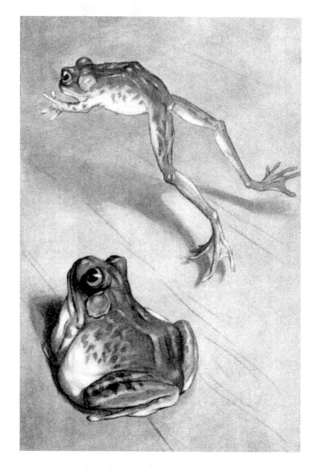

"The feller took the money and started away; and when he was going out at the door, he sorter jerked his thumb over his shoulder—so—at Dan'l, and says again, very deliberate, 'Well,' he says, '*I* don't see no p'ints about that frog that's any better'n any other frog.'

"Smiley he stood scratching his head and looking down at Dan'l a long time, and at last he says, 'I do wonder what in the nation that frog throw'd off for—I wonder if there ain't something the matter with him—he 'pears to look mighty baggy, somehow.' And he ketched Dan'l by the nap of the neck, and hefted him, and says, 'Why blame my cats if he don't weigh five pound!' and turned him upside down and he belched out a double handful of shot. And then he see how it was, and he was the maddest man—he set the frog down and took out after that feller, but he never ketched him. And—"

[Here Simon Wheeler heard his name called from the front yard, and got up to see what was wanted.] And turning to me as he moved away, he said: "Just set where you are, stranger, and rest easy—I ain't going to be gone a second."

But, by your leave, I did not think that a continuation of the history of the enterprising vagabond *Jim* Smiley would be likely to afford me much information concerning the Rev. *Leonidas* W. Smiley, and so I started away.

At the door I met the sociable Wheeler returning, and he button-holed me and recommenced:

"Well, thish-yer Smiley had a yaller one-eyed cow that didn't have no tail, only jest a short stump like a bannanner, and—"

However, lacking both time and inclination, I did not wait to hear about the afflicted cow, but took my leave.

# ABOUT MAGNANIMOUS-INCIDENT LITERATURE

All my life, from boyhood up, I have had the habit of reading a certain set of anecdotes, written in the quaint vein of The World's ingenious Fabulist, for the lesson they taught me and the pleasure they gave me. They lay always convenient to my hand, and whenever I thought meanly of my kind I turned to them, and they banished that sentiment; whenever I felt myself to be selfish, sordid, and ignoble I turned to them, and they told me what to do to win back my self-respect. Many times I wished that the charming anecdotes had not stopped with their happy climaxes, but had continued the pleasing history of the several benefactors and beneficiaries. This wish rose in my breast so persistently that at last I determined to satisfy it by seeking out the sequels of those anecdotes myself. So I set about it, and after great labor and tedious research accomplished my task. I will lay the result before you, giving you each anecdote in its turn, and following it with its sequel as I gathered it through my investigations.

## THE GRATEFUL POODLE

One day a benevolent physician (who had read the books) having found a stray poodle suffering from a broken leg, conveyed the poor creature to his home, and after setting and bandaging the injured limb gave the little outcast its liberty again, and thought no more about the matter. But how great was his surprise, upon opening his door one morning, some days later, to find the grateful poodle patiently waiting there, and in its company another stray dog, one of whose legs, by some accident, had been broken. The kind physician at once relieved the distressed animal, nor did he forget to admire the inscrutable goodness and mercy of God, who had been willing to use so humble an instrument as the poor outcast poodle for the inculcating of, etc., etc., etc.

## SEQUEL

The next morning the benevolent physician found the two dogs, beaming with gratitude, waiting at his door, and with them two other dogs-cripples. The cripples were speedily healed, and the four went their way, leaving the benevolent physician more overcome by pious wonder than ever. The day passed, the morning came. There at the door sat now the four reconstructed dogs, and with them four others requiring reconstruction. This day also passed, and another morning came; and now sixteen dogs, eight of them newly crippled, occupied the sidewalk, and the people were going around. By noon the broken legs were all set, but the pious wonder in the good physician's breast was beginning to get mixed with involuntary profanity. The sun rose once more, and exhibited thirty-two dogs, sixteen of them with broken legs, occupying the sidewalk and half of the street; the human spectators took up the rest of the room. The cries of the wounded, the songs of the healed brutes, and the comments of the onlooking citizens made great and inspiring cheer, but traffic was interrupted in that street. The good physician hired a couple of assistant surgeons and got through his benevolent work before dark, first taking the precaution to cancel his church membership, so that he might express himself with the latitude which the case required.

But some things have their limits. When once more the morning dawned, and the good physician looked out upon a massed and far-reaching multitude of clamorous and beseeching dogs, he said, "I might as well acknowledge it, I have been fooled by the books; they only tell the pretty part of the story, and then stop. Fetch me the shotgun; this thing has gone along far enough."

He issued forth with his weapon, and chanced to step upon the tail of the original poodle, who promptly bit him in the leg. Now the great and good work which this poodle had been engaged in had engendered in him such a mighty and augmenting enthusiasm as to turn his weak head at last and drive him mad. A month later, when the benevolent physician lay in the death-throes of hydrophobia, he called his weeping friends about him, and said:—

"Beware of the books. They tell but half of the story. Whenever a poor wretch asks you for help, and you feel a doubt as to what result may flow from your benevolence, give yourself the benefit of the doubt and kill the applicant."

And so saying he turned his face to the wall and gave up the ghost.

## THE BENEVOLENT AUTHOR

A poor and young literary beginner had tried in vain to get his manuscripts accepted. At last, when the horrors of starvation were staring him in the face, he laid his sad case before a celebrated author, beseeching his counsel and assistance. This generous man immediately put aside his own matters and proceeded to peruse one of the despised manuscripts. Having completed his kindly task, he shook the poor young man cordially by the hand, saying, "I perceive merit in this; come again to me on Monday." At the time specified, the celebrated author, with a sweet smile, but saying nothing, spread open a magazine which was damp from the press. What was the poor young man's astonishment to discover upon the printed page his own article. "How can I ever," said he, falling upon his knees and bursting into tears, "testify my gratitude for this noble conduct!"

The celebrated author was the renowned Snodgrass; the poor young beginner thus rescued from obscurity and starvation was the afterward equally renowned Snagsby. Let this pleasing incident admonish us to turn a charitable ear to all beginners that need help.

## SEQUEL

The next week Snagsby was back with five rejected manuscripts. The celebrated author was a little surprised, because in the books the young struggler had needed but one lift, apparently. However, he plowed through these papers, removing unnecessary flowers and digging up some acres of adjective-stumps, and then succeeded in getting two of the articles accepted.

A week or so drifted by, and the grateful Snagsby arrived with another cargo. The celebrated author had felt a mighty glow of satisfaction within himself the first time he had successfully befriended the poor young struggler, and had compared himself with the generous people in the books with high gratification; but he was beginning to suspect now that he had struck upon something fresh in the noble-episode line. His enthusiasm took a chill. Still, he could not bear to repulse this struggling young author, who clung to him with such pretty simplicity and trustfulness.

Well, the upshot of it all was that the celebrated author presently found himself permanently freighted with the poor young beginner. All his mild efforts to unload this cargo went for nothing. He had to give daily counsel, daily encouragement; he had to keep on procuring magazine acceptances, and then revamping the manuscripts to make them presentable. When the young aspirant got a start at last, he rode into sudden fame by describing the celebrated author's private life with such a caustic humor and such minuteness of blistering detail that the book sold a prodigious edition, and broke the celebrated author's heart with mortification. With his latest gasp he said, "Alas, the books deceived me; they do not tell the whole story. Beware of the struggling young author, my friends. Whom God sees fit to starve, let not man presumptuously rescue to his own undoing."

## THE GRATEFUL HUSBAND

One day a lady was driving through the principal street of a great city with her little boy, when the horses took fright and dashed madly away, hurling the coachman from his box and leaving the occupants of the carnage paralyzed with terror. But a brave youth who was driving a grocery-wagon threw himself before the plunging animals, and succeeded in arresting their flight at the peril of his own.—[This is probably a misprint.—M. T.]—The grateful lady took his number, and upon arriving at her home she related the heroic act to her husband (who had read the books), who listened with streaming eyes to the moving recital, and who, after returning thanks, in conjunction with his restored loved ones, to Him who suffereth not even a sparrow to fall to the ground unnoticed, sent for the brave young person, and, placing a check for five hundred dollars in his hand, said, "Take this as a reward for your noble act, William Ferguson, and if ever you shall need a friend, remember that Thompson McSpadden has a grateful heart." Let us learn from this that a good deed cannot fail to benefit the doer, however humble he may be.

## SEQUEL

William Ferguson called the next week and asked Mr. McSpadden to use his influence to get him a higher employment, he feeling capable of better things than driving a grocer's wagon. Mr. McSpadden got him an under-clerkship at a good salary.

Presently William Ferguson's mother fell sick, and William—Well, to cut the story short, Mr. McSpadden consented to take her into his house. Before long she yearned for the society of her younger children; so Mary and Julia were admitted also, and little Jimmy, their brother. Jimmy had a pocket knife, and he wandered into the drawing-room with it one day, alone, and reduced ten thousand dollars' worth of furniture to an indeterminable value in rather less than three-quarters of an hour. A day or two later he fell down-stairs and broke his neck, and seventeen of his family's relatives came to the house to attend the funeral. This made them acquainted, and they kept the kitchen occupied after that, and likewise kept the McSpaddens busy hunting up situations of various sorts for them, and hunting up more when they wore these out. The old woman drank a good deal and swore a good deal; but the grateful McSpaddens knew it was their duty to reform her, considering what her son had done for them, so they clave nobly to their generous task. William came often and got decreasing sums of money, and asked for higher and more lucrative employments—which the grateful McSpadden more or less promptly procured for him. McSpadden consented also, after some demur, to fit William for college; but when the first vacation came and the hero requested to be sent to Europe for his health, the persecuted McSpadden rose against the tyrant and revolted. He plainly and squarely refused. William Ferguson's mother was so astounded that she let her gin-bottle drop, and her profane lips refused to do their office. When she recovered she said in a half-gasp, "Is this your gratitude? Where would your wife and boy be now, but for my son?"

William said, "Is this your gratitude? Did I save your wife's life or not? Tell me that!"

Seven relations swarmed in from the kitchen and each said, "And this is his gratitude!"

William's sisters stared, bewildered, and said, "And this is his grat—" but were interrupted by their mother, who burst into tears and exclaimed,

"To think that my sainted little Jimmy threw away his life in the service of such a reptile!"

Then the pluck of the revolutionary McSpadden rose to the occasion, and he replied with fervor, "Out of my house, the whole beggarly tribe of you! I was beguiled by the books, but shall never be beguiled again—once is sufficient for me." And turning to William he shouted, "Yes, you did save my wife's life, and the next man that does it shall die in his tracks!"

Not being a clergyman, I place my text at the end of my sermon instead of at the beginning. Here it is, from Mr. Noah Brooks's Recollections of President Lincoln in "Scribners Monthly":

> *J.H. Hackett, in his part of Falstaff, was an actor who gave Mr. Lincoln great delight. With his usual desire to signify to others his sense of obligation, Mr. Lincoln wrote a genial little note to the actor expressing his pleasure at witnessing his performance. Mr. Hackett, in reply, sent a book of some sort; perhaps it was one of his own authorship. He also wrote several notes to the President. One night, quite late, when the episode had passed out of my mind, I went to the White House in answer to a message. Passing into the President's office, I noticed, to my surprise, Hackett sitting in the anteroom as if waiting for an audience. The President asked me if any one was outside. On being told, he said, half sadly, "Oh, I can't see him, I can't see him; I was in hopes he had gone away." Then he added, "Now this just illustrates the difficulty of having pleasant friends and acquaintances in this place. You know how I liked Hackett as an actor, and how I wrote to tell him so. He sent me that book, and there I thought the matter would end. He is a master of his place in the profession, I suppose, and well fixed in it; but just because we had a little friendly correspondence, such as any two men might have, he wants something. What do you suppose he wants?" I could not guess, and Mr. Lincoln added, "well, he wants to be consul to London. Oh, dear!"*

I will observe, in conclusion, that the William Ferguson incident occurred, and within my personal knowledge—though I have changed the nature of the details, to keep William from recognizing himself in it.

All the readers of this article have in some sweet and gushing hour of their lives played the role of Magnanimous-Incident hero. I wish I knew how many there are among them who are willing to talk about that episode and like to be reminded of the consequences that flowed from it.

❧

# PUNCH, BROTHERS, PUNCH

Will the reader please to cast his eye over the following lines, and see if he can discover anything harmful in them?

*Conductor, when you receive a fare,*
*Punch in the presence of the passenjare!*
*A blue trip slip for an eight-cent fare,*
*A buff trip slip for a six-cent fare,*
*A pink trip slip for a three-cent fare,*
*Punch in the presence of the passenjare!*

*CHORUS*

*Punch, brothers! punch with care!*
*Punch in the presence of the passenjare!*

I came across these jingling rhymes in a newspaper, a little while ago, and read them a couple of times. They took instant and entire possession of me. All through breakfast they went waltzing through my brain; and when, at last, I rolled up my napkin, I could not tell whether I had eaten anything or not. I had carefully laid out my day's work the day before—thrilling tragedy in the novel which I am writing. I went to my den to begin my deed of blood. I took up my pen, but all I could get it to say was, "Punch in the presence of the passenjare." I fought hard for an hour, but it was useless. My head kept humming, "A blue trip slip for an eight-cent fare, a buff trip slip for a six-cent fare," and so on and so on, without peace or respite. The day's work was ruined—I could see that plainly enough. I gave up and drifted down-town, and presently discovered that my feet were keeping time to that relentless jingle. When I could stand it no longer I altered my step. But it did no good; those rhymes accommodated themselves to the new step and went on harassing me just as before. I returned home, and suffered all the afternoon; suffered all through an unconscious and unrefreshing dinner; suffered, and cried, and jingled all through the evening; went to bed and rolled, tossed, and jingled right along, the same as ever; got up at midnight frantic, and tried to read; but there was nothing visible upon the whirling page except "Punch! punch in the presence of the passenjare." By sunrise I was out of my mind, and everybody marveled and was distressed at the idiotic burden of my ravings— "Punch! oh, punch! punch in the presence of the passenjare!"

Two days later, on Saturday morning, I arose, a tottering wreck, and went forth to fulfil an engagement with a valued friend, the Rev. Mr.————, to walk to the Talcott Tower, ten miles distant. He stared at me, but asked no questions. We started. Mr.———— talked, talked, talked as is his wont. I said nothing; I heard nothing. At the end of a mile, Mr.———— said "Mark, are you sick? I never saw a man look so haggard and worn and absent-minded. Say something, do!"

Drearily, without enthusiasm, I said: "Punch brothers, punch with care! Punch in the presence of the passenjare!"

My friend eyed me blankly, looked perplexed, then said:

"I do not think I get your drift, Mark. There does not seem to be any relevancy in what you have said, certainly nothing sad; and yet—maybe it was the way you said the words—I never heard anything that sounded so pathetic. What is—"

But I heard no more. I was already far away with my pitiless, heartbreaking "blue trip slip for an eight-cent fare, buff trip slip for a six-cent fare, pink trip slip for a three-cent fare; punch in the presence of the passenjare." I do not know what occurred during the other nine miles. However, all of a sudden Mr.———— laid his hand on my shoulder and shouted:—

"Oh, wake up! wake up! wake up! Don't sleep all day! Here we are at the Tower, man! I have talked myself deaf and dumb and blind, and never got a response. Just look at this magnificent autumn landscape! Look at it! look at it! Feast your eye on it! You have traveled; you have seen boasted landscapes elsewhere. Come, now, deliver an honest opinion. What do you say to this?"

I sighed wearily; and murmured:—

"A buff trip slip for a six-cent fare, a pink trip slip for a three-cent fare, punch in the presence of the passenjare."

Rev. Mr. ———— stood there, very grave, full of concern, apparently, and looked long at me; then he said:—

"Mark, there is something about this that I cannot understand. Those are about the same words you said before; there does not seem to be anything in them, and yet they nearly break my heart when you say them. Punch in the— how is it they go?"

I began at the beginning and repeated all the lines.

My friend's face lighted with interest. He said:—

"Why, what a captivating jingle it is! It is almost music. It flows along so nicely. I have nearly caught the rhymes myself. Say them over just once more, and then I'll have them, sure."

I said them over. Then Mr. ———— said them. He made one little mistake, which I corrected. The next time and the next he got them right. Now a great burden seemed to tumble from my shoulders. That torturing jingle departed out of my brain, and a grateful sense of rest and peace descended upon me. I was light-hearted enough to sing; and I did sing for half an hour, straight along, as we went jogging homeward. Then my freed tongue found blessed speech again, and the pent talk of many a weary hour began to gush and flow. It flowed on and on, joyously, jubilantly, until the fountain was empty and dry. As I wrung my friend's hand at parting, I said:—

"Haven't we had a royal good time! But now I remember, you haven't said a word for two hours. Come, come, out with something!"

The Rev. Mr.——— turned a lack-lustre eye upon me, drew a deep sigh, and said, without animation, without apparent consciousness:

"Punch, brothers, punch with care! Punch in the presence of the passenjare!"

A pang shot through me as I said to myself, "Poor fellow, poor fellow! he has got it, now."

I did not see Mr.——— for two or three days after that. Then, on Tuesday evening, he staggered into my presence and sank dejectedly into a seat. He was pale, worn; he was a wreck. He lifted his faded eyes to my face and said:—

"Ah, Mark, it was a ruinous investment that I made in those heartless rhymes. They have ridden me like a nightmare, day and night, hour after hour, to this very moment. Since I saw you I have suffered the torments of the lost. Saturday evening I had a sudden call, by telegraph, and took the night train for Boston. The occasion was the death of a valued old friend who had requested that I should preach his funeral sermon. I took my seat in the cars and set myself to framing the discourse. But I never got beyond the opening paragraph; for then the train started and the car-wheels began their 'clack, clack-clack-clack-clack! clack-clack!—clack-clack-clack!' and right away those odious rhymes fitted themselves to that accom-paniment. For an hour I sat there and set a syllable of those rhymes to every separate and distinct clack the car-wheels made. Why, I was as fagged out, then, as if I had been chopping wood all day. My skull was splitting with headache. It seemed to me that I must go mad if I sat there any longer; so I undressed and went to bed. I stretched myself out in my berth, and—well, you know what the result was. The thing went right along, just the same. 'Clack-clack clack, a blue trip slip, clack-clack-clack, for an eight-cent fare; clack-clack-clack, a buff trip slip, clack clack-clack, for a six-cent fare, and so on, and so on, and so on punch in the presence of the passenjare!' Sleep? Not a single wink! I was almost a lunatic when I got to Boston. Don't ask me about the funeral. I did the best I could, but every solemn individual sentence was meshed and tangled and woven in and out with 'Punch, brothers, punch with care, punch in the presence of the passenjare.' And the most distressing thing was that my delivery dropped into the undulating rhythm of those pulsing rhymes, and I could actually catch absent-minded people nodding time to the swing of it with their stupid heads. And, Mark, you may believe it or not, but before I got through the entire assemblage were placidly bobbing their heads in solemn unison, mourners, undertaker, and all. The moment I had finished, I fled to the anteroom in a state bordering on frenzy. Of course it would be my luck to find a sorrowing and aged maiden aunt of the deceased there, who had arrived from Springfield too late to get into the church. She began to sob, and said:—

"'Oh, oh, he is gone, he is gone, and I didn't see him before he died!'

"'Yes!' I said, 'he is gone, he is gone, he is gone—oh, will this suffering never cease!'

"'You loved him, then! Oh, you too loved him!'

"'Loved him! Loved who?'

"'Why, my poor George! my poor nephew!'

"'Oh—him! Yes—oh, yes, yes. Certainly—certainly. Punch—punch—oh, this misery will kill me!'

"'Bless you! bless you, sir, for these sweet words! I, too, suffer in this dear loss. Were you present during his last moments?'

"'Yes. I—whose last moments?'

"'His. The dear departed's.'

"'Yes! Oh, yes—yes—yes! I suppose so, I think so, I don't know! Oh, certainly—I was there—I was there!'

"'Oh, what a privilege! what a precious privilege! And his last words—oh, tell me, tell me his last words! What did he say?'

"'He said—he said—oh, my head, my head, my head! He said—he said—he never said anything but Punch, punch, punch in the presence of the passenjare! Oh, leave me, madam! In the name of all that is generous, leave me to my madness, my misery, my despair!—a buff trip slip for a six-cent fare, a pink trip slip for a three-cent fare—endu—rance can no fur—ther go!—PUNCH in the presence of the passenjare!"

My friend's hopeless eyes rested upon mine a pregnant minute, and then he said impressively:—

"Mark, you do not say anything. You do not offer me any hope. But, ah me, it is just as well—it is just as well. You could not do me any good. The time has long gone by when words could comfort me. Something tells me that my tongue is doomed to wag forever to the jigger of that remorseless jingle. There—there it is coming on me again: a blue trip slip for an eight-cent fare, a buff trip slip for a—"

Thus murmuring faint and fainter, my friend sank into a peaceful trance and forgot his sufferings in a blessed respite.

How did I finally save him from an asylum? I took him to a neighboring university and made him discharge the burden of his persecuting rhymes into the eager ears of the poor, unthinking students. How is it with them, now? The result is too sad to tell. Why did I write this article? It was for a worthy, even a noble, purpose. It was to warn you, reader, if you should came across those merciless rhymes, to avoid them—avoid them as you would a pestilence!

# AN ENCOUNTER WITH AN INTERVIEWER

The nervous, dapper, "peart" young man took the chair I offered him, and said he was connected with the *Daily Thunderstorm*, and added:

"Hoping it's no harm, I've come to interview you."

"Come to what?"

"Interview you."

"Ah! I see. Yes—yes. Um! Yes—yes."

I was not feeling bright that morning. Indeed, my powers seemed a bit under a cloud. However, I went to the bookcase, and when I had been looking six or seven minutes I found I was obliged to refer to the young man. I said:—

"How do you spell it?"

"Spell what?"

"Interview."

"Oh, my goodness! what do you want to spell it for?"

"I don't want to spell it; I want to see what it means."

"Well, this is astonishing, I must say. I can tell you what it means, if you—if you—"

"Oh, all right! That will answer, and much obliged to you, too."

"In, in, ter, ter, inter—"

"Then you spell it with an I?"

"Why certainly!"

"Oh, that is what took me so long."

"Why, my dear sir, what did you propose to spell it with?"

"Well, I—I—hardly know. I had the Unabridged, and I was ciphering around in the back end, hoping I might tree her among the pictures. But it's a very old edition."

"Why, my friend, they wouldn't have a picture of it in even the latest e—My dear sir, I beg your pardon, I mean no harm in the world, but you do not look as—as—intelligent as I had expected you would. No harm—I mean no harm at all."

"Oh, don't mention it! It has often been said, and by people who would not flatter and who could have no inducement to flatter, that I am quite remarkable in that way. Yes—yes; they always speak of it with rapture."

"I can easily imagine it. But about this interview. You know it is the custom, now, to interview any man who has become notorious."

"Indeed, I had not heard of it before. It must be very interesting. What do you do it with?"

"Ah, well—well—well—this is disheartening. It ought to be done with a club in some cases; but customarily it consists in the interviewer asking questions and the interviewed answering them. It is all the rage now. Will you let me ask you certain questions calculated to bring out the salient points of your public and private history?"

"Oh, with pleasure—with pleasure. I have a very bad memory, but I hope you will not mind that. That is to say, it is an irregular memory—singularly irregular. Sometimes it goes in a gallop, and then again it will be as much as a fortnight passing a given point. This is a great grief to me."

"Oh, it is no matter, so you will try to do the best you can."

"I will. I will put my whole mind on it."

"Thanks. Are you ready to begin?"

"Ready."

Q. How old are you?

A. Nineteen, in June.

Q. Indeed. I would have taken you to be thirty-five or six. Where were you born?

A. In Missouri.

Q. When did you begin to write?

A. In 1836.

Q. Why, how could that be, if you are only nineteen now?

A. I don't know. It does seem curious, somehow.

Q. It does, indeed. Whom do you consider the most remarkable man you ever met?

A. Aaron Burr.

Q. But you never could have met Aaron Burr, if you are only nineteen years!—

A. Now, if you know more about me than I do, what do you ask me for?

Q. Well, it was only a suggestion; nothing more. How did you happen to meet Burr?

A. Well, I happened to be at his funeral one day, and he asked me to make less noise, and—

Q. But, good heavens! if you were at his funeral, he must have been dead, and if he was dead how could he care whether you made a noise or not?

A. I don't know. He was always a particular kind of a man that way.

Q. Still, I don't understand it at all. You say he spoke to you, and that he was dead.

A. I didn't say he was dead.

Q. But wasn't he dead?

A. Well, some said he was, some said he wasn't.

Q. What did you think?

A. Oh, it was none of my business! It wasn't any of my funeral.

Q. Did you—However, we can never get this matter straight. Let me ask about something else. What was the date of your birth?

A. Monday, October 31, 1693.

Q. What! Impossible! That would make you a hundred and eighty years old. How do you account for that?

A. I don't account for it at all.

Q. But you said at first you were only nineteen, and now you make yourself out to be one hundred and eighty. It is an awful discrepancy.

A. Why, have you noticed that? (Shaking hands.) Many a time it has seemed to me like a discrepancy, but somehow I couldn't make up my mind. How quick you notice a thing!

Q. Thank you for the compliment, as far as it goes. Had you, or have you, any brothers or sisters?

A. Eh! I—I—I think so—yes—but I don't remember.

Q. Well, that is the most extraordinary statement I ever heard!

A. Why, what makes you think that?

Q. How could I think otherwise? Why, look here! Who is this a picture of on the wall? Isn't that a brother of yours?

A. Oh, yes, yes, yes! Now you remind me of it; that was a brother of mine. That's William—Bill we called him. Poor old Bill!

Q. Why? Is he dead, then?

A. Ah! well, I suppose so. We never could tell. There was a great mystery about it.

Q. That is sad, very sad. He disappeared, then?

A. Well, yes, in a sort of general way. We buried him—

Q. Buried him! Buried him, without knowing whether he was dead or not?

A. Oh, no! Not that. He was dead enough.

Q. Well, I confess that I can't understand this. If you buried him, and you knew he was dead.

A. No! no! We only thought he was.

Q. Oh, I see! He came to life again?

A. I bet he didn't.

Q. Well, I never heard anything like this. Somebody was dead. Somebody was buried. Now, where was the mystery?

A. Ah! that's just it! That's it exactly. You see, we were twins—defunct and I—and we got mixed in the bathtub when we were only two weeks old, and one of us was drowned. But we didn't know which. Some think it was Bill. Some think it was me.

Q. Well, that is remarkable. What do you think?

A. Goodness knows! I would give whole worlds to know. This solemn, this awful mystery has cast a gloom over my whole life. But I will tell you a secret now, which I never have revealed to any creature before. One of us had a peculiar mark—a large mole on the back of his left hand; that was me. That child was the one that was drowned!

Q. Very well, then, I don't see that there is any mystery about it, after all.

A. You don't? Well, I do. Anyway, I don't see how they could ever have been such a blundering lot as to go and bury the wrong child. But, 'sh!—don't mention it where the family can hear of it. Heaven knows they have heartbreaking troubles enough without adding this.

Q. Well, I believe I have got material enough for the present, and I am very much obliged to you for the pains you have taken. But I was a good deal interested in that account of Aaron Burr's funeral. Would you mind telling me what particular circumstance it was that made you think Burr was such a remarkable man?

A. Oh! it was a mere trifle! Not one man in fifty would have noticed it at all. When the sermon was over, and the procession all ready to start for the cemetery, and the body all arranged nice in the hearse, he said he wanted to take a last look at the scenery, and so he got up and rode with the driver.

Then the young man reverently withdrew. He was very pleasant company, and I was sorry to see him go.

❧

# LEGEND OF SAGENFELD, IN GERMANY

More than a thousand years ago this small district was a kingdom—a little bit of a kingdom, a sort of dainty little toy kingdom, as one might say. It was far removed from the jealousies, strifes, and turmoils of that old warlike day, and so its life was a simple life, its people a gentle and guileless race; it lay always in a deep dream of peace, a soft Sabbath tranquillity; there was no malice, there was no envy, there was no ambition, consequently there were no heart-burnings, there was no unhappiness in the land.

In the course of time the old king died and his little son Hubert came to the throne. The people's love for him grew daily; he was so good and so pure and so noble, that by and by his love became a passion, almost a worship. Now at his birth the soothsayers had diligently studied the stars and found something written in that shining book to this effect:

*In Hubert's fourteenth year a pregnant event will happen; the animal whose singing shall sound sweetest in Hubert's ear shall save Hubert's life. So long as the king and the nation shall honor this animal's race for this good deed, the ancient dynasty shall not fail of an heir, nor the nation know war or pestilence or poverty. But beware an erring choice!*

All through the king's thirteenth year but one thing was talked of by the soothsayers, the statesmen, the little parliament, and the general people. That one thing was this: How is the last sentence of the prophecy to be understood? What goes before seems to mean that the saving animal will choose itself at the proper time; but the closing sentence seems to mean that the king must choose beforehand, and say what singer among the animals pleases him best, and that if he choose wisely the chosen animal will save his life, his dynasty, his people, but that if he should make "an erring choice"—beware!

By the end of the year there were as many opinions about this matter as there had been in the beginning; but a majority of the wise and the simple were agreed that the safest plan would be for the little king to make choice beforehand, and the earlier the better. So an edict was sent forth commanding all persons who owned singing creatures to bring them to the great hall of the palace in the morning of the first day of the new year. This command was obeyed. When everything was in readiness for the trial, the king made his solemn entry with the great officers of the crown, all clothed in their robes of state. The king mounted his golden throne and prepared to give judgment. But he presently said:—

"These creatures all sing at once; the noise is unendurable; no one can choose in such a turmoil. Take them all away, and bring back one at a time."

This was done. One sweet warbler after another charmed the young king's ear and was removed to make way for another candidate. The precious minutes slipped by; among so many bewitching songsters he found it hard to choose, and all the harder because the promised penalty for an error was so terrible that it unsettled his judgment and made him afraid to trust his own ears. He grew nervous and his face showed distress. His ministers saw this, for they never took their eyes from him a moment. Now they began to say in their hearts:

"He has lost courage—the cool head is gone—he will err—he and his dynasty and his people are doomed!"

At the end of an hour the king sat silent awhile, and then said:—

"Bring back the linnet."

The linnet trilled forth her jubilant music. In the midst of it the king was about to uplift his scepter in sign of choice, but checked himself and said:—

"But let us be sure. Bring back the thrush; let them sing together."

The thrush was brought, and the two birds poured out their marvels of song together. The king wavered, then his inclination began to settle and strengthen—one could see it in his countenance. Hope budded in the hearts of the old ministers, their pulses began to beat quicker, the scepter began to rise slowly, when: There was a hideous interruption! It was a sound like this—just at the door:

"Waw...he! waw...he! waw-he!-waw he!-waw-he!"

Everybody was sorely startled—and enraged at himself for showing it.

The next instant the dearest, sweetest, prettiest little peasant-maid of nine years came tripping in, her brown eyes glowing with childish eagerness; but when she saw that august company and those angry faces she stopped and hung her head and put her poor coarse apron to her eyes. Nobody gave her welcome, none pitied her. Presently she looked up timidly through her tears, and said:—

"My lord the king, I pray you pardon me, for I meant no wrong. I have no father and no mother, but I have a goat and a donkey, and they are all in all to me. My goat gives me the sweetest milk, and when my dear good donkey brays it seems to me there is no music like to it. So when my lord the king's jester said the sweetest singer among all the animals should save the crown and nation, and moved me to bring him here—"

All the court burst into a rude laugh, and the child fled away crying, without trying to finish her speech. The chief minister gave a private order that she and her disastrous donkey be flogged beyond the precincts of the palace and commanded to come within them no more.

Then the trial of the birds was resumed. The two birds sang their best, but the scepter lay motionless in the king's hand. Hope died slowly out in the breasts of all. An hour went by; two hours, still no decision. The day waned to its close, and the waiting multitudes outside the palace grew crazed with anxiety and apprehension. The twilight came on, the shadows fell deeper and deeper. The king and his court could no longer see each other's faces. No one spoke—none called for lights. The great trial had been made; it had failed; each and all wished to hide their faces from the light and cover up their deep trouble in their own hearts.

Finally-hark! A rich, full strain of the divinest melody streamed forth from a remote part of the hall—the nightingale's voice!

"Up!" shouted the king, "let all the bells make proclamation to the people, for the choice is made and we have not erred. King, dynasty, and nation are saved. From henceforth let the nightingale be honored throughout the land forever. And publish it among all the people that whosoever shall insult a nightingale, or injure it, shall suffer death. The king hath spoken."

All that little world was drunk with joy. The castle and the city blazed with bonfires all night long, the people danced and drank and sang; and the triumphant clamor of the bells never ceased.

From that day the nightingale was a sacred bird. Its song was heard in every house; the poets wrote its praises; the painters painted it; its sculptured image adorned every arch and turret and fountain and public building. It was even taken into the king's councils; and no grave matter of state was decided until the soothsayers had laid the thing before the state nightingale and translated to the ministry what it was that the bird had sung about it.

The young king was very fond of the chase. When the summer was come he rode forth with hawk and hound, one day, in a brilliant company of his nobles. He got separated from them by and by, in a great forest, and took what he imagined a near cut, to find them again; but it was a mistake. He rode on and on, hopefully at first, but with sinking courage finally. Twilight came on, and still he was plunging through a lonely and unknown land. Then came a catastrophe. In the dim light he forced his horse through a tangled thicket overhanging a steep and rocky declivity. When horse and rider reached the bottom, the former had a broken neck and the latter a broken leg. The poor little king lay there suffering agonies of pain, and each hour seemed a long month to him. He kept his ear strained to hear any sound that might promise hope of rescue; but he heard no voice, no sound of horn or bay of hound. So at last he gave up all hope, and said, "Let death come, for come it must."

Just then the deep, sweet song of a nightingale swept across the still wastes of the night.

"Saved!" the king said. "Saved! It is the sacred bird, and the prophecy is come true. The gods themselves protected me from error in the choice."

He could hardly contain his joy; he could not word his gratitude. Every few moments now he thought he caught the sound of approaching succor. But each time it was a disappointment; no succor came. The dull hours drifted on. Still no help came—but still the sacred bird sang on. He began to have misgivings about his choice, but he stifled them. Toward dawn the bird ceased. The morning came, and with it thirst and hunger; but no succor. The day waxed and waned. At last the king cursed the nightingale.

Immediately the song of the thrush came from out the wood. The king said in his heart, "This was the true-bird—my choice was false—succor will come now."

But it did not come. Then he lay many hours insensible. When he came to himself, a linnet was singing. He listened with apathy. His faith was gone. "These birds," he said, "can bring no help; I and my house and my people are doomed." He turned him about to die; for he was grown very feeble from hunger and thirst and suffering, and felt that his end was near. In truth, he wanted to die, and be released from pain. For long hours he lay without thought or feeling or motion. Then his senses returned. The dawn of the third morning was breaking. Ah, the world seemed very beautiful to those worn eyes. Suddenly a great longing to live rose up in the lad's heart, and from his soul welled a deep and fervent prayer that Heaven would have mercy upon him and let him see his home and his friends once more. In that instant a soft, a faint, a far-off sound, but oh, how inexpressibly sweet to his waiting ear, came floating out of the distance:

"Waw...he! waw...he! Waw-he!—waw-he!—waw-he!"

"That, oh, that song is sweeter, a thousand times sweeter than the voice of the nightingale, thrush, or linnet, for it brings not mere hope, but certainty of succor; and now, indeed, am I saved! The sacred singer has chosen itself, as the oracle intended; the prophecy is fulfilled, and my life, my house, and my people are redeemed. The ass shall be sacred from this day!"

The divine music grew nearer and nearer, stronger—and stronger and ever sweeter and sweeter to the perishing sufferer's ear. Down the declivity the docile little donkey wandered, cropping herbage and singing as he went; and when at last he saw the dead horse and the wounded king, he came and snuffed at them with simple and marveling curiosity. The king petted him, and he knelt down as had been his wont when his little mistress desired to mount. With great labor and pain the lad drew himself upon the creature's back, and held himself there by aid of the generous ears. The ass went singing forth from the place and carried the king to the little peasant-maid's hut. She gave him her pallet for a bed, refreshed him with goat's milk, and then flew to tell the great news to the first scouting-party of searchers she might meet.

The king got well. His first act was to proclaim the sacredness and inviolability of the ass; his second was to add this particular ass to his cabinet and make him chief minister of the crown; his third was to have all the statues and effigies of nightingales throughout his kingdom destroyed, and replaced by statues and effigies of the sacred donkey; and, his fourth was to announce that when the little peasant maid should reach her fifteenth year he would make her his queen and he kept his word.

Such is the legend. This explains why the moldering image of the ass adorns all these old crumbling walls and arches; and it explains why, during many centuries, an ass was always the chief minister in that royal cabinet, just as is still the case in most cabinets to this day; and it also explains why, in that little kingdom, during many centuries, all great poems, all great speeches, all great books, all public solemnities, and all royal proclamations, always began with these stirring words:

"Waw...he! waw...he!—waw he! Waw-he!"

*[Left out of "A Tramp Abroad" because its authenticity seemed doubtful, and could not at that time be proved.—M. T.]*

# CONCERNING THE AMERICAN LANGUAGE

There was as Englishman in our compartment, and he complimented me on—on what? But you would never guess. He complimented me on my English. He said Americans in general did not speak the English language as correctly as I did. I said I was obliged to him for his compliment, since I knew he meant it for one, but that I was not fairly entitled to it, for I did not speak English at all—I only spoke American.

He laughed, and said it was a distinction without a difference. I said no, the difference was not prodigious, but still it was considerable. We fell into a friendly dispute over the matter. I put my case as well as I could, and said:—

"The languages were identical several generations ago, but our changed conditions and the spread of our people far to the south and far to the west have made many alterations in our pronunciation, and have introduced new words among us and changed the meanings of many old ones. English people talk through their noses; we do not. We say know, English people say nao; we say cow, the Briton says kaow; we—"

"Oh, come! that is pure Yankee; everybody knows that."

"Yes, it is pure Yankee; that is true. One cannot hear it in America outside of the little corner called New England, which is Yankee land. The English themselves planted it there, two hundred and fifty years ago, and there it remains; it has never spread. But England talks through her nose yet; the Londoner and the backwoods New-Englander pronounce 'know' and 'cow' alike, and then the Briton unconsciously satirizes himself by making fun of the Yankee's pronunciation."

We argued this point at some length; nobody won; but no matter, the fact remains Englishmen say nao and kaow for "know" and "cow," and that is what the rustic inhabitant of a very small section of America does.

"You conferred your 'a' upon New England, too, and there it remains; it has not traveled out of the narrow limits of those six little states in all these two hundred and fifty years. All England uses it, New England's small population—say four millions—use it, but we have forty-five millions who do not use it. You say 'glahs of wawtah,' so does New England; at least, New England says 'glahs.' America at large flattens the 'a', and says 'glass of water.' These sounds are pleasanter than yours; you may think they are not right—well, in English they are not right, but in 'American' they are. You say 'flahsk' and 'bahsket,' and 'jackahss'; we say 'flask,' 'basket,' 'jackass'—sounding the 'a' as it is in 'tallow,' 'fallow,' and so on. Up to as late as 1847 Mr. Webster's Dictionary had the impudence to still pronounce 'basket' bahsket, when he knew that outside of his little New England all America shortened the 'a' and paid no attention to his English broadening of it. However, it called itself an English Dictionary, so it was proper enough that it should stick to English forms, perhaps. It still calls itself an English Dictionary today, but it has quietly ceased to pronounce 'basket' as if it were spelt 'bahsket.' In the American language the 'h' is respected; the 'h' is not dropped or added improperly."

"The same is the case in England—I mean among the educated classes, of course."

"Yes, that is true; but a nation's language is a very large matter. It is not simply a manner of speech obtaining among the educated handful; the manner obtaining among the vast uneducated multitude must be considered also. Your uneducated masses speak English, you will not deny that; our uneducated masses speak American—it won't be fair for you to deny that, for you can see, yourself, that when your stable-boy says, 'It isn't the 'unting that 'urts the 'orse, but the 'ammer, 'ammer, 'ammer on the 'ard 'ighway,' and our stable-boy makes the same remark without suffocating a single h, these two people are manifestly talking two different languages. But if the signs are to be trusted, even your educated classes used to drop the 'h.' They say humble, now, and heroic, and historic etc., but I judge that they used to drop those h's because your writers still keep up the fashion of putting an AN before those words instead of A. This is what Mr. Darwin might call a 'rudimentary' sign that as an was justifiable once, and useful when your educated classes used to say 'umble, and 'eroic, and 'istorical. Correct writers of the American language do not put an before those words."

The English gentleman had something to say upon this matter, but never mind what he said—I'm not arguing his case. I have him at a disadvantage, now. I proceeded:

"In England you encourage an orator by exclaiming, 'H'yaah! h'yaah!' We pronounce it heer in some sections, 'h'yer' in others, and so on; but our whites do not say 'h'yaah,' pronouncing the a's like the a in ah. I have heard English ladies say 'don't you'—making two separate and distinct words of it; your Mr. Burnand has satirized it. But we always say 'dontchu.' This is much better. Your ladies say, 'Oh, it's oful nice!' Ours say, 'Oh, it's awful nice!' We say, 'Four hundred,' you say 'For'—as in the word or. Your clergymen speak of 'the Lawd,' ours of 'the Lord'; yours speak of 'the gawds of the heathen,' ours of 'the gods of the heathen.' When you are exhausted, you say you are 'knocked up.' We don't. When you say you will do a thing 'directly,' you mean 'immediately'; in the American language—generally speaking—the word signifies 'after a little.' When you say 'clever,' you mean 'capable'; with us the word used to mean 'accommodating,' but I don't know what it means now. Your word 'stout' means 'fleshy'; our word 'stout' usually means 'strong.' Your words 'gentleman' and 'lady' have a very restricted meaning; with us they include the barmaid, butcher, burglar, harlot, and horse-thief. You say, 'I haven't got any stockings on,' 'I haven't got any memory,' 'I haven't got any money in my purse; we usually say, 'I haven't any stockings on,' 'I haven't any memory!' 'I haven't any money in my purse.' You say 'out of window'; we always put in a the. If one asks 'How old is that man?' the Briton answers, 'He will be about forty'; in the American language we should say, 'He is about forty.' However, I won't tire you, sir; but if I wanted to, I could pile up differences here until I not only convinced you that English and American are separate languages, but that when I speak my native tongue in its utmost purity an Englishman can't understand me at all."

"I don't wish to flatter you, but it is about all I can do to understand you now."

That was a very pretty compliment, and it put us on the pleasantest terms directly—I use the word in the English sense.

[Later—1882. Esthetes in many of our schools are now beginning to teach the pupils to broaden the 'a,' and to say "don't you," in the elegant foreign way.]

# THE $30,000 BEQUEST

### CHAPTER 1

Lakeside was a pleasant little town of five or six thousand inhabitants, and a rather pretty one, too, as towns go in the Far West. It had church accommodations for thirty-five thousand, which is the way of the Far West and the South, where everybody is religious, and where each of the Protestant sects is represented and has a plant of its own. Rank was unknown in Lakeside—unconfessed, anyway; everybody knew everybody and his dog, and a sociable friendliness was the prevailing atmosphere.

Saladin Foster was book-keeper in the principal store, and the only high-salaried man of his profession in Lakeside. He was thirty-five years old, now; he had served that store for fourteen years; he had begun in his marriage-week at four hundred dollars a year, and had climbed steadily up, a hundred dollars a year, for four years; from that time forth his wage had remained eight hundred—a handsome figure indeed, and everybody conceded that he was worth it.

His wife, Electra, was a capable helpmeet, although—like himself—a dreamer of dreams and a private dabbler in romance. The first thing she did, after her marriage—child as she was, aged only nineteen—was to buy an acre of ground on the edge of the town, and pay down the cash for it—twenty-five dollars, all her fortune. Saladin had less, by fifteen. She instituted a vegetable garden there, got it farmed on shares by the nearest neighbor, and made it pay her a hundred per cent. a year. Out of Saladin's first year's wage she put thirty dollars in the savings-bank, sixty out of his second, a hundred out of his third, a hundred and fifty out of his fourth. His wage went to eight hundred a year, then, and meantime two children had arrived and increased the expenses, but she banked two hundred a year from the salary, nevertheless, thenceforth. When she had been married seven years she built and furnished a pretty and comfortable two-thousand-dollar house in the midst of her garden-acre, paid half of the money down and moved her family in. Seven years later she was out of debt and had several hundred dollars out earning its living.

Earning it by the rise in landed estate; for she had long ago bought another acre or two and sold the most of it at a profit to pleasant people who were willing to build, and would be good neighbors and furnish a general comradeship for herself and her growing family. She had an independent income from safe investments of about a hundred dollars a year; her children were growing in years and grace; and she was a pleased and happy woman. Happy in her husband, happy in her children, and the husband and the children were happy in her. It is at this point that this history begins.

The youngest girl, Clytemnestra—called Clytie for short—was eleven; her sister, Gwendolen—called Gwen for short—was thirteen; nice girls, and comely. The names betray the latent romance-tinge in the parental blood, the parents' names indicate that the tinge was an inheritance. It was an affectionate family, hence all four of its members had pet names, Saladin's was a curious and unsexing one—Sally; and so was Electra's—Aleck. All day long Sally was a good and diligent book-keeper and salesman; all day long Aleck was a good and faithful mother and housewife, and thoughtful and calculating business woman; but in the cozy living-room at night they put the plodding world away, and lived in another and a fairer, reading romances to each other, dreaming dreams, comrading with kings and princes and stately lords and ladies in the flash and stir and splendor of noble palaces and grim and ancient castles.

## CHAPTER 2

Now came great news! Stunning news—joyous news, in fact. It came from a neighboring state, where the family's only surviving relative lived. It was Sally's relative—a sort of vague and indefinite uncle or second or third cousin by the name of Tilbury Foster, seventy and a bachelor, reputed well off and corresponding sour and crusty. Sally had tried to make up to him once, by letter, in a bygone time, and had not made that mistake again. Tilbury now wrote to Sally, saying he should shortly die, and should leave him thirty thousand dollars, cash; not for love, but because money had given him most of his troubles and exasperations, and he wished to place it where there was good hope that it would continue its malignant work. The bequest would be found in his will, and would be paid over. PROVIDED, that Sally should be able to prove to the executors that he had TAKEN NO NOTICE OF THE GIFT BY SPOKEN WORD OR BY LETTER, HAD MADE NO INQUIRIES CONCERNING THE MORIBUND'S PROGRESS TOWARD THE EVERLASTING TROPICS, AND HAD NOT ATTENDED THE FUNERAL.

As soon as Aleck had partially recovered from the tremendous emotions created by the letter, she sent to the relative's habitat and subscribed for the local paper.

Man and wife entered into a solemn compact, now, to never mention the great news to any one while the relative lived, lest some ignorant person carry the fact to the death-bed and distort it and make it appear that they were disobediently thankful for the bequest, and just the same as confessing it and publishing it, right in the face of the prohibition.

For the rest of the day Sally made havoc and confusion with his books, and Aleck could not keep her mind on her affairs, not even take up a flower-pot or book or a stick of wood without forgetting what she had intended to do with it. For both were dreaming.

"Thir-ty thousand dollars!"

All day long the music of those inspiring words sang through those people's heads.

From his marriage-day forth, Aleck's grip had been upon the purse, and Sally had seldom known what it was to be privileged to squander a dime on non-necessities.

"Thir-ty thousand dollars!" the song went on and on. A vast sum, an unthinkable sum!

All day long Aleck was absorbed in planning how to invest it, Sally in planning how to spend it.

There was no romance-reading that night. The children took themselves away early, for their parents were silent, distraught, and strangely unentertaining. The good-night kisses might as well have been impressed upon vacancy, for all the response they got; the parents were not aware of the kisses, and the children had been gone an hour before their absence was noticed. Two pencils had been busy during that hour—note-making; in the way of plans. It was Sally who broke the stillness at last. He said, with exultation:

"Ah, it'll be grand, Aleck! Out of the first thousand we'll have a horse and a buggy for summer, and a cutter and a skin lap-robe for winter."

Aleck responded with decision and composure—

"Out of the CAPITAL? Nothing of the kind. Not if it was a million!"

Sally was deeply disappointed; the glow went out of his face.

"Oh, Aleck!" he said, reproachfully. "We've always worked so hard and been so scrimped: and now that we are rich, it does seem—"

He did not finish, for he saw her eye soften; his supplication had touched her. She said, with gentle persuasiveness:

"We must not spend the capital, dear, it would not be wise. Out of the income from it—"

"That will answer, that will answer, Aleck! How dear and good you are! There will be a noble income and if we can spend that—"

"Not ALL of it, dear, not all of it, but you can spend a part of it. That is, a reasonable part. But the whole of the capital—every penny of it—must be put right to work, and kept at it. You see the reasonableness of that, don't you?"

"Why, ye-s. Yes, of course. But we'll have to wait so long. Six months before the first interest falls due."

"Yes—maybe longer."

"Longer, Aleck? Why? Don't they pay half-yearly?"

"THAT kind of an investment—yes; but I sha'n't invest in that way."

"What way, then?"

"For big returns."

"Big. That's good. Go on, Aleck. What is it?"

"Coal. The new mines. Cannel. I mean to put in ten thousand. Ground floor. When we organize, we'll get three shares for one."

"By George, but it sounds good, Aleck! Then the shares will be worth—how much? And when?"

"About a year. They'll pay ten per cent. half yearly, and be worth thirty thousand. I know all about it; the advertisement is in the Cincinnati paper here."

"Land, thirty thousand for ten—in a year! Let's jam in the whole capital and pull out ninety! I'll write and subscribe right now—tomorrow it maybe too late."

He was flying to the writing-desk, but Aleck stopped him and put him back in his chair. She said:

"Don't lose your head so. WE mustn't subscribe till we've got the money; don't you know that?"

Sally's excitement went down a degree or two, but he was not wholly appeased.

"Why, Aleck, we'll HAVE it, you know—and so soon, too. He's probably out of his troubles before this; it's a hundred to nothing he's selecting his brimstone-shovel this very minute. Now, I think—"

Aleck shuddered, and said:

"How CAN you, Sally! Don't talk in that way, it is perfectly scandalous."

"Oh, well, make it a halo, if you like, I don't care for his outfit, I was only just talking. Can't you let a person talk?"

"But why should you WANT to talk in that dreadful way? How would you like to have people talk so about YOU, and you not cold yet?"

"Not likely to be, for ONE while, I reckon, if my last act was giving away money for the sake of doing somebody a harm with it. But never mind about

Tilbury, Aleck, let's talk about something worldly. It does seem to me that that mine is the place for the whole thirty. What's the objection?"

"All the eggs in one basket—that's the objection."

"All right, if you say so. What about the other twenty? What do you mean to do with that?"

"There is no hurry; I am going to look around before I do anything with it."

"All right, if your mind's made up," signed Sally. He was deep in thought awhile, then he said:

"There'll be twenty thousand profit coming from the ten a year from now. We can spend that, can we, Aleck?"

Aleck shook her head.

"No, dear," she said, "it won't sell high till we've had the first semi-annual dividend. You can spend part of that."

"Shucks, only THAT—and a whole year to wait! Confound it, I—"

"Oh, do be patient! It might even be declared in three months—it's quite within the possibilities."

"Oh, jolly! oh, thanks!" and Sally jumped up and kissed his wife in gratitude. "It'll be three thousand—three whole thousand! how much of it can we spend, Aleck? Make it liberal!—do, dear, that's a good fellow."

Aleck was pleased; so pleased that she yielded to the pressure and conceded a sum which her judgment told her was a foolish extravagance—a thousand dollars. Sally kissed her half a dozen times and even in that way could not express all his joy and thankfulness. This new access of gratitude and affection carried Aleck quite beyond the bounds of prudence, and before she could restrain herself she had made her darling another grant—a couple of thousand out of the fifty or sixty which she meant to clear within a year of the twenty which still remained of the bequest. The happy tears sprang to Sally's eyes, and he said:

"Oh, I want to hug you!" And he did it. Then he got his notes and sat down and began to check off, for first purchase, the luxuries which he should earliest wish to secure. "Horse—buggy—cutter—lap-robe—patent-leathers—dog—plug-hat— church-pew—stem-winder—new teeth—SAY, Aleck!"

"Well?"

"Ciphering away, aren't you? That's right. Have you got the twenty thousand invested yet?"

"No, there's no hurry about that; I must look around first, and think."

"But you are ciphering; what's it about?"

"Why, I have to find work for the thirty thousand that comes out of the coal, haven't I?"

"Scott, what a head! I never thought of that. How are you getting along? Where have you arrived?"

"Not very far—two years or three. I've turned it over twice; once in oil and once in wheat."

"Why, Aleck, it's splendid! How does it aggregate?"

"I think—well, to be on the safe side, about a hundred and eighty thousand clear, though it will probably be more."

"My! isn't it wonderful? By gracious! luck has come our way at last, after all the hard sledding, Aleck!"

"Well?"

"I'm going to cash in a whole three hundred on the missionaries—what real right have we care for expenses!"

"You couldn't do a nobler thing, dear; and it's just like your generous nature, you unselfish boy."

The praise made Sally poignantly happy, but he was fair and just enough to say it was rightfully due to Aleck rather than to himself, since but for her he should never have had the money.

Then they went up to bed, and in their delirium of bliss they forgot and left the candle burning in the parlor. They did not remember until they were undressed; then Sally was for letting it burn; he said they could afford it, if it was a thousand. But Aleck went down and put it out.

A good job, too; for on her way back she hit on a scheme that would turn the hundred and eighty thousand into half a million before it had had time to get cold.


CHAPTER 3

The little newspaper which Aleck had subscribed for was a Thursday sheet; it would make the trip of five hundred miles from Tilbury's village and arrive on Saturday. Tilbury's letter had started on Friday, more than a day too late for the benefactor to die and get into that week's issue, but in plenty of time to make connection for the next output. Thus the Fosters had to wait almost a complete week to find out whether anything of a satisfactory nature had happened to him or not. It was a long, long week, and the strain was a heavy one. The pair could hardly have borne it if their minds had not had the relief of wholesome diversion. We have seen that they had that. The woman was piling up fortunes right along, the man was spending them—spending all his wife would give him a chance at, at any rate.

At last the Saturday came, and the *Weekly Sagamore* arrived. Mrs. Eversly Bennett was present. She was the Presbyterian parson's wife, and was working the Fosters for a charity. Talk now died a sudden death—on the Foster side. Mrs. Bennett presently discovered that her hosts were not hearing a word she was saying; so she got up, wondering and indignant, and went away. The moment she was out of the house, Aleck eagerly tore the wrapper from the paper, and her eyes and Sally's swept the columns for the death-notices. Disappointment! Tilbury was not anywhere mentioned. Aleck was a Christian from the cradle, and duty and the force of habit required her to go through the motions. She pulled herself together and said, with a pious two-per-cent. trade joyousness:

"Let us be humbly thankful that he has been spared; and—"

"Damn his treacherous hide, I wish—"

"Sally! For shame!"

"I don't care!" retorted the angry man. "It's the way YOU feel, and if you weren't so immorally pious you'd be honest and say so."

Aleck said, with wounded dignity:

"I do not see how you can say such unkind and unjust things. There is no such thing as immoral piety."

Sally felt a pang, but tried to conceal it under a shuffling attempt to save his case by changing the form of it—as if changing the form while retaining the juice could deceive the expert he was trying to placate. He said:

"I didn't mean so bad as that, Aleck; I didn't really mean immoral piety, I only meant—meant—well, conventional piety, you know; er—shop piety; the—the—why, YOU know what I mean. Aleck—the—well, where you put up that plated article and play it for solid, you know, without intending anything improper, but just out of trade habit, ancient policy, petrified custom, loyalty to—to—hang it, I can't find the right words, but YOU know what I mean, Aleck, and that there isn't any harm in it. I'll try again. You see, it's this way. If a person—"

"You have said quite enough," said Aleck, coldly; "let the subject be dropped."

"I'M willing," fervently responded Sally, wiping the sweat from his forehead and looking the thankfulness he had no words for. Then, musingly, he apologized to himself. "I certainly held threes—I KNOW it—but I drew and didn't fill. That's where I'm so often weak in the game. If I had stood pat—but I didn't. I never do. I don't know enough."

Confessedly defeated, he was properly tame now and subdued. Aleck forgave him with her eyes.

The grand interest, the supreme interest, came instantly to the front again; nothing could keep it in the background many minutes on a stretch. The couple took up the puzzle of the absence of Tilbury's death-notice. They discussed it every which way, more or less hopefully, but they had to finish where they began, and concede that the only really sane explanation of the absence of the notice must be—and without doubt was—that Tilbury was not dead. There was something sad about it, something even a little unfair, maybe, but there it was, and had to be put up with. They were agreed as to that. To Sally it seemed a strangely inscrutable dispensation; more inscrutable than usual, he thought; one of the most unnecessary inscrutable he could call to mind, in fact—and said so, with some feeling; but if he was hoping to draw Aleck he failed; she reserved her opinion, if she had one; she had not the habit of taking injudicious risks in any market, worldly or other.

The pair must wait for next week's paper—Tilbury had evidently postponed. That was their thought and their decision. So they put the subject away and went about their affairs again with as good heart as they could.

Now, if they had but known it, they had been wronging Tilbury all the time. Tilbury had kept faith, kept it to the letter; he was dead, he had died to schedule. He was dead more than four days now and used to it; entirely dead, perfectly dead, as dead as any other new person in the cemetery; dead in abundant time to get into that week's *Sagamore*, too, and only shut out by an accident; an accident which could not happen to a metropolitan journal, but which happens easily to a poor little village rag like the *Sagamore*. On this occasion, just as the editorial page was being locked up, a gratis quart of strawberry ice-water arrived from Hostetter's Ladies and Gents Ice-Cream Parlors, and the stickful of rather chilly regret over Tilbury's translation got crowded out to make room for the editor's frantic gratitude.

On its way to the standing-galley Tilbury's notice got pied. Otherwise it would have gone into some future edition, for *Weekly Sagamores* do not waste "live" matter, and in their galleys "live" matter is immortal, unless a pi accident intervenes. But a thing that gets pied is dead, and for such there is no resurrection; its chance of seeing print is gone, forever and ever. And so, let Tilbury like it or not, let him rave in his grave to his fill, no matter—no mention of his death would ever see the light in the *Weekly Sagamore*.

## CHAPTER 4

Five weeks drifted tediously along. The *Sagamore* arrived regularly on the Saturdays, but never once contained a mention of Tilbury Foster. Sally's patience broke down at this point, and he said, resentfully:

"Damn his livers, he's immortal!"

Aleck give him a very severe rebuke, and added with icy solemnity:

"How would you feel if you were suddenly cut out just after such an awful remark had escaped out of you?"

Without sufficient reflection Sally responded:

"I'd feel I was lucky I hadn't got caught with it IN me."

Pride had forced him to say something, and as he could not think of any rational thing to say he flung that out. Then he stole a base—as he called it—that is, slipped from the presence, to keep from being brayed in his wife's discussion-mortar.

Six months came and went. The *Sagamore* was still silent about Tilbury. Meantime, Sally had several times thrown out a feeler—that is, a hint that he would like to know. Aleck had ignored the hints. Sally now resolved to brace up and risk a frontal attack. So he squarely proposed to disguise himself and go to Tilbury's village and surreptitiously find out as to the prospects. Aleck put her foot on the dangerous project with energy and decision. She said:

"What can you be thinking of? You do keep my hands full! You have to be watched all the time, like a little child, to keep you from walking into the fire. You'll stay right where you are!"

"Why, Aleck, I could do it and not be found out—I'm certain of it."

"Sally Foster, don't you know you would have to inquire around?"

"Of course, but what of it? Nobody would suspect who I was."

"Oh, listen to the man! Some day you've got to prove to the executors that you never inquired. What then?"

He had forgotten that detail. He didn't reply; there wasn't anything to say. Aleck added:

"Now then, drop that notion out of your mind, and don't ever meddle with it again. Tilbury set that trap for you. Don't you know it's a trap? He is on the watch, and fully expecting you to blunder into it. Well, he is going to be disappointed—at least while I am on deck. Sally!"

"Well?"

"As long as you live, if it's a hundred years, don't you ever make an inquiry. Promise!"

"All right," with a sigh and reluctantly.

Then Aleck softened and said:

"Don't be impatient. We are prospering; we can wait; there is no hurry. Our small dead-certain income increases all the time; and as to futures, I have not made a mistake yet—they are piling up by the thousands and tens of thousands. There is not another family in the state with such prospects as ours. Already we are beginning to roll in eventual wealth. You know that, don't you?"

"Yes, Aleck, it's certainly so."

"Then be grateful for what God is doing for us and stop worrying. You do not believe we could have achieved these prodigious results without His special help and guidance, do you?"

Hesitatingly, "N-no, I suppose not." Then, with feeling and admiration, "And yet, when it comes to judiciousness in watering a stock or putting up a hand to skin Wall Street I don't give in that *you* need any outside amateur help, if I do wish I—"

"Oh, *do* shut up! I know you do not mean any harm or any irreverence, poor boy, but you can't seem to open your mouth without letting out things to make a person shudder. You keep me in constant dread. For you and for all of us. Once I had no fear of the thunder, but now when I hear it I—"

Her voice broke, and she began to cry, and could not finish. The sight of this smote Sally to the heart and he took her in his arms and petted her and comforted her and promised better conduct, and upbraided himself and remorsefully pleaded for forgiveness. And he was in earnest, and sorry for what he had done and ready for any sacrifice that could make up for it.

And so, in privacy, he thought long and deeply over the matter, resolving to do what should seem best. It was easy to *promise* reform; indeed he had already promised it. But would that do any real good, any permanent good? No, it would be but temporary—he knew his weakness, and confessed it to himself with sorrow—he could not keep the promise. Something surer and better must be devised; and he devised it. At cost of precious money which he had long been saving up, shilling by shilling, he put a lightning-rod on the house.

At a subsequent time he relapsed.

What miracles habit can do! and how quickly and how easily habits are acquired—both trifling habits and habits which profoundly change us. If by accident we wake at two in the morning a couple of nights in succession, we have need to be uneasy, for another repetition can turn the accident into a habit; and a month's dallying with whiskey—but we all know these commonplace facts.

The castle-building habit, the day-dreaming habit—how it grows! what a luxury it becomes; how we fly to its enchantments at every idle moment, how we revel in them, steep our souls in them, intoxicate ourselves with their beguiling fantasies—oh yes, and how soon and how easily our dream life and our material life become so intermingled and so fused together that we can't quite tell which is which, any more.

By and by Aleck subscribed to a Chicago daily and for the *Wall Street Pointer*. With an eye single to finance she studied these as diligently all the week as she studied her Bible Sundays. Sally was lost in admiration, to note with what swift and sure strides her genius and judgment developed and expanded in the forecasting and handling of the securities of both the material and spiritual markets. He was proud of her nerve and daring in exploiting worldly stocks, and just as proud of her conservative caution in working her spiritual deals. He noted that she never lost her head in either case; that with a splendid courage she often went short on worldly futures, but heedfully drew the line there—she was always long on the others. Her policy was quite sane and simple, as she explained it to him: what she put into earthly futures was for speculation, what she put into spiritual futures was for investment; she was willing to go into the one on a margin, and take chances, but in the case of the other, "margin her no margins"—she wanted to cash in a hundred cents per dollar's worth, and have the stock transferred on the books.

It took but a very few months to educate Aleck's imagination and Sally's. Each day's training added something to the spread and effectiveness of the two machines. As a consequence, Aleck made imaginary money much faster than at first she had dreamed of making it, and Sally's competency in spending the overflow of it kept pace with the strain put upon it, right along. In the beginning, Aleck had given the coal speculation a twelvemonth in which to materialize, and had been loath to grant that this term might possibly be shortened by nine months. But that was the feeble work, the nursery work, of a financial fancy that had had no teaching, no experience, no practice. These aids soon came, then that nine months vanished, and the imaginary ten-thousand-dollar investment came marching home with three hundred per cent. profit on its back!

It was a great day for the pair of Fosters. They were speechless for joy. Also speechless for another reason: after much watching of the market, Aleck had lately, with fear and trembling, made her first flyer on a "margin," using the remaining twenty thousand of the bequest in this risk. In her mind's eye she had seen it climb, point by point—always with a chance that the market would break—until at last her anxieties were too great for further endurance— she being new to the margin business and unhardened, as yet—and she gave her imaginary broker an imaginary order by imaginary telegraph to sell. She said forty thousand dollars' profit was enough. The sale was made on the very day that the coal venture had returned with its rich freight. As I have said, the couple were speechless, they sat dazed and blissful that night, trying to realize that they were actually worth a hundred thousand dollars in clean, imaginary cash. Yet so it was.

It was the last time that ever Aleck was afraid of a margin; at least afraid enough to let it break her sleep and pale her cheek to the extent that this first experience in that line had done.

Indeed it was a memorable night. Gradually the realization that they were rich sank securely home into the souls of the pair, then they began to place the money. If we could have looked out through the eyes of these dreamers, we should have seen their tidy little wooden house disappear, and two-story brick with a cast-iron fence in front of it take its place; we should have seen a three-globed gas-chandelier grow down from the parlor ceiling; we should have seen the homely rag carpet turn to noble Brussels, a dollar and a half a yard; we should have seen the plebeian fireplace vanish away and a recherche, big base-burner with isinglass windows take position and spread awe around. And we should have seen other things, too; among them the buggy, the lap-robe, the stove-pipe hat, and so on.

From that time forth, although the daughters and the neighbors saw only the same old wooden house there, it was a two-story brick to Aleck and Sally and not a night went by that Aleck did not worry about the imaginary gas-bills, and get for all comfort Sally's reckless retort: "What of it? We can afford it."

Before the couple went to bed, that first night that they were rich, they had decided that they must celebrate. They must give a party—that was the idea. But how to explain it—to the daughters and the neighbors? They could not expose the fact that they were rich. Sally was willing, even anxious, to do it; but Aleck kept her head and would not allow it. She said that although the money was as good as in, it would be as well to wait until it was actually in. On that policy she took her stand, and would not budge. The great secret must be kept, she said—kept from the daughters and everybody else.

The pair were puzzled. They must celebrate, they were determined to celebrate, but since the secret must be kept, what could they celebrate? No birthdays were due for three months. Tilbury wasn't available, evidently he was going to live forever; what the nation *could* they celebrate? That was Sally's way of putting it; and he was getting impatient, too, and harassed. But at last he hit it—just by sheer inspiration, as it seemed to him—and all their troubles were gone in a moment; they would celebrate the Discovery of America. A splendid idea!

Aleck was almost too proud of Sally for words—she said *she* never would have thought of it. But Sally, although he was bursting with delight in the compliment and with wonder at himself, tried not to let on, and said it wasn't really anything, anybody could have done it. Whereat Aleck, with a prideful toss of her happy head, said:

"Oh, certainly! Anybody could—oh, anybody! Hosannah Dilkins, for instance! Or maybe Adelbert Peanut—oh, *dear*—yes! Well, I'd like to see them try it, that's all. Dear-me-suz, if they could think of the discovery of a forty-acre island it's more than *I* believe they could; and as for the whole continent, why, Sally Foster, you know perfectly well it would strain the livers and lights out of them and *then* they couldn't!"

The dear woman, she knew he had talent; and if affection made her over-estimate the size of it a little, surely it was a sweet and gentle crime, and forgivable for its source's sake.


CHAPTER 5

The celebration went off well. The friends were all present, both the young and the old. Among the young were Flossie and Gracie Peanut and their brother

Adelbert, who was a rising young journeyman tinner, also Hosannah Dilkins, Jr., journeyman plasterer, just out of his apprenticeship. For many months Adelbert and Hosannah had been showing interest in Gwendolen and Clytemnestra Foster, and the parents of the girls had noticed this with private satisfaction. But they suddenly realized now that that feeling had passed. They recognized that the changed financial conditions had raised up a social bar between their daughters and the young mechanics. The daughters could now look higher—and must. Yes, must. They need marry nothing below the grade of lawyer or merchant; poppa and momma would take care of this; there must be no mesalliances.

However, these thinkings and projects of their were private, and did not show on the surface, and therefore threw no shadow upon the celebration. What showed upon the surface was a serene and lofty contentment and a dignity of carriage and gravity of deportment which compelled the admiration and likewise the wonder of the company. All noticed it and all commented upon it, but none was able to divine the secret of it. It was a marvel and a mystery. Three several persons remarked, without suspecting what clever shots they were making:

"It's as if they'd come into property."

That was just it, indeed.

Most mothers would have taken hold of the matrimonial matter in the old regulation way; they would have given the girls a talking to, of a solemn sort and untactful—a lecture calculated to defeat its own purpose, by producing tears and secret rebellion; and the said mothers would have further damaged the business by requesting the young mechanics to discontinue their attentions. But this mother was different. She was practical. She said nothing to any of the young people concerned, nor to any one else except Sally. He listened to her and understood; understood and admired. He said:

"I get the idea. Instead of finding fault with the samples on view, thus hurting feelings and obstructing trade without occasion, you merely offer a higher class of goods for the money, and leave nature to take her course. It's wisdom, Aleck, solid wisdom, and sound as a nut. Who's your fish? Have you nominated him yet?"

No, she hadn't. They must look the market over—which they did. To start with, they considered and discussed Brandish, rising young lawyer, and Fulton, rising young dentist. Sally must invite them to dinner. But not right away; there was no hurry, Aleck said. Keep an eye on the pair, and wait; nothing would be lost by going slowly in so important a matter.

It turned out that this was wisdom, too; for inside of three weeks Aleck made a wonderful strike which swelled her imaginary hundred thousand to four hundred thousand of the same quality. She and Sally were in the clouds that evening. For the first time they introduced champagne at dinner. Not real champagne, but plenty real enough for the amount of imagination expended on it. It was Sally that did it, and Aleck weakly submitted. At bottom both were troubled and ashamed, for he was a high-up Son of Temperance, and at funerals wore an apron which no dog could look upon and retain his reason and his opinion; and she was a W. C. T. U., with all that that implies of boiler-iron virtue and unendurable holiness. But there is was; the pride of riches was beginning its disintegrating work. They had lived to prove, once more, a sad truth which had been proven many times before in the world: that whereas principle is a great and noble protection against showy and degrading vanities and vices, poverty is worth six of it. More than four hundred thousand dollars to the good. They took up the matrimonial matter again. Neither the dentist nor the lawyer was mentioned; there was no occasion, they were out of the running. Disqualified. They discussed the son of the pork-packer and the son of the village banker. But finally, as in the previous case, they concluded to wait and think, and go cautiously and sure.

Luck came their way again. Aleck, ever watchful saw a great and risky chance, and took a daring flyer. A time of trembling, of doubt, of awful uneasiness followed, for non-success meant absolute ruin and nothing short of it. Then came the result, and Aleck, faint with joy, could hardly control her voice when she said:

"The suspense is over, Sally—and we are worth a cold million!"

Sally wept for gratitude, and said:

"Oh, Electra, jewel of women, darling of my heart, we are free at last, we roll in wealth, we need never scrimp again. It's a case for Veuve Cliquot!" and he got out a pint of spruce-beer and made sacrifice, he saying "Damn the expense," and she rebuking him gently with reproachful but humid and happy eyes.

They shelved the pork-packer's son and the banker's son, and sat down to consider the Governor's son and the son of the Congressman.

## CHAPTER 6

It were a weariness to follow in detail the leaps and bounds the Foster fictitious finances took from this time forth. It was marvelous, it was dizzying, it was dazzling. Everything Aleck touched turned to fairy gold, and heaped itself glittering toward the firmament. Millions upon millions poured in, and still the mighty stream flowed thundering along, still its vast volume increased. Five millions—ten millions—twenty—thirty—was there never to be an end?

Two years swept by in a splendid delirium, the intoxicated Fosters scarcely noticing the flight of time. They were now worth three hundred million dollars; they were in every board of directors of every prodigious combine in the country; and still as time drifted along, the millions went on piling up, five at a time, ten at a time, as fast as they could tally them off, almost. The three hundred double itself—then doubled again—and yet again—and yet once more.

Twenty-four hundred millions!

The business was getting a little confused. It was necessary to take an account of stock, and straighten it out. The Fosters knew it, they felt it, they realized that it was imperative; but they also knew that to do it properly and perfectly the task must be carried to a finish without a break when once it was begun. A ten-hours' job; and where could THEY find ten leisure hours in a bunch? Sally was selling pins and sugar and calico all day and every day; Aleck was cooking and washing dishes and sweeping and making beds all day and every day, with none to help, for the daughters were being saved up for high society. The Fosters knew there was one way to get the ten hours, and only one. Both were ashamed to name it; each waited for the other to do it. Finally Sally said:

"Somebody's got to give in. It's up to me. Consider that I've named it—never mind pronouncing it out aloud."

Aleck colored, but was grateful. Without further remark, they fell. Fell, and—broke the Sabbath. For that was their only free ten-hour stretch. It was but another step in the downward path. Others would follow. Vast wealth has temptations which fatally and surely undermine the moral structure of persons not habituated to its possession.

They pulled down the shades and broke the Sabbath. With hard and patient labor they overhauled their holdings and listed them. And a long-drawn procession of formidable names it was! Starting with the Railway Systems, Steamer Lines, Standard Oil, Ocean Cables, Diluted Telegraph, and all the rest, and winding up with Klondike, De Beers, Tammany Graft, and Shady Privileges in the Post-office Department.

Twenty-four hundred millions, and all safely planted in Good Things, gilt-edged and interest-bearing. Income, $120,000,000 a year. Aleck fetched a long purr of soft delight, and said:

"Is it enough?"

"It is, Aleck."

"What shall we do?"

"Stand pat."

"Retire from business?"

"That's it."

"I am agreed. The good work is finished; we will take a long rest and enjoy the money."

"Good! Aleck!"

"Yes, dear?"

"How much of the income can we spend?"

"The whole of it."

It seemed to her husband that a ton of chains fell from his limbs. He did not say a word; he was happy beyond the power of speech.

After that, they broke the Sabbaths right along as fast as they turned up. It is the first wrong step that counts. Every Sunday they put in the whole day, after morning service, on inventions—inventions of ways to spend the money. They got to continuing this delicious dissipation until past midnight; and at every seance Aleck lavished millions upon great charities and religious enterprises, and Sally lavished like sums upon matters to which (at first) he gave definite names. Only at first. Later the names gradually lost sharpness of outline, and eventually faded into "sundries," thus becoming entirely—but safely—undescriptive. For Sally was crumbling. The placing of these millions added seriously and most uncomfortably to the family expenses—in tallow candles. For a while Aleck was worried. Then, after a little, she ceased to worry, for the occasion of it was gone. She was pained, she was grieved, she was ashamed; but she said nothing, and so became an accessory. Sally was taking candles; he was robbing the store. It is ever thus. Vast wealth, to the person unaccustomed to it, is a bane; it eats into the flesh and bone of his morals. When the Fosters were poor, they could have been trusted with untold candles. But now they—but let us not dwell upon it. From candles to apples is but a step: Sally got to taking apples; then soap; then maple-sugar; then canned goods; then crockery. How easy it is to go from bad to worse, when once we have started upon a downward course!

Meantime, other effects had been milestoning the course of the Fosters' splendid financial march. The fictitious brick dwelling had given place to an imaginary granite one with a checker-board mansard roof; in time this one disappeared and gave place to a still grander home—and so on and so on. Mansion after mansion, made of air, rose, higher, broader, finer, and each in its turn vanished away; until now in these latter great days, our dreamers were in fancy housed, in a distant region, in a sumptuous vast palace which looked out from a leafy summit upon a noble prospect of vale and river and receding hills steeped in tinted mists—and all private, all the property of the dreamers; a palace swarming with liveried servants, and populous with guests of fame and power, hailing from all the world's capitals, foreign and domestic.

This palace was far, far away toward the rising sun, immeasurably remote, astronomically remote, in Newport, Rhode Island, Holy Land of High Society, ineffable Domain of the American Aristocracy. As a rule they spent a part of every Sabbath—after morning service—in this sumptuous home, the rest of it they spent in Europe, or in dawdling around in their private yacht. Six days of sordid and plodding fact life at home on the ragged edge of Lakeside and straitened means, the seventh in Fairyland—such had been their program and their habit.

In their sternly restricted fact life they remained as of old—plodding, diligent, careful, practical, economical. They stuck loyally to the little Presbyterian Church, and labored faithfully in its interests and stood by its high and tough doctrines with all their mental and spiritual energies. But in their dream life they obeyed the invitations of their fancies, whatever they might be, and howsoever the fancies might change. Aleck's fancies were not very capricious, and not frequent, but Sally's scattered a good deal. Aleck, in her dream life, went over to the Episcopal camp, on account of its large official titles; next she became High-church on account of the candles and shows; and next she naturally changed to Rome, where there were cardinals and more candles. But these excursions were a nothing to Sally's. His dream life was a glowing and continuous and persistent excitement, and he kept every part of it fresh and sparkling by frequent changes, the religious part along with the rest. He worked his religions hard, and changed them with his shirt.

The liberal spendings of the Fosters upon their fancies began early in their prosperities, and grew in prodigality step by step with their advancing fortunes. In time they became truly enormous. Aleck built a university or two per Sunday; also a hospital or two; also a Rowton hotel or so; also a batch of churches; now and then a cathedral; and once, with untimely and ill-chosen playfulness, Sally said, "It was a cold day when she didn't ship a cargo of missionaries to persuade unreflecting Chinamen to trade off twenty-four carat Confucianism for counterfeit Christianity."

This rude and unfeeling language hurt Aleck to the heart, and she went from the presence crying. That spectacle went to his own heart, and in his pain and shame he would have given worlds to have those unkind words back. She had uttered no syllable of reproach—and that cut him. Not one suggestion that he look at his own record—and she could have made, oh, so many, and such blistering ones! Her generous silence brought a swift revenge, for it turned his thoughts upon himself, it summoned before him a spectral procession, a moving vision of his life as he had been leading it these past few years of limitless prosperity, and as he sat there reviewing it his cheeks burned and his soul was steeped in humiliation. Look at her life—how fair it was, and tending ever upward; and look at his own—how frivolous, how charged with mean vanities, how selfish, how empty, how ignoble! And its trend—never upward, but downward, ever downward!

He instituted comparisons between her record and his own. He had found fault with her—so he mused—*he*! And what could he say for himself? When she built her first church what was he doing? Gathering other blase multimillionaires into a Poker Club; defiling his own palace with it; losing hundreds of thousands to it at every sitting, and sillily vain of the admiring notoriety it made for him. When she was building her first university, what was he doing? Polluting himself with a gay and dissipated secret life in the company of other fast bloods, multimillionaires in money and paupers in character. When she was building her first foundling asylum, what was he doing? Alas! When she was projecting her noble Society for the Purifying of the Sex, what was he doing? Ah, what, indeed! When she and the W. C. T. U. and the Woman with the Hatchet, moving with resistless march, were sweeping the fatal bottle from the land, what was he doing? Getting drunk three times a day. When she, builder of a hundred cathedrals, was being gratefully welcomed and blest in papal Rome and decorated with the Golden Rose which she had so honorably earned, what was he doing? Breaking the bank at Monte Carlo.

He stopped. He could go no farther; he could not bear the rest. He rose up, with a great resolution upon his lips: this secret life should be revealing, and confessed; no longer would he live it clandestinely, he would go and tell her All.

And that is what he did. He told her All; and wept upon her bosom; wept, and moaned, and begged for her forgiveness. It was a profound shock, and she staggered under the blow, but he was her own, the core of her heart, the blessing of her eyes, her all in all, she could deny him nothing, and she forgave him. She felt that he could never again be quite to her what he had been before; she knew that he could only repent, and not reform; yet all morally defaced and decayed as he was, was he not her own, her very own, the idol of her deathless worship? She said she was his serf, his slave, and she opened her yearning heart and took him in.


CHAPTER 7

One Sunday afternoon some time after this they were sailing the summer seas in their dream yacht, and reclining in lazy luxury under the awning of the after-deck. There was silence, for each was busy with his own thoughts. These seasons of silence had insensibly been growing more and more frequent of late;

the old nearness and cordiality were waning. Sally's terrible revelation had done its work; Aleck had tried hard to drive the memory of it out of her mind, but it would not go, and the shame and bitterness of it were poisoning her gracious dream life. She could see now (on Sundays) that her husband was becoming a bloated and repulsive Thing. She could not close her eyes to this, and in these days she no longer looked at him, Sundays, when she could help it.

But she—was she herself without blemish? Alas, she knew she was not. She was keeping a secret from him, she was acting dishonorably toward him, and many a pang it was costing her. *She was breaking the compact, and concealing it from him.* Under strong temptation she had gone into business again; she had risked their whole fortune in a purchase of all the railway systems and coal and steel companies in the country on a margin, and she was now trembling, every Sabbath hour, lest through some chance word of hers he find it out. In her misery and remorse for this treachery she could not keep her heart from going out to him in pity; she was filled with compunctions to see him lying there, drunk and contented, and ever suspecting. Never suspecting—trusting her with a perfect and pathetic trust, and she holding over him by a thread a possible calamity of so devastating a—

"*Say*—Aleck?"

The interrupting words brought her suddenly to herself. She was grateful to have that persecuting subject from her thoughts, and she answered, with much of the old-time tenderness in her tone:

"Yes, dear."

"Do you know, Aleck, I think we are making a mistake—that is, you are. I mean about the marriage business." He sat up, fat and froggy and benevolent, like a bronze Buddha, and grew earnest. "Consider—it's more than five years. You've continued the same policy from the start: with every rise, always holding on for five points higher. Always when I think we are going to have some weddings, you see a bigger thing ahead, and I undergo another disappointment. *I* think you are too hard to please. Some day we'll get left. First, we turned down the dentist and the lawyer. That was all right—it was sound. Next, we turned down the banker's son and the pork-butcher's heir—right again, and sound. Next, we turned down the Congressman's son and the Governor's—right as a trivet, I confess it. Next the Senator's son and the son of the Vice-President of the United States—perfectly right, there's no permanency about those little distinctions. Then you went for the aristocracy; and I thought we had struck oil at last—yes. We would make a plunge at the Four Hundred, and pull in some ancient lineage, venerable, holy, ineffable, mellow with the antiquity of a hundred and fifty years, disinfected of the ancestral odors of salt-cod and pelts all of a century ago, and unsmirched by a day's work since, and then! why, then the marriages, of course. But no, along comes a pair a real aristocrats from Europe, and straightway you throw over the half-breeds. It was awfully discouraging, Aleck! Since then, what a procession! You turned down the baronets for a pair of barons; you turned down the barons for a pair of viscounts; the viscounts for a pair of earls; the earls for a pair of marquises; the marquises for a brace of dukes. *now*, Aleck, cash in!—you've played the limit. You've got a job lot of four dukes under the hammer; of four nationalities; all sound in the wind and limb and pedigree, all bankrupt and in debt up to the ears. They come high, but we can afford it. Come, Aleck, don't delay any longer, don't keep up the suspense: take the whole lay-out, and leave the girls to choose!"

Aleck had been smiling blandly and contentedly all through this arraignment of her marriage policy, a pleasant light, as of triumph with perhaps a nice surprise peeping out through it, rose in her eyes, and she said, as calmly as she could:

"Sally, what would you say to—*royalty*?"

Prodigious! Poor man, it knocked him silly, and he fell over the garboard-strake and barked his shin on the cat-heads. He was dizzy for a moment, then he gathered himself up and limped over and sat down by his wife and beamed his old-time admiration and affection upon her in floods, out of his bleary eyes.

"By George!" he said, fervently, "Aleck, you *are* great—the greatest woman in the whole earth! I can't ever learn the whole size of you. I can't ever learn the immeasurable deeps of you. Here I've been considering myself qualified to criticize your game. *I!* Why, if I had stopped to think, I'd have known you had a lone hand up your sleeve. Now, dear heart, I'm all red-hot impatience—tell me about it!"

The flattered and happy woman put her lips to his ear and whispered a princely name. It made him catch his breath, it lit his face with exultation.

"Land!" he said, "it's a stunning catch! He's got a gambling-hall, and a graveyard, and a bishop, and a cathedral—all his very own. And all gilt-edged five-hundred-per-cent. stock, every detail of it; the tidiest little property in Europe; and that graveyard—it's the selectest in the world: none but suicides admitted; *yes*, sir, and the free-list suspended, too, *all* the time. There isn't much land in the principality, but there's enough: eight hundred acres in the graveyard and forty-two outside. It's a *sovereignty*—that's the main thing; *land's* nothing. There's plenty land, Sahara's drugged with it."

Aleck glowed; she was profoundly happy. She said:

"Think of it, Sally—it is a family that has never married outside the Royal and Imperial Houses of Europe: our grandchildren will sit upon thrones!"

"True as you live, Aleck—and bear scepters, too; and handle them as naturally and nonchantly as I handle a yardstick. It's a grand catch, Aleck. He's corralled, is he? Can't get away? You didn't take him on a margin?"

"No. Trust me for that. He's not a liability, he's an asset. So is the other one."

"Who is it, Aleck?"

"His Royal Highness Sigismund-Siegfriend-Lauenfeld-Dinkelspiel-Schwartzenberg Blutwurst, Hereditary Grant Duke of Katzenyammer."

"No! You can't mean it!"

"It's as true as I'm sitting here, I give you my word," she answered.

His cup was full, and he hugged her to his heart with rapture, saying:

"How wonderful it all seems, and how beautiful! It's one of the oldest and noblest of the three hundred and sixty-four ancient German principalities, and one of the few that was allowed to retain its royal estate when Bismarck got done trimming them. I know that farm, I've been there. It's got a rope-walk and a candle-factory and an army. Standing army. Infantry and cavalry. Three soldier and a horse. Aleck, it's been a long wait, and full of heartbreak and hope deferred, but God knows I am happy now. Happy, and grateful to you, my own, who have done it all. When is it to be?"

"Next Sunday."

"Good. And we'll want to do these weddings up in the very regalest style that's going. It's properly due to the royal quality of the parties of the first part. Now as I understand it, there is only one kind of marriage that is sacred to royalty, exclusive to royalty: it's the morganatic."

"What do they call it that for, Sally?"

"I don't know; but anyway it's royal, and royal only."

"Then we will insist upon it. More—I will compel it. It is morganatic marriage or none."

"That settles it!" said Sally, rubbing his hands with delight. "And it will be the very first in America. Aleck, it will make Newport sick."

Then they fell silent, and drifted away upon their dream wings to the far regions of the earth to invite all the crowned heads and their families and provide gratis transportation to them.

CHAPTER 8

During three days the couple walked upon air, with their heads in the clouds. They were but vaguely conscious of their surroundings; they saw all things dimly, as through a veil; they were steeped in dreams, often they did not hear when they were spoken to; they often did not understand when they heard; they answered confusedly or at random; Sally sold molasses by weight, sugar by the yard, and furnished soap when asked for candles, and Aleck put the cat in the wash and fed milk to the soiled linen. Everybody was stunned and amazed, and went about muttering, "What *can* be the matter with the Fosters?"

Three days. Then came events! Things had taken a happy turn, and for forty-eight hours Aleck's imaginary corner had been booming. Up—up—still up! Cost point was passed. Still up—and up—and up! Cost point was passed. STill up—and up—and up! Five points above cost—then ten—fifteen—twenty! Twenty points cold profit on the vast venture, now, and Aleck's imaginary brokers were shouting frantically by imaginary long-distance, "Sell! sell! for Heaven's sake *sell*!"

She broke the splendid news to Sally, and he, too, said, "Sell! sell—oh, don't make a blunder, now, you own the earth!—sell, sell!" But she set her iron will and lashed it amidships, and said she would hold on for five points more if she died for it.

It was a fatal resolve. The very next day came the historic crash, the record crash, the devastating crash, when the bottom fell out of Wall Street, and the whole body of gilt-edged stocks dropped ninety-five points in five hours, and the multimillionaire was seen begging his bread in the Bowery. Aleck sternly held her grip and "put up" as long as she could, but at last there came a call which she was powerless to meet, and her imaginary brokers sold her out. Then, and not till then, the man in her was vanished, and the woman in her resumed sway. She put her arms about her husband's neck and wept, saying:

"I am to blame, do not forgive me, I cannot bear it. We are paupers! Paupers, and I am so miserable. The weddings will never come off; all that is past; we could not even buy the dentist, now."

A bitter reproach was on Sally's tongue: "I *begged* you to sell, but you—" He did not say it; he had not the heart to add a hurt to that broken and repentant spirit. A nobler thought came to him and he said:

"Bear up, my Aleck, all is not lost! You really never invested a penny of my uncle's bequest, but only its unmaterialized future; what we have lost was only the incremented harvest from that future by your incomparable financial judgment and sagacity. Cheer up, banish these griefs; we still have the thirty thousand untouched; and with the experience which you have acquired, think what you will be able to do with it in a couple years! The marriages are not off, they are only postponed."

These are blessed words. Aleck saw how true they were, and their influence was electric; her tears ceased to flow, and her great spirit rose to its full stature again. With flashing eye and grateful heart, and with hand uplifted in pledge and prophecy, she said:

"Now and here I proclaim—"

But she was interrupted by a visitor. It was the editor and proprietor of the *Sagamore*. He had happened into Lakeside to pay a duty-call upon an obscure grandmother of his who was nearing the end of her pilgrimage, and with the idea of combining business with grief he had looked up the Fosters, who had been so absorbed in other things for the past four years that they neglected to pay up their subscription. Six dollars due. No visitor could have been more welcome. He would know all about Uncle Tilbury and what his chances might be getting to be, cemeterywards. They could, of course, ask no questions, for that would squelch the bequest, but they could nibble around on the edge of the subject and hope for results. The scheme did not work. The obtuse editor did not know he was being nibbled at; but at last, chance accomplished what art had failed in. In illustration of something under discussion which required the help of metaphor, the editor said:

"Land, it's a tough as Tilbury Foster!—as *we* say."

It was sudden, and it made the Fosters jump. The editor noticed, and said, apologetically:

"No harm intended, I assure you. It's just a saying; just a joke, you know—nothing of it. Relation of yours?"

Sally crowded his burning eagerness down, and answered with all the indifference he could assume:

"I—well, not that I know of, but we've heard of him." The editor was thankful, and resumed his composure. Sally added: "Is he—is he—well?"

"Is he *well*? Why, bless you he's in Sheol these five years!"

The Fosters were trembling with grief, though it felt like joy. Sally said, non-committally—and tentatively:

"Ah, well, such is life, and none can escape—not even the rich are spared."

The editor laughed.

"If you are including Tilbury," said he, "it don't apply. *he* hadn't a cent; the town had to bury him."

The Fosters sat petrified for two minutes; petrified and cold. Then, white-faced and weak-voiced, Sally asked:

"Is it true? Do you *know* it to be true?"

"Well, I should say! I was one of the executors. He hadn't anything to leave but a wheelbarrow, and he left that to me. It hadn't any wheel, and wasn't any good. Still, it was something, and so, to square up, I scribbled off a sort of a little obituarial send-off for him, but it got crowded out."

The Fosters were not listening—their cup was full, it could contain no more. They sat with bowed heads, dead to all things but the ache at their hearts.

An hour later. Still they sat there, bowed, motionless, silent, the visitor long ago gone, they unaware.

Then they stirred, and lifted their heads wearily, and gazed at each other wistfully, dreamily, dazed; then presently began to twaddle to each other in a wandering and childish way. At intervals they lapsed into silences, leaving a sentence unfinished, seemingly either unaware of it or losing their way. Sometimes, when they woke out of these silences they had a dim and transient consciousness that something had happened to their minds; then with a dumb and yearning solicitude they would softly caress each other's hands in mutual compassion and support, as if they would say: "I am near you, I will not forsake you, we will bear it together; somewhere there is release and forgetfulness, somewhere there is a grave and peace; be patient, it will not be long."

They lived yet two years, in mental night, always brooding, steeped in vague regrets and melancholy dreams, never speaking; then release came to both on the same day.

Toward the end the darkness lifted from Sally's ruined mind for a moment, and he said:

"Vast wealth, acquired by sudden and unwholesome means, is a snare. It did us no good, transient were its feverish pleasures; yet for its sake we threw away our sweet and simple and happy life—let others take warning by us."

He lay silent awhile, with closed eyes; then as the chill of death crept upward toward his heart, and consciousness was fading from his brain, he muttered:

"Money had brought him misery, and he took his revenge upon us, who had done him no harm. He had his desire: with base and cunning calculation he left us but thirty thousand, knowing we would try to increase it, and ruin our life and break our hearts. Without added expense he could have left us far above desire of increase, far above the temptation to speculate, and a kinder soul would have done it; but in him was no generous spirit, no pity, no—"

# THE CANVASSER'S TALE

Poor, sad-eyed stranger! There was that about his humble mien, his tired look, his decayed-gentility clothes, that almost reached the mustard-seed of charity that still remained, remote and lonely, in the empty vastness of my heart, notwithstanding I observed a portfolio under his arm, and said to myself, Behold, Providence hath delivered his servant into the hands of another canvasser.

Well, these people always get one interested. Before I well knew how it came about, this one was telling me his history, and I was all attention and sympathy. He told it something like this:—

My parents died, alas, when I was a little, sinless child. My uncle Ithuriel took me to his heart and reared me as his own. He was my only relative in the wide world; but he was good and rich and generous. He reared me in the lap of luxury. I knew no want that money could satisfy.

In the fullness of time I was graduated, and went with two of my servants— my chamberlain and my valet—to travel in foreign countries. During four years I flitted upon careless wing amid the beauteous gardens of the distant strand, if you will permit this form of speech in one whose tongue was ever attuned to poesy; and indeed I so speak with confidence, as one unto his kind, for I perceive by your eyes that you too, sir, are gifted with the divine inflation. In those far lands I reveled in the ambrosial food that fructifies the soul, the mind, the heart. But of all things, that which most appealed to my inborn esthetic taste was the prevailing custom there, among the rich, of making collections of elegant and costly rarities, dainty objets de vertu, and in an evil hour I tried to uplift my uncle Ithuriel to a plane of sympathy with this exquisite employment.

I wrote and told him of one gentleman's vast collection of shells; another's noble collection of meerschaum pipes; another's elevating and refining collection of undecipherable autographs; another's priceless collection of old china; another's enchanting collection of postage-stamps—and so forth and so on. Soon my letters yielded fruit. My uncle began to look about for something to make a collection of. You may know, perhaps, how fleetly a taste like this dilates. His soon became a raging fever, though I knew it not. He began to neglect his great pork business; presently he wholly retired and turned an elegant leisure into a rabid search for curious things. His wealth was vast, and he spared it not. First he tried cow-bells. He made a collection which filled five large salons, and comprehended all the different sorts of cow-bells that ever had been contrived, save one. That one—an antique, and the only specimen extant—was possessed by another collector. My uncle offered enormous sums for it, but the gentleman would not sell. Doubtless you know what necessarily resulted. A true collector attaches no value to a collection that is not complete. His great heart breaks, he sells his hoard, he turns his mind to some field that seems unoccupied.

Thus did my uncle. He next tried brickbats. After piling up a vast and intensely interesting collection, the former difficulty supervened; his great heart broke again; he sold out his soul's idol to the retired brewer who possessed the missing brick. Then he tried flint hatchets and other implements of Primeval Man, but by and by discovered that the factory where they were made was supplying other collectors as well as himself. He tried Aztec inscriptions and stuffed whales—another failure, after incredible labor and expense. When his collection seemed at last perfect, a stuffed whale arrived from Greenland and an Aztec inscription from the Cundurango regions of Central America that made all former specimens insignificant. My uncle hastened to secure these noble gems. He got the stuffed whale, but another collector got the inscription. A real Cundurango, as possibly you know, is a possession of such supreme value that, when once a collector gets it, he will rather part with his family than with it. So my uncle sold out, and saw his darlings go forth, never more to return; and his coal-black hair turned white as snow in a single night.

Now he waited, and thought. He knew another disappointment might kill him. He was resolved that he would choose things next time that no other man was collecting. He carefully made up his mind, and once more entered the field-this time to make a collection of echoes.

"Of what?" said I.

Echoes, sir. His first purchase was an echo in Georgia that repeated four times; his next was a six-repeater in Maryland; his next was a thirteen-repeater in Maine; his next was a nine-repeater in Kansas; his next was a twelve-repeater in Tennessee, which he got cheap, so to speak, because it was out of repair, a portion of the crag which reflected it having tumbled down. He believed he could repair it at a cost of a few thousand dollars, and, by increasing the elevation with masonry, treble the repeating capacity; but the architect who undertook the job had never built an echo before, and so he utterly spoiled this one. Before he meddled with it, it used to talk back like a mother-in-law, but now it was only fit for the deaf-and-dumb asylum. Well, next he bought a lot of cheap little double-barreled echoes, scattered around over various states and territories; he got them at twenty per cent off by taking the lot. Next he bought a perfect Gatling-gun of an echo in Oregon, and it cost a fortune, I can tell you. You may know, sir, that in the echo market the scale of prices is cumulative, like the carat-scale in diamonds; in fact, the same phraseology is used. A single-carat echo is worth but ten dollars over and above the value of the land it is on; a two-carat or double-barreled echo is worth thirty dollars; a five-carat is worth nine hundred and fifty; a ten-carat is worth thirteen thousand. My uncle's Oregon-echo, which he called the Great Pitt Echo, was a twenty-two carat gem, and cost two hundred and sixteen thousand dollars—they threw the land in, for it was four hundred miles from a settlement.

Well, in the mean time my path was a path of roses. I was the accepted suitor of the only and lovely daughter of an English earl, and was beloved to distraction. In that dear presence I swam in seas of bliss. The family were content, for it was known that I was sole heir to an uncle held to be worth five millions of dollars. However, none of us knew that my uncle had become a collector, at least in anything more than a small way, for esthetic amusement.

Now gathered the clouds above my unconscious head. That divine echo, since known throughout the world as the Great Koh-i-noor, or Mountain of Repetitions, was discovered. It was a sixty-five carat gem. You could utter a word and it would talk back at you for fifteen minutes, when the day was otherwise quiet. But behold, another fact came to light at the same time: another echo-collector was in the field. The two rushed to make the peerless purchase. The property consisted of a couple of small hills with a shallow swale between, out yonder among the back settlements of New York State. Both men arrived on the ground at the same time, and neither knew the other was there. The echo was not all owned by one man; a person by the name of Williamson Bolivar Jarvis owned the east hill, and a person by the name of Harbison J. Bledso owned the west hill; the swale between was the dividing-line. So while my uncle was buying Jarvis's hill for three million two hundred and eighty-five thousand dollars, the other party was buying Bledso's hill for a shade over three million.

Now, do you perceive the natural result? Why, the noblest collection of echoes on earth was forever and ever incomplete, since it possessed but the one-half of the king echo of the universe. Neither man was content with this divided ownership, yet neither would sell to the other. There were jawings, bickerings, heart-burnings. And at last that other collector, with a malignity which only a collector can ever feel toward a man and a brother, proceeded to cut down his hill!

You see, as long as he could not have the echo, he was resolved that nobody should have it. He would remove his hill, and then there would be nothing to reflect my uncle's echo. My uncle remonstrated with him, but the man said, "I own one end of this echo; I choose to kill my end; you must take care of your own end yourself."

Well, my uncle got an injunction put on him. The other man appealed and fought it in a higher court. They carried it on up, clear to the Supreme Court of the United States. It made no end of trouble there. Two of the judges believed that an echo was personal property, because it was impalpable to sight and touch, and yet was purchasable, salable, and consequently taxable; two others believed that an echo was real estate, because it was manifestly attached to the land, and was not removable from place to place; other of the judges contended that an echo was not property at all.

It was finally decided that the echo was property; that the hills were property; that the two men were separate and independent owners of the two hills, but tenants in common in the echo; therefore defendant was at full liberty to cut down his hill, since it belonged solely to him, but must give bonds in three million dollars as indemnity for damages which might result to my uncle's half of the echo. This decision also debarred my uncle from using defendant's hill to reflect his part of the echo, without defendant's consent; he must use only his own hill; if his part of the echo would not go, under these circumstances, it was sad, of course, but the court could find no remedy. The court also debarred defendant from using my uncle's hill to reflect his end of the echo, without consent. You see the grand result! Neither man would give consent, and so that astonishing and most noble echo had to cease from its great powers; and since that day that magnificent property is tied up and unsalable.

A week before my wedding-day, while I was still swimming in bliss and the nobility were gathering from far and near to honor our espousals, came news of my uncle's death, and also a copy of his will, making me his sole heir. He was gone; alas, my dear benefactor was no more. The thought surcharges my heart even at this remote day. I handed the will to the earl; I could not read it for the blinding tears. The earl read it; then he sternly said, "Sir, do you call this wealth?—but doubtless you do in your inflated country. Sir, you are left sole heir to a vast collection of echoes—if a thing can be called a collection that is scattered far and wide over the huge length and breadth of the American continent; sir, this is not all; you are head and ears in debt; there is not an echo in the lot but has a mortgage on it; sir, I am not a hard man, but I must look to my child's interest; if you had but one echo which you could honestly call your own, if you had but one echo which was free from incumbrance, so that you could retire to it with my child, and by humble, painstaking industry cultivate and improve it, and thus wrest from it a maintenance, I would not say you nay; but I cannot marry my child to a beggar. Leave his side, my darling; go, sir, take your mortgage-ridden echoes and quit my sight forever."

My noble Celestine clung to me in tears, with loving arms, and swore she would willingly, nay gladly, marry me, though I had not an echo in the world. But it could not be. We were torn asunder, she to pine and die within the twelvemonth, I to toil life's long journey sad and alone, praying daily, hourly, for that release which shall join us together again in that dear realm where the wicked cease from troubling and the weary are at rest. Now, sir, if you will be so kind as to look at these maps and plans in my portfolio, I am sure I can sell you an echo for less money than any man in the trade. Now this one, which cost my uncle ten dollars, thirty years ago, and is one of the sweetest things in Texas, I will let you have for—

"Let me interrupt you," I said. "My friend, I have not had a moment's respite from canvassers this day. I have bought a sewing-machine which I did not want; I have bought a map which is mistaken in all its details; I have bought a clock which will not go; I have bought a moth poison which the moths prefer to any other beverage; I have bought no end of useless inventions, and now I have had enough of this foolishness. I would not have one of your echoes if you were even to give it to me. I would not let it stay on the place. I always hate a man that tries to sell me echoes. You see this gun? Now take your collection and move on; let us not have bloodshed."

But he only smiled a sad, sweet smile, and got out some more diagrams. You know the result perfectly well, because you know that when you have once opened the door to a canvasser, the trouble is done and you have got to suffer defeat.

I compromised with this man at the end of an intolerable hour. I bought two double-barreled echoes in good condition, and he threw in another, which he said was not salable because it only spoke German. He said, "She was a perfect polyglot once, but somehow her palate got down."

❧

# A DOG'S TALE

## CHAPTER 1

My father was a St. Bernard, my mother was a collie, but I am a Presbyterian. This is what my mother told me, I do not know these nice distinctions myself. To me they are only fine large words meaning nothing. My mother had a fondness for such; she liked to say them, and see other dogs look surprised and envious, as wondering how she got so much education. But, indeed, it was not real education; it was only show: she got the words by listening in the dining-room and drawing-room when there was company, and by going with the children to Sunday-school and listening there; and whenever she heard a large word she said it over to herself many times, and so was able to keep it until there was a dogmatic gathering in the neighborhood, then she would get it off, and surprise and distress them all, from pocket-pup to mastiff, which rewarded her for all her trouble. If there was a stranger he was nearly sure to be suspicious, and when he got his breath again he would ask her what it meant. And she always told him. He was never expecting this but thought he would catch her; so when she told him, he was the one that looked ashamed, whereas he had thought it was going to be she. The others were always waiting for this, and glad of it and proud of her, for they knew what was going to happen, because they had had experience. When she told the meaning of a big word they were all so taken up with admiration that it never occurred to any dog to doubt if it was the right one; and that was natural, because, for one thing, she answered up so promptly that it seemed like a dictionary speaking, and for another thing, where could they find out whether it was right or not? for she was the only cultivated dog there was. By and by, when I was older, she brought home the word Unintellectual, one time, and worked it pretty hard all the week at different gatherings, making much unhappiness and despondency; and it was at this time that I noticed that during that week she was asked for the meaning at eight different assemblages, and flashed out a fresh definition every time, which showed me that she had more presence of mind than culture, though I said nothing, of course. She had one word which she always kept on hand, and ready, like a life-preserver, a kind of emergency word to strap on when she was likely to get washed overboard in a sudden way—that was the word Synonymous. When she happened to fetch out a long word which had had its day weeks before and its prepared meanings gone to her dump-pile, if there was a stranger there of course it knocked him groggy for a couple of minutes, then he would come to, and by that time she would be away down wind on another tack, and not expecting anything; so when he'd hail and ask her to cash in, I (the only dog on the inside of her game) could see her canvas flicker a moment—but only just a moment—then it would belly out taut and full, and she would say, as calm as a summer's day, "It's synonymous with supererogation," or some godless long reptile of a word like that, and go placidly about and skim away on the next tack, perfectly comfortable, you know, and leave that stranger looking profane and embarrassed, and the initiated slatting the floor with their tails in unison and their faces transfigured with a holy joy.

And it was the same with phrases. She would drag home a whole phrase, if it had a grand sound, and play it six nights and two matinees, and explain it a new way every time—which she had to, for all she cared for was the phrase; she wasn't interested in what it meant, and knew those dogs hadn't wit enough to catch her, anyway. Yes, she was a daisy! She got so she wasn't afraid of anything, she had such confidence in the ignorance of those creatures. She even brought anecdotes that she had heard the family and the dinner-guests laugh and shout over; and as a rule she got the nub of one chestnut hitched onto another chestnut, where, of course, it didn't fit and hadn't any point; and when she delivered the nub she fell over and rolled on the floor and laughed and barked in the most insane way, while I could see that she was wondering to herself why it didn't seem as funny as it did when she first heard it. But no harm was done; the others rolled and barked too, privately ashamed of themselves for not seeing the point, and never suspecting that the fault was not with them and there wasn't any to see.

You can see by these things that she was of a rather vain and frivolous character; still, she had virtues, and enough to make up, I think. She had a kind heart and gentle ways, and never harbored resentments for injuries done her, but put them easily out of her mind and forgot them; and she taught her children her kindly way, and from her we learned also to be brave and prompt in time of danger, and not to run away, but face the peril that threatened friend or stranger, and help him the best we could without stopping to think what the cost might be to us. And she taught us not by words only, but by example, and that is the best way and the surest and the most lasting. Why, the brave things she did, the splendid things! she was just a soldier; and so modest about it—well, you couldn't help admiring her, and you couldn't help imitating her; not even a King Charles spaniel could remain entirely despicable in her society. So, as you see, there was more to her than her education.

## CHAPTER 2

When I was well grown, at last, I was sold and taken away, and I never saw her again. She was broken-hearted, and so was I, and we cried; but she comforted me as well as she could, and said we were sent into this world for a wise and good purpose, and must do our duties without repining, take our life as we might find it, live it for the best good of others, and never mind about the results; they were not our affair. She said men who did like this would have a noble and beautiful reward by and by in another world, and although we animals would not go there, to do well and right without reward would give to our brief lives a worthiness and dignity which in itself would be a reward. She had gathered these things from time to time when she had gone to the Sunday-school with the children, and had laid them up in her memory more carefully than she had done with those other words and phrases; and she had studied them deeply, for her good and ours. One may see by this that she had a wise and thoughtful head, for all there was so much lightness and vanity in it.

So we said our farewells, and looked our last upon each other through our tears; and the last thing she said—keeping it for the last to make me remember it the better, I think—was, "In memory of me, when there is a time of danger to another do not think of yourself, think of your mother, and do as she would do."

Do you think I could forget that? No.

## CHAPTER 3

It was such a charming home!—my new one; a fine great house, with pictures, and delicate decorations, and rich furniture, and no gloom anywhere, but all the wilderness of dainty colors lit up with flooding sunshine; and the spacious

grounds around it, and the great garden—oh, greensward, and noble trees, and flowers, no end! And I was the same as a member of the family; and they loved me, and petted me, and did not give me a new name, but called me by my old one that was dear to me because my mother had given it me—Aileen Mavoureen. She got it out of a song; and the Grays knew that song, and said it was a beautiful name.

Mrs. Gray was thirty, and so sweet and so lovely, you cannot imagine it; and Sadie was ten, and just like her mother, just a darling slender little copy of her, with auburn tails down her back, and short frocks; and the baby was a year old, and plump and dimpled, and fond of me, and never could get enough of hauling on my tail, and hugging me, and laughing out its innocent happiness; and Mr. Gray was thirty-eight, and tall and slender and handsome, a little bald in front, alert, quick in his movements, business-like, prompt, decided, unsentimental, and with that kind of trim-chiseled face that just seems to glint and sparkle with frosty intellectuality! He was a renowned scientist. I do not know what the word means, but my mother would know how to use it and get effects. She would know how to depress a rat-terrier with it and make a lap-dog look sorry he came. But that is not the best one; the best one was Laboratory. My mother could organize a Trust on that one that would skin the tax-collars off the whole herd. The laboratory was not a book, or a picture, or a place to wash your hands in, as the college president's dog said—no, that is the lavatory; the laboratory is quite different, and is filled with jars, and bottles, and electrics, and wires, and strange machines; and every week other scientists came there and sat in the place, and used the machines, and discussed, and made what they called experiments and discoveries; and often I came, too, and stood around and listened, and tried to learn, for the sake of my mother, and in loving memory of her, although it was a pain to me, as realizing what she was losing out of her life and I gaining nothing at all; for try as I might, I was never able to make anything out of it at all.

Other times I lay on the floor in the mistress's work-room and slept, she gently using me for a foot-stool, knowing it pleased me, for it was a caress; other times I spent an hour in the nursery, and got well tousled and made happy; other times I watched by the crib there, when the baby was asleep and the nurse out for a few minutes on the baby's affairs; other times I romped and raced through the grounds and the garden with Sadie till we were tired out, then slumbered on the grass in the shade of a tree while she read her book; other times I went visiting among the neighbor dogs—for there were some most pleasant ones not far away, and one very handsome and courteous and graceful one, a curly-haired

"BY-AND-BY CAME MY LITTLE PUPPY"

Irish setter by the name of Robin Adair, who was a Presbyterian like me, and belonged to the Scotch minister.

The servants in our house were all kind to me and were fond of me, and so, as you see, mine was a pleasant life. There could not be a happier dog that I was, nor a gratefuler one. I will say this for myself, for it is only the truth: I tried in all ways to do well and right, and honor my mother's memory and her teachings, and earn the happiness that had come to me, as best I could.

By and by came my little puppy, and then my cup was full, my happiness was perfect. It was the dearest little waddling thing, and so smooth and soft and velvety, and had such cunning little awkward paws, and such affectionate eyes, and such a sweet and innocent face; and it made me so proud to see how the children and their mother adored it, and fondled it, and exclaimed over every little wonderful thing it did. It did seem to me that life was just too lovely to—

Then came the winter. One day I was standing a watch in the nursery. That is to say, I was asleep on the bed. The baby was asleep in the crib, which was alongside the bed, on the side next the fireplace. It was the kind of crib that has a lofty tent over it made of gauzy stuff that you can see through. The nurse was out, and we two sleepers were alone. A spark from the wood-fire was shot out, and it lit on the slope of the tent. I suppose a quiet interval followed, then a scream from the baby awoke me, and there was that tent flaming up toward the ceiling! Before I could think, I sprang to the floor in my fright, and in a second was half-way to the door; but in the next half-second my mother's farewell was sounding in my ears, and I was back on the bed again., I reached my head through the flames and dragged the baby out by the waist-band, and tugged it along, and we fell to the floor together in a cloud of smoke; I snatched a new hold, and dragged the screaming little creature along and out at the door and around the bend of the hall, and was still tugging away, all excited and happy and proud, when the master's voice shouted:

"Begone you cursed beast!" and I jumped to save myself; but he was furiously quick, and chased me up, striking furiously at me with his cane, I dodging this way and that, in terror, and at last a strong blow fell upon my left foreleg, which made me shriek and fall, for the moment, helpless; the cane went up for another blow, but never descended, for the nurse's voice rang wildly out, "The nursery's on fire!" and the master rushed away in that direction, and my other bones were saved.

The pain was cruel, but, no matter, I must not lose any time; he might come back at any moment; so I limped on three legs to the other end of the hall, where there was a dark little stairway leading up into a garret where old boxes and such things were kept, as I had heard say, and where people seldom went. I managed to climb up there, then I searched my way through the dark among the piles of things, and hid in the secretest place I could find. It was foolish to be afraid there, yet still I was; so afraid that I held in and hardly even whimpered, though it would have been such a comfort to whimper, because that eases the pain, you know. But I could lick my leg, and that did some good.

For half an hour there was a commotion downstairs, and shoutings, and rushing footsteps, and then there was quiet again. Quiet for some minutes, and that was grateful to my spirit, for then my fears began to go down; and fears are worse than pains—oh, much worse. Then came a sound that froze me. They were calling me—calling me by name—hunting for me!

It was muffled by distance, but that could not take the terror out of it, and it was the most dreadful sound to me that I had ever heard. It went all about, everywhere, down there: along the halls, through all the rooms, in both stories, and in the basement and the cellar; then outside, and farther and farther away—then back, and all about the house again, and I thought it would never, never stop. But at last it did, hours and hours after the vague twilight of the garret had long ago been blotted out by black darkness.

Then in that blessed stillness my terrors fell little by little away, and I was at peace and slept. It was a good rest I had, but I woke before the twilight had come again. I was feeling fairly comfortable, and I could think out a plan now. I made a very good one; which was, to creep down, all the way down the back stairs, and hide behind the cellar door, and slip out and escape when the iceman came at dawn, while he was inside filling the refrigerator; then I would hide all day, and start on my journey when night came; my journey to—well, anywhere where they would not know me and betray me to the master. I was feeling almost cheerful now; then suddenly I thought: Why, what would life be without my puppy!

That was despair. There was no plan for me; I saw that; I must say where I was; stay, and wait, and take what might come—it was not my affair; that was what life is—my mother had said it. Then—well, then the calling began again! All my sorrows came back. I said to myself, the master will never forgive. I did not know what I had done to make him so bitter and so unforgiving, yet I judged it was something a dog could not understand, but which was clear to a man and dreadful.

They called and called—days and nights, it seemed to me. So long that the hunger and thirst near drove me mad, and I recognized that I was getting very weak. When you are this way you sleep a great deal, and I did. Once I woke in an awful fright—it seemed to me that the calling was right there in the garret! And so it was: it was Sadie's voice, and she was crying; my name was falling from her lips all broken, poor thing, and I could not believe my ears for the joy of it when I heard her say:

"Come back to us—oh, come back to us, and forgive—it is all so sad without our—"

I broke in with SUCH a grateful little yelp, and the next moment Sadie was plunging and stumbling through the darkness and the lumber and shouting for the family to hear, "She's found, she's found!"

The days that followed—well, they were wonderful. The mother and Sadie and the servants—why, they just seemed to worship me. They couldn't seem to make me a bed that was fine enough; and as for food, they couldn't be satisfied with anything but game and delicacies that were out of season; and every day the friends and neighbors flocked in to hear about my heroism—that was the name they called it by, and it means agriculture. I remember my mother pulling it on a kennel once, and explaining it in that way, but didn't say what agriculture was, except that it was synonymous with intramural incandescence; and a dozen times a day Mrs. Gray and Sadie would tell the tale to new-comers, and say I risked my life to save the baby's, and both of us had burns to prove it, and then the company would pass me around and pet me and exclaim about me, and you could see the pride in the eyes of Sadie and her mother; and when the people wanted to know what made me limp, they looked ashamed and changed the subject, and sometimes when people hunted them this way and that way with questions about it, it looked to me as if they were going to cry.

And this was not all the glory; no, the master's friends came, a whole twenty of the most distinguished people, and had me in the laboratory, and discussed me as if I was a kind of discovery; and some of them said it was wonderful in a dumb beast, the finest exhibition of instinct they could call to mind; but the master said, with vehemence, "It's far above instinct; it's *reason*, and many a man, privileged to be saved and go with you and me to a better world by right of its possession, has less of it that this poor silly quadruped that's foreordained to perish"; and then he laughed, and said: "Why, look at me—I'm a sarcasm! bless you, with all my grand intelligence, the only think I inferred was that the dog had gone mad and was destroying the child, whereas but for the beast's intelligence—it's *reason*, I tell you!—the child would have perished!"

They disputed and disputed, and *I* was the very center of subject of it all, and I wished my mother could know that this grand honor had come to me; it would have made her proud.

Then they discussed optics, as they called it, and whether a certain injury to the brain would produce blindness or not, but they could not agree about it, and said they must test it by experiment by and by; and next they discussed plants, and that interested me, because in the summer Sadie and I had planted seeds—I helped her dig the holes, you know—and after days and days a little shrub or a flower came up there, and it was a wonder how that could happen; but it did, and I wished I could talk—I would have told those people about it and shown then how much I knew, and been all alive with the subject; but I didn't care for the optics; it was dull, and when they came back to it again it bored me, and I went to sleep.

Pretty soon it was spring, and sunny and pleasant and lovely, and the sweet mother and the children patted me and the puppy good-by, and went away on a journey and a visit to their kin, and the master wasn't any company for us, but we played together and had good times, and the servants were kind and friendly, so we got along quite happily and counted the days and waited for the family.

And one day those men came again, and said, now for the test, and they took the puppy to the laboratory, and I limped three-leggedly along, too, feeling proud, for any attention shown to the puppy was a pleasure to me, of course. They discussed and experimented, and then suddenly the puppy shrieked, and they set him on the floor, and he went staggering around, with his head all bloody, and the master clapped his hands and shouted:

"There, I've won—confess it! He's a blind as a bat!"

And they all said:

"It's so—you've proved your theory, and suffering humanity owes you a great debt from henceforth," and they crowded around him, and wrung his hand cordially and thankfully, and praised him.

But I hardly saw or heard these things, for I ran at once to my little darling, and snuggled close to it where it lay, and licked the blood, and it put its head against mine, whimpering softly, and I knew in my heart it was a comfort to it in its pain and trouble to feel its mother's touch, though it could not see me. Then it dropped down, presently, and its little velvet nose rested upon the floor, and it was still, and did not move any more.

Soon the master stopped discussing a moment, and rang  in the footman, and said, "Bury it in the far corner of the garden," and then went on with the discussion, and I trotted after the footman, very happy and grateful, for I knew the puppy was out of its pain now, because it was asleep. We went far down the garden to the farthest end, where the children and the nurse and the puppy and I used to play in the summer in the shade of a great elm, and there the footman dug a hole, and I saw he was going to plant the puppy, and I was glad, because it would grow and come up a fine handsome dog, like Robin Adair, and be a beautiful surprise for the family when they came home; so I tried to help him dig, but my lame leg was no good, being stiff, you know, and you have to have two, or it is no use. When the footman had finished and covered little Robin up, he patted my head, and there were tears in his eyes, and he said: "Poor little doggie, you saved *his* child!"

I have watched two whole weeks, and he doesn't come up! This last week a fright has been stealing upon me. I think there is something terrible about this. I do not know what it is, but the fear makes me sick, and I cannot eat, though the servants bring me the best of food; and they pet me so, and even come in the night, and cry, and say, "Poor doggie—do give it up and come home; *don't* break our hearts!" and all this terrifies me the more, and makes me sure something has happened. And I am so weak; since yesterday I cannot stand on my feet anymore. And within this hour the servants, looking toward the sun where it was sinking out of sight and the night chill coming on, said things I could not understand, but they carried something cold to my heart.

"Those poor creatures! They do not suspect. They will come home in the morning, and eagerly ask for the little doggie that did the brave deed, and who of us will be strong enough to say the truth to them: 'The humble little friend is gone where go the beasts that perish.'"

# WAS IT HEAVEN? OR HELL?

## CHAPTER 1

"You told a LIE?"

"You confess it—you actually confess it—you told a lie!"

## CHAPTER 2

The family consisted of four persons: Margaret Lester, widow, aged thirty six; Helen Lester, her daughter, aged sixteen; Mrs. Lester's maiden aunts, Hannah and Hester Gray, twins, aged sixty-seven. Waking and sleeping, the three women spent their days and night in adoring the young girl; in watching the movements of her sweet spirit in the mirror of her face; in refreshing their souls with the vision of her bloom and beauty; in listening to the music of her voice; in gratefully recognizing how rich and fair for them was the world with this presence in it; in shuddering to think how desolate it would be with this light gone out of it.

By nature—and inside—the aged aunts were utterly dear and lovable and good, but in the matter of morals and conduct their training had been so uncompromisingly strict that it had made them exteriorly austere, not to say stern. Their influence was effective in the house; so effective that the mother and the daughter conformed to its moral and religious requirements cheerfully, contentedly, happily, unquestionably. To do this was become second nature to them. And so in this peaceful heaven there were no clashings, no irritations, no fault-finding, no heart-burnings.

In it a lie had no place. In it a lie was unthinkable. In it speech was restricted to absolute truth, iron-bound truth, implacable and uncompromising truth, let the resulting consequences be what they might. At last, one day, under stress of circumstances, the darling of the house sullied her lips with a lie—and confessed it, with tears and self-upbraidings. There are not any words that can paint the consternation of the aunts. It was as if the sky had crumpled up and collapsed and the earth had tumbled to ruin with a crash. They sat side by side, white and stern, gazing speechless upon the culprit, who was on her knees before them with her face buried first in one lap and then the other, moaning and sobbing, and appealing for sympathy and forgiveness and getting no response, humbly kissing the hand of the one, then of the other, only to see it withdrawn as suffering defilement by those soiled lips.

Twice, at intervals, Aunt Hester said, in frozen amazement:

"You told a LIE?"

Twice, at intervals, Aunt Hannah followed with the muttered and amazed ejaculation:

"You confess it—you actually confess it—you told a lie!"

It was all they could say. The situation was new, unheard of, incredible; they could not understand it, they did not know how to take hold of it, it approximately paralyzed speech.

At length it was decided that the erring child must be taken to her mother, who was ill, and who ought to know what had happened. Helen begged, besought, implored that she might be spared this further disgrace, and that her mother might be spared the grief and pain of it; but this could not be: duty required this sacrifice, duty takes precedence of all things, nothing can absolve one from a duty, with a duty no compromise is possible.

Helen still begged, and said the sin was her own, her mother had had no hand in it—why must she be made to suffer for it?

But the aunts were obdurate in their righteousness, and said the law that visited the sins of the parent upon the child was by all right and reason reversible; and therefore it was but just that the innocent mother of a sinning child should suffer her rightful share of the grief and pain and shame which were the allotted wages of the sin.

The three moved toward the sick-room.

At this time the doctor was approaching the house. He was still a good distance away, however. He was a good doctor and a good man, and he had a good heart, but one had to know him a year to get over hating him, two years to learn to endure him, three to learn to like him, and four and five to learn to love him. It was a slow and trying education, but it paid. He was of great stature; he had a leonine head, a leonine face, a rough voice, and an eye which was sometimes a pirate's and sometimes a woman's, according to the mood. He knew nothing about etiquette, and cared nothing about it; in speech, manner, carriage, and conduct he was the reverse of conventional. He was frank, to the limit; he had opinions on all subjects; they were always on tap and ready for delivery, and he cared not a farthing whether his listener liked them or didn't. Whom he loved he loved, and manifested it; whom he didn't love he hated, and published it from the housetops. In his young days he had been a sailor, and the salt-airs of all the seas blew from him yet. He was a sturdy and loyal Christian, and believed he was the best one in the land, and the only one whose Christianity was perfectly sound, healthy, full-charged with common sense, and had no decayed places in it. People who had an ax to grind, or people who for any reason wanted to get on the soft side of him, called him The Christian—a phrase whose delicate flattery was music to his ears, and whose capital T was such an enchanting and vivid object to him that he could *see* it when it fell out of a person's mouth even in the dark. Many who were fond of him stood on their consciences with both feet and brazenly called him by that large title habitually, because it was a pleasure to them to do anything that would please him; and with eager and cordial malice his extensive and diligently cultivated crop of enemies gilded it, beflowered it, expanded it to "The *Only* Christian." Of these two titles, the latter had the wider currency; the enemy, being greatly in the majority, attended to that. Whatever the doctor believed, he believed with all his heart, and would fight for it whenever he got the chance; and if the intervals between chances grew to be irksomely wide, he would invent ways of shortening them himself. He was severely conscientious, according to his rather independent lights, and whatever he took to be a duty he performed, no matter whether the judgment of the professional moralists agreed with his own or not. At sea, in his young days, he had used profanity freely, but as soon as he was converted he made a rule, which he rigidly stuck to ever afterward, never to use it except on the rarest occasions, and then only when duty commanded. He had been a hard drinker at sea, but after his conversion he became a firm and outspoken teetotaler, in order to be an example to the young, and from that time forth he seldom drank; never, indeed, except when it seemed to him to be a duty—a condition which sometimes occurred a couple of times a year, but never as many as five times.

Necessarily, such a man is impressionable, impulsive, emotional. This one was, and had no gift at hiding his feelings; or if he had it he took no trouble to exercise it. He carried his soul's prevailing weather in his face, and when he entered a room the parasols or the umbrellas went up—figuratively speaking—according to the indications. When the soft light was in his eye it meant approval, and delivered a benediction; when he came with a frown he lowered the temperature ten degrees. He was a well-beloved man in the house of his friends, but sometimes a dreaded one.

He had a deep affection for the Lester household and its several members returned this feeling with interest. They mourned over his kind of Christianity, and he frankly scoffed at theirs; but both parties went on loving each other just the same.

He was approaching the house—out of the distance; the aunts and the culprit were moving toward the sick-chamber.

## CHAPTER 3

The three last named stood by the bed; the aunts austere, the transgressor softly sobbing. The mother turned her head on the pillow; her tired eyes flamed up instantly with sympathy and passionate mother-love when they fell upon her child, and she opened the refuge and shelter of her arms.

"Wait!" said Aunt Hannah, and put out her hand and stayed the girl from leaping into them.

"Helen," said the other aunt, impressively, "tell your mother all. Purge your soul; leave nothing unconfessed."

Standing stricken and forlorn before her judges, the young girl mourned her sorrowful tale through the end, then in a passion of appeal cried out:

"Oh, mother, can't you forgive me? won't you forgive me?—I am so desolate!"

"Forgive you, my darling? Oh, come to my arms!—there, lay your head upon my breast, and be at peace. If you had told a thousand lies—"

There was a sound—a warning—the clearing of a throat. The aunts glanced up, and withered in their clothes—there stood the doctor, his face a thunder-cloud. Mother and child knew nothing of his presence; they lay locked together, heart to heart, steeped in immeasurable content, dead to all things else. The physician stood many moments glaring and glooming upon the scene before him; studying it, analyzing it, searching out its genesis; then he put up his hand and beckoned to the aunts. They came trembling to him, and stood humbly before him and waited. He bent down and whispered:

"Didn't I tell you this patient must be protected from all excitement? What the hell have you been doing? Clear out of the place!"

They obeyed. Half an hour later he appeared in the parlor, serene, cheery, clothed in sunshine, conducting Helen, with his arm about her waist, petting her, and saying gentle and playful things to her; and she also was her sunny and happy self again.

"Now, then;" he said, "good-by, dear. Go to your room, and keep away from your mother, and behave yourself. But wait—put out your tongue. There, that will do—you're as sound as a nut!" He patted her cheek and added, "Run along now; I want to talk to these aunts."

She went from the presence. His face clouded over again at once; and as he sat down he said:

"You too have been doing a lot of damage—and maybe some good. Some good, yes—such as it is. That woman's disease is typhoid! You've brought it to a show-up, I think, with your insanities, and that's a service—such as it is. I hadn't been able to determine what it was before."

With one impulse the old ladies sprang to their feet, quaking with terror.

"Sit down! What are you proposing to do?"

"Do? We must fly to her. We—"

"You'll do nothing of the kind; you've done enough harm for one day. Do you want to squander all your capital of crimes and follies on a single deal? Sit down, I tell you. I have arranged for her to sleep; she needs it; if you disturb her without my orders, I'll brain you—if you've got the materials for it."

They sat down, distressed and indignant, but obedient, under compulsion. He proceeded:

"Now, then, I want this case explained. *they* wanted to explain it to me—as if there hadn't been emotion or excitement enough already. You knew my orders; how did you dare to go in there and get up that riot?"

Hester looked appealing at Hannah; Hannah returned a beseeching look at Hester—neither wanted to dance to this unsympathetic orchestra. The doctor came to their help. He said:

"Begin, Hester."

Fingering at the fringes of her shawl, and with lowered eyes, Hester said, timidly:

"We should not have disobeyed for any ordinary cause, but this was vital. This was a duty. With a duty one has no choice; one must put all lighter considerations aside and perform it. We were obliged to arraign her before her mother. She had told a lie."

The doctor glowered upon the woman a moment, and seemed to be trying to work up in his mind an understand of a wholly incomprehensible proposition; then he stormed out:

"She told a lie! *Did* she? God bless my soul! I tell a million a day! And so does every doctor. And so does everybody—including you—for that matter. And *that* was the important thing that authorized you to venture to disobey my orders and imperil that woman's life! Look here, Hester Gray, this is pure lunacy; that girl *couldn't* tell a lie that was intended to injure a person. The thing is impossible—absolutely impossible. You know it yourselves—both of you; you know it perfectly well."

Hannah came to her sister's rescue:

"Hester didn't mean that it was that kind of a lie, and it wasn't. But it was a lie."

"Well, upon my word, I never heard such nonsense! Haven't you got sense enough to discriminate between lies! Don't you know the difference between a lie that helps and a lie that hurts?"

"*All* lies are sinful," said Hannah, setting her lips together like a vise; "all lies are forbidden."

The Only Christian fidgeted impatiently in his chair. He went to attack this proposition, but he did not quite know how or where to begin. Finally he made a venture:

"Hester, wouldn't you tell a lie to shield a person from an undeserved injury or shame?"

"No."

"Not even a friend?"

"No."

"Not even your dearest friend?"

"No. I would not."

The doctor struggled in silence awhile with this situation; then he asked:

"Not even to save him from bitter pain and misery and grief?"

"No. Not even to save his life."

Another pause. Then:

"Nor his soul?"

There was a hush—a silence which endured a measurable interval—then Hester answered, in a low voice, but with decision:

"Nor his soul."

No one spoke for a while; then the doctor said:

"Is it with you the same, Hannah?"

"Yes," she answered.

"I ask you both—why?"

"Because to tell such a lie, or any lie, is a sin, and could cost us the loss of our own souls—*would*, indeed, if we died without time to repent."

"Strange... strange... it is past belief." Then he asked, roughly: "Is such a soul as that *worth* saving?" He rose up, mumbling and grumbling, and started for the door, stumping vigorously along. At the threshold he turned and rasped out an admonition: "Reform! Drop this mean and sordid and selfish devotion to the saving of your shabby little souls, and hunt up something to do that's got some dignity to it! *Risk* your souls! risk them in good causes; then if you lose them, why should you care? Reform!"

The good old gentlewomen sat paralyzed, pulverized, outraged, insulted, and brooded in bitterness and indignation over these blasphemies. They were hurt to the heart, poor old ladies, and said they could never forgive these injuries.

"Reform!"

They kept repeating that word resentfully. "Reform—and learn to tell lies!"

Time slipped along, and in due course a change came over their spirits. They had completed the human being's first duty—which is to think about himself until he has exhausted the subject, then he is in a condition to take up minor interests and think of other people. This changes the complexion of his spirits—generally wholesomely. The minds of the two old ladies reverted to their beloved niece and the fearful disease which had smitten her; instantly they forgot the hurts their self-love had received, and a passionate desire rose in their hearts to go to the help of the sufferer and comfort her with their love, and minister to her, and labor for her the best they could with their weak hands, and joyfully and affectionately wear out their poor old bodies in her dear service if only they might have the privilege.

"And we shall have it!" said Hester, with the tears running down her face. "There are no nurses comparable to us, for there are no others that will stand their watch by that bed till they drop and die, and God knows we would do that."

"Amen," said Hannah, smiling approval and endorsement through the mist of moisture that blurred her glasses. "The doctor knows us, and knows we will not disobey again; and he will call no others. He will not dare!"

"Dare?" said Hester, with temper, and dashing the water from her eyes; "he will dare anything—that Christian devil! But it will do no good for him to try it this time—but, laws! Hannah! after all's said and done, he is gifted and wise and good, and he would not think of such a thing. . . . It is surely time for one of us to go to that room. What is keeping him? Why doesn't he come and say so?"

They caught the sound of his approaching step. He entered, sat down, and began to talk.

"Margaret is a sick woman," he said. "She is still sleeping, but she will wake presently; then one of you must go to her. She will be worse before she is better. Pretty soon a night-and-day watch must be set. How much of it can you two undertake?"

"All of it!" burst from both ladies at once.

The doctor's eyes flashed, and he said, with energy:

"You *do* ring true, you brave old relics! And you *shall* do all of the nursing you can, for there's none to match you in that divine office in this town; but you can't do all of it, and it would be a crime to let you." It was grand praise, golden praise, coming from such a source, and it took nearly all the resentment out of the aged twin's hearts. "Your Tilly and my old Nancy shall do the rest—good nurses both, white souls with black skins, watchful, loving, tender—just perfect nurses!—and competent liars from the cradle. . . . Look you! keep a little watch on Helen; she is sick, and is going to be sicker."

The ladies looked a little surprised, and not credulous; and Hester said:

"How is that? It isn't an hour since you said she was as sound as a nut."

The doctor answered, tranquilly:

"It was a lie."

The ladies turned upon him indignantly, and Hannah said:

"How can you make an odious confession like that, in so indifferent a tone, when you know how we feel about all forms of—"

"Hush! You are as ignorant as cats, both of you, and you don't know what you are talking about. You are like all the rest of the moral moles; you lie from morning till night, but because you don't do it with your mouths, but only with your lying eyes, your lying inflections, your deceptively misplaced emphasis, and your misleading gestures, you turn up your complacent noses and parade before God and the world as saintly and unsmirched Truth-Speakers, in whose cold-storage souls a lie would freeze to death if it got there! Why will you humbug yourselves with that foolish notion that no lie is a lie except a spoken one? What is the difference between lying with your eyes and lying with your mouth? There is none; and if you would reflect a moment you would see that it is so. There isn't a human being that doesn't tell a gross of lies every day of his life; and you—why, between you, you tell thirty thousand; yet you flare up here in a lurid hypocritical horror because I tell that child a benevolent and sinless lie to protect her from her imagination, which would get to work and warm up her blood to a fever in an hour, if I were disloyal enough to my duty to let it. Which I should probably do if I were interested in saving my soul by such disreputable means.

"Come, let us reason together. Let us examine details. When you two were in the sick-room raising that riot, what would you have done if you had known I was coming?"

"Well, what?"

"You would have slipped out and carried Helen with you—wouldn't you?"

The ladies were silent.

"What would be your object and intention?"

"Well, what?"

"To keep me from finding out your guilt; to beguile me to infer that Margaret's excitement proceeded from some cause not known to you. In a word, to tell me a lie—a silent lie. Moreover, a possibly harmful one."

The twins colored, but did not speak.

"You not only tell myriads of silent lies, but you tell lies with your mouths—you two."

"*That* is not so!"

"It is so. But only harmless ones. You never dream of uttering a harmful one. Do you know that that is a concession—and a confession?"

"How do you mean?"

"It is an unconscious concession that harmless lies are not criminal; it is a confession that you constantly *make* that discrimination. For instance, you declined old Mrs. Foster's invitation last week to meet those odious Higbies at supper—in a polite note in which you expressed regret and said you were very sorry you could not go. It was a lie. It was as unmitigated a lie as was ever uttered. Deny it, Hester—with another lie."

Hester replied with a toss of her head.

"That will not do. Answer. Was it a lie, or wasn't it?"

The color stole into the cheeks of both women, and with a struggle and an effort they got out their confession:

"It was a lie."

"Good—the reform is beginning; there is hope for you yet; you will not tell a lie to save your dearest friend's soul, but you will spew out one without a scruple to save yourself the discomfort of telling an unpleasant truth."

He rose. Hester, speaking for both, said; coldly:

"We have lied; we perceive it; it will occur no more. To lie is a sin. We shall never tell another one of any kind whatsoever, even lies of courtesy or benevolence, to save any one a pang or a sorrow decreed for him by God."

"Ah, how soon you will fall! In fact, you have fallen already; for what you have just uttered is a lie. Good-by. Reform! One of you go to the sick-room now."


CHAPTER 4

Twelve days later.

Mother and child were lingering in the grip of the hideous disease. Of hope for either there was little. The aged sisters looked white and worn, but they would not give up their posts. Their hearts were breaking, poor old things, but their grit was steadfast and indestructible. All the twelve days the mother had pined for the child, and the child for the mother, but both knew that the prayer of these longings could not be granted. When the mother was told—on the first day—that her disease was typhoid, she was frightened, and asked if there was danger that Helen could have contracted it the day before, when she was in the sick-chamber on that confession visit. Hester told her the doctor had poo-pooed the idea. It troubled Hester to say it, although it was true, for she had not believed the doctor; but when she saw the mother's joy in the news, the pain in her conscience lost something of its force—a result which made her ashamed of the constructive deception which she had practiced, though not ashamed enough to make her distinctly and definitely wish she had refrained from it. From that moment the sick woman understood that her daughter must remain away, and she said she would reconcile herself to the separation the best she could, for she would rather suffer death than have her child's health imperiled.

That afternoon Helen had to take to her bed, ill. She grew worse during the night. In the morning her mother asked after her:

"Is she well?"

Hester turned cold; she opened her lips, but the words refused to come. The mother lay languidly looking, musing, waiting; suddenly she turned white and gasped out:

"Oh, my God! what is it? is she sick?"

Then the poor aunt's tortured heart rose in rebellion, and words came:

"No—be comforted; she is well."

The sick woman put all her happy heart in her gratitude:

"Thank God for those dear words! Kiss me. How I worship you for saying them!"

Hester told this incident to Hannah, who received it with a rebuking look, and said, coldly:

"Sister, it was a lie."

Hester's lips trembled piteously; she choked down a sob, and said:

"Oh, Hannah, it was a sin, but I could not help it. I could not endure the fright and the misery that were in her face."

"No matter. It was a lie. God will hold you to account for it."

"Oh, I know it, I know it," cried Hester, wringing her hands, "but even if it were now, I could not help it. I know I should do it again."

"Then take my place with Helen in the morning. I will make the report myself."

Hester clung to her sister, begging and imploring.

"Don't, Hannah, oh, don't—you will kill her."

"I will at least speak the truth."

In the morning she had a cruel report to bear to the mother, and she braced herself for the trial. When she returned from her mission, Hester was waiting, pale and trembling, in the hall. She whispered:

"Oh, how did she take it—that poor, desolate mother?"

Hannah's eyes were swimming in tears. She said:

"God forgive me, I told her the child was well!"

Hester gathered her to her heart, with a grateful "God bless you, Hannah!" and poured out her thankfulness in an inundation of worshiping praises.

After that, the two knew the limit of their strength, and accepted their fate. They surrendered humbly, and abandoned themselves to the hard requirements of the situation. Daily they told the morning lie, and confessed their sin in prayer; not asking forgiveness, as not being worthy of it, but only wishing to make record that they realized their wickedness and were not desiring to hide it or excuse it.

Daily, as the fair young idol of the house sank lower and lower, the sorrowful old aunts painted her glowing bloom and her fresh young beauty to the wan mother, and winced under the stabs her ecstasies of joy and gratitude gave them.

In the first days, while the child had strength to hold a pencil, she wrote fond little love-notes to her mother, in which she concealed her illness; and these the mother read and reread through happy eyes wet with thankful tears, and kissed them over and over again, and treasured them as precious things under her pillow.

Then came a day when the strength was gone from the hand, and the mind wandered, and the tongue babbled pathetic incoherences. This was a sore dilemma for the poor aunts. There were no love-notes for the mother. They did not know what to do. Hester began a carefully studied and plausible explanation, but lost the track of it and grew confused; suspicion began to show in the mother's face, then alarm. Hester saw it, recognized the imminence of the danger, and descended to the emergency, pulling herself resolutely together and plucking victor from the open jaws of defeat. In a placid and convincing voice she said:

"I thought it might distress you to know it, but Helen spent the night at the Sloanes'. There was a little party there, and, although she did not want to go, and you so sick, we persuaded her, she being young and needing the innocent pastimes of youth, and we believing you would approve. Be sure she will write the moment she comes."

"How good you are, and how dear and thoughtful for us both! Approve? Why, I thank you with all my heart. My poor little exile! Tell her I want her to have every pleasure she can—I would not rob her of one. Only let her keep her health, that is all I ask. Don't let that suffer; I could not bear it. How thankful I am that she escaped this infection—and what a narrow risk she ran, Aunt Hester! Think of that lovely face all dulled and burned with fever. I can't bear the thought of it. Keep her health. Keep her bloom! I can see her now, the dainty creature—with the big, blue, earnest eyes; and sweet, oh, so sweet and gentle and winning! Is she as beautiful as ever, dear Aunt Hester?"

"Oh, more beautiful and bright and charming than ever she was before, if such a thing can be"—and Hester turned away and fumbled with the medicine-bottles, to hide her shame and grief.

CHAPTER 5

After a little, both aunts were laboring upon a difficult and baffling work in Helen's chamber. Patiently and earnestly, with their stiff old fingers, they were trying to forge the required note. They made failure after failure, but they improved little by little all the time. The pity of it all, the pathetic humor of it, there was none to see; they themselves were unconscious of it. Often their tears fell upon the notes and spoiled them; sometimes a single misformed word made a note risky which could have been ventured but for that; but at last Hannah produced one whose script was a good enough imitation of Helen's to pass any but a suspicious eye, and bountifully enriched it with the petting phrases and loving nicknames that had been familiar on the child's lips from her nursery days. She carried it to the mother, who took it with avidity, and kissed it, and fondled it, reading its precious words over and over again, and dwelling with deep contentment upon its closing paragraph:

"Mousie darling, if I could only see you, and kiss your eyes, and feel your arms about me! I am so glad my practicing does not disturb you. Get well soon. Everybody is good to me, but I am so lonesome without you, dear mamma."

"The poor child, I know just how she feels. She cannot be quite happy without me; and I—oh, I live in the light of her eyes! Tell her she must practice all she pleases; and, Aunt Hannah—tell her I can't hear the piano this far, nor hear dear voice when she sings: God knows I wish I could. No one knows how sweet that voice is to me; and to think—some day it will be silent! What are you crying for?"

"Only because—because—it was just a memory. When I came away she was singing, 'Loch Lomond.' The pathos of it! It always moves me so when she sings that."

"And me, too. How heartbreakingly beautiful it is when some youthful sorrow is brooding in her breast and she sings it for the mystic healing it brings. . . . Aunt Hannah?"

"Dear Margaret?"

"I am very ill. Sometimes it comes over me that I shall never hear that dear voice again."

"Oh, don't—don't, Margaret! I can't bear it!"

Margaret was moved and distressed, and said, gently:

"There—there—let me put my arms around you. Don't cry. There—put your cheek to mine. Be comforted. I wish to live. I will live if I can. Ah, what could she do without me! . . . Does she often speak of me?—but I know she does."

"Oh, all the time—all the time!"

"My sweet child! She wrote the note the moment she came home?"

"Yes—the first moment. She would not wait to take off her things."

"I knew it. It is her dear, impulsive, affectionate way. I knew it without asking, but I wanted to hear you say it. The petted wife knows she is loved, but she makes her husband tell her so every day, just for the joy of hearing it. . . . She used the pen this time. That is better; the pencil-marks could rub out, and I should grieve for that. Did you suggest that she use the pen?"

"Y—no—she—it was her own idea."

The mother looked her pleasure, and said:

"I was hoping you would say that. There was never such a dear and thoughtful child! . . . Aunt Hannah?"

"Dear Margaret?"

"Go and tell her I think of her all the time, and worship her. Why—you are crying again. Don't be so worried about me, dear; I think there is nothing to fear, yet."

The grieving messenger carried her message, and piously delivered it to unheeding ears. The girl babbled on unaware; looking up at her with wondering and startled eyes flaming with fever, eyes in which was no light of recognition:

"Are you—no, you are not my mother. I want her—oh, I want her! She was here a minute ago—I did not see her go. Will she come? will she come quickly? will she come now? . . . There are so many houses . . . and they oppress me so . . . and everything whirls and turns and whirls . . . oh, my head, my head!"— and so she wandered on and on, in her pain, flitting from one torturing fancy to another, and tossing her arms about in a weary and ceaseless persecution of unrest.

Poor old Hannah wetted the parched lips and softly stroked the hot brow, murmuring endearing and pitying words, and thanking the Father of all that the mother was happy and did not know.

## CHAPTER 6

Daily the child sank lower and steadily lower towards the grave, and daily the sorrowing old watchers carried gilded tidings of her radiant health and loveliness to the happy mother, whose pilgrimage was also now nearing its end. And daily they forged loving and cheery notes in the child's hand, and stood by with remorseful consciences and bleeding hearts, and wept to see the grateful mother devour them and adore them and treasure them away as things beyond price, because of their sweet source, and sacred because her child's hand had touched them.

At last came that kindly friend who brings healing and peace to all. The lights were burning low. In the solemn hush which precedes the dawn vague figures flitted soundless along the dim hall and gathered silent and awed in Helen's chamber, and grouped themselves about her bed, for a warning had gone forth, and they knew. The dying girl lay with closed lids, and unconscious, the drapery upon her breast faintly rising and falling as her wasting life ebbed away. At intervals a sigh or a muffled sob broke upon the stillness. The same haunting thought was in all minds there: the pity of this death, the going out into the great darkness, and the mother not here to help and hearten and bless.

Helen stirred; her hands began to grope wistfully about as if they sought something—she had been blind some hours. The end was come; all knew it. With a great sob Hester gathered her to her breast, crying, "Oh, my child, my darling!" A rapturous light broke in the dying girl's face, for it was mercifully vouchsafed her to mistake those sheltering arms for another's; and she went to her rest murmuring, "Oh, mamma, I am so happy—I longed for you—now I can die."

Two hours later Hester made her report. The mother asked:

"How is it with the child?"

"She is well."

## CHAPTER 7

A sheaf of white crape and black was hung upon the door of the house, and there it swayed and rustled in the wind and whispered its tidings. At noon the preparation of the dead was finished, and in the coffin lay the fair young form, beautiful, and in the sweet face a great peace. Two mourners sat by it, grieving and worshipping—Hannah and the black woman Tilly. Hester came, and she was trembling, for a great trouble was upon her spirit. She said:

"She asks for a note."

Hannah's face blanched. She had not thought of this; it had seemed that that pathetic service was ended. But she realized now that that could not be. For a little while the two women stood looking into each other's face, with vacant eyes; then Hannah said:

"There is no way out of it—she must have it; she will suspect, else."

"And she would find out."

"Yes. It would break her heart." She looked at the dead face, and her eyes filled. "I will write it," she said.

Hester carried it. The closing line said:

"Darling Mousie, dear sweet mother, we shall soon be together again. Is not that good news? And it is true; they all say it is true."

The mother mourned, saying:

"Poor child, how will she bear it when she knows? I shall never see her again in life. It is hard, so hard. She does not suspect? You guard her from that?"

"She thinks you will soon be well."

"How good you are, and careful, dear Aunt Hester! None goes near her who could carry the infection?"

"It would be a crime."

"But you *see* her?"

"With a distance between—yes."

"That is so good. Others one could not trust; but you two guardian angels—steel is not so true as you. Others would be unfaithful; and many would deceive, and lie."

Hester's eyes fell, and her poor old lips trembled.

"Let me kiss you for her, Aunt Hester; and when I am gone, and the danger is past, place the kiss upon her dear lips some day, and say her mother sent it, and all her mother's broken heart is in it."

Within the hour, Hester, raining tears upon the dead face, performed her pathetic mission.

## CHAPTER 8

Another day dawned, and grew, and spread its sunshine in the earth. Aunt Hannah brought comforting news to the failing mother, and a happy note, which said again, "We have but a little time to wait, darling mother, then we shall be together."

The deep note of a bell came moaning down the wind.

"Aunt Hannah, it is tolling. Some poor soul is at rest. As I shall be soon. You will not let her forget me?"

"Oh, God knows she never will!"

"Do not you hear strange noises, Aunt Hannah? It sounds like the shuffling of many feet."

"We hoped you would not hear it, dear. It is a little company gathering, for—for Helen's sake, poor little prisoner. There will be music—and she loves it so. We thought you would not mind."

"Mind? Oh no, no—oh, give her everything her dear heart can desire. How good you two are to her, and how good to me! God bless you both always!"

After a listening pause:

"How lovely! It is her organ. Is she playing it herself, do you think?" Faint and rich and inspiring the chords floating to her ears on the still air. "Yes, it is her touch, dear heart, I recognize it. They are singing. Why—it is a hymn! and the sacredest of all, the most touching, the most consoling . . . . It seems to open the gates of paradise to me . . . . If I could die now . . . ."

Faint and far the words rose out of the stillness:

*Nearer, my God, to Thee,*

*Nearer to Thee,*
*E'en though it be a cross*
*That raiseth me.*

With the closing of the hymn another soul passed to its rest, and they that had been one in life were not sundered in death. The sisters, mourning and rejoicing, said:

"How blessed it was that she never knew!"

## CHAPTER 9

At midnight they sat together, grieving, and the angel of the Lord appeared in the midst transfigured with a radiance not of earth; and speaking, said:

"For liars a place is appointed. There they burn in the fires of hell from everlasting unto everlasting. Repent!"

The bereaved fell upon their knees before him and clasped their hands and bowed their gray heads, adoring. But their tongues clove to the roof of their mouths, and they were dumb.

"Speak! that I may bear the message to the chancery of heaven and bring again the decree from which there is no appeal."

Then they bowed their heads yet lower, and one said:

"Our sin is great, and we suffer shame; but only perfect and final repentance can make us whole; and we are poor creatures who have learned our human weakness, and we know that if we were in those hard straits again our hearts would fail again, and we should sin as before. The strong could prevail, and so be saved, but we are lost."

They lifted their heads in supplication. The angel was gone. While they marveled and wept he came again; and bending low, he whispered the decree.

## CHAPTER 10

Was it Heaven? Or Hell?

# A CURE FOR THE BLUES

By courtesy of Mr. Cable I came into possession of a singular book eight or ten years ago. It is likely that mine is now the only copy in existence. Its title-page, unabbreviated, reads as follows:

"The Enemy Conquered; or, Love Triumphant. By G. Ragsdale McClintock,[1] author of 'An Address,' etc., delivered at Sunflower Hill, South Carolina, and member of the Yale Law School. New Haven: published by T. H. Pease, 83 Chapel Street, 1845."

No one can take up this book and lay it down again unread. Whoever reads one line of it is caught, is chained; he has become the contented slave of its fascinations; and he will read and read, devour and devour, and will not let it go out of his hand till it is finished to the last line, though the house be on fire over his head. And after a first reading he will not throw it aside, but will keep it by him, with his Shakespeare and his Homer, and will take it up many and many a time, when the world is dark and his spirits are low, and be straightway cheered and refreshed. Yet this work has been allowed to lie wholly neglected, unmentioned, and apparently unregretted, for nearly half a century.

The reader must not imagine that he is to find in it wisdom, brilliancy, fertility of invention, ingenuity of construction, excellence of form, purity of style, perfection of imagery, truth to nature, clearness of statement, humanly possible situations, humanly possible people, fluent narrative, connected sequence of events—or philosophy, or logic, or sense. No; the rich, deep, beguiling charm of the book lies in the total and miraculous *absence* from it of all these qualities—a charm which is completed and perfected by the evident fact that the author, whose naive innocence easily and surely wins our regard, and almost our worship, does not know that they are absent, does not even suspect that they are absent. When read by the light of these helps to an understanding of the situation, the book is delicious—profoundly and satisfyingly delicious.

I call it a book because the author calls it a book, I call it a work because he calls it a work; but, in truth, it is merely a duodecimo pamphlet of thirty-one pages. It was written for fame and money, as the author very frankly—yes, and very hopefully, too, poor fellow—says in his preface. The money never came—no penny of it ever came; and how long, how pathetically long, the fame has been deferred—forty-seven years! He was young then, it would have been so much to him then; but will he care for it now?

As time is measured in America, McClintock's epoch is antiquity. In his long-vanished day the Southern author had a passion for "eloquence"; it was his pet, his darling. He would be eloquent, or perish. And he recognized only one kind of eloquence—the lurid, the tempestuous, the volcanic. He liked words—big words, fine words, grand words, rumbling, thundering, reverberating words; with sense attaching if it could be got in without marring the sound, but not otherwise. He loved to stand up before a dazed world, and pour forth flame and smoke and lava and pumice-stone into the skies, and work his subterranean thunders, and shake himself with earthquakes, and stench himself with sulphur fumes. If he consumed his own fields and vineyards, that was a pity, yes; but he would have his eruption at any cost. Mr. McClintock's eloquence—and he is always eloquent, his crater is always spouting—is of the pattern common to his day, but he departs from the custom of the time in one respect: his brethren allowed sense to intrude when it did not mar the sound, but he does not allow it to intrude at all. For example, consider this figure, which he used in the village "Address" referred to with such candid complacency in the title-page above quoted—"like the topmost topaz of an ancient tower." Please read it again; contemplate it; measure it; walk around it; climb up it; try to get at an approximate realization of the size of it. Is the fellow to that to be found in literature, ancient or modern, foreign or domestic, living or dead, drunk or sober? One notices how fine and grand it sounds. We know that if it was loftily uttered, it got a noble burst of applause from the villagers; yet there isn't a ray of sense in it, or meaning to it.

McClintock finished his education at Yale in 1843, and came to Hartford on a visit that same year. I have talked with men who at that time talked with him, and felt of him, and knew he was real. One needs to remember that fact and to keep fast hold of it; it is the only way to keep McClintock's book from undermining one's faith in McClintock's actuality.

As to the book. The first four pages are devoted to an inflamed eulogy of Woman—simply woman in general, or perhaps as an institution—wherein, among other compliments to her details, he pays a unique one to her voice. He says it "fills the breast with fond alarms, echoed by every rill." It sounds well enough, but it is not true. After the eulogy he takes up his real work and the novel begins. It begins in the woods, near the village of Sunflower Hill.

Brightening clouds seemed to rise from the mist of the fair Chattahoochee, to spread their beauty over the thick forest, to guide the hero whose bosom beats with aspirations to conquer the enemy that would tarnish his name, and to win back the admiration of his long-tried friend.

It seems a general remark, but it is not general; the hero mentioned is the to-be hero of the book; and in this abrupt fashion, and without name or description, he is shoveled into the tale. "With aspirations to conquer the enemy that would tarnish his name" is merely a phrase flung in for the sake of the sound—let it not mislead the reader. No one is trying to tarnish this person; no one has thought of it. The rest of the sentence is also merely a phrase; the man has no friend as yet, and of course has had no chance to try him, or win back his admiration, or disturb him in any other way.

The hero climbs up over "Sawney's Mountain," and down the other side, making for an old Indian "castle"—which becomes "the red man's hut" in the next sentence; and when he gets there at last, he "surveys with wonder and astonishment" the invisible structure, "which time has buried in the dust, and thought to himself his happiness was not yet complete." One doesn't know why it wasn't, nor how near it came to being complete, nor what was still wanting to round it up and make it so. Maybe it was the Indian; but the book does not say. At this point we have an episode:

Beside the shore of the brook sat a young man, about eighteen or twenty, who seemed to be reading some favorite book, and who had a remarkably noble countenance—eyes which betrayed more than a common mind. This of course made the youth a welcome guest, and gained him friends in whatever condition of his life he might be placed. The traveler observed that he was a well-built figure which showed strength and grace in every movement. He accordingly addressed him in quite a gentlemanly manner, and inquired of him the way to the village. After he had received the desired information, and was about taking his leave, the youth said, "Are you not Major Elfonzo, the great musician[2]—the champion of a noble cause—the modern Achilles, who gained so many victories in the Florida War?" "I bear that name," said the Major, "and those titles, trusting at the same time that the ministers of grace will carry me triumphantly through all my laudable undertakings, and if," continued the Major, "you, sir, are the patronizer of noble deeds, I should like to make you my confidant and learn your address." The youth looked somewhat amazed, bowed low, mused for a moment, and began: "My name is Roswell. I have been recently admitted to the bar, and can only give a faint outline of my future success in that honorable profession; but I trust, sir, like the Eagle, I shall look down from the lofty rocks upon the dwellings of man, and shall ever be ready to give you any assistance in my official capacity, and whatever this muscular arm of mine can do, whenever it shall be called from its buried *greatness*." The Major grasped him by the hand, and exclaimed: "O! thou exalted spirit of inspiration—thou flame of burning prosperity, may the Heaven-directed blaze be the glare of thy soul, and battle down every rampart that seems to impede your progress!"

There is a strange sort of originality about McClintock; he imitates other people's styles, but nobody can imitate his, not even an idiot. Other people can be windy, but McClintock blows a gale; other people can blubber sentiment, but McClintock spews it; other people can mishandle metaphors, but only McClintock knows how to make a business of it. McClintock is always McClintock, he is always consistent, his style is always his own style. He does not make the mistake of being relevant on one page and irrelevant on another; he is irrelevant on all of them. He does not make the mistake of being lucid in one place and obscure in another; he is obscure all the time. He does not make the mistake of slipping in a name here and there that is out of character with his work; he always uses names that exactly and fantastically fit his lunatics. In the matter of undeviating consistency he stands alone in authorship. It is this that makes his style unique, and entitles it to a name of its own—McClintockian. It is this that protects it from being mistaken for anybody else's. Uncredited quotations from other writers often leave a reader in doubt as to their authorship, but McClintock is safe from that accident; an uncredited quotation from him would always be recognizable. When a boy nineteen years old, who had just been admitted to the bar, says, "I trust, sir, like the Eagle, I shall look down from lofty rocks upon the dwellings of man," we know who is speaking through that boy; we should recognize that note anywhere. There be myriads of instruments in this world's literary orchestra, and a multitudinous confusion of sounds that they make, wherein fiddles are drowned, and guitars smothered, and one sort of drum mistaken for another sort; but whensoever the brazen note of the McClintockian trombone breaks through that fog of music, that note is recognizable, and about it there can be no blur of doubt.

The novel now arrives at the point where the Major goes home to see his father. When McClintock wrote this interview he probably believed it was pathetic.

The road which led to the town presented many attractions Elfonzo had bid farewell to the youth of deep feeling, and was now wending his way to the dreaming spot of his fondness. The south winds whistled through the woods, as the waters dashed against the banks, as rapid fire in the pent furnace roars. This brought him to remember while alone, that he quietly left behind the hospitality of a father's house, and gladly entered the world, with higher hopes than are often realized. But as he journeyed onward, he was mindful of the advice of his father, who had often looked sadly on the ground, when tears of cruelly deceived hope moistened his eyes. Elfonzo had been somewhat a dutiful son; yet fond of the amusements of life—had been in distant lands—had enjoyed the pleasure of the world, and had frequently returned to the scenes of his boyhood, almost destitute of many of the comforts of life. In this condition, he would frequently say to his father, "Have I offended you, that you look upon me as a stranger, and frown upon me with stinging looks? Will you not favor me with the sound of your voice? If I have trampled upon your veneration, or have spread a humid veil of darkness around your expectations, send me back into the world, where no heart beats for me—where the foot of man had never yet trod; but give me at least one kind word—allow me to come into the presence sometimes of thy winter-worn locks." "Forbid it, Heaven, that I should be angry with thee," answered the father, "my son, and yet I send thee back to the children of the world—to the cold charity of the combat, and to a land of victory. I read another destiny in thy countenance—I learn thy inclinations from the flame that has already kindled in my soul a strange sensation. It will seek thee, my dear Elfonzo, it will find thee—thou canst not escape that lighted torch, which shall blot out from the remembrance of men a long train of prophecies which they have foretold against thee. I once thought not so. Once, I was blind; but now the path of life is plain before me, and my sight is clear; yet, Elfonzo, return to thy worldly occupation—take again in thy hand that chord of sweet sounds—struggle with the civilized world and with your own heart; fly swiftly to the enchanted ground—let the night-owl send forth its screams from the stubborn oak—let the sea sport upon the beach, and the stars sing together; but learn of these, Elfonzo, thy doom, and thy hiding-place. Our most innocent as well as our most lawful *desires* must often be denied us, that we may learn to sacrifice them to a Higher will."

Remembering such admonitions with gratitude, Elfonzo was immediately urged by the recollection of his father's family to keep moving.

McClintock has a fine gift in the matter of surprises; but as a rule they are not pleasant ones, they jar upon the feelings. His closing sentence in the last quotation is of that sort. It brings one down out of the tinted clouds in too sudden and collapsed a fashion. It incenses one against the author for a moment. It makes the reader want to take him by this winter-worn locks, and trample on his veneration, and deliver him over to the cold charity of combat, and blot him out with his own lighted torch. But the feeling does not last. The master takes again in his hand that concord of sweet sounds of his, and one is reconciled, pacified.

His steps became quicker and quicker—he hastened through the *piny* woods, dark as the forest was, and with joy he very soon reached the little village of repose, in whose bosom rested the boldest chivalry. His close attention to every important object—his modest questions about whatever was new to him—his reverence for wise old age, and his ardent desire to learn many of the fine arts, soon brought him into respectable notice.

One mild winter day, as he walked along the streets toward the Academy, which stood upon a small eminence, surrounded by native growth—some venerable in its appearance, others young and prosperous—all seemed inviting, and seemed to be the very place for learning as well as for genius to spend its research beneath its spreading shades. He entered its classic walls in the usual mode of southern manners.

The artfulness of this man! None knows so well as he how to pique the curiosity of the reader—and how to disappoint it. He raises the hope, here, that he is going to tell all about how one enters a classic wall in the usual mode of Southern manners; but does he? No; he smiles in his sleeve, and turns aside to other matters.

The principal of the Institution begged him to be seated and listen to the recitations that were going on. He accordingly obeyed the request, and seemed to be much pleased. After the school was dismissed, and the young hearts regained their freedom, with the songs of the evening, laughing at the anticipated pleasures of a happy home, while others tittered at the actions of the past day, he addressed the teacher in a tone that indicated a resolution—with an undaunted mind. He said he had determined to become a student, if he could meet with his approbation. "Sir," said he, "I have spent much time in the world. I have traveled among the uncivilized inhabitants of America. I have met with friends, and combated with foes; but none of these gratify my ambition, or decide what is to be my destiny. I see the learned world have an influence with the voice of the people themselves. The despoilers of the remotest kingdoms of the earth refer their differences to this class of persons. This the illiterate and inexperienced little dream of; and now if you will receive me as I am, with these deficiencies—with all my misguided opinions, I will give you my honor, sir, that I will never disgrace the Institution, or those who have placed you in this honorable station." The instructor, who had met with many disappointments, knew how to feel for a stranger who had been thus turned upon the charities of an unfeeling community. He looked at him earnestly, and said: "Be of good cheer—look forward, sir, to the high destination you may attain. Remember, the more elevated the mark at which you aim, the more sure, the more glorious, the more magnificent the prize." From wonder to wonder, his encouragement led the impatient listener. A strange nature bloomed before him—giant streams promised him success—gardens of hidden treasures opened to his view. All this, so vividly described, seemed to gain a new witchery from his glowing fancy.

It seems to me that this situation is new in romance. I feel sure it has not been attempted before. Military celebrities have been disguised and set at lowly occupations for dramatic effect, but I think McClintock is the first to send one of them to school. Thus, in this book, you pass from wonder to wonder, through gardens of hidden treasure, where giant streams bloom before you, and behind you, and all around, and you feel as happy, and groggy, and satisfied with your quart of mixed metaphor aboard as you would if it had been mixed in a sample-room and delivered from a jug.

Now we come upon some more McClintockian surprise—a sweetheart who is sprung upon us without any preparation, along with a name for her which is even a little more of a surprise than she herself is.

In 1842 he entered the class, and made rapid progress in the English and Latin departments. Indeed, he continued advancing with such rapidity that he was like to become the first in his class, and made such unexpected progress, and was so studious, that he had almost forgotten the pictured saint of his affections. The fresh wreaths of the pine and cypress had waited anxiously to drop once more the dews of Heaven upon the heads of those who had so often poured forth the tender emotions of their souls under its boughs. He was aware of the pleasure that he had seen there. So one evening, as he was returning from his reading, he concluded he would pay a visit to this enchanting spot. Little did he think of witnessing a shadow of his former happiness, though no doubt he wished it might be so. He continued sauntering by the roadside, meditating on the past. The nearer he approached the spot, the more anxious he became. At that moment a tall female figure flitted across his path, with a bunch of roses in her hand; her countenance showed uncommon vivacity, with a resolute spirit; her ivory teeth already appeared as she smiled beautifully, promenading—while her ringlets of hair dangled unconsciously around her snowy neck. Nothing was wanting to complete her beauty. The tinge of the rose was in full bloom upon her cheek; the charms of sensibility and tenderness were always her associates. In Ambulinia's bosom dwelt a noble soul—one that never faded—one that never was conquered.

Ambulinia! It can hardly be matched in fiction. The full name is Ambulinia Valeer. Marriage will presently round it out and perfect it. Then it will be Mrs. Ambulinia Valeer Elfonzo. It takes the chromo.

Her heart yielded to no feeling but the love of Elfonzo, on whom she gazed with intense delight, and to whom she felt herself more closely bound, because he sought the hand of no other. Elfonzo was roused from his apparent reverie. His books no longer were his inseparable companions—his thoughts arrayed themselves to encourage him to the field of victory. He endeavored to speak to his supposed Ambulinia, but his speech appeared not in words. No, his effort was a stream of fire, that kindled his soul into a flame of admiration, and carried his senses away captive. Ambulinia had disappeared, to make him more mindful of his duty. As she walked speedily away through the piny woods, she calmly echoed: "O! Elfonzo, thou wilt now look from thy sunbeams. Thou shalt now walk in a new path—perhaps thy way leads through darkness; but fear not, the stars foretell happiness."

To McClintock that jingling jumble of fine words meant something, no doubt, or seemed to mean something; but it is useless for us to try to divine what it was. Ambulinia comes—we don't know whence nor why; she mysteriously intimates—we don't know what; and then she goes echoing away—we don't know whither; and down comes the curtain. McClintock's art is subtle; McClintock's art is deep.

Not many days afterward, as surrounded by fragrant flowers she sat one evening at twilight, to enjoy the cool breeze that whispered notes of melody along the distant groves, the little birds perched on every side, as if to watch the movements of their new visitor. The bells were tolling, when Elfonzo silently stole along by the wild wood flowers, holding in his hand his favorite instrument of music—his eye continually searching for Ambulinia, who hardly seemed to perceive him, as she played carelessly with the songsters that hopped from branch to branch. Nothing could be more striking than the difference between the two. Nature seemed to have given the more tender soul to Elfonzo, and the stronger and more courageous to Ambulinia. A deep feeling spoke from the eyes of Elfonzo—such a feeling as can only be expressed by those who are blessed as admirers, and by those who are able to return the same with sincerity of heart. He was a few years older than Ambulinia: she had turned a little into her seventeenth. He had almost grown up in the Cherokee country, with the same equal proportions as one of the natives. But little intimacy had existed between them until the year forty-one—because the youth felt that the character of such a lovely girl was too exalted to inspire any other feeling than that of quiet reverence. But as lovers will not always be insulted, at all times and under all circumstances, by the frowns and cold looks of crabbed old age, which should continually reflect dignity upon those around, and treat the unfortunate as well as the fortunate with a graceful mien, he continued to use diligence and perseverance. All this lighted a spark in his heart that changed his whole character, and like the unyielding Deity that follows the storm to check its rage in the forest, he resolves for the first time to shake off his embarrassment and return where he had before only worshiped.

At last we begin to get the Major's measure. We are able to put this and that casual fact together, and build the man up before our eyes, and look at him. And after we have got him built, we find him worth the trouble. By the above comparison between his age and Ambulinia's, we guess the war-worn veteran to be twenty-two; and the other facts stand thus: he had grown up in the Cherokee country with the same equal proportions as one of the natives—how flowing and graceful the language, and yet how tantalizing as to meaning!—he had been turned adrift by his father, to whom he had been "somewhat of a dutiful son"; he wandered in distant lands; came back frequently "to the scenes of his boyhood, almost destitute of many of the comforts of life," in order to get into the presence of his father's winter-worn locks, and spread a humid veil of darkness around his expectations; but he was always promptly sent back to the cold charity of the combat again; he learned to play the fiddle, and made a name for himself in that line; he had dwelt among the wild tribes; he had philosophized about the despoilers of the kingdoms of the earth, and found out—the cunning creature—that they refer their differences to the learned for settlement; he had achieved a vast fame as a military chieftain, the Achilles of the Florida campaigns, and then had got him a spelling-book and started to school; he had fallen in love with Ambulinia Valeer while she was teething, but had kept it to himself awhile, out of the reverential awe which he felt for the child; but now at last, like the unyielding Deity who follows the storm to check its rage in the forest, he resolves to shake off his embarrassment, and to return where before he had only worshiped. The Major, indeed, has made up his mind to rise up and shake his faculties together, and to see if *he* can't do that thing himself. This is not clear. But no matter about that: there stands the hero, compact and visible; and he is no mean structure, considering that his creator had never structure, considering that his creator had never created anything before, and hadn't anything but rags and wind to build with this time. It seems to me that no one can contemplate this odd creature, this quaint and curious blatherskite, without admiring McClintock, or, at any rate, loving him and feeling grateful to him; for McClintock made him, he gave him to us; without McClintock we could not have had him, and would now be poor.

But we must come to the feast again. Here is a courtship scene, down there in the romantic glades among the raccoons, alligators, and things, that has merit, peculiar literary merit. See how Achilles woos. Dwell upon the second sentence (particularly the close of it) and the beginning of the third. Never mind the new personage, Leos, who is intruded upon us unheralded and unexplained. That is McClintock's way; it is his habit; it is a part of his genius; he cannot help it; he never interrupts the rush of his narrative to make introductions.

It could not escape Ambulinia's penetrating eye that he sought an interview with her, which she as anxiously avoided, and assumed a more distant calmness than before, seemingly to destroy all hope. After many efforts and struggles with his own person, with timid steps the Major approached the damsel, with the same caution as he would have done in a field of battle. "Lady Ambulinia," said he, trembling, "I have long desired a moment like this. I dare not let it escape. I fear the consequences; yet I hope your indulgence will at least hear my petition. Can you not anticipate what I would say, and what I am about to express? Will not you, like Minerva, who sprung from the brain of Jupiter, release me from thy winding chains or cure me—" "Say no more, Elfonzo," answered Ambulinia, with a serious look, raising her hand as if she intended to swear eternal hatred against the whole world; "another lady in my place would have perhaps answered your question in bitter coldness. I know not the little arts of my sex. I care but little for the vanity of those who would chide me, and am unwilling as well as ashamed to be guilty of anything that would lead you to think 'all is not gold that glitters'; so be no rash in your resolution. It is better to repent now, than to do it in a more solemn hour. Yes, I know what you would say. I know you have a costly gift for me—the noblest that man can make—*your heart*! You should not offer it to one so unworthy. Heaven, you know, has allowed my father's house to be made a house of solitude, a home of silent obedience, which my parents say is more to be admired than big names and high-sounding titles. Notwithstanding all this, let me speak the emotions of an honest heart—allow me to say in the fullness of my hopes that I anticipate better days. The bird may stretch its wings toward the sun, which it can never reach; and flowers of the field appear to ascend in the same direction, because they cannot do otherwise; but man confides his complaints to the saints in whom he believes; for in their abodes of light they know no more sorrow. From your confession and indicative looks, I must be that person; if so deceive not yourself."

Elfonzo replied, "Pardon me, my dear madam, for my frankness. I have loved you from my earliest days—everything grand and beautiful hath borne the image of Ambulinia; while precipices on every hand surrounded me, your *guardian angel* stood and beckoned me away from the deep abyss. In every trial, in every misfortune, I have met with your helping hand; yet I never dreamed or dared to cherish thy love, till a voice impaired with age encouraged the cause, and declared they who acquired thy favor should win a victory. I saw how Leos worshiped thee. I felt my own unworthiness. I began to *know jealousy*, a strong guest—indeed, in my bosom,—yet I could see if I gained your admiration Leos was to be my rival. I was aware that he had the influence of your parents, and the wealth of a deceased relative, which is too often mistaken for permanent and regular tranquillity; yet I have determined by your permission to beg an interest in your prayers—to ask you to animate my drooping spirits by your smiles and your winning looks; for if you but speak I shall be conqueror, my enemies shall stagger like Olympus shakes. And though earth and sea may tremble, and the charioteer of the sun may forget his dashing steed, yet I am assured that it is only to arm me with divine weapons which will enable me to complete my long-tried intention."

"Return to yourself, Elfonzo," said Ambulinia, pleasantly: "a dream of vision has disturbed your intellect; you are above the atmosphere, dwelling in the celestial regions; nothing is there that urges or hinders, nothing that brings discord into our present litigation. I entreat you to condescend a little, and be a man, and forget it all. When Homer describes the battle of the gods and noble men fighting with giants and dragons, they represent under this image our struggles with the delusions of our passions. You have exalted me, an unhappy girl, to the skies; you have called me a saint, and portrayed in your imagination an angel in human form. Let her remain such to you, let her continue to be as you have supposed, and be assured that she will consider a share in your esteem as her highest treasure. Think not that I would allure you from the path in which your conscience leads you; for you know I respect the conscience of others, as I would die for my own. Elfonzo, if I am worthy of thy love, let such conversation never again pass between us. Go, seek a nobler theme! we will seek it in the stream of time, as the sun set in the Tigris." As she spake these words she grasped the hand of Elfonzo, saying at the same time—"Peace and prosperity attend you, my hero; be up and doing!" Closing her remarks with this expression, she walked slowly away, leaving Elfonzo astonished and amazed. He ventured not to follow or detain her. Here he stood alone, gazing at the stars; confounded as he was, here he stood.

Yes; there he stood. There seems to be no doubt about that. Nearly half of this delirious story has now been delivered to the reader. It seems a pity to reduce the other half to a cold synopsis. Pity! it is more than a pity, it is a crime; for to synopsize McClintock is to reduce a sky-flushing conflagration to dull embers, it is to reduce barbaric splendor to ragged poverty. McClintock never wrote a line that was not precious; he never wrote one that could be spared; he never framed one from which a word could be removed without damage. Every sentence that this master has produced may be likened to a perfect set of teeth, white, uniform, beautiful. If you pull one, the charm is gone.

Still, it is now necessary to begin to pull, and to keep it up; for lack of space requires us to synopsize.

We left Elfonzo standing there amazed. At what, we do not know. Not at the girl's speech. No; we ourselves should have been amazed at it, of course, for none of us has ever heard anything resembling it; but Elfonzo was used to speeches made up of noise and vacancy, and could listen to them with undaunted mind like the "topmost topaz of an ancient tower"; he was used to making them himself; he—but let it go, it cannot be guessed out; we shall never know what it was that astonished him. He stood there awhile; then he said, "Alas! am I now Grief's disappointed son at last?" He did not stop to examine his mind, and to try to find out what he probably meant by that, because, for one reason, "a mixture of ambition and greatness of soul moved upon his young heart," and started him for the village. He resumed his bench in school, "and reasonably progressed in his education." His heart was heavy, but he went into society, and sought surcease of sorrow in its light distractions. He made himself popular with his violin, "which seemed to have a thousand chords—more symphonious than the Muses of Apollo, and more enchanting than the ghost of the Hills." This is obscure, but let it go.

During this interval Leos did some unencouraged courting, but at last, "choked by his undertaking," he desisted.

Presently "Elfonzo again wends his way to the stately walls and new-built village." He goes to the house of his beloved; she opens the door herself. To my surprise—for Ambulinia's heart had still seemed free at the time of their last interview—love beamed from the girl's eyes. One sees that Elfonzo was surprised, too; for when he caught that light, "a halloo of smothered shouts ran through every vein." A neat figure—a very neat figure, indeed! Then he kissed her. "The scene was overwhelming." They went into the parlor. The girl said it was safe, for her parents were abed, and would never know. Then we have this fine picture—flung upon the canvas with hardly an effort, as you will notice.

Advancing toward him, she gave a bright display of her rosy neck, and from her head the ambrosial locks breathed divine fragrance; her robe hung waving to his view, while she stood like a goddess confessed before him.

There is nothing of interest in the couple's interview. Now at this point the girl invites Elfonzo to a village show, where jealousy is the motive of the play, for she wants to teach him a wholesome lesson, if he is a jealous person. But this is a sham, and pretty shallow. McClintock merely wants a pretext to drag in a plagiarism of his upon a scene or two in "Othello."

The lovers went to the play. Elfonzo was one of the fiddlers. He and Ambulinia must not been seen together, lest trouble follow with the girl's malignant father; we are made to understand that clearly. So the two sit together in the orchestra, in the midst of the musicians. This does not seem to be good art. In the first place, the girl would be in the way, for orchestras are always packed closely together, and there is no room to spare for people's girls; in the next place, one cannot conceal a girl in an orchestra without everybody taking notice of it. There can be no doubt, it seems to me, that this is bad art.

Leos is present. Of course, one of the first things that catches his eye is the maddening spectacle of Ambulinia "leaning upon Elfonzo's chair." This poor girl does not seem to understand even the rudiments of concealment. But she is "in her seventeenth," as the author phrases it, and that is her justification.

Leos meditates, constructs a plan—with personal violence as a basis, of course. It was their way down there. It is a good plain plan, without any imagination in it. He will go out and stand at the front door, and when these two come out he will "arrest Ambulinia from the hands of the insolent Elfonzo," and thus make for himself a "more prosperous field of immortality than ever was decreed by Omnipotence, or ever pencil drew or artist imagined." But, dear me, while he is waiting there the couple climb out at the back window and scurry home! This is romantic enough, but there is a lack of dignity in the situation.

At this point McClintock puts in the whole of his curious play—which we skip.

Some correspondence follows now. The bitter father and the distressed lovers write the letters. Elopements are attempted. They are idiotically planned, and they fail. Then we have several pages of romantic powwow and confusion dignifying nothing. Another elopement is planned; it is to take place on Sunday, when everybody is at church. But the "hero" cannot keep the secret; he tells everybody. Another author would have found another instrument when he decided to defeat this elopement; but that is not McClintock's way. He uses the person that is nearest at hand.

The evasion failed, of course. Ambulinia, in her flight, takes refuge in a neighbor's house. Her father drags her home. The villagers gather, attracted by the racket.

Elfonzo was moved at this sight. The people followed on to see what was going to become of Ambulinia, while he, with downcast looks, kept at a distance, until he saw them enter the abode of the father, thrusting her, that was the sigh of his soul, out of his presence into a solitary apartment, when she exclaimed, "Elfonzo! Elfonzo! oh, Elfonzo! where art thou, with all thy heroes? haste, oh! haste, come thou to my relief. Ride on the wings of the wind! Turn thy force loose like a tempest, and roll on thy army like a whirlwind, over this mountain of trouble and confusion. Oh friends! if any pity me, let your last efforts throng upon the green hills, and come to the relief of Ambulinia, who is guilty of nothing but innocent love." Elfonzo called out with a loud voice, "My God, can I stand this! arouse up, I beseech you, and put an end to this tyranny. Come, my brave boys," said he, "are you ready to go forth to your duty?" They stood around him. "Who," said he, "will call us to arms? Where are my thunderbolts of war? Speak ye, the first who will meet the foe! Who will go forward with me in this ocean of grievous temptation? If there is one who desires to go, let him come and shake hands upon the altar of devotion, and swear that he will be a hero; yes, a Hector in a cause like this, which calls aloud for a speedy remedy." "Mine be the deed," said a young lawyer, "and mine alone; Venus alone shall quit her station before I will forsake one jot or tittle of my promise to you; what is death to me? what is all this warlike army, if it is not to win a victory? I love the sleep of the lover and the mighty; nor would I give it over till the blood of my enemies should wreak with that of my own. But God forbid that our fame should soar on the blood of the slumberer." Mr. Valeer stands at his door with the frown of a demon upon his brow, with his dangerous weapon[3] ready to strike the first man who should enter his door. "Who will arise and go forward through blood and carnage to the rescue of my Ambulinia?" said Elfonzo. "All," exclaimed the multitude; and onward they went, with their implements of battle. Others, of a more timid nature, stood among the distant hills to see the result of the contest.

It will hardly be believed that after all this thunder and lightning not a drop of rain fell; but such is the fact. Elfonzo and his gang stood up and black-guarded Mr. Valeer with vigor all night, getting their outlay back with interest; then in the early morning the army and its general retired from the field, leaving the victory with their solitary adversary and his crowbar. This is the first time this has happened in romantic literature. The invention is original. Everything in this book is original; there is nothing hackneyed about it anywhere. Always, in other romances, when you find the author leading up to a climax, you know what is going to happen. But in this book it is different; the thing which seems inevitable and unavoidable never happens; it is circumvented by the art of the author every time.

Another elopement was attempted. It failed.

We have now arrived at the end. But it is not exciting. McClintock thinks it is; but it isn't. One day Elfonzo sent Ambulinia another note—a note proposing elopement No. 16. This time the plan is admirable; admirable, sagacious, ingenious, imaginative, deep—oh, everything, and perfectly easy. One wonders why it was never thought of before. This is the scheme. Ambulinia is to leave the breakfast-table, ostensibly to "attend to the placing of those flowers, which should have been done a week ago"—artificial ones, of course; the others wouldn't keep so long—and then, instead of fixing the flowers, she is to walk out to the grove, and go off with Elfonzo. The invention of this plan overstrained the author that is plain, for he straightway shows failing powers. The details of the plan are not many or elaborate. The author shall state them himself—this good soul, whose intentions are always better than his English:

"You walk carelessly toward the academy grove, where you will find me with a lightning steed, elegantly equipped to bear you off where we shall be joined in wedlock with the first connubial rights."

Last scene of all, which the author, now much enfeebled, tries to smarten up and make acceptable to his spectacular heart by introducing some new properties—silver bow, golden harp, olive branch—things that can all come good in an elopement, no doubt, yet are not to be compared to an umbrella for real handiness and reliability in an excursion of that kind.

And away she ran to the sacred grove, surrounded with glittering pearls, that indicated her coming. Elfonzo hails her with his silver bow and his golden harp. They meet—Ambulinia's countenance brightens—Elfonzo leads up the winged steed. "Mount," said he, "ye true-hearted, ye fearless soul—the day is ours." She sprang upon the back of the young thunderbolt, a brilliant star sparkles upon her head, with one hand she grasps the reins, and with the other she holds an olive branch. "Lend thy aid, ye strong winds," they exclaimed, "ye moon, ye sun, and all ye fair host of heaven, witness the enemy conquered." "Hold," said Elfonzo, "thy dashing steed." "Ride on," said Ambulinia, "the voice of thunder is behind us." And onward they went, with such rapidity that they very soon arrived at Rural Retreat, where they dismounted, and were united with all the solemnities that usually attended such divine operations.

There is but one Homer, there is but one Shakespeare, there is but one McClintock—and his immortal book is before you. Homer could not have written this book, Shakespeare could not have written it, I could not have done it myself. There is nothing just like it in the literature of any country or of any epoch. It stands alone; it is monumental. It adds G. Ragsdale McClintock's to the sum of the republic's imperishable names.

[1] The name here given is a substitute for the one actually attached to the pamphlet.

[2] Further on it will be seen that he is a country expert on the fiddle, and has a three-township fame.

[3] It is a crowbar.

# THE CURIOUS BOOK

Complete

(The foregoing review of the great work of G. Ragsdale McClintock is liberally illuminated with sample extracts, but these cannot appease the appetite. Only the complete book, unabridged, can do that. Therefore it is here printed.—M.T.)

THE ENEMY CONQUERED; OR, LOVE TRIUMPHANT

*Sweet girl, thy smiles are full of charms,*
*Thy voice is sweeter still,*
*It fills the breast with fond alarms,*
*Echoed by every rill.*

I begin this little work with an eulogy upon woman, who has ever been distinguished for her perseverance, her constancy, and her devoted attention to those upon whom she has been pleased to place her *affections*. Many have been the themes upon which writers and public speakers have dwelt with intense and increasing interest. Among these delightful themes stands that of woman, the balm to all our sighs and disappointments, and the most pre-eminent of all other topics. Here the poet and orator have stood and gazed with wonder and with admiration; they have dwelt upon her innocence, the ornament of all her virtues. First viewing her external charms, such as set forth in her form and benevolent countenance, and then passing to the deep hidden springs of loveliness and disinterested devotion. In every clime, and in every age, she has been the pride of her *nation*. Her watchfulness is untiring; she who guarded the sepulcher was the first to approach it, and the last to depart from its awful yet sublime scene. Even here, in this highly favored land, we look to her for the security of our institutions, and for our future greatness as a nation. But, strange as it may appear, woman's charms and virtues are but slightly appreciated by thousands. Those who should raise the standard of female worth, and paint her value with her virtues, in living colors, upon the banners that are fanned by the zephyrs of heaven, and hand them down to posterity as emblematical of a rich inheritance, do not properly estimate them.

Man is not sensible, at all times, of the nature and the emotions which bear that name; he does not understand, he will not comprehend; his intelligence has not expanded to that degree of glory which drinks in the vast revolution of humanity, its end, its mighty destination, and the causes which operated, and are still operating, to produce a more elevated station, and the objects which energize and enliven its consummation. This he is a stranger to; he is not aware that woman is the recipient of celestial love, and that man is dependent upon her to perfect his character; that without her, philosophically and truly speaking, the brightest of his intelligence is but the coldness of a winter moon, whose beams can produce no fruit, whose solar light is not its own, but borrowed from the great dispenser of effulgent beauty. We have no disposition in the world to flatter the fair sex, we would raise them above those dastardly principles which only exist in little souls, contracted hearts, and a distracted brain. Often does she unfold herself in all her fascinating loveliness, presenting the most captivating charms; yet we find man frequently treats such purity of purpose with indifference. Why does he do it? Why does he baffle that which is inevitably the source of his better days? Is he so much of a stranger to those excellent qualities as not to appreciate woman, as not to have respect to her dignity? Since her art and beauty first captivated man, she has been his delight and his comfort; she has shared alike in his misfortunes and in his prosperity.

Whenever the billows of adversity and the tumultuous waves of trouble beat high, her smiles subdue their fury. Should the tear of sorrow and the mournful sigh of grief interrupt the peace of his mind, her voice removes them all, and she bends from her circle to encourage him onward. When darkness would obscure his mind, and a thick cloud of gloom would bewilder its operations, her intelligent eye darts a ray of streaming light into his heart. Mighty and charming is that disinterested devotion which she is ever ready to exercise toward man, not waiting till the last moment of his danger, but seeks to relieve him in his early afflictions. It gushes forth from the expansive fullness of a tender and devoted heart, where the noblest, the purest, and the most elevated and refined feelings are matured and developed in those many kind offices which invariably make her character.

In the room of sorrow and sickness, this unequaled characteristic may always been seen, in the performance of the most charitable acts; nothing that she can

112

do to promote the happiness of him who she claims to be her protector will be omitted; all is invigorated by the animating sunbeams which awaken the heart to songs of gaiety. Leaving this point, to notice another prominent consideration, which is generally one of great moment and of vital importance. Invariably she is firm and steady in all her pursuits and aims. There is required a combination of forces and extreme opposition to drive her from her position; she takes her stand, not to be moved by the sound of Apollo's lyre or the curved bow of pleasure.

Firm and true to what she undertakes, and that which she requires by her own aggrandizement, and regards as being within the strict rules of propriety, she will remain stable and unflinching to the last. A more genuine principle is not to be found in the most determined, resolute heart of man. For this she deserves to be held in the highest commendation, for this she deserves the purest of all other blessings, and for this she deserves the most laudable reward of all others. It is a noble characteristic and is worthy of imitation of any age. And when we look at it in one particular aspect, it is still magnified, and grows brighter and brighter the more we reflect upon its eternal duration. What will she not do, when her word as well as her affections and *love* are pledged to her lover? Everything that is dear to her on earth, all the hospitalities of kind and loving parents, all the sincerity and loveliness of sisters, and the benevolent devotion of brothers, who have surrounded her with every comfort; she will forsake them all, quit the harmony and sweet sound of the lute and the harp, and throw herself upon the affections of some devoted admirer, in whom she fondly hopes to find more than she has left behind, which is not often realized by many. Truth and virtue all combined! How deserving our admiration and love! Ah cruel would it be in man, after she has thus manifested such an unshaken confidence in him, and said by her determination to abandon all the endearments and blandishments of home, to act a villainous part, and prove a traitor in the revolution of his mission, and then turn Hector over the innocent victim whom he swore to protect, in the presence of Heaven, recorded by the pen of an angel.

Striking as this train may unfold itself in her character, and as pre-eminent as it may stand among the fair display of her other qualities, yet there is another, which struggles into existence, and adds an additional luster to what she already possesses. I mean that disposition in woman which enables her, in sorrow, in grief, and in distress, to bear all with enduring patience. This she has done, and can and will do, amid the din of war and clash of arms. Scenes and occurrences which, to every appearance, are calculated to rend the heart with the profoundest emotions of trouble, do not fetter that exalted principle imbued in her very nature. It is true, her tender and feeling heart may often be moved (as she is thus constituted), but she is not conquered, she has not given up to the harlequin of disappointments, her energies have not become clouded in the last movement of misfortune, but she is continually invigorated by the archetype of her affections. She may bury her face in her hands, and let the tear of anguish roll, she may promenade the delightful walks of some garden, decorated with all the flowers of nature, or she may steal out along some gently rippling stream, and there, as the silver waters uninterruptedly move forward, shed her silent tears;

they mingle with the waves, and take a last farewell of their agitated home, to seek a peaceful dwelling among the rolling floods; yet there is a voice rushing from her breast, that proclaims *victory* along the whole line and battlement of her affections. That voice is the voice of patience and resignation; that voice is one that bears everything calmly and dispassionately, amid the most distressing scenes; when the fates are arrayed against her peace, and apparently plotting for her destruction, still she is resigned.

Woman's affections are deep, consequently her troubles may be made to sink deep. Although you may not be able to mark the traces of her grief and the furrowings of her anguish upon her winning countenance, yet be assured they are nevertheless preying upon her inward person, sapping the very foundation of that heart which alone was made for the weal and not the woe of man. The deep recesses of the soul are fields for their operation. But they are not destined simply to take the regions of the heart for their dominion, they are not satisfied merely with interrupting her better feelings; but after a while you may see the blooming cheek beginning to droop and fade, her intelligent eye no longer sparkles with the starry light of heaven, her vibrating pulse long since changed its regular motion, and her palpitating bosom beats once more for the midday of her glory. Anxiety and care ultimately throw her into the arms of the haggard and grim monster death. But, oh, how patient, under every pining influence! Let us view the matter in bolder colors; see her when the dearest object of her affections recklessly seeks every bacchanalian pleasure, contents himself with the last rubbish of creation. With what solicitude she awaits his return! Sleep fails to perform its office—she weeps while the nocturnal shades of the night triumph in the stillness. Bending over some favorite book, whilst the author throws before her mind the most beautiful imagery, she startles at every sound. The midnight silence is broken by the solemn announcement of the return of another morning. He is still absent; she listens for that voice which has so often been greeted by the melodies of her own; but, alas! stern silence is all that she receives for her vigilance.

Mark her unwearied watchfulness, as the night passes away. At last, brutalized by the accursed thing, he staggers along with rage, and, shivering with cold, he makes his appearance. Not a murmur is heard from her lips. On the contrary, she meets him with a smile—she caresses him with tender arms, with all the gentleness and softness of her sex. Here, then, is seen her disposition, beautifully arrayed. Woman, thou art more to be admired than the spicy gales of Arabia, and more sought for than the gold of Golconda. We believe that Woman should associate freely with man, and we believe that it is for the preservation of her rights. She should become acquainted with the metaphysical designs of those who condescended to sing the siren song of flattery. This, we think, should be according to the unwritten law of decorum, which is stamped upon every innocent heart. The precepts of prudery are often steeped in the guilt of contamination, which blasts the expectations of better moments. Truth, and beautiful dreams—loveliness, and delicacy of character, with cherished affections of the ideal woman—gentle hopes and aspirations, are enough to uphold her in the storms of darkness, without the transferred colorings of a stained sufferer. How often have we seen it in our public prints, that woman occupies a false station in the world! and some have gone so far as to say it was an unnatural one. So long has she been regarded a weak creature, by the rabble and illiterate—they have looked upon her as an insufficient actress on the great stage of human life—a mere puppet, to fill up the drama of human existence—a thoughtless, inactive being—that she has too often come to the same conclusion herself, and has sometimes forgotten her high destination, in the meridian of her glory. We have but little sympathy or patience for those who treat her as a mere Rosy Melindi—who are always fishing for pretty complements—who are satisfied by the gossamer of Romance, and who can be allured by the verbosity of high-flown words, rich in language, but poor and barren in sentiment. Beset, as she has been, by the intellectual vulgar, the selfish, the designing, the cunning, the hidden, and the artful—no wonder she has sometimes folded her wings in despair, and forgotten her *heavenly* mission in the delirium of imagination; no wonder she searches out some wild desert, to find a peaceful home. But this cannot always continue. A new era is moving gently onward, old things are rapidly passing away; old superstitions, old prejudices, and old notions are now bidding farewell to their old associates and companions, and giving way to one whose wings are plumed with the light of heaven and tinged by the dews of the morning. There is a remnant of blessedness that clings to her in spite of all evil influence, there is enough of the Divine Master left to accomplish the noblest work ever achieved under the canopy of the vaulted skies; and that time is fast approaching, when the picture of the true woman will shine from its frame of glory, to captivate, to win back, to restore, and to call into being once more, *the object of her mission.*

> *Star of the brave! thy glory shed,*
> *O'er all the earth, thy army led—*
> *Bold meteor of immortal birth!*
> *Why come from Heaven to dwell on Earth?*

Mighty and glorious are the days of youth; happy the moments of the *lover*, mingled with smiles and tears of his devoted, and long to be remembered are the achievements which he gains with a palpitating heart and a trembling hand. A bright and lovely dawn, the harbinger of a fair and prosperous day, had arisen over the beautiful little village of Cumming, which is surrounded by the most romantic scenery in the Cherokee country. Brightening clouds seemed to rise from the mist of the fair Chattahoochee, to spread their beauty over the thick forest, to guide the hero whose bosom beats with aspirations to conquer the enemy that would tarnish his name, and to win back the admiration of his long-tried friend. He endeavored to make his way through Sawney's Mountain, where many meet to catch the gales that are continually blowing for the refreshment of the stranger and the traveler. Surrounded as he was by hills on every side, naked rocks dared the efforts of his energies. Soon the sky became overcast, the sun buried itself in the clouds, and the fair day gave place to gloomy twilight, which lay heavily on the Indian Plains. He remembered an old Indian Castle, that once stood at the foot of the mountain. He thought if he could make his way to this, he would rest contented for a short time. The mountain air breathed fragrance—a rosy tinge rested on the glassy waters that murmured at its base. His resolution soon brought him to the remains of the red man's hut: he surveyed with wonder and astonishment the decayed building, which time had buried in the dust, and thought to himself, his happiness was not yet complete. Beside the shore of the brook sat a young man, about eighteen or twenty, who seemed to be reading some favorite book, and who had a remarkably noble countenance—eyes which betrayed more than a common mind. This of course made the youth a welcome guest, and gained him friends in whatever condition of life he might be placed. The traveler observed that he was a well-built figure, which showed strength and grace in every movement. He accordingly addressed him in quite a gentlemanly manner, and inquired of him the way to the village. After he had received the desired information, and was about taking his leave, the youth said, "Are you not Major Elfonzo, the great musician—the champion of a noble cause—the modern Achilles, who gained so many victories in the Florida War?" "I bear that name," said the Major, "and those titles, trusting at the same time that the ministers of grace will carry me triumphantly through all my laudable undertakings, and if," continued the Major, "you, sir, are the patronizer of noble deeds, I should like to make you my confidant and learn your address." The youth looked somewhat amazed, bowed low, mused for a moment, and began: "My name is Roswell. I have been recently admitted to the bar, and can only give a faint outline of my future success in that honorable profession; but I trust, sir, like the Eagle, I shall look down from lofty rocks upon the dwellings of man, and shall ever be ready to give you any assistance in my official capacity, and whatever this muscular arm of mine can do, whenever it shall be called from its buried *greatness*." The Major grasped him by the hand, and exclaimed: "O! thou exalted spirit of inspiration— thou flame of burning prosperity, may the Heaven-directed blaze be the glare of thy soul, and battle down every rampart that seems to impede your progress!"

The road which led to the town presented many attractions. Elfonzo had bid farewell to the youth of deep feeling, and was not wending his way to the dreaming spot of his fondness. The south winds whistled through the woods, as the waters dashed against the banks, as rapid fire in the pent furnace roars. This brought him to remember while alone, that he quietly left behind the hospitality of a father's house, and gladly entered the world, with higher hopes than are often realized. But as he journeyed onward, he was mindful of the advice of his father, who had often looked sadly on the ground when tears of cruelly deceived hope moistened his eye. Elfonzo had been somewhat of a dutiful son; yet fond of the amusements of life—had been in distant lands—had enjoyed the pleasure of the world and had frequently returned to the scenes of his boyhood, almost destitute of many of the comforts of life. In this condition, he would frequently say to his father, "Have I offended you, that you look upon me as a stranger, and frown upon me with stinging looks? Will you not favor me with the sound of your voice? If I have trampled upon your veneration, or have spread a humid veil of darkness around your expectations, send me back into the world where no heart beats for me—where the foot of man has never yet trod; but give me at least one kind word—allow me to come into the presence sometimes of thy winter-worn locks." "Forbid it, Heaven, that I should be angry with thee," answered the father, "my son, and yet I send thee back to the children of the world—to the cold charity of the combat, and to a land of victory. I read another destiny in thy countenance—I learn thy inclinations from the flame that has already kindled in my soul a stranger sensation. It will seek thee, my dear Elfonzo, it will find thee—thou canst not escape that lighted torch, which shall blot out from the remembrance of men a long train of prophecies which they have foretold against thee. I once thought not so. Once, I was blind; but now the path of life is plain before me, and my sight is clear; yet Elfonzo, return to thy worldly occupation—take again in thy hand that chord of sweet sounds—struggle with the civilized world, and with your own heart; fly swiftly to the enchanted ground—let the night-owl send forth its screams from the stubborn oak—let the sea sport upon the beach, and the stars sing together; but learn of these, Elfonzo, thy doom, and thy hiding-place. Our most innocent as well as our most lawful *desires* must often be denied us, that we may learn to sacrifice them to a Higher will."

Remembering such admonitions with gratitude, Elfonzo was immediately urged by the recollection of his father's family to keep moving. His steps became quicker and quicker—he hastened through the *piny* woods, dark as the forest was, and with joy he very soon reached the little village or repose, in whose bosom rested the boldest chivalry. His close attention to every important object—his modest questions about whatever was new to him—his reverence for wise old age, and his ardent desire to learn many of the fine arts, soon brought him into respectable notice.

One mild winter day as he walked along the streets toward the Academy, which stood upon a small eminence, surrounded by native growth—some venerable in its appearance, others young and prosperous—all seemed inviting, and seemed to be the very place for learning as well as for genius to spend its research beneath its spreading shades. He entered its classic walls in the usual mode of southern manners. The principal of the Institution begged him to be seated and listen to the recitations that were going on. He accordingly obeyed the request, and seemed to be much pleased. After the school was dismissed, and the young hearts regained their freedom, with the songs of the evening, laughing at the anticipated pleasures of a happy home, while others tittered at the actions of the past day, he addressed the teacher in a tone that indicated a resolution—with an undaunted mind. He said he had determined to become a student, if he could meet with his approbation. "Sir," said he, "I have spent much time in the world. I have traveled among the uncivilized inhabitants of America. I have met with friends, and combated with foes; but none of these gratify my ambition, or decide what is to be my destiny. I see the learned would have an influence with the voice of the people themselves. The despoilers of the remotest kingdoms of the earth refer their differences to this class of persons. This the illiterate and inexperienced little dream of; and now if you will receive me as I am, with these deficiencies—with all my misguided opinions, I will give you my honor, sir, that I will never disgrace the Institution, or those who have placed you in this honorable station." The instructor, who had met with many disappointments, knew how to feel for a stranger who had been thus turned upon the charities of an unfeeling community. He looked at him earnestly, and said: "Be of good cheer—look forward, sir, to the high destination you may attain. Remember, the more elevated the mark at which you aim, the more sure, the more glorious, the more magnificent the prize." From wonder to wonder, his encouragement led the impatient listener. A stranger nature bloomed before him—giant streams promised him success—gardens of hidden treasures opened to his view. All this, so vividly described, seemed to gain a new witchery from his glowing fancy.

In 1842 he entered the class, and made rapid progress in the English and Latin departments. Indeed, he continued advancing with such rapidity that he was like to become the first in his class, and made such unexpected progress, and was so studious, that he had almost forgotten the pictured saint of his affections. The fresh wreaths of the pine and cypress had waited anxiously to drop once more the dews of Heavens upon the heads of those who had so often poured forth the tender emotions of their souls under its boughs. He was aware of the pleasure that he had seen there. So one evening, as he was returning from his reading, he concluded he would pay a visit to this enchanting spot. Little did he think of witnessing a shadow of his former happiness, though no doubt he wished it might be so. He continued sauntering by the roadside, meditating on the past. The nearer he approached the spot, the more anxious he became. At the moment a tall female figure flitted across his path, with a bunch of roses in her hand; her countenance showed uncommon vivacity, with a resolute spirit; her ivory teeth already appeared as she smiled beautifully, promenading—while her ringlets of hair dangled unconsciously around her snowy neck. Nothing was wanting to complete her beauty. The tinge of the rose was in full bloom upon her cheek; the charms of sensibility and tenderness were always her associates. In Ambulinia's bosom dwelt a noble soul—one that never faded—one that never was conquered. Her heart yielded to no feeling but the love of Elfonzo, on whom she gazed with intense delight, and to whom she felt herself more closely bound, because he sought the hand of no other. Elfonzo was roused from his apparent reverie. His books no longer were his inseparable companions—his thoughts arrayed themselves to encourage him in the field of victory. He endeavored to speak to his supposed Ambulinia, but his speech appeared not in words. No, his effort was a stream of fire, that kindled his soul into a flame of admiration, and carried his senses away captive. Ambulinia had disappeared, to make him more mindful of his duty. As she walked speedily away through the piny woods she calmly echoed: "O! Elfonzo, thou wilt now look from thy sunbeams. Thou shalt now walk in a new path—perhaps thy way leads through darkness; but fear not, the stars foretell happiness."

Not many days afterward, as surrounded by fragrant flowers she sat one evening at twilight, to enjoy the cool breeze that whispered notes of melody along the distant groves, the little birds perched on every side, as if to watch the movements of their new visitor. The bells were tolling when Elfonzo silently stole along by the wild wood flowers, holding in his hand his favorite instrument of music—his eye continually searching for Ambulinia, who hardly seemed to perceive him, as she played carelessly with the songsters that hopped from branch to branch. Nothing could be more striking than the difference between the two. Nature seemed to have given the more tender soul to Elfonzo, and the stronger and more courageous to Ambulinia. A deep feeling spoke from the eyes of Elfonzo—such a feeling as can only be expressed by those who are blessed as admirers, and by those who are able to return the same with sincerity of heart. He was a few years older than Ambulinia: she had turned a little into her seventeenth. He had almost grown up in the Cherokee country, with the same equal proportions as one of the natives. But little intimacy had existed between them until the year forty-one—because the youth felt that the character of such a lovely girl was too exalted to inspire any other feeling than that of quiet reverence. But as lovers will not always be insulted, at all times and under all circumstances, by the frowns and cold looks of crabbed old age, which should continually reflect dignity upon those around, and treat unfortunate as well as the fortunate with a graceful mien, he continued to use diligence and perseverance. All this lighted a spark in his heart that changed his whole character, and like the unyielding Deity that follows the storm to check its rage in the forest, he resolves for the first time to shake off his embarrassment and return where he had before only worshiped.

It could not escape Ambulinia's penetrating eye that he sought an interview with her, which she as anxiously avoided, and assumed a more distant calmness than before, seemingly to destroy all hope. After many efforts and struggles with his own person, with timid steps the Major approached the damsel, with the same caution as he would have done in a field of battle. "Lady Ambulinia," said he, trembling, "I have long desired a moment like this. I dare not let it escape. I fear the consequences; yet I hope your indulgence will at least hear my petition. Can you not anticipate what I would say, and what I am about to express? Will not you, like Minerva, who sprung from the brain of Jupiter, release me from thy winding chains or cure me—" "Say no more, Elfonzo," answered Ambulinia, with a serious look, raising her hand as if she intended to swear eternal hatred against the whole world; "another lady in my place would have perhaps answered your question in bitter coldness. I know not the little arts of my sex. I care but little for the vanity of those who would chide me, and am unwilling as well as shamed to be guilty of anything that would lead you to think 'all is not gold that glitters'; so be not rash in your resolution. It is better to repent now than to do it in a more solemn hour. Yes, I know what you would say. I know you have a costly gift for me—the noblest that man can make—*your heart*! You should not offer it to one so unworthy. Heaven, you know, has allowed my father's house to be made a house of solitude, a home of silent obedience, which my parents say is more to be admired than big names and high-sounding titles. Notwithstanding all this, let me speak the emotions of an honest heart; allow me to say in the fullness of my hopes that I anticipate better days. The bird may stretch its wings toward the sun, which it can never reach; and flowers of the field appear to ascend in the same direction, because they cannot do otherwise; but man confides his complaints to the saints in whom he believes; for in their abodes of light they know no more sorrow. From your confession and indicative looks, I must be that person; if so, deceive not yourself."

Elfonzo replied, "Pardon me, my dear madam, for my frankness. I have loved you from my earliest days; everything grand and beautiful hath borne the image of Ambulinia; while precipices on every hand surrounded me, your *guardian angel* stood and beckoned me away from the deep abyss. In every trial, in every misfortune, I have met with your helping hand; yet I never dreamed or dared to cherish thy love till a voice impaired with age encouraged the cause, and declared they who acquired thy favor should win a victory. I saw how Leos worshipped thee. I felt my own unworthiness. I began to *know jealousy*—a strong guest, indeed, in my bosom—yet I could see if I gained your admiration Leos was to be my rival. I was aware that he had the influence of your parents, and the wealth of a deceased relative, which is too often mistaken for permanent and regular tranquillity; yet I have determined by your permission to beg an interest in your prayers—to ask you to animate my dropping spirits by your smiles and your winning looks; for if you but speak I shall be conqueror, my enemies shall stagger like Olympus shakes. And though earth and sea may tremble, and the charioteer of the sun may forget his dashing steed, yet I am assured that it is only to arm me with divine weapons which will enable me to complete my long-tried intention."

"Return to your self, Elfonzo," said Ambulinia, pleasantly; "a dream of vision has disturbed your intellect; you are above the atmosphere, dwelling in the celestial regions; nothing is there that urges or hinders, nothing that brings discord into our present litigation. I entreat you to condescend a little, and be a man, and forget it all. When Homer describes the battle of the gods and noble men fighting with giants and dragons, they represent under this image our struggles with the delusions of our passions. You have exalted me, an unhappy girl, to the skies; you have called me a saint, and portrayed in your imagination an angel in human form. Let her remain such to you, let her continue to be as you have supposed, and be assured that she will consider a share in your esteem as her highest treasure. Think not that I would allure you from the path in which your conscience leads you; for you know I respect the conscience of others, as I would die for my own. Elfonzo, if I am worthy of thy love, let such conversation never again pass between us. Go, seek a nobler theme! we will seek it in the stream of time as the sun set in the Tigris." As she spake these words she grasped the hand of Elfonzo, saying at the same time, "Peace and prosperity attend you, my hero: be up and doing!" Closing her remarks with this expression, she walked slowly away, leaving Elfonzo astonished and amazed. He ventured not to follow or detain her. Here he stood alone, gazing at the stars; confounded as he was, here he stood. The rippling stream rolled on at his feet. Twilight had already begun to draw her sable mantle over the earth, and now and then the fiery smoke would ascend from the little town which lay spread out before him. The citizens seemed to be full of life and good-humor; but poor Elfonzo saw not a brilliant scene. No; his future life stood before him, stripped of the hopes that once adorned all his sanguine desires. "Alas!" said he, "am I now Grief's disappointed son at last." Ambulinia's image rose before his fancy. A mixture of ambition and greatness of soul moved upon his young heart, and encouraged him to bear all his crosses with the patience of a Job, notwithstanding he had to encounter with so many obstacles. He still endeavored to prosecute his studies, and reasonably progressed in his education. Still, he was not content; there was something yet to be done before his happiness was complete. He would visit his friends and acquaintances. They would invite him to social parties, insisting that he should partake of the amusements that were going on. This he enjoyed tolerably well. The ladies and gentlemen were generally well pleased with the Major; as he delighted all with his violin, which seemed to have a thousand chords—more symphonious than the Muses of Apollo and more enchanting than the ghost of the Hills. He passed some days in the country. During that time Leos had made many calls upon Ambulinia, who was generally received with a great deal of courtesy by the family. They thought him to be a young man worthy of attention, though he had but little in his soul to attract the attention or even win the affections of her whose graceful manners had almost made him a slave to every bewitching look that fell from her eyes. Leos made several attempts to tell her of his fair prospects—how much he loved her, and how much it would add to his bliss if he could but think she would be willing to share these blessings with him; but, choked by his undertaking, he made himself more like an inactive drone than he did like one who bowed at beauty's shrine.

Elfonzo again wends his way to the stately walls and new-built village. He now determines to see the end of the prophesy which had been foretold to him. The clouds burst from his sight; he believes if he can but see his Ambulinia, he can open to her view the bloody altars that have been misrepresented to stigmatize his name. He knows that her breast is transfixed with the sword of reason, and ready at all times to detect the hidden villainy of her enemies. He resolves to see her in her own home, with the consoling theme: "'I can but perish if I go.' Let the consequences be what they may," said he, "if I die, it shall be contending and struggling for my own rights."

Night had almost overtaken him when he arrived in town. Colonel Elder, a noble-hearted, high-minded, and independent man, met him at his door as usual, and seized him by the hand. "Well, Elfonzo," said the Colonel, "how does the world use you in your efforts?" "I have no objection to the world," said Elfonzo, "but the people are rather singular in some of their opinions." "Aye, well," said the Colonel, "you must remember that creation is made up of many mysteries; just take things by the right handle; be always sure you know which is the smooth side before you attempt your polish; be reconciled to your fate, be it what it may; and never find fault with your condition, unless your complaining will benefit it. Perseverance is a principle that should be commendable in those who have judgment to govern it. I should never had been so successful in my hunting excursions had I waited till the deer, by some magic dream, had been drawn to the muzzle of the gun before I made an attempt to fire at the game that dared my boldness in the wild forest. The great mystery in hunting seems to be—a good marksman, a resolute mind, a fixed determination, and my world for it, you will never return home without sounding your horn with the breath of a new victory. And so with every other undertaking. Be confident that your ammunition is of the right kind—always pull your trigger with a steady hand, and so soon as you perceive a calm, touch her off, and the spoils are yours."

This filled him with redoubled vigor, and he set out with a stronger anxiety than ever to the home of Ambulinia. A few short steps soon brought him to the door, half out of breath. He rapped gently. Ambulinia, who sat in the parlor alone, suspecting Elfonzo was near, ventured to the door, opened it, and beheld the hero, who stood in an humble attitude, bowed gracefully, and as they caught each other's looks the light of peace beamed from the eyes of Ambulinia. Elfonzo caught the expression; a halloo of smothered shouts ran through every vein, and for the first time he dared to impress a kiss upon her cheek. The scene was overwhelming; had the temptation been less animating, he would not have ventured to have acted so contrary to the desired wish of his Ambulinia; but who could have withstood the irrestistable temptation! What society condemns the practice but a cold, heartless, uncivilized people that know nothing of the warm attachments of refined society? Here the dead was raised to his long-cherished hopes, and the lost was found. Here all doubt and danger were buried in the vortex of oblivion; sectional differences no longer disunited their opinions; like the freed bird from the cage, sportive claps its rustling wings, wheels about to heaven in a joyful strain, and raises its notes to the upper sky. Ambulinia insisted upon Elfonzo to be seated, and give her a history of his unnecessary absence; assuring him the family had retired, consequently they would ever remain ignorant of his visit. Advancing toward him, she gave a bright display of her rosy neck, and from her head the ambrosial locks breathed divine fragrance; her robe hung waving to his view, while she stood like a goddess confessed before him.

"It does seem to me, my dear sir," said Ambulinia, "that you have been gone an age. Oh, the restless hours I have spent since I last saw you, in yon beautiful grove. There is where I trifled with your feelings for the express purpose of trying your attachment for me. I now find you are devoted; but ah! I trust you live not unguarded by the powers of Heaven. Though oft did I refuse to join my hand with thine, and as oft did I cruelly mock thy entreaties with borrowed shapes: yes, I feared to answer thee by terms, in words sincere and undissembled. O! could I pursue, and you have leisure to hear the annals of my woes, the evening star would shut Heaven's gates upon the impending day before my tale would be finished, and this night would find me soliciting your forgiveness."

"Dismiss thy fears and thy doubts," replied Elfonzo.

"Look, O! look: that angelic look of thine—bathe not thy visage in tears; banish those floods that are gathering; let my confession and my presence bring thee some relief." "Then, indeed, I will be cheerful," said Ambulinia, "and I think if we will go to the exhibition this evening, we certainly will see something worthy of our attention. One of the most tragical scenes is to be acted that has ever been witnessed, and one that every jealous-hearted person should learn a lesson from. It cannot fail to have a good effect, as it will be performed by those who are young and vigorous, and learned as well as enticing. You are aware, Major Elfonzo, who are to appear on the stage, and what the characters are to represent." "I am acquainted with the circumstances," replied Elfonzo, "and as I am to be one of the musicians upon that interesting occasion, I should be much gratified if you would favor me with your company during the hours of the exercises."

"What strange notions are in your mind?" inquired Ambulinia. "Now I know you have something in view, and I desire you to tell me why it is that you are so anxious that I should continue with you while the exercises are going on; though if you think I can add to your happiness and predilections, I have no particular objection to acquiesce in your request. Oh, I think I foresee, now, what you anticipate." "And will you have the goodness to tell me what you think it will be?" inquired Elfonzo. "By all means," answered Ambulinia; "a rival, sir, you would fancy in your own mind; but let me say for you, fear not! fear not! I will be one of the last persons to disgrace my sex by thus encouraging every one who may feel disposed to visit me, who may honor me with their graceful bows and their choicest compliments. It is true that young men too often mistake civil politeness for the finer emotions of the heart, which is tantamount to courtship; but, ah! how often are they deceived, when they come to test the weight of sunbeams with those on whose strength hangs the future happiness of an untried life."

The people were now rushing to the Academy with impatient anxiety; the band of music was closely followed by the students; then the parents and guardians; nothing interrupted the glow of spirits which ran through every bosom, tinged with the songs of a Virgil and the tide of a Homer. Elfonzo and Ambulinia soon repaired to the scene, and fortunately for them both the house was so crowded that they took their seats together in the music department, which was not in view of the auditory. This fortuitous circumstances added more the bliss of the Major than a thousand such exhibitions would have done. He forgot that he was man; music had lost its charms for him; whenever he attempted to carry his part, the string of the instrument would break, the bow became stubborn, and refused to obey the loud calls of the audience. Here, he said, was the paradise of his home, the long-sought-for opportunity; he felt as though he could send a million supplications to the throne of Heaven for such an exalted privilege. Poor Leos, who was somewhere in the crowd, looking as attentively as if he was searching for a needle in a haystack; here is stood, wondering to himself why Ambulinia was not there. "Where can she be? Oh! if she was only here, how I could relish the scene! Elfonzo is certainly not in town; but what if he is? I have got the wealth, if I have not the dignity, and I am sure that the squire and his lady have always been particular friends of mine, and I think with this assurance I shall be able to get upon the blind side of the rest of the family and make the heaven-born Ambulinia the mistress of all I possess." Then, again, he would drop his head, as if attempting to solve the most difficult problem in Euclid. While he was thus conjecturing in his own mind, a very interesting part of the exhibition was going on, which called the attention of all present. The curtains of the stage waved continually by the repelled forces that were given to them, which caused Leos to behold Ambulinia leaning upon the chair of Elfonzo. Her lofty beauty, seen by the glimmering of the chandelier, filled his heart with rapture, he knew not how to contain himself; to go where they were would expose him to ridicule; to continue where he was, with such an object before him, without being allowed an explanation in that trying hour, would be to the great injury of his mental as well as of his physical powers; and, in the name of high heaven, what must he do? Finally, he resolved to contain himself as well as he conveniently could, until the scene was over, and then he would plant himself at the door, to arrest Ambulinia from the hands of the insolent Elfonzo, and thus make for himself a more prosperous field of immortality than ever was decreed by Omnipotence, or ever pencil drew or artist imagined. Accordingly he made himself sentinel, immediately after the performance of the evening—retained his position apparently in defiance of all the world; he waited, he gazed at every lady, his whole frame trembled; here he stood, until everything like human shape had disappeared from the institution, and he had done nothing; he had failed to accomplish that which he so eagerly sought for. Poor, unfortunate creature! he had not the eyes of an Argus, or he might have seen his Juno and Elfonzo, assisted by his friend Sigma, make their escape from the window, and, with the rapidity of a race-horse, hurry through the blast of the storm to the residence of her father, without being recognized. He did not tarry long, but assured Ambulinia the endless chain of their existence was more closely connected than ever, since he had seen the virtuous, innocent, imploring, and the constant Amelia murdered by the jealous-hearted Farcillo, the accursed of the land.

The following is the tragical scene, which is only introduced to show the subject-matter that enabled Elfonzo to come to such a determinate resolution that nothing of the kind should ever dispossess him of his true character, should he be so fortunate as to succeed in his present undertaking.

Amelia was the wife of Farcillo, and a virtuous woman; Gracia, a young lady, was her particular friend and confidant. Farcillo grew jealous of Amelia, murders her, finds out that he was deceived, *and stabs himself.* Amelia appears alone, talking to herself.

A. Hail, ye solitary ruins of antiquity, ye sacred tombs and silent walks! it is your aid I invoke; it is to you, my soul, wrapt in deep mediating, pours forth its prayer. Here I wander upon the stage of mortality, since the world hath turned against me. Those whom I believed to be my friends, alas! are now my enemies, planting thorns in all my paths, poisoning all my pleasures, and turning the past to pain. What a lingering catalogue of sighs and tears lies just before me, crowding my aching bosom with the fleeting dream of humanity, which must shortly terminate. And to what purpose will all this bustle of life, these agitations and emotions of the heart have conduced, if it leave behind it nothing of utility, if it leave no traces of improvement? Can it be that I am deceived in my conclusions? No, I see that I have nothing to hope for, but everything for fear, which tends to drive me from the walks of time.

> Oh! in this dead night, if loud winds arise,
> To lash the surge and bluster in the skies,
> May the west its furious rage display,
> Toss me with storms in the watery way.

(Enter Gracia.)

G. Oh, Amelia, is it you, the object of grief, the daughter of opulence, of wisdom and philosophy, that thus complaineth? It cannot be you are the child of misfortune, speaking of the monuments of former ages, which were allotted not for the reflection of the distressed, but for the fearless and bold.

A. Not the child of poverty, Gracia, or the heir of glory and peace, but of fate. Remember, I have wealth more than wit can number; I have had power more than kings could encompass; yet the world seems a desert; all nature appears an afflictive spectacle of warring passions. This blind fatality, that capriciously sports with the rules and lives of mortals, tells me that the mountains will never again send forth the water of their springs to my thirst. Oh, that I might be freed and set at liberty from wretchedness! But I fear, I fear this will never be.

G. Why, Amelia, this untimely grief? What has caused the sorrows that bespeak better and happier days, to those lavish out such heaps of misery? You are aware that your instructive lessons embellish the mind with holy truths, by wedding its attention to none but great and noble affections.

A. This, of course, is some consolation. I will ever love my own species with feelings of a fond recollection, and while I am studying to advance the universal philanthropy, and the spotless name of my own sex, I will try to build my own upon the pleasing belief that I have accelerated the advancement of one who whispers of departed confidence.

> *And I, like some poor peasant fated to reside*
> *Remote from friends, in a forest wide.*
> *Oh, see what woman's woes and human wants require,*
> *Since that great day hath spread the seed of sinful fire.*

G. Look up, thou poor disconsolate; you speak of quitting earthly enjoyments. Unfold thy bosom to a friend, who would be willing to sacrifice every enjoyment for the restoration of the dignity and gentleness of mind which used to grace your walks, and which is so natural to yourself; not only that, but your paths were strewed with flowers of every hue and of every order.

> *With verdant green the mountains glow,*
> *For thee, for thee, the lilies grow;*
> *Far stretched beneath the tented hills,*
> *A fairer flower the valley fills.*

A. Oh, would to Heaven I could give you a short narrative of my former prospects for happiness, since you have acknowledged to be an unchangeable confidant—the richest of all other blessings. Oh, ye names forever glorious, ye celebrated scenes, ye renowned spot of my hymeneal moments; how replete is your chart with sublime reflections! How many profound vows, decorated with immaculate deeds, are written upon the surface of that precious spot of earth where I yielded up my life of celibacy, bade youth with all its beauties a final adieu, took a last farewell of the laurels that had accompanied me up the hill of my juvenile career. It was then I began to descend toward the valley of disappointment and sorrow; it was then I cast my little bark upon a mysterious ocean of wedlock, with him who then smiled and caressed me, but, alas! now frowns with bitterness, and has grown jealous and cold toward me, because the ring he gave me is misplaced or lost. Oh, bear me, ye flowers of memory, softly through the eventful history of past times; and ye places that have witnessed the progression of man in the circle of so many societies, and, of, aid my recollection, while I endeavor to trace the vicissitudes of a life devoted in endeavoring to comfort him that I claim as the object of my wishes.

> *Ah! ye mysterious men, of all the world, how few*
> *Act just to Heaven and to your promise true!*
> *But He who guides the stars with a watchful eye,*
> *The deeds of men lay open without disguise;*
> *Oh, this alone will avenge the wrongs I bear,*
> *For all the oppressed are His peculiar care.*

(F. makes a slight noise.)

A. Who is there—Farcillo?

G. Then I must gone. Heaven protect you. Oh, Amelia, farewell, be of good cheer.

> *May you stand like Olympus' towers,*
> *Against earth and all jealous powers!*
> *May you, with loud shouts ascend on high*
> *Swift as an eagle in the upper sky.*

A. Why so cold and distant tonight, Farcillo? Come, let us each other greet, and forget all the past, and give security for the future.

F. Security! talk to me about giving security for the future—what an insulting requisition! Have you said your prayers tonight, Madam Amelia?

A. Farcillo, we sometimes forget our duty, particularly when we expect to be caressed by others.

F. If you bethink yourself of any crime, or of any fault, that is yet concealed from the courts of Heaven and the thrones of grace, I bid you ask and solicit forgiveness for it now.

A. Oh, be kind, Farcillo, don't treat me so. What do you mean by all this?

F. Be kind, you say; you, madam, have forgot that kindness you owe to me, and bestowed it upon another; you shall suffer for your conduct when you make your peace with your God. I would not slay thy unprotected spirit. I call to Heaven to be my guard and my watch—I would not kill thy soul, in which all once seemed just, right, and perfect; but I must be brief, woman.

A. What, talk you of killing? Oh, Farcillo, Farcillo, what is the matter?

F. Aye, I do, without doubt; mark what I say, Amelia.

A. Then, O God, O Heaven, and Angels, be propitious, and have mercy upon me.

F. Amen to that, madam, with all my heart, and with all my soul.

A. Farcillo, listen to me one moment; I hope you will not kill me.

F. Kill you, aye, that I will; attest it, ye fair host of light, record it, ye dark imps of hell!

A. Oh, I fear you—you are fatal when darkness covers your brow; yet I know not why I should fear, since I never wronged you in all my life. I stand, sir, guiltless before you.

F. You pretend to say you are guiltless! Think of thy sins, Amelia; think, oh, think, hidden woman.

A. Wherein have I not been true to you? That death is unkind, cruel, and unnatural, that kills for living.

F. Peace, and be still while I unfold to thee.

A. I will, Farcillo, and while I am thus silent, tell me the cause of such cruel coldness in an hour like this.

F. That *ring*, oh, that ring I so loved, and gave thee as the ring of my heart; the allegiance you took to be faithful, when it was presented; the kisses and smiles with which you honored it. You became tired of the donor, despised it as a plague, and finally gave it to Malos, the hidden, the vile traitor.

A. No, upon my word and honor, I never did; I appeal to the Most High to bear me out in this matter. Send for Malos, and ask him.

F. Send for Malos, aye! Malos you wish to see; I thought so. I knew you could not keep his name concealed. Amelia, sweet Amelia, take heed, take heed of perjury; you are on the stage of death, to suffer for *your sins*.

A. What, not to die I hope, my Farcillo, my ever beloved.

F. Yes, madam, to die a traitor's death. Shortly your spirit shall take its exit; therefore confess freely thy sins, for to deny tends only to make me groan under the bitter cup thou hast made for me. Thou art to die with the name of traitor on thy brow!

A. Then, O Lord, have mercy upon me; give me courage, give me grace and fortitude to stand this hour of trial.

F. Amen, I say, with all my heart.

A. And, oh, Farcillo, will you have mercy, too? I never intentionally offended you in all my life, never *loved* Malos, never gave him cause to think so, as the high court of Justice will acquit me before its tribunal.

F. Oh, false, perjured woman, thou didst chill my blood, and makest me a demon like thyself. I saw the ring.

A. He found it, then, or got it clandestinely; send for him, and let him confess the truth; let his confession be sifted.

F. And you still wish to see him! I tell you, madam, he hath already confessed, and thou knowest the darkness of thy heart.

A. What, my deceived Farcillo, that I gave him the ring, in which all my affections were concentrated? Oh, surely not.

F. Aye, he did. Ask thy conscience, and it will speak with a voice of thunder to thy soul.

A. He will not say so, he dare not, he cannot.

F. No, he will not say so now, because his mouth, I trust, is hushed in death, and his body stretched to the four winds of heaven, to be torn to pieces by carnivorous birds.

A. What, he is dead, and gone to the world of spirits with that declaration in his mouth? Oh, unhappy man! Oh, insupportable hour!

F. Yes, and had all his sighs and looks and tears been lives, my great revenge could have slain them all, without the least condemnation.

A. Alas! he is ushered into eternity without testing the matter for which I am abused and sentenced and condemned to die.

F. Cursed, infernal woman! Weepest thou for him to my face? He that hath robbed me of my peace, my energy, the whole love of my life? Could I call the fabled Hydra, I would have him live and perish, survive and die, until the sun itself would grow dim with age. I would make him have the thirst of a Tantalus, and roll the wheel of an Ixion, until the stars of heaven should quit their brilliant stations.

A. Oh, invincible God, save me! Oh, unsupportable moment! Oh, heavy hour! Banish me, Farcillo—send me where no eye can ever see me, where no sound shall ever great my ear; but, oh, slay me not, Farcillo; vent thy rage and thy spite upon this emaciated frame of mine, only spare my life.

F. Your petitions avail nothing, cruel Amelia.

A. Oh, Farcillo, perpetrate the dark deed tomorrow; let me live till then, for my past kindness to you, and it may be some kind angel will show to you that I am not only the object of innocence, but one who never loved another but your noble self.

F. Amelia, the decree has gone forth, it is to be done, and that quickly; thou art to die, madam.

A. But half an hour allow me, to see my father and my only child, to tell her the treachery and vanity of this world.

F. There is no alternative, there is no pause: my daughter shall not see its deceptive mother die; your father shall not know that his daughter fell disgraced, despised by all but her enchanting Malos.

A. Oh, Farcillo, put up thy threatening dagger into its scabbard; let it rest and be still, just while I say one prayer for thee and for my child.

F. It is too late, thy doom is fixed, thou hast not confessed to Heaven or to me, my child's protector—thou art to die. Ye powers of earth and heaven, protect and defend me in this alone. (*stabs her while imploring for mercy.*)

A. Oh, Farcillo, Farcillo, a guiltless death I die.

F. Die! die! die!

(Gracia enters running, falls on her knees weeping, and kisses Amelia.)

G. Oh, Farcillo, Farcillo! oh, Farcillo!

F. I am here, the genius of the age, and the avenger of my wrongs.

G. Oh, lady, speak once more; sweet Amelia, on, speak again. Gone, gone— yes, forever gone! Farcillo, oh, cold-hearted Farcillo, some evil fiend hath urged you to do this, Farcillo.

F. Say not so again, or you shall receive the same fate. I did the glorious deed, madam—beware, then, how you talk.

G. I fear not your implements of war; I will let you know you have not the power to do me harm. If you have a heart of triple brass, it shall be reached and melted, and thy blood shall chill thy veins and grow stiff in thy arteries. Here is the ring of the virtuous and innocent murdered Amelia; I obtained it from Malos, who yet lives, in hopes that he will survive the wound given him, and says he got it clandestinely—declares Amelia to be the princess of truth and virtue, invulnerable to anything like forgetting her first devotion to thee. The world has heard of your conduct and your jealousy, and with one universal voice declares her to be the best of all in piety; that she is the star of this great universe, and a more virtuous woman never lived since the wheels of time began. Oh, had you waited till tomorrow, or until I had returned, some kind window would have been opened to her relief. But, alas! she is gone—yes, forever gone, to try the realities of an unknown world!

(Farcillo leaning over the body of Amelia.)

F. Malos not dead, and here is my ring! Oh, Amelia! falsely murdered! Oh, bloody deed! Oh, wretch that I am! Oh, angels forgive me! Oh, God, withhold thy vengeance! Oh, Amelia! if Heaven would make a thousand worlds like this, set with diamonds, and all of one perfect chrysolite, I would not have done this for them all, I would not have frowned and cursed as I did. Oh, she was heavenly true, nursed in the very lap of bright angels! Cursed slave that I am! Jealousy, oh! thou infernal demon! Lost, lost to every sense of honor! Oh! Amelia—heaven-born Amelia—dead, dead! Oh! oh! oh!—then let me die with thee. Farewell! farewell! ye world that deceived me! (*stabs himself.*)

Soon after the excitement of this tragical scene was over, and the enlisted feeling for Amelia had grown more buoyant with Elfonzo and Ambulinia, he determined to visit his retired home, and make the necessary improvements to enjoy a better day; consequently he conveyed the following lines to Ambulinia:

> Go tell the world that hope is glowing,
> Go bid the rocks their silence break,
> Go tell the stars that love is glowing,
> Then bid the hero his lover take.

In the region where scarcely the foot of man hath ever trod, where the woodman hath not found his way, lies a blooming grove, seen only by the sun when he mounts his lofty throne, visited only by the light of the stars, to whom are entrusted the guardianship of earth, before the sun sinks to rest in his rosy bed. High cliffs of rocks surround the romantic place, and in the small cavity of the rocky wall grows the daffodil clear and pure; and as the wind blows along the enchanting little mountain which surrounds the lonely spot, it nourishes the flowers with the dew-drops of heaven. Here is the seat of Elfonzo; darkness claims but little victory over this dominion, and in vain does she spread out her gloomy wings. Here the waters flow perpetually, and the trees lash their tops together to bid the welcome visitor a happy muse. Elfonzo, during his short stay in the country, had fully persuaded himself that it was his duty to bring this solemn matter to an issue. A duty that he individually owed, as a gentleman, to the parents of Ambulinia, a duty in itself involving not only his own happiness and his own standing in society, but one that called aloud the act of the parties to make it perfect and complete. How he should communicate his intentions to get a favorable reply, he was at a loss to know; he knew not whether to address Esq. Valeer in prose or in poetry, in a jocular or an argumentative manner, or whether he should use moral suasion, legal injunction, or seizure and take by reprisal; if it was to do the latter, he would have no difficulty in deciding in his own mind, but his gentlemanly honor was at stake; so he concluded to address the following letter to the father and mother of Ambulinia, as his address in person he knew would only aggravate the old gentleman, and perhaps his lady.

Cumming, Ga., January 22, 1844
Mr. and Mrs. Valeer—
Again I resume the pleasing task of addressing you, and once more beg an immediate answer to my many salutations. From every circumstance that has taken place, I feel in duty bound to comply with my obligations; to forfeit my word would be more than I dare do; to break my pledge, and my vows that have been witnessed, sealed, and delivered in the presence of an unseen Deity, would be disgraceful on my part, as well as ruinous to Ambulinia. I wish no longer to be kept in suspense about this matter. I wish to act gentlemanly in every particular. It is true, the promises I have made are unknown to any but Ambulinia, and I think it unnecessary to here enumerate them, as they who promise the most generally perform the least. Can you for a moment doubt my sincerity or my character? My only wish is, sir, that you may calmly and dispassionately look at the situation of the case, and if your better judgment should dictate otherwise, my obligations may induce me to pluck the flower that you so diametrically opposed. We have sworn by the saints—by the gods of battle, and by that faith whereby just men are made perfect—to be united. I hope, my dear sir, you will find it convenient as well as agreeable to give me a favorable answer, with the signature of Mrs. Valeer, as well as yourself.
With very great esteem,
your humble servant,
J. I. Elfonzo.

The moon and stars had grown pale when Ambulinia had retired to rest. A crowd of unpleasant thoughts passed through her bosom. Solitude dwelt in her chamber—no sound from the neighboring world penetrated its stillness; it appeared a temple of silence, of repose, and of mystery. At that moment she heard a still voice calling her father. In an instant, like the flash of lightning, a thought ran through her mind that it must be the bearer of Elfonzo's communication. "It is not a dream!" she said, "no, I cannot read dreams. Oh! I would to Heaven I was near that glowing eloquence—that poetical language—it charms the mind in an inexpressible manner, and warms the coldest heart." While consoling herself with this strain, her father rushed into her room almost frantic with rage, exclaiming: "Oh, Ambulinia! Ambulinia!! undutiful, ungrateful daughter! What does this mean? Why does this letter bear such heart-rending intelligence? Will you quit a father's house with this debased wretch, without a place to lay his distracted head; going up and down the country, with every novel object that many chance to wander through this region. He is a pretty man to make love known to his superiors, and you, Ambulinia, have done but little credit to yourself by honoring his visits. Oh, wretchedness! can it be that my hopes of happiness are forever blasted! Will you not listen to a father's entreaties, and pay some regard to a mother's tears. I know, and I do pray that God will give me fortitude to bear with this sea of troubles, and rescue my daughter, my Ambulinia, as a brand from the eternal burning." "Forgive me, father, oh! forgive thy child," replied Ambulinia. "My heart is ready to break, when I see you in this grieved state of agitation. Oh! think not so meanly of me, as that I mourn for my own danger. Father, I am only woman. Mother, I am only the templement of thy youthful years, but will suffer courageously whatever punishment you think proper to inflict upon me, if you will but allow me to comply with my most sacred promises—if you will but give me my personal right and my personal liberty. Oh, father! if your generosity will but give me these, I ask nothing more. When Elfonzo offered me his heart, I gave him my hand, never to forsake him, and now may the mighty God banish me before I leave him in adversity. What a heart must I have to rejoice in prosperity with him whose offers I have accepted, and then, when poverty comes, haggard as it may be, for me to trifle with the oracles of Heaven, and change with every fluctuation that may interrupt our happiness—like the politician who runs the political gantlet for office one day, and the next day, because the horizon is darkened a little, he is seen running for his life, for fear he might perish in its ruins. Where is the philosophy, where is the consistency, where is the charity, in conduct like this? Be happy then, my beloved father, and forget me; let the sorrow of parting break down the wall of separation and make us equal in our feeling; let me now say how ardently I love you; let me kiss that age-worn cheek, and should my tears bedew thy face, I will wipe them away. Oh, I never can forget you; no, never, never!"

"Weep not," said the father, "Ambulinia. I will forbid Elfonzo my house, and desire that you may keep retired a few days. I will let him know that my friendship for my family is not linked together by cankered chains; and if he ever enters upon my premises again, I will send him to his long home." "Oh, father! let me entreat you to be calm upon this occasion, and though Elfonzo may be the sport of the clouds and winds, yet I feel assured that no fate will send him to the silent tomb until the God of the Universe calls him hence with a triumphant voice."

Here the father turned away, exclaiming: "I will answer his letter in a very few words, and you, madam, will have the goodness to stay at home with your mother; and remember, I am determined to protect you from the consuming fire that looks so fair to your view."

Cumming, January 22, 1844.

Sir—In regard to your request, I am as I ever have been, utterly opposed to your marrying into my family; and if you have any regard for yourself, or any gentlemanly feeling, I hope you will mention it to me no more; but seek some other one who is not so far superior to you in standing.

W. W. Valeer.

When Elfonzo read the above letter, he became so much depressed in spirits that many of his friends thought it advisable to use other means to bring about the happy union. "Strange," said he, "that the contents of this diminutive letter should cause me to have such depressed feelings; but there is a nobler theme than this. I know not why my *military title* is not as great as that of *squire Valeer*. For my life I cannot see that my ancestors are inferior to those who are so bitterly opposed to my marriage with Ambulinia. I know I have seen huge mountains before me, yet, when I think that I know gentlemen will insult me upon this delicate matter, should I become angry at fools and babblers, who pride themselves in their impudence and ignorance? No. My equals! I know not where to find them. My inferiors! I think it beneath me; and my superiors! I think it presumption; therefore, if this youthful heart is protected by any of the divine rights, I never will betray my trust."

He was aware that Ambulinia had a confidence that was, indeed, as firm and as resolute as she was beautiful and interesting. He hastened to the cottage of Louisa, who received him in her usual mode of pleasantness, and informed him that Ambulinia had just that moment left. "Is it possible?" said Elfonzo. "Oh, murdered hours! Why did she not remain and be the guardian of my secrets? But hasten and tell me how she has stood this trying scene, and what are her future determinations." "You know," said Louisa, "Major Elfonzo, that you have Ambulinia's first love, which is of no small consequence. She came here about twilight, and shed many precious tears in consequence of her own fate with yours. We walked silently in yon little valley you see, where we spent a momentary repose. She seemed to be quite as determined as ever, and before we left that beautiful spot she offered up a prayer to Heaven for thee." "I will see her then," replied Elfonzo, "though legions of enemies may oppose. She is mine by foreordination—she is mine by prophesy—she is mine by her own free will, and I will rescue her from the hands of her oppressors. Will you not, Miss Louisa, assist me in my capture?"

"I will certainly, by the aid of Divine Providence," answered Louisa, "endeavor to break those slavish chains that bind the richest of prizes; though allow me, Major, to entreat you to use no harsh means on this important occasion; take a decided stand, and write freely to Ambulinia upon this subject, and I will see that no intervening cause hinders its passage to her. God alone will save a mourning people. Now is the day and now is the hour to obey a command of such valuable worth." The Major felt himself grow stronger after this short interview with Louisa. He felt as if he could whip his weight in wildcats—he knew he was master of his own feelings, and could now write a letter that would bring this litigation to *an issue*.

Cumming, January 24, 1844.

Dear Ambulinia—

We have now reached the most trying moment of our lives; we are pledged not to forsake our trust; we have waited for a favorable hour to come, thinking your friends would settle the matter agreeably among themselves, and finally be reconciled to our marriage; but as I have waited in vain, and looked in vain, I have determined in my own mind to make a proposition to you, though you may think it not in accord with your station, or compatible with your rank; yet, "sub loc signo vinces." You know I cannot resume my visits, in consequence of the utter hostility that your father has to me; therefore the consummation of our union will have to be sought for in a more sublime sphere, at the residence of a respectable friend of this village. You cannot have any scruples upon this mode of proceeding, if you will but remember it emanates from one who loves you better than his own life—who is more than anxious to bid you welcome to a new and happy home. Your warmest associates say come; the talented, the learned, the wise, and the experienced say come;—all these with their friends say, come. Viewing these, with many other inducements, I flatter myself that you will come to the embraces of your Elfonzo; for now is the time of your acceptance of the day of your liberation. You cannot be ignorant, Ambulinia, that thou art the desire of my heart; its thoughts are too noble, and too pure, to conceal themselves from you. I shall wait for your answer to this impatiently, expecting that you will set the time to make your departure, and to be in readiness at a moment's warning to share the joys of a more preferable life. This will be handed to you by Louisa, who will take a pleasure in communicating anything to you that may relieve your dejected spirits, and will assure you that I now stand ready, willing, and waiting to make good my vows.

I am, dear Ambulinia, yours

truly, and forever,

J. I. Elfonzo.


Louisa made it convenient to visit Mr. Valeer's, though they did not suspect her in the least the bearer of love epistles; consequently, she was invited in the room to console Ambulinia, where they were left alone. Ambulinia was seated by a small table—her head resting on her hand—her brilliant eyes were bathed in tears. Louisa handed her the letter of Elfonzo, when another spirit animated her features—the spirit of renewed confidence that never fails to strengthen the female character in an hour of grief and sorrow like this, and as she pronounced the last accent of his name, she exclaimed, "And does he love me yet! I never will forget your generosity, Louisa. Oh, unhappy and yet blessed Louisa! may you never feel what I have felt—may you never know the pangs of love. Had I never loved, I never would have been unhappy; but I turn to Him who can save, and if His wisdom does not will my expected union, I know He will give me strength to bear my lot. Amuse yourself with this little book, and take it as an apology for my silence," said Ambulinia, "while I attempt to answer this volume of consolation." "Thank you," said Louisa, "you are excusable upon this occasion; but I pray you, Ambulinia, to be expert upon this momentous subject,

133

that there may be nothing mistrustful upon my part." "I will," said Ambulinia, and immediately resumed her seat and addressed the following to Elfonzo:

Cumming, Ga., January 28, 1844.
Devoted Elfonzo—

I hail your letter as a welcome messenger of faith, and can now say truly and firmly that my feelings correspond with yours. Nothing shall be wanting on my part to make my obedience your fidelity. Courage and perseverance will accomplish success. Receive this as my oath, that while I grasp your hand in my own imagination, we stand united before a higher tribunal than any on earth. All the powers of my life, soul, and body, I devote to thee. Whatever dangers may threaten me, I fear not to encounter them. Perhaps I have determined upon my own destruction, by leaving the house of the best of parents; be it so; I flee to you; I share your destiny, faithful to the end. The day that I have concluded upon for this task is *Sabbath* next, when the family with the citizens are generally at church. For Heaven's sake let not that day pass unimproved: trust not till tomorrow, it is the cheat of life—the future that never comes—the grave of many noble births—the cavern of ruined enterprise: which like the lightning's flash is born, and dies, and perishes, ere the voice of him who sees can cry, *Behold! Behold!!* You may trust to what I say, no power shall tempt me to betray confidence. Suffer me to add one word more.

> *I will soothe thee, in all thy grief,*
> *Beside the gloomy river;*
> *And though thy love may yet be brief;*
> *Mine is fixed forever.*

Receive the deepest emotions of my heart for thy constant love, and may the power of inspiration by thy guide, thy portion, and thy all. In great haste,
Yours faithfully,
Ambulinia.

"I now take my leave of you, sweet girl," said Louisa, "sincerely wishing you success on Sabbath next." When Ambulinia's letter was handed to Elfonzo, he perused it without doubting its contents. Louisa charged him to make but few confidants; but like most young men who happened to win the heart of a beautiful girl, he was so elated with the idea that he felt as a commanding general on parade, who had confidence in all, consequently gave orders to all. The appointed Sabbath, with a delicious breeze and cloudless sky, made its appearance. The people gathered in crowds to the church—the streets were filled with neighboring citizens, all marching to the house of worship. It is entirely useless for me to attempt to describe the feelings of Elfonzo and Ambulinia, who were silently watching the movements of the multitude, apparently counting them as then entered the house of God, looking for the last one to darken the door. The impatience and anxiety with which they waited, and the bliss they anticipated on the eventful day, is altogether indescribable. Those that have been so fortunate as to embark in such a noble enterprise know all its realities; and those who have not had this inestimable privilege will have to taste its sweets before they can tell to others its joys, its comforts, and its Heaven-born worth. Immediately after Ambulinia had assisted the family off to church, she took advantage of that opportunity to make good her promises. She left a home of enjoyment to be wedded to one whose love had been justifiable. A few short steps brought her to the presence of Louisa, who urged her to make good use of her time, and not to delay a moment, but to go with her to her brother's house, where Elfonzo would forever make her happy. With lively speed, and yet a graceful air, she entered the door and found herself protected by the champion of her confidence. The necessary arrangements were fast making to have the two lovers united—everything was in readiness except the parson; and as they are generally very sanctimonious on such occasions, the news got to the parents of Ambulinia before the everlasting knot was tied, and they both came running, with uplifted hands and injured feelings, to arrest their daughter from an unguarded and hasty resolution. Elfonzo desired to maintain his ground, but Ambulinia thought it best for him to leave, to prepare for a greater contest. He accordingly obeyed, as it would have been a vain endeavor for him to have battled against a man who was armed with deadly weapons; and besides, he could not resist the request of such a pure heart. Ambulinia concealed herself in the upper story of the house, fearing the rebuke of her father; the door was locked, and no chastisement was now expected. Esquire Valeer, whose pride was already touched, resolved to preserve the dignity of his family. He entered the house almost exhausted, looking wildly for Ambulinia. "Amazed and astonished indeed I am," said he, "at a people who call themselves civilized, to allow such behavior as this. Ambulinia, Ambulinia!" he cried, "come to the calls of your first, your best, and your only friend. I appeal to you, sir," turning to the gentleman of the house, "to know where Ambulinia has gone, or where is she?" "Do you mean to insult me, sir, in my own house?" inquired the gentleman. "I will burst," said Mr. V., "asunder every door in your dwelling, in search of my daughter, if you do not speak quickly, and tell me where she is. I care nothing about that outcast rubbish of creation, that mean, low-lived Elfonzo, if I can but obtain Ambulinia. Are you not going to open this door?" said he. "By the Eternal that made Heaven and earth! I will go about the work instantly, if this is not done!" The confused citizens gathered from all parts of the village, to know the cause of this commotion. Some rushed into the house; the door that was locked flew open, and there stood Ambulinia, weeping. "Father, be still," said she, "and I will follow thee home." But the agitated man seized her, and bore her off through the gazing multitude. "Father!" she exclaimed, "I humbly beg your pardon—I will be dutiful—I will obey thy commands. Let the sixteen years I have lived in obedience to thee by my future security." "I don't like to be always giving credit, when the old score is not paid up, madam," said the father. The mother followed almost in a state of derangement, crying and imploring her to think beforehand, and ask advice from experienced persons, and they would tell her it was a rash undertaking. "Oh!" said she, "Ambulinia, my daughter, did you know what I have suffered—did you know how many nights I have whiled away in agony, in pain, and in fear, you would pity the sorrows of a heartbroken mother."

"Well, mother," replied Ambulinia, "I know I have been disobedient; I am aware that what I have done might have been done much better; but oh! what shall I do with my honor? it is so dear to me; I am pledged to Elfonzo. His high moral worth is certainly worth some attention; moreover, my vows, I have no doubt, are recorded in the book of life, and must I give these all up? must my fair hopes be forever blasted? Forbid it, father; oh! forbid it, mother; forbid it, Heaven." "I have seen so many beautiful skies overclouded," replied the mother, "so many blossoms nipped by the frost, that I am afraid to trust you to the care of those fair days, which may be interrupted by thundering and tempestuous nights. You no doubt think as I did—life's devious ways were strewn with sweet-scented flowers, but ah! how long they have lingered around me and took their flight in the vivid hope that laughs at the drooping victims it has murdered." Elfonzo was moved at this sight. The people followed on to see what was going to become of Ambulinia, while he, with downcast looks, kept at a distance, until he saw them enter the abode of the father, thrusting her, that was the sigh of his soul, out of his presence into a solitary apartment, when she exclaimed, "Elfonzo! Elfonzo! oh, Elfonzo! where art thou, with all thy heroes? haste, oh! haste, come thou to my relief. Ride on the wings of the wind! Turn thy force loose like a tempest, and roll on thy army like a whirlwind, over this mountain of trouble and confusion. Oh, friends! if any pity me, let your last efforts throng upon the green hills, and come to the relief of Ambulinia, who is guilty of nothing but innocent love." Elfonzo called out with a loud voice, "My God, can I stand this! arise up, I beseech you, and put an end to this tyranny. Come, my brave boys," said he, "are you ready to go forth to your duty?" They stood around him. "Who," said he, "will call us to arms? Where are my thunderbolts of war? Speak ye, the first who will meet the foe! Who will go forward with me in this ocean of grievous temptation? If there is one who desires to go, let him come and shake hands upon the altar of devotion, and swear that he will be a hero; yes, a Hector in a cause like this, which calls aloud for a speedy remedy." "Mine be the deed," said a young lawyer, "and mine alone; Venus alone shall quit her station before I will forsake one jot or tittle of my promise to you; what is death to me? what is all this warlike army, if it is not to win a victory? I love the sleep of the lover and the mighty; nor would I give it over till the blood of my enemies should wreak with that of my own. But God forbid that our fame should soar on the blood of the slumberer." Mr. Valeer stands at his door with the frown of a demon upon his brow, with his dangerous weapon ready to strike the first man who should enter his door. "Who will arise and go forward through blood and carnage to the rescue of my Ambulinia?" said Elfonzo. "All," exclaimed the multitude; and onward they went, with their implements of battle. Others, of a more timid nature, stood among the distant hills to see the result of the contest.

Elfonzo took the lead of his band. Night arose in clouds; darkness concealed the heavens; but the blazing hopes that stimulated them gleamed in every bosom. All approached the anxious spot; they rushed to the front of the house and, with one exclamation, demanded Ambulinia. "Away, begone, and disturb my peace no more," said Mr. Valeer. "You are a set of base, insolent, and infernal rascals. Go, the northern star points your path through the dim twilight of the night; go, and vent your spite upon the lonely hills; pour forth your love, you poor, weak-minded wretch, upon your idleness and upon your guitar, and your fiddle; they are fit subjects for your admiration, for let me assure you, though this sword and iron lever are cankered, yet they frown in sleep, and let one of you dare to enter my house this night and you shall have the contents and the weight of these instruments." "Never yet did base dishonor blur my name," said Elfonzo; "mine is a cause of renown; here are my warriors; fear and tremble, for this night, though hell itself should oppose, I will endeavor to avenge her whom thou hast banished in solitude. The voice of Ambulinia shall be heard from that dark dungeon." At that moment Ambulinia appeared at the window above, and with a tremulous voice said, "Live, Elfonzo! oh! live to raise my stone of moss! why should such language enter your heart? why should thy voice rend the air with such agitation? I bid thee live, once more remembering these tears of mine are shed alone for thee, in this dark and gloomy vault, and should I perish under this load of trouble, join the song of thrilling accents with the raven above my grave, and lay this tattered frame beside the banks of the Chattahoochee or the stream of Sawney's brook; sweet will be the song of death to your Ambulinia. My ghost shall visit you in the smiles of Paradise, and tell your high fame to the minds of that region, which is far more preferable than this lonely cell. My heart shall speak for thee till the latest hour; I know faint and broken are the sounds of sorrow, yet our souls, Elfonzo, shall hear the peaceful songs together. One bright name shall be ours on high, if we are not permitted to be united here; bear in mind that I still cherish my old sentiments, and the poet will mingle the names of Elfonzo and Ambulinia in the tide of other days." "Fly, Elfonzo," said the voices of his united band, "to the wounded heart of your beloved. All enemies shall fall beneath thy sword. Fly through the clefts, and the dim spark shall sleep in death." Elfonzo rushes forward and strikes his shield against the door, which was barricaded, to prevent any intercourse. His brave sons throng around him. The people pour along the streets, both male and female, to prevent or witness the melancholy scene.

"To arms, to arms!" cried Elfonzo; "here is a victory to be won, a prize to be gained that is more to me that the whole world beside." "It cannot be done tonight," said Mr. Valeer. "I bear the clang of death; my strength and armor shall prevail. My Ambulinia shall rest in this hall until the break of another day, and if we fall, we fall together. If we die, we die clinging to our tattered rights, and our blood alone shall tell the mournful tale of a murdered daughter and a ruined father." Sure enough, he kept watch all night, and was successful in defending his house and family. The bright morning gleamed upon the hills, night vanished away, the Major and his associates felt somewhat ashamed that they had not been as fortunate as they expected to have been; however, they still leaned upon their arms in dispersed groups; some were walking the streets, others were talking in the Major's behalf. Many of the citizen suspended business, as the town presented nothing but consternation. A novelty that might end in the destruction of some worthy and respectable citizens. Mr. Valeer ventured in the streets, though not without being well armed. Some of his friends congratulated him on the decided stand he had taken, and hoped he would settle the matter amicably with Elfonzo, without any serious injury. "Me," he replied, "what, me, condescend to fellowship with a coward, and a low-lived, lazy, undermining villain? no, gentlemen, this cannot be; I had rather be borne off, like the bubble upon the dark blue ocean, with Ambulinia by my side, than to have him in the ascending or descending line of relationship. Gentlemen," continued he, "if Elfonzo is so much of a distinguished character, and is so learned in the fine arts, why do you not patronize such men? why not introduce him into your families, as a gentleman of taste and of unequaled magnanimity? why are you so very anxious that he should become a relative of mine? Oh, gentlemen, I fear you yet are tainted with the curiosity of our first parents, who were beguiled by the poisonous kiss of an old ugly serpent, and who, for one *apple, damned* all mankind. I wish to divest myself, as far as possible, of that untutored custom. I have long since learned that the perfection of wisdom, and the end of true philosophy, is to proportion our wants to our possessions, our ambition to our capacities; we will then be a happy and a virtuous people." Ambulinia was sent off to prepare for a long and tedious journey. Her new acquaintances had been instructed by her father how to treat her, and in what manner, and to keep the anticipated visit entirely secret. Elfonzo was watching the movements of everybody; some friends had told him of the plot that was laid to carry off Ambulinia. At night, he rallied some two or three of his forces, and went silently along to the stately mansion; a faint and glimmering light showed through the windows; lightly he steps to the door; there were many voices rallying fresh in fancy's eye; he tapped the shutter; it was opened instantly, and he beheld once more, seated beside several ladies, the hope of all his toils; he rushed toward her, she rose from her seat, rejoicing; he made one mighty grasp, when Ambulinia exclaimed, "Huzza for Major Elfonzo! I will defend myself and you, too, with this conquering instrument I hold in my hand; huzza, I say, I now invoke time's broad wing to shed around us some dewdrops of verdant spring."

But the hour had not come for this joyous reunion; her friends struggled with Elfonzo for some time, and finally succeeded in arresting her from his hands. He dared not injure them, because they were matrons whose courage needed no spur; she was snatched from the arms of Elfonzo, with so much eagerness, and yet with such expressive signification, that he calmly withdrew from this lovely enterprise, with an ardent hope that he should be lulled to repose by the zephyrs which whispered peace to his soul. Several long days and night passed unmolested, all seemed to have grounded their arms of rebellion, and no callidity appeared to be going on with any of the parties. Other arrangements were made by Ambulinia; she feigned herself to be entirely the votary of a mother's care, and she, by her graceful smiles, that manhood might claim his stern dominion in some other region, where such boisterous love was not so prevalent. This gave the parents a confidence that yielded some hours of sober joy; they believed that Ambulinia would now cease to love Elfonzo, and that her stolen affections would now expire with her misguided opinions. They therefore declined the idea of sending her to a distant land. But oh! they dreamed not of the rapture that dazzled the fancy of Ambulinia, who would say, when alone, youth should not fly away on his rosy pinions, and leave her to grapple in the conflict with unknown admirers.

> *No frowning age shall control*
> *The constant current of my soul,*
> *Nor a tear from pity's eye*
> *Shall check my sympathetic sigh.*

With this resolution fixed in her mind, one dark and dreary night, when the winds whistled and the tempest roared, she received intelligence that Elfonzo was then waiting, and every preparation was then ready, at the residence of Dr. Tully, and for her to make a quick escape while the family was reposing. Accordingly she gathered her books, went the wardrobe supplied with a variety of ornamental dressing, and ventured alone in the streets to make her way to Elfonzo, who was near at hand, impatiently looking and watching her arrival. "What forms," said she, "are those rising before me? What is that dark spot on the clouds? I do wonder what frightful ghost that is, gleaming on the red tempest? Oh, be merciful and tell me what region you are from. Oh, tell me, ye strong spirits, or ye dark and fleeting clouds, that I yet have a friend." "A friend," said a low, whispering voice. "I am thy unchanging, thy aged, and thy disappointed mother. Why brandish in that hand of thine a javelin of pointed steel? Why suffer that lip I have kissed a thousand times to equivocate? My daughter, let these tears sink deep into thy soul, and no longer persist in that which may be your destruction and ruin. Come, my dear child, retract your steps, and bear me company to your welcome home." Without one retorting word, or frown from her brow, she yielded to the entreaties of her mother, and with all the mildness of her former character she went along with the silver lamp of age, to the home of candor and benevolence. Her father received her cold and formal politeness—"Where has Ambulinia been, this blustering evening, Mrs. Valeer?" inquired he. "Oh, she and I have been taking a solitary walk," said the mother; "all things, I presume, are now working for the best."

Elfonzo heard this news shortly after it happened. "What," said he, "has heaven and earth turned against me? I have been disappointed times without number. Shall I despair?—must I give it over? Heaven's decrees will not fade; I will write again—I will try again; and if it traverses a gory field, I pray forgiveness at the altar of justice."

Desolate Hill, Cumming, Geo., 1844.

Unconquered and Beloved Ambulinia— I have only time to say to you, not to despair; thy fame shall not perish; my visions are brightening before me. The whirlwind's rage is past, and we now shall subdue our enemies without doubt. On Monday morning, when your friends are at breakfast, they will not suspect your departure, or even mistrust me being in town, as it has been reported advantageously that I have left for the west. You walk carelessly toward the academy grove, where you will find me with a lightning steed, elegantly equipped to bear you off where we shall be joined in wedlock with the first connubial rights. Fail not to do this—think not of the tedious relations of our wrongs—be invincible. You alone occupy all my ambition, and I alone will make you my happy spouse, with the same unimpeached veracity. I remain, forever, your devoted friend and admirer, J. L. Elfonzo.

The appointed day ushered in undisturbed by any clouds; nothing disturbed Ambulinia's soft beauty. With serenity and loveliness she obeys the request of Elfonzo. The moment the family seated themselves at the table—"Excuse my absence for a short time," said she, "while I attend to the placing of those flowers, which should have been done a week ago." And away she ran to the sacred grove, surrounded with glittering pearls, that indicated her coming. Elfonzo hails her with his silver bow and his golden harp. They meet—Ambulinia's countenance brightens—Elfonzo leads up his winged steed. "Mount," said he, "ye true-hearted, ye fearless soul—the day is ours." She sprang upon the back of the young thunder bolt, a brilliant star sparkles upon her head, with one hand she grasps the reins, and with the other she holds an olive branch. "Lend thy aid, ye strong winds," they exclaimed, "ye moon, ye sun, and all ye fair host of heaven, witness the enemy conquered." "Hold," said Elfonzo, "thy dashing steed." "Ride on," said Ambulinia, "the voice of thunder is behind us." And onward they went, with such rapidity that they very soon arrived at Rural Retreat, where they dismounted, and were united with all the solemnities that usually attend such divine operations. They passed the day in thanksgiving and great rejoicing, and on that evening they visited their uncle, where many of their friends and acquaintances had gathered to congratulate them in the field of untainted bliss. The kind old gentleman met them in the yard: "Well," said he, "I wish I may die, Elfonzo, if you and Ambulinia haven't tied a knot with your tongue that you can't untie with your teeth. But come in, come in, never mind, all is right—the world still moves on, and no one has fallen in this great battle."

Happy now is their lot! Unmoved by misfortune, they live among the fair beauties of the South. Heaven spreads their peace and fame upon the arch of the rainbow, and smiles propitiously at their triumph, *through the tears of the storm.*

# THE CALIFORNIAN'S TALE

Thirty-five years ago I was out prospecting on the Stanislaus, tramping all day long with pick and pan and horn, and washing a hatful of dirt here and there, always expecting to make a rich strike, and never doing it. It was a lovely region, woodsy, balmy, delicious, and had once been populous, long years before, but now the people had vanished and the charming paradise was a solitude. They went away when the surface diggings gave out. In one place, where a busy little city with banks and newspapers and fire companies and a mayor and aldermen had been, was nothing but a wide expanse of emerald turf, with not even the faintest sign that human life had ever been present there. This was down toward Tuttletown. In the country neighborhood thereabouts, along the dusty roads, one found at intervals the prettiest little cottage homes, snug and cozy, and so cobwebbed with vines snowed thick with roses that the doors and windows were wholly hidden from sight—sign that these were deserted homes, forsaken years ago by defeated and disappointed families who could neither sell them nor give them away. Now and then, half an hour apart, one came across solitary log cabins of the earliest mining days, built by the first gold-miners, the predecessors of the cottage-builders. In some few cases these cabins were still occupied; and when this was so, you could depend upon it that the occupant was the very pioneer who had built the cabin; and you could depend on another thing, too—that he was there because he had once had his opportunity to go home to the States rich, and had not done it; had rather lost his wealth, and had then in his humiliation resolved to sever all communication with his home relatives and friends, and be to them thenceforth as one dead. Round about California in that day were scattered a host of these living dead men—pride-smitten poor fellows, grizzled and old at forty, whose secret thoughts were made all of regrets and longings—regrets for their wasted lives, and longings to be out of the struggle and done with it all.

It was a lonesome land! Not a sound in all those peaceful expanses of grass and woods but the drowsy hum of insects; no glimpse of man or beast; nothing to keep up your spirits and make you glad to be alive. And so, at last, in the early part of the afternoon, when I caught sight of a human creature, I felt a most grateful uplift. This person was a man about forty-five years old, and he was standing at the gate of one of those cozy little rose-clad cottages of the sort already referred to. However, this one hadn't a deserted look; it had the look of being lived in and petted and cared for and looked after; and so had its front yard, which was a garden of flowers, abundant, gay, and flourishing. I was invited in, of course, and required to make myself at home—it was the custom of the country.

It was delightful to be in such a place, after long weeks of daily and nightly familiarity with miners' cabins—with all which this implies of dirt floor, never-made beds, tin plates and cups, bacon and beans and black coffee, and nothing of ornament but war pictures from the Eastern illustrated papers tacked to the log walls. That was all hard, cheerless, materialistic desolation, but here was a nest which had aspects to rest the tired eye and refresh that something in one's nature which, after long fasting, recognizes, when confronted by the belongings of art, howsoever cheap and modest they may be, that it has unconsciously been famishing and now has found nourishment. I could not have believed that a rag carpet could feast me so, and so content me; or that there could be such solace to the soul in wall-paper and framed lithographs, and bright-colored tidies and lamp-mats, and Windsor chairs, and varnished what-nots, with sea-shells and books and china vases on them, and the score of little unclassifiable tricks and touches that a woman's hand distributes about a home, which one sees without knowing he sees them, yet would miss in a moment if they were taken away. The delight that was in my heart showed in my face, and the man saw it and was pleased; saw it so plainly that he answered it as if it had been spoken.

"All her work," he said, caressingly; "she did it all herself—every bit," and he took the room in with a glance which was full of affectionate worship. One of those soft Japanese fabrics with which women drape with careful negligence the upper part of a picture-frame was out of adjustment. He noticed it, and rearranged it with cautious pains, stepping back several times to gauge the effect before he got it to suit him. Then he gave it a light finishing pat or two with his hand, and said: "She always does that. You can't tell just what it lacks, but it does lack something until you've done that—you can see it yourself after it's done, but that is all you know; you can't find out the law of it. It's like the finishing pats a mother gives the child's hair after she's got it combed and brushed, I reckon. I've seen her fix all these things so much that I can do them all just her way, though I don't know the law of any of them. But she knows the law. She knows the why and the how both; but I don't know the why; I only know the how."

He took me into a bedroom so that I might wash my hands; such a bedroom as I had not seen for years: white counterpane, white pillows, carpeted floor, papered walls, pictures, dressing-table, with mirror and pin-cushion and dainty toilet things; and in the corner a wash-stand, with real china-ware bowl and pitcher, and with soap in a china dish, and on a rack more than a dozen towels—towels too clean and white for one out of practice to use without some vague sense of profanation. So my face spoke again, and he answered with gratified words:

"All her work; she did it all herself—every bit. Nothing here that hasn't felt the touch of her hand. Now you would think—But I mustn't talk so much."

By this time I was wiping my hands and glancing from detail to detail of the room's belongings, as one is apt to do when he is in a new place, where everything he sees is a comfort to his eye and his spirit; and I became conscious, in one of those unaccountable ways, you know, that there was something there somewhere that the man wanted me to discover for myself. I knew it perfectly, and I knew he was trying to help me by furtive indications with his eye, so I tried hard to get on the right track, being eager to gratify him. I failed several times, as I could see out of the corner of my eye without being told; but at last I knew I must be looking straight at the thing—knew it from the pleasure issuing in invisible waves from him. He broke into a happy laugh, and rubbed his hands together, and cried out:

"That's it! You've found it. I knew you would. It's her picture."

I went to the little black-walnut bracket on the farther wall, and did find there what I had not yet noticed—a daguerreotype-case. It contained the sweetest girlish face, and the most beautiful, as it seemed to me, that I had ever seen. The man drank the admiration from my face, and was fully satisfied.

"Nineteen her last birthday," he said, as he put the picture back; "and that was the day we were married. When you see her—ah, just wait till you see her!"

"Where is she? When will she be in?"

"Oh, she's away now. She's gone to see her people. They live forty or fifty miles from here. She's been gone two weeks today."

"When do you expect her back?"

"This is Wednesday. She'll be back Saturday, in the evening—about nine o'clock, likely."

I felt a sharp sense of disappointment.

"I'm sorry, because I'll be gone then," I said, regretfully.

"Gone? No—why should you go? Don't go. She'll be disappointed."

She would be disappointed—that beautiful creature! If she had said the words herself they could hardly have blessed me more. I was feeling a deep, strong longing to see her—a longing so supplicating, so insistent, that it made me afraid. I said to myself: "I will go straight away from this place, for my peace of mind's sake."

"You see, she likes to have people come and stop with us—people who know things, and can talk—people like you. She delights in it; for she knows—oh, she knows nearly everything herself, and can talk, oh, like a bird—and the books she reads, why, you would be astonished. Don't go; it's only a little while, you know, and she'll be so disappointed."

I heard the words, but hardly noticed them, I was so deep in my thinkings and strugglings. He left me, but I didn't know. Presently he was back, with the picture case in his hand, and he held it open before me and said:

"There, now, tell her to her face you could have stayed to see her, and you wouldn't."

That second glimpse broke down my good resolution. I would stay and take the risk. That night we smoked the tranquil pipe, and talked till late about various things, but mainly about her; and certainly I had had no such pleasant and restful time for many a day. The Thursday followed and slipped comfortably away. Toward twilight a big miner from three miles away came—one of the grizzled, stranded pioneers—and gave us warm salutation, clothed in grave and sober speech. Then he said:

"I only just dropped over to ask about the little madam, and when is she coming home. Any news from her?"

"Oh, yes, a letter. Would you like to hear it, Tom?"

"Well, I should think I would, if you don't mind, Henry!"

Henry got the letter out of his wallet, and said he would skip some of the private phrases, if we were willing; then he went on and read the bulk of it—a loving, sedate, and altogether charming and gracious piece of handiwork, with a postscript full of affectionate regards and messages to Tom, and Joe, and Charley, and other close friends and neighbors.

As the reader finished, he glanced at Tom, and cried out:

"Oho, you're at it again! Take your hands away, and let me see your eyes. You always do that when I read a letter from her. I will write and tell her."

"Oh no, you mustn't, Henry. I'm getting old, you know, and any little disappointment makes me want to cry. I thought she'd be here herself, and now you've got only a letter."

"Well, now, what put that in your head? I thought everybody knew she wasn't coming till Saturday."

"Saturday! Why, come to think, I did know it. I wonder what's the matter with me lately? Certainly I knew it. Ain't we all getting ready for her? Well, I must be going now. But I'll be on hand when she comes, old man!"

Late Friday afternoon another gray veteran tramped over from his cabin a mile or so away, and said the boys wanted to have a little gaiety and a good time Saturday night, if Henry thought she wouldn't be too tired after her journey to be kept up.

"Tired? She tired! Oh, hear the man! Joe, *you* know she'd sit up six weeks to please any one of you!"

When Joe heard that there was a letter, he asked to have it read, and the loving messages in it for him broke the old fellow all up; but he said he was such an old wreck that *that* would happen to him if she only just mentioned his name. "Lord, we miss her so!" he said.

Saturday afternoon I found I was taking out my watch pretty often. Henry noticed it, and said, with a startled look:

"You don't think she ought to be here soon, do you?"

I felt caught, and a little embarrassed; but I laughed, and said it was a habit of mine when I was in a state of expenctancy. But he didn't seem quite satisfied; and from that time on he began to show uneasiness. Four times he walked me up the road to a point whence we could see a long distance; and there he would stand, shading his eyes with his hand, and looking. Several times he said:

"I'm getting worried, I'm getting right down worried. I know she's not due till about nine o'clock, and yet something seems to be trying to warn me that something's happened. You don't think anything has happened, do you?"

I began to get pretty thoroughly ashamed of him for his childishness; and at last, when he repeated that imploring question still another time, I lost my patience for the moment, and spoke pretty brutally to him. It seemed to shrivel him up and cow him; and he looked so wounded and so humble after that, that I detested myself for having done the cruel and unnecessary thing. And so I was glad when Charley, another veteran, arrived toward the edge of the evening, and nestled up to Henry to hear the letter read, and talked over the preparations for the welcome. Charley fetched out one hearty speech after another, and did his best to drive away his friend's bodings and apprehensions.

"Anything *happened* to her? Henry, that's pure nonsense. There isn't anything going to happen to her; just make your mind easy as to that. What did the letter say? Said she was well, didn't it? And said she'd be here by nine o'clock, didn't it? Did you ever know her to fail of her word? Why, you know you never did. Well, then, don't you fret; she'll *be* here, and that's absolutely certain, and as sure as you are born. Come, now, let's get to decorating—not much time left."

Pretty soon Tom and Joe arrived, and then all hands set about adoring the house with flowers. Toward nine the three miners said that as they had brought their instruments they might as well tune up, for the boys and girls would soon be arriving now, and hungry for a good, old-fashioned break-down. A fiddle, a banjo, and a clarinet—these were the instruments. The trio took their places side by side, and began to play some rattling dance-music, and beat time with their big boots.

It was getting very close to nine. Henry was standing in the door with his eyes directed up the road, his body swaying to the torture of his mental distress. He had been made to drink his wife's health and safety several times, and now Tom shouted:

"All hands stand by! One more drink, and she's here!"

Joe brought the glasses on a waiter, and served the party. I reached for one of the two remaining glasses, but Joe growled under his breath:

"Drop that! Take the other."

Which I did. Henry was served last. He had hardly swallowed his drink when the clock began to strike. He listened till it finished, his face growing pale and paler; then he said:

"Boys, I'm sick with fear. Help me—I want to lie down!"

They helped him to the sofa. He began to nestle and drowse, but presently spoke like one talking in his sleep, and said: "Did I hear horses' feet? Have they come?"

One of the veterans answered, close to his ear: "It was Jimmy Parish come to say the party got delayed, but they're right up the road a piece, and coming along. Her horse is lame, but she'll be here in half an hour."

"Oh, I'm SO thankful nothing has happened!"

He was asleep almost before the words were out of his mouth. In a moment those handy men had his clothes off, and had tucked him into his bed in the chamber where I had washed my hands. They closed the door and came back. Then they seemed preparing to leave; but I said: "Please don't go, gentlemen. She won't know me; I am a stranger."

They glanced at each other. Then Joe said:

"She? Poor thing, she's been dead nineteen years!"

"Dead?"

"That or worse. She went to see her folks half a year after she was married, and on her way back, on a Saturday evening, the Indians captured her within five miles of this place, and she's never been heard of since."

"And he lost his mind in consequence?"

"Never has been sane an hour since. But he only gets bad when that time of year comes round. Then we begin to drop in here, three days before she's due, to encourage him up, and ask if he's heard from her, and Saturday we all come and fix up the house with flowers, and get everything ready for a dance. We've done it every year for nineteen years. The first Saturday there was twenty-seven of us, without counting the girls; there's only three of us now, and the girls are gone. We drug him to sleep, or he would go wild; then he's all right for another year—thinks she's with him till the last three or four days come round; then he begins to look for her, and gets out his poor old letter, and we come and ask him to read it to us. Lord, she was a darling!"

# A BURLESQUE BIOGRAPHY

Two or three persons having at different times intimated that if I would write an autobiography they would read it when they got leisure, I yield at last to this frenzied public demand and herewith tender my history.

Ours is a noble house, and stretches a long way back into antiquity. The earliest ancestor the Twains have any record of was a friend of the family by the name of Higgins. This was in the eleventh century, when our people were living in Aberdeen, county of Cork, England. Why it is that our long line has ever since borne the maternal name (except when one of them now and then took a playful refuge in an alias to avert foolishness), instead of Higgins, is a mystery which none of us has ever felt much desire to stir. It is a kind of vague, pretty romance, and we leave it alone. All the old families do that way.

Arthour Twain was a man of considerable note—a solicitor on the highway in William Rufus's time. At about the age of thirty he went to one of those fine old English places of resort called Newgate, to see about something, and never returned again. While there he died suddenly.

Augustus Twain seems to have made something of a stir about the year 1160. He was as full of fun as he could be, and used to take his old saber and sharpen it up, and get in a convenient place on a dark night, and stick it through people as they went by, to see them jump. He was a born humorist. But he got to going too far with it; and the first time he was found stripping one of these parties, the authorities removed one end of him, and put it up on a nice high place on Temple Bar, where it could contemplate the people and have a good time. He never liked any situation so much or stuck to it so long.

Then for the next two hundred years the family tree shows a succession of soldiers—noble, high-spirited fellows, who always went into battle singing, right behind the army, and always went out a-whooping, right ahead of it.

This is a scathing rebuke to old dead Froissart's poor witticism that our family tree never had but one limb to it, and that that one stuck out at right angles, and bore fruit winter and summer.

Early in the fifteenth century we have Beau Twain, called "the Scholar." He wrote a beautiful, beautiful hand. And he could imitate anybody's hand so closely that it was enough to make a person laugh his head off to see it. He had infinite sport with his talent. But by and by he took a contract to break stone for a road, and the roughness of the work spoiled his hand. Still, he enjoyed life all the time he was in the stone business, which, with inconsiderable intervals, was some forty-two years. In fact, he died in harness. During all those long years he gave such satisfaction that he never was through with one contract a week till the government gave him another. He was a perfect pet. And he was always a favorite with his fellow-artists, and was a conspicuous member of their benevolent secret society, called the Chain Gang. He always wore his hair short, had a preference for striped clothes, and died lamented by the government. He was a sore loss to his country. For he was so regular.

Some years later we have the illustrious John Morgan Twain. He came over to this country with Columbus in 1492 as a passenger. He appears to have been of a crusty, uncomfortable disposition. He complained of the food all the way over, and was always threatening to go ashore unless there was a change. He wanted fresh shad. Hardly a day passed over his head that he did not go idling about the ship with his nose in the air, sneering about the commander, and saying he did not believe Columbus knew where he was going to or had ever been there before. The memorable cry of "Land ho!" thrilled every heart in the ship but his. He gazed awhile through a piece of smoked glass at the penciled line lying on the distant water, and then said: "Land be hanged—it's a raft!"

When this questionable passenger came on board the ship, he brought nothing with him but an old newspaper containing a handkerchief marked "B.G.," one cotton sock marked "L.W.C.," one woolen one marked "D.F.," and a night-shirt marked "O.M.R." And yet during the voyage he worried more about his "trunk," and gave himself more airs about it, than all the rest of the passengers put together. If the ship was "down by the head," and would not steer, he would go and move his "trunk" further aft, and then watch the effect. If the ship was "by the stern," he would suggest to Columbus to detail some men to "shift that baggage." In storms he had to be gagged, because his wailings about his "trunk" made it impossible for the men to hear the orders. The man does not appear to have been openly charged with any gravely unbecoming thing, but it is noted in the ship's log as a "curious circumstance" that albeit he brought his baggage on board the ship in a newspaper, he took it ashore in four trunks, a queensware crate, and a couple of champagne baskets. But when he came back insinuating, in an insolent, swaggering way, that some of this things were missing, and was going to search the other passengers' baggage, it was too much, and they threw him overboard. They watched long and wonderingly for him to come up, but not even a bubble rose on the quietly ebbing tide. But while every one was most absorbed in gazing over the side, and the interest was momentarily increasing, it was observed with consternation that the vessel was adrift and the anchor-cable hanging limp from the bow. Then in the ship's dimmed and ancient log we find this quaint note:

"In time it was discouvered yt ye troblesome passenger hadde gone downe and got ye anchor, and toke ye same and solde it to ye dam sauvages from ye interior, saying yt he hadde founde it, ye sonne of a ghun!"

Yet this ancestor had good and noble instincts, and it is with pride that we call to mind the fact that he was the first white person who ever interested himself in the work of elevating and civilizing our Indians. He built a commodious jail and put up a gallows, and to his dying day he claimed with satisfaction that he had had a more restraining and elevating influence on the Indians than any other reformer that ever labored among them. At this point the chronicle becomes less frank and chatty, and closes abruptly by saying that the old voyager went to see his gallows perform on the first white man ever hanged in America, and while there received injuries which terminated in his death.

The great-grandson of the "Reformer" flourished in sixteen hundred and something, and was known in our annals as "the old Admiral," though in history he had other titles. He was long in command of fleets of swift vessels, well armed and manned, and did great service in hurrying up merchantmen. Vessels which he followed and kept his eagle eye on, always made good fair time across the ocean. But if a ship still loitered in spite of all he could do, his indignation would grow till he could contain himself no longer—and then he would take that ship home where he lived and keep it there carefully, expecting the owners to come for it, but they never did. And he would try to get the idleness and sloth out of the sailors of that ship by compelling them to take invigorating exercise and a bath. He called it "walking a plank." All the pupils liked it. At any rate, they never found any fault with it after trying it. When the owners were late coming for their ships, the Admiral always burned them, so that the insurance money should not be lost. At last this fine old tar was cut down in the fullness of his years and honors. And to her dying day, his poor heart-broken widow believed that if he had been cut down fifteen minutes sooner he might have been resuscitated.

Charles Henry Twain lived during the latter part of the seventeenth century, and was a zealous and distinguished missionary. He converted sixteen thousand South Sea islanders, and taught them that a dog-tooth necklace and a pair of spectacles was not enough clothing to come to divine service in. His poor flock loved him very, very dearly; and when his funeral was over, they got up in a body (and came out of the restaurant) with tears in their eyes, and saying, one to another, that he was a good tender missionary, and they wished they had some more of him.

Pah-go-to-wah-wah-pukketekeewis (Mighty-Hunter-with-a-Hog-Eye-Twain) adorned the middle of the eighteenth century, and aided General Braddock with all his heart to resist the oppressor Washington. It was this ancestor who fired seventeen times at our Washington from behind a tree. So far the beautiful romantic narrative in the moral story-books is correct; but when that narrative goes on to say that at the seventeenth round the awe-stricken savage said solemnly that that man was being reserved by the Great Spirit for some mighty mission, and he dared not lift his sacrilegious rifle against him again, the narrative seriously impairs the integrity of history. What he did say was:

"It ain't no (hic) no use. 'At man's so drunk he can't stan' still long enough for a man to hit him. I (hic) I can't 'ford to fool away any more am'nition on him."

That was why he stopped at the seventeenth round, and it was a good, plain, matter-of-fact reason, too, and one that easily commends itself to us by the eloquent, persuasive flavor of probability there is about it.

I also enjoyed the story-book narrative, but I felt a marring misgiving that every Indian at Braddock's Defeat who fired at a soldier a couple of times (two easily grows to seventeen in a century), and missed him, jumped to the conclusion that the Great Spirit was reserving that soldier for some grand mission; and so I somehow feared that the only reason why Washington's case is remembered and the others forgotten is, that in his the prophecy came true, and in that of the others it didn't. There are not books enough on earth to contain the record of the prophecies Indians and other unauthorized parties have made; but one may carry in his overcoat pockets the record of all the prophecies that have been fulfilled.

I will remark here, in passing, that certain ancestors of mine are so thoroughly well-known in history by their aliases, that I have not felt it to be worth while to dwell upon them, or even mention them in the order of their birth. Among these may be mentioned Richard Brinsley Twain, alias Guy Fawkes; John Wentworth Twain, alias Sixteen-String Jack; William Hogarth Twain, alias Jack Sheppard; Ananias Twain, alias Baron Munchausen; John George Twain, alias Captain Kydd; and then there are George Francis Twain, Tom Pepper, Nebuchadnezzar, and Baalam's Ass—they all belong to our family, but to a branch of it somewhat distinctly removed from the honorable direct line—in fact, a collateral branch, whose members chiefly differ from the ancient stock in that, in order to acquire the notoriety we have always yearned and hungered for, they have got into a low way of going to jail instead of getting hanged.

It is not well, when writing an autobiography, to follow your ancestry down too close to your own time—it is safest to speak only vaguely of your great-grandfather, and then skip from there to yourself, which I now do.

I was born without teeth—and there Richard III had the advantage of me; but I was born without a humpback, likewise, and there I had the advantage of him. My parents were neither very poor nor conspicuously honest.

But now a thought occurs to me. My own history would really seem so tame contrasted with that of my ancestors, that it is simply wisdom to leave it unwritten until I am hanged. If some other biographies I have read had stopped with the ancestry until a like event occurred, it would have been a felicitous thing for the reading public. How does it strike you?

# WIT INSPIRATIONS OF THE "TWO-YEAR-OLDS"

All infants appear to have an impertinent and disagreeable fashion nowadays of saying "smart" things on most occasions that offer, and especially on occasions when they ought not to be saying anything at all. Judging by the average published specimens of smart sayings, the rising generation of children are little better than idiots. And the parents must surely be but little better than the children, for in most cases they are the publishers of the sunbursts of infantile imbecility which dazzle us from the pages of our periodicals. I may seem to speak with some heat, not to say a suspicion of personal spite; and I do admit that it nettles me to hear about so many gifted infants in these days, and remember that I seldom said anything smart when I was a child. I tried it once or twice, but it was not popular. The family were not expecting brilliant remarks from me, and so they snubbed me sometimes and spanked me the rest. But it makes my flesh creep and my blood run cold to think what might have happened to me if I had dared to utter some of the smart things of this generation's "four-year-olds" where my father could hear me. To have simply skinned me alive and considered his duty at an end would have seemed to him criminal leniency toward one so sinning. He was a stern, unsmiling man, and hated all forms of precocity. If I had said some of the things I have referred to, and said them in his hearing, he would have destroyed me. He would, indeed. He would, provided the opportunity remained with him. But it would not, for I would have had judgment enough to take some strychnine first and say my smart thing afterward. The fair record of my life has been tarnished by just one pun. My father overheard that, and he hunted me over four or five townships seeking to take my life. If I had been full-grown, of course he would have been right; but, child as I was, I could not know how wicked a thing I had done.

I made one of those remarks ordinarily called "smart things" before that, but it was not a pun. Still, it came near causing a serious rupture between my father and myself. My father and mother, my uncle Ephraim and his wife, and one or two others were present, and the conversation turned on a name for me. I was lying there trying some India-rubber rings of various patterns, and endeavoring to make a selection, for I was tired of trying to cut my teeth on people's fingers, and wanted to get hold of something that would enable me to hurry the thing through and get something else. Did you ever notice what a nuisance it was cutting your teeth on your nurse's finger, or how back-breaking and tiresome it was trying to cut them on your big toe? And did you never get out of patience and wish your teeth were in Jerico long before you got them half cut? To me it seems as if these things happened yesterday. And they did, to some children. But I digress. I was lying there trying the India-rubber rings. I remember looking at the clock and noticing that in an hour and twenty-five minutes I would be two weeks old, and thinking how little I had done to merit the blessings that were so unsparingly lavished upon me. My father said:

"Abraham is a good name. My grandfather was named Abraham."

My mother said:

"Abraham is a good name. Very well. Let us have Abraham for one of his names."

I said:

"Abraham suits the subscriber."

My father frowned, my mother looked pleased; my aunt said:

"What a little darling it is!"

My father said:

"Isaac is a good name, and Jacob is a good name."

My mother assented, and said:

150

"No names are better. Let us add Isaac and Jacob to his names."

I said:

"All right. Isaac and Jacob are good enough for yours truly. Pass me that rattle, if you please. I can't chew India-rubber rings all day."

Not a soul made a memorandum of these sayings of mine, for publication. I saw that, and did it myself, else they would have been utterly lost. So far from meeting with a generous encouragement like other children when developing intellectually, I was now furiously scowled upon by my father; my mother looked grieved and anxious, and even my aunt had about her an expression of seeming to think that maybe I had gone too far. I took a vicious bite out of an India-rubber ring, and covertly broke the rattle over the kitten's head, but said nothing. Presently my father said:

"Samuel is a very excellent name."

I saw that trouble was coming. Nothing could prevent it. I laid down my rattle; over the side of the cradle I dropped my uncle's silver watch, the clothes-brush, the toy dog, my tin soldier, the nutmeg-grater, and other matters which I was accustomed to examine, and meditate upon and make pleasant noises with, and bang and batter and break when I needed wholesome entertainment. Then I put on my little frock and my little bonnet, and took my pygmy shoes in one hand and my licorice in the other, and climbed out on the floor. I said to myself, Now, if the worse comes to worst, I am ready. Then I said aloud, in a firm voice:

"Father, I cannot, cannot wear the name of Samuel."

"My son!"

"Father, I mean it. I cannot."

"Why?"

"Father, I have an invincible antipathy to that name."

"My son, this is unreasonable. Many great and good men have been named Samuel."

"Sir, I have yet to hear of the first instance."

"What! There was Samuel the prophet. Was not he great and good?"

"Not so very."

"My son! With His own voice the Lord called him."

"Yes, sir, and had to call him a couple times before he could come!"

And then I sallied forth, and that stern old man sallied forth after me. He overtook me at noon the following day, and when the interview was over I had acquired the name of Samuel, and a thrashing, and other useful information; and by means of this compromise my father's wrath was appeased and a misunderstanding bridged over which might have become a permanent rupture if I had chosen to be unreasonable. But just judging by this episode, what would my father have done to me if I had ever uttered in his hearing one of the flat, sickly things these "two-years-olds" say in print nowadays? In my opinion there would have been a case of infanticide in our family.

# AN ENTERTAINING ARTICLE

I take the following paragraph from an article in the Boston *Advertiser*:

## AN ENGLISH CRITIC ON MARK TWAIN

Perhaps the most successful flights of humor of Mark Twain have been descriptions of the persons who did not appreciate his humor at all. We have become familiar with the Californians who were thrilled with terror by his burlesque of a newspaper reporter's way of telling a story, and we have heard of the Pennsylvania clergyman who sadly returned his *Innovents Abroad* to the book-agent with the remark that "the man who could shed tears over the tomb of Adam must be an idiot." But Mark Twain may now add a much more glorious instance to his string of trophies. The *Saturday Review*, in its number of October 8th, reviews his book of travels, which has been republished in England, and reviews it seriously. We can imagine the delight of the humorist in reading this tribute to his power; and indeed it is so amusing in itself that he can hardly do better than reproduce the article in full in his next monthly Memoranda.

(Publishing the above paragraph thus, gives me a sort of authority for reproducing the *Saturday Review*'s article in full in these pages. I dearly wanted to do it, for I cannot write anything half so delicious myself. If I had a cast-iron dog that could read this English criticism and preserve his austerity, I would drive him off the door-step.)

(From the London "Saturday Review.")

## REVIEWS OF NEW BOOKS

*The Innocents Abroad*. A Book of Travels. By Mark Twain. London: Hotten, publisher. 1870.

Lord Macaulay died too soon. We never felt this so deeply as when we finished the last chapter of the above-named extravagant work. Macaulay died too soon—for none but he could mete out complete and comprehensive justice to the insolence, the impertinence, the presumption, the mendacity, and, above all, the majestic ignorance of this author.

To say that the *Innocents Abroad* is a curious book, would be to use the faintest language—would be to speak of the Matterhorn as a neat elevation or of Niagara as being "nice" or "pretty." "Curious" is too tame a word wherewith to describe the imposing insanity of this work. There is no word that is large enough or long enough. Let us, therefore, photograph a passing glimpse of book and author, and trust the rest to the reader. Let the cultivated English student of human nature picture to himself this Mark Twain as a person capable of doing the following-described things—and not only doing them, but with incredible innocence *printing them* calmly and tranquilly in a book. For instance:

He states that he entered a hair-dresser's in Paris to get shaved, and the first "rake" the barber gave him with his razor it *loosened his "hide"* and *lifted him out of the chair.*

This is unquestionably exaggerated. In Florence he was so annoyed by beggars that he pretends to have seized and eaten one in a frantic spirit of revenge. There is, of course, no truth in this. He gives at full length a theatrical program seventeen or eighteen hundred years old, which he professes to have found in the ruins of the Coliseum, among the dirt and mold and rubbish. It is a sufficient comment upon this statement to remark that even a cast-iron program would not have lasted so long under such circumstances. In Greece he plainly betrays both fright and flight upon one occasion, but with frozen effrontery puts the latter in this falsely tamed form: "We *sidled* toward the Piraeus." "Sidled," indeed! He does not hesitate to intimate that at Ephesus, when his mule strayed from the proper course, he got down, took him under his arm, carried him to the road again, pointed him right, remounted, and went to sleep contentedly till it was time to restore the beast to the path once more. He states that a growing youth among his ship's passengers was in the constant habit of appeasing his hunger with soap and oakum between meals. In Palestine he tells of ants that came eleven miles to spend the summer in the desert and brought their provisions with them; yet he shows by his description of the country that the feat was an impossibility. He mentions, as if it were the most commonplace of matters, that he cut a Moslem in two in broad daylight in Jerusalem, with Godfrey de Bouillon's sword, and would have shed more blood *if he had had a graveyard of his own.* These statements are unworthy a moment's attention. Mr. Twain or any other foreigner who did such a thing in Jerusalem would be mobbed, and would infallibly lose his life. But why go on? Why repeat more of his audacious and exasperating falsehoods? Let us close fittingly with this one: he affirms that "in the mosque of St. Sophia at Constantinople I got my feet so stuck up with a complication of gums, slime, and general impurity, that I wore out more than two thousand pair of bootjacks getting my boots off that night, and even then some Christian hide peeled off with them." It is monstrous. Such statements are simply lies—there is no other name for them. Will the reader longer marvel at the brutal ignorance that pervades the American nation when we tell him that we are informed upon perfectly good authority that this extravagant compilation of falsehoods, this exhaustless mine of stupendous lies, this *Innocents Abroad,* has actually been adopted by the schools and colleges of several of the states as a text-book!

But if his falsehoods are distressing, his innocence and his ignorance are enough to make one burn the book and despise the author. In one place he was so appalled at the sudden spectacle of a murdered man, unveiled by the moonlight, that he jumped out of the window, going through sash and all, and then remarks with the most childlike simplicity that he "was not scared, but was considerably agitated." It puts us out of patience to note that the simpleton is densely unconscious that Lucrezia Borgia ever existed off the stage. He is vulgarly ignorant of all foreign languages, but is frank enough to criticize, the Italians' use of their own tongue. He says they spell the name of their great painter "Vinci, but pronounce it Vinchy"—and then adds with a naivete possible only to helpless ignorance, "foreigners always spell better than they pronounce." In another place he commits the bald absurdity of putting the phrase "tare an ouns" into an Italian's mouth. In Rome he unhesitatingly believes the legend that St. Philip Neri's heart was so inflamed with divine love that it burst his ribs—believes it wholly because an author with a learned list of university degrees strung after his name endorses it—"otherwise," says this gentle idiot, "I should have felt a curiosity to know what Philip had for dinner." Our author makes a long, fatiguing journey to the Grotto del Cane on purpose to test its poisoning powers on a dog—got elaborately ready for the experiment, and then discovered that he had no dog. A wiser person would have kept such a thing discreetly to himself, but with this harmless creature everything comes out. He hurts his foot in a rut two thousand years old in exhumed Pompeii, and presently, when staring at one of the cinder-like corpses unearthed in the next square, conceives the idea that maybe it is the remains of the ancient Street Commissioner, and straightway his horror softens down to a sort of chirpy contentment with the condition of things. In Damascus he visits the well of Ananias, three thousand years old, and is as surprised and delighted as a child to find that the water is "as pure and fresh as if the well had been dug yesterday." In the Holy Land he gags desperately at the hard Arabic and Hebrew Biblical names, and finally concludes to call them Baldwinsville, Williamsburgh, and so on, "for convenience of spelling."

We have thus spoken freely of this man's stupefying simplicity and innocence, but we cannot deal similarly with his colossal ignorance. We do not know where to begin. And if we knew where to begin, we certainly would not know where to leave off. We will give one specimen, and one only. He did not know, until he got to Rome, that Michael Angelo was dead! And then, instead of crawling away and hiding his shameful ignorance somewhere, he proceeds to express a pious, grateful sort of satisfaction that he is gone and out of his troubles!

No, the reader may seek out the author's exhibition of his uncultivation for himself. The book is absolutely dangerous, considering the magnitude and variety of its misstatements, and the convincing confidence with which they are made. And yet it is a text-book in the schools of America.

The poor blunderer mouses among the sublime creations of the Old Masters, trying to acquire the elegant proficiency in art-knowledge, which he has a groping sort of comprehension is a proper thing for a traveled man to be able to display. But what is the manner of his study? And what is the progress he achieves? To what extent does he familiarize himself with the great pictures of Italy, and what degree of appreciation does he arrive at? Read:

"When we see a monk going about with a lion and looking up into heaven, we know that that is St. Mark. When we see a monk with a book and a pen, looking tranquilly up to heaven, trying to think of a word, we know that that is St. Matthew. When we see a monk sitting on a rock, looking tranquilly up to heaven, with a human skull beside him, and without other baggage, we know that that is St. Jerome. Because we know that he always went flying light in the matter of baggage. When we see other monks looking tranquilly up to heaven, but having no trade-mark, we always ask who those parties are. We do this because we humbly wish to learn."

He then enumerates the thousands and thousand of copies of these several pictures which he has seen, and adds with accustomed simplicity that he feels encouraged to believe that when he has seen "Some More" of each, and had a larger experience, he will eventually "begin to take an absorbing interest in them"—the vulgar boor.

That we have shown this to be a remarkable book, we think no one will deny. That is a pernicious book to place in the hands of the confiding and uniformed, we think we have also shown. That the book is a deliberate and wicked creation of a diseased mind, is apparent upon every page. Having placed our judgment thus upon record, let us close with what charity we can, by remarking that even in this volume there is some good to be found; for whenever the author talks of his own country and lets Europe alone, he never fails to make himself interesting, and not only interesting but instructive. No one can read without benefit his occasional chapters and paragraphs, about life in the gold and silver mines of California and Nevada; about the Indians of the plains and deserts of the West, and their cannibalism; about the raising of vegetables in kegs of gunpowder by the aid of two or three teaspoons of guano; about the moving of small arms from place to place at night in wheelbarrows to avoid taxes; and about a sort of cows and mules in

the Humboldt mines, that climb down chimneys and disturb the people at night. These matters are not only new, but are well worth knowing. It is a pity the author did not put in more of the same kind. His book is well written and is exceedingly entertaining, and so it just barely escaped being quite valuable also.

(One month later)

Latterly I have received several letters, and see a number of newspaper paragraphs, all upon a certain subject, and all of about the same tenor. I here give honest specimens. One is from a New York paper, one is from a letter from an old friend, and one is from a letter from a New York publisher who is a stranger to me. I humbly endeavor to make these bits toothsome with the remark that the article they are praising (which appeared in the December *Galaxy*, and *pretended* to be a criticism from the London *Saturday Review* on my *Innocents Abroad*) *was written by myself, every line of it*:

The *Herald* says the richest thing out is the "serious critique" in the London *Saturday Review*, on Mark Twain's *Innocents Abroad*. We thought before we read it that it must be "serious," as everybody said so, and were even ready to shed a few tears; but since perusing it, we are bound to confess that next to Mark Twain's "Jumping Frog" it's the finest bit of humor and sarcasm that we've come across in many a day.

(I do not get a compliment like that every day.)

I used to think that your writings were pretty good, but after reading the criticism in *The Galaxy* from the *London Review*, have discovered what an ass I must have been. If suggestions are in order, mine is, that you put that article in your next edition of the *Innocents*, as an extra chapter, if you are not afraid to put your own humor in competition with it. It is as rich a thing as I ever read.

(Which is strong commendation from a book publisher.)

The London Reviewer, my friend, is not the stupid, "serious" creature he pretends to be, *I* think; but, on the contrary, has a keen appreciation and enjoyment of your book. As I read his article in *The Galaxy*, I could imagine him giving vent to many a hearty laugh. But he is writing for Catholics and Established Church people, and high-toned, antiquated, conservative gentility, whom it is a delight to him to help you shock, while he pretends to shake his head with owlish density. He is a magnificent humorist himself.

(Now that is graceful and handsome. I take off my hat to my life-long friend and comrade, and with my feet together and my fingers spread over my heart, I say, in the language of Alabama, "You do me proud.")

I stand guilty of the authorship of the article, but I did not mean any harm. I saw by an item in the Boston *Advertiser* that a solemn, serious critique on the English edition of my book had appeared in the London *Saturday Review*, and the idea of *such* a literary breakfast by a stolid, ponderous British ogre of the quill was too much for a naturally weak virtue, and I went home and burlesqued it—reveled in it, I may say. I never saw a copy of the real *Saturday Review* criticism until after my burlesque was written and mailed to the printer. But when I did get hold of a copy, I found it to be vulgar, awkwardly written, ill-natured, and entirely serious and in earnest. The gentleman who wrote the newspaper paragraph above quoted had not been misled as to its character.

If any man doubts my word now, I will kill him. No, I will not kill him; I will win his money. I will bet him twenty to one, and let any New York publisher hold the stakes, that the statements I have above made as to the authorship of the article in question are entirely true. Perhaps I may get wealthy at this, for I am willing to take all the bets that offer; and if a man wants larger odds, I will give him all he requires. But he ought to find out whether I am betting on what is termed "a sure thing" or not before he ventures his money, and he can do that by going to a public library and examining the London *Saturday Review* of October 8th, which contains the real critique.

Bless me, some people thought that *I* was the "sold" person!

P.S.—I cannot resist the temptation to toss in this most savory thing of all—this easy, graceful, philosophical disquisition, with his happy, chirping confidence. It is from the Cincinnati *Enquirer*:

Nothing is more uncertain than the value of a fine cigar. Nine smokers out of ten would prefer an ordinary domestic article, three for a quarter, to fifty-cent Partaga, if kept in ignorance of the cost of the latter. The flavor of the Partaga is too delicate for palates that have been accustomed to Connecticut seed leaf. So it is with humor. The finer it is in quality, the more danger of its not being recognized at all. Even Mark Twain has been taken in by an English review of his *Innocents Abroad*. Mark Twain is by no means a coarse humorist, but the Englishman's humor is so much finer than his, that he mistakes it for solid earnest, and "lafts most consumedly."

A man who cannot learn stands in his own light. Hereafter, when I write an article which I know to be good, but which I may have reason to fear will not, in some quarters, be considered to amount to much, coming from an American, I will aver that an Englishman wrote it and that it is copied from a London journal. And then I will occupy a back seat and enjoy the cordial applause.

(Still later)

Mark Twain at last sees that the *Saturday Review*'s criticism of his *Innocents Abroad* was not serious, and he is intensely mortified at the thought of having been so badly sold. He takes the only course left him, and in the last *Galaxy* claims that *he* wrote the criticism himself, and published it in *The Galaxy* to sell the public. This is ingenious, but unfortunately it is not true. If any of our readers will take the trouble to call at this office we sill show them the original article in the *Saturday Review* of October 8th, which, on comparison, will be found to be identical with the one published in *The Galaxy*. The best thing for Mark to do will be to admit that he was sold, and say no more about it.

The above is from the Cincinnati *Enquirer*, and is a falsehood. Come to the proof. If the *Enquirer* people, through any agent, will produce at *The Galaxy* office a London *Saturday Review* of October 8th, containing an article which, on comparison, will be found to be identical with the one published in *The Galaxy*, I will pay to that agent five hundred dollars cash. Moreover, if at any specified time I fail to produce at the same place a copy of the London *Saturday Review* of October 8th, containing a lengthy criticism upon the *Innocents Abroad*, entirely different, in every paragraph and sentence, from the one I published in *The Galaxy*, I will pay to the *Enquirer* agent another five hundred dollars cash. I offer Sheldon & Co., publishers, 500 Broadway, New York, as my "backers." Any one in New York, authorized by the *Enquirer*, will receive prompt attention. It is an easy and profitable way for the *Enquirer* people to prove that they have not uttered a pitiful, deliberate falsehood in the above paragraphs. Will they swallow that falsehood ignominiously, or will they send an agent to *The Galaxy* office? I think the Cincinnati *Enquirer* must be edited by children.

# AMENDED OBITUARIES

*To the Editor*:

Sir,—I am approaching seventy; it is in sight; it is only three years away. Necessarily, I must go soon. It is but matter-of-course wisdom, then, that I should begin to set my worldly house in order now, so that it may be done calmly and with thoroughness, in place of waiting until the last day, when, as we have often seen, the attempt to set both houses in order at the same time has been marred by the necessity for haste and by the confusion and waste of time arising from the inability of the notary and the ecclesiastic to work together harmoniously, taking turn about and giving each other friendly assistance—not perhaps in fielding, which could hardly be expected, but at least in the minor offices of keeping game and umpiring; by consequence of which conflict of interests and absence of harmonious action a draw has frequently resulted where this ill-fortune could not have happened if the houses had been set in order one at a time and hurry avoided by beginning in season, and giving to each the amount of time fairly and justly proper to it.

In setting my earthly house in order I find it of moment that I should attend in person to one or two matters which men in my position have long had the habit of leaving wholly to others, with consequences often most regrettable. I wish to speak of only one of these matters at this time: Obituaries. Of necessity, an Obituary is a thing which cannot be so judiciously edited by any hand as by that of the subject of it. In such a work it is not the Facts that are of chief importance, but the light which the obituarist shall throw upon them, the meaning which he shall dress them in, the conclusions which he shall draw from them, and the judgments which he shall deliver upon them. The Verdicts, you understand: that is the danger-line.

In considering this matter, in view of my approaching change, it has seemed to me wise to take such measures as may be feasible, to acquire, by courtesy of the press, access to my standing obituaries, with the privilege—if this is not asking too much—of editing, not their Facts, but their Verdicts. This, not for the present profit, further than as concerns my family, but as a favorable influence usable on the Other Side, where there are some who are not friendly to me.

With this explanation of my motives, I will now ask you of your courtesy to make an appeal for me to the public press. It is my desire that such journals and periodicals as have obituaries of me lying in their pigeonholes, with a view to sudden use some day, will not wait longer, but will publish them now, and kindly send me a marked copy. My address is simply New York City—I have no other that is permanent and not transient.

I will correct them—not the Facts, but the Verdicts—striking out such clauses as could have a deleterious influence on the Other Side, and replacing them with clauses of a more judicious character. I should, of course, expect to pay double rates for both the omissions and the substitutions; and I should also expect to pay quadruple rates for all obituaries which proved to be rightly and wisely worded in the originals, thus requiring no emendations at all.

It is my desire to leave these Amended Obituaries neatly bound behind me as a perennial consolation and entertainment to my family, and as an heirloom which shall have a mournful but definite commercial value for my remote posterity.

I beg, sir, that you will insert this Advertisement (1t-eow, agate, inside), and send the bill to

Yours very respectfully.

Mark Twain.


P.S.—For the best Obituary—one suitable for me to read in public, and calculated to inspire regret—I desire to offer a Prize, consisting of a Portrait of me done entirely by myself in pen and ink without previous instructions. The ink warranted to be the kind used by the very best artists.


&#9753;


# THE DANGER OF LYING IN BED


The man in the ticket-office said:

"Have an accident insurance ticket, also?"

"No," I said, after studying the matter over a little. "No, I believe not; I am going to be traveling by rail all day today. However, tomorrow I don't travel. Give me one for tomorrow."

The man looked puzzled. He said:

"But it is for accident insurance, and if you are going to travel by rail—"

"If I am going to travel by rail I sha'n't need it. Lying at home in bed is the thing *I* am afraid of."

I had been looking into this matter. Last year I traveled twenty thousand miles, almost entirely by rail; the year before, I traveled over twenty-five thousand miles, half by sea and half by rail; and the year before that I traveled in the neighborhood of ten thousand miles, exclusively by rail. I suppose if I put in all the little odd journeys here and there, I may say I have traveled sixty thousand miles during the three years I have mentioned. *And never an accident.*

For a good while I said to myself every morning: "Now I have escaped thus far, and so the chances are just that much increased that I shall catch it this time. I will be shrewd, and buy an accident ticket." And to a dead moral certainty I drew a blank, and went to bed that night without a joint started or a bone splintered. I got tired of that sort of daily bother, and fell to buying accident tickets that were good for a month. I said to myself, "A man *can't* buy thirty blanks in one bundle."

But I was mistaken. There was never a prize in the the lot. I could read of railway accidents every day—the newspaper atmosphere was foggy with them; but somehow they never came my way. I found I had spent a good deal of money in the accident business, and had nothing to show for it. My suspicions were aroused, and I began to hunt around for somebody that had won in this lottery. I found plenty of people who had invested, but not an individual that had ever had an accident or made a cent. I stopped buying accident tickets and went to ciphering. The result was astounding. *The peril lay not in traveling, but in staying at home.*

I hunted up statistics, and was amazed to find that after all the glaring newspaper headlines concerning railroad disasters, less than *three hundred* people had really lost their lives by those disasters in the preceding twelve months. The Erie road was set down as the most murderous in the list. It had killed forty-six—or twenty-six, I do not exactly remember which, but I know the number was double that of any other road. But the fact straightway suggested itself that the Erie was an immensely long road, and did more business than any other line in the country; so the double number of killed ceased to be matter for surprise.

By further figuring, it appeared that between New York and Rochester the Erie ran eight passenger-trains each way every day—16 altogether; and carried a daily average of 6,000 persons. That is about a million in six months—the population of New York City. Well, the Erie kills from 13 to 23 persons of *its* million in six months; and in the same time 13,000 of New York's million die in their beds! My flesh crept, my hair stood on end. "This is appalling!" I said. "The danger isn't in traveling by rail, but in trusting to those deadly beds. I will never sleep in a bed again."

I had figured on considerably less than one-half the length of the Erie road. It was plain that the entire road must transport at least eleven or twelve thousand people every day. There are many short roads running out of Boston that do fully half as much; a great many such roads. There are many roads scattered about the Union that do a prodigious passenger business. Therefore it was fair to presume that an average of 2,500 passengers a day for each road in the country would be almost correct. There are 846 railway lines in our country, and 846 times 2,500 are 2,115,000. So the railways of America move more than two millions of people every day; six hundred and fifty millions of people a year, without counting the Sundays. They do that, too—there is no question about it; though where they get the raw material is clear beyond the jurisdiction of my arithmetic; for I have hunted the census through and through, and I find that there are not that many people in the United States, by a matter of six hundred and ten millions at the very least. They must use some of the same people over again, likely.

San Francisco is one-eighth as populous as New York; there are 60 deaths a week in the former and 500 a week in the latter—if they have luck. That is 3,120 deaths a year in San Francisco, and eight times as many in New York—say about 25,000 or 26,000. The health of the two places is the same. So we will let it stand as a fair presumption that this will hold good all over the country, and that consequently 25,000 out of every million of people we have must die every year. That amounts to one-fortieth of our total population. One million of us, then, die annually. Out of this million ten or twelve thousand are stabbed, shot, drowned, hanged, poisoned, or meet a similarly violent death in some other popular way, such as perishing by kerosene-lamp and hoop-skirt conflagrations, getting buried in coal-mines, falling off house-tops, breaking through church, or lecture-room floors, taking patent medicines, or committing suicide in other forms. The Erie railroad kills 23 to 46; the other 845 railroads kill an average of one-third of a man each; and the rest of that million, amounting in the aggregate to that appalling figure of 987,631 corpses, die naturally in their beds!

You will excuse me from taking any more chances on those beds. The railroads are good enough for me.

And my advice to all people is, Don't stay at home any more than you can help; but when you have *got* to stay at home a while, buy a package of those insurance tickets and sit up nights. You cannot be too cautious.

(One can see now why I answered that ticket-agent in the manner recorded at the top of this sketch.)

The moral of this composition is, that thoughtless people grumble more than is fair about railroad management in the United States. When we consider that every day and night of the year full fourteen thousand railway-trains of various kinds, freighted with life and armed with death, go thundering over the land, the marvel is, *not* that they kill three hundred human beings in a twelvemonth, but that they do not kill three hundred times three hundred!

# ADVICE TO LITTLE GIRLS

Good little girls ought not to make mouths at their teachers for every trifling offense. This retaliation should only be resorted to under peculiarly aggravated circumstances.

If you have nothing but a rag-doll stuffed with sawdust, while one of your more fortunate little playmates has a costly China one, you should treat her with a show of kindness nevertheless. And you ought not to attempt to make a forcible swap with her unless your conscience would justify you in it, and you know you are able to do it.

You ought never to take your little brother's "chewing-gum" away from him by main force; it is better to rope him in with the promise of the first two dollars and a half you find floating down the river on a grindstone. In the artless simplicity natural to this time of life, he will regard it as a perfectly fair transaction. In all ages of the world this eminently plausible fiction has lured the obtuse infant to financial ruin and disaster.

If at any time you find it necessary to correct your brother, do not correct him with mud—never, on any account, throw mud at him, because it will spoil his clothes. It is better to scald him a little, for then you obtain desirable results. You secure his immediate attention to the lessons you are inculcating, and at the same time your hot water will have a tendency to move impurities from his person, and possibly the skin, in spots.

If your mother tells you to do a thing, it is wrong to reply that you won't. It is better and more becoming to intimate that you will do as she bids you, and then afterward act quietly in the matter according to the dictates of your best judgment.

You should ever bear in mind that it is to your kind parents that you are indebted for your food, and for the privilege of staying home from school when you let on that you are sick. Therefore you ought to respect their little prejudices, and humor their little whims, and put up with their little foibles until they get to crowding you too much.

Good little girls always show marked deference for the aged. You ought never to "sass" old people unless they "sass" you first.

<br>

# DOES THE RACE OF MAN LOVE A LORD?

Often a quite assified remark becomes sanctified by use and petrified by custom; it is then a permanency, its term of activity a geologic period.

The day after the arrival of Prince Henry I met an English friend, and he rubbed his hands and broke out with a remark that was charged to the brim with joy—joy that was evidently a pleasant salve to an old sore place:

"Many a time I've had to listen without retort to an old saying that is irritatingly true, and until now seemed to offer no chance for a return jibe: 'An Englishman does dearly love a lord'; but after this I shall talk back, and say, 'How about the Americans?'"

It is a curious thing, the currency that an idiotic saying can get. The man that first says it thinks he has made a discovery. The man he says it to, thinks the same. It departs on its travels, is received everywhere with admiring acceptance, and not only as a piece of rare and acute observation, but as being exhaustively true and profoundly wise; and so it presently takes its place in the world's list of recognized and established wisdoms, and after that no one thinks of examining it to see whether it is really entitled to its high honors or not. I call to mind instances of this in two well-established proverbs, whose dullness is not surpassed by the one about the Englishman and his love for a lord: one of them records the American's Adoration of the Almighty Dollar, the other the American millionaire-girl's ambition to trade cash for a title, with a husband thrown in.

It isn't merely the American that adores the Almighty Dollar, it is the human race. The human race has always adored the hatful of shells, or the bale of calico, or the half-bushel of brass rings, or the handful of steel fish-hooks, or the houseful of black wives, or the zareba full of cattle, or the two-score camels and asses, or the factory, or the farm, or the block of buildings, or the railroad bonds, or the bank stock, or the hoarded cash, or—anything that stands for wealth and consideration and independence, and can secure to the possessor that most precious of all things, another man's envy. It was a dull person that invented the idea that the American's devotion to the dollar is more strenuous than another's.

Rich American girls do buy titles, but they did not invent that idea; it had been worn threadbare several hundred centuries before America was discovered. European girls still exploit it as briskly as ever; and, when a title is not to be had for the money in hand, they buy the husband without it. They must put up the "dot," or there is no trade. The commercialization of brides is substantially universal, except in America. It exists with us, to some little extent, but in no degree approaching a custom.

"The Englishman dearly loves a lord."

What is the soul and source of this love? I think the thing could be more correctly worded:

"The human race dearly envies a lord."

That is to say, it envies the lord's place. Why? On two accounts, I think: its Power and its Conspicuousness.

Where Conspicuousness carries with it a Power which, by the light of our own observation and experience, we are able to measure and comprehend, I think our envy of the possessor is as deep and as passionate as is that of any other nation. No one can care less for a lord than the backwoodsman, who has had no personal contact with lords and has seldom heard them spoken of; but I will not allow that any Englishman has a profounder envy of a lord than has the average American who has lived long years in a European capital and fully learned how immense is the position the lord occupies.

Of any ten thousand Americans who eagerly gather, at vast inconvenience, to get a glimpse of Prince Henry, all but a couple of hundred will be there out of an immense curiosity; they are burning up with desire to see a personage who is so much talked about. They envy him; but it is Conspicuousness they envy mainly, not the Power that is lodged in his royal quality and position, for they have but a vague and spectral knowledge and appreciation of that; through their environment and associations they have been accustomed to regard such things lightly, and as not being very real; consequently, they are not able to value them enough to consumingly envy them.

But, whenever an American (or other human being) is in the presence, for the first time, of a combination of great Power and Conspicuousness which he thoroughly understands and appreciates, his eager curiosity and pleasure will be well-sodden with that other passion—envy—whether he suspects it or not. At any time, on any day, in any part of America, you can confer a happiness upon any passing stranger by calling his attention to any other passing stranger and saying:

"Do you see that gentleman going along there? It is Mr. Rockefeller."

Watch his eye. It is a combination of power and conspicuousness which the man understands.

When we understand rank, we always like to rub against it. When a man is conspicuous, we always want to see him. Also, if he will pay us an attention we will manage to remember it. Also, we will mention it now and then, casually; sometimes to a friend, or if a friend is not handy, we will make out with a stranger.

Well, then, what is rank, and what is conspicuousness? At once we think of kings and aristocracies, and of world-wide celebrities in soldierships, the arts, letters, etc., and we stop there. But that is a mistake. Rank holds its court and receives its homage on every round of the ladder, from the emperor down to the rat-catcher; and distinction, also, exists on every round of the ladder, and commands its due of deference and envy.

To worship rank and distinction is the dear and valued privilege of all the human race, and it is freely and joyfully exercised in democracies as well as in monarchies—and even, to some extent, among those creatures whom we impertinently call the Lower Animals. For even they have some poor little vanities and foibles, though in this matter they are paupers as compared to us.

A Chinese Emperor has the worship of his four hundred millions of subjects, but the rest of the world is indifferent to him. A Christian Emperor has the worship of his subjects and of a large part of the Christian world outside of his domains; but he is a matter of indifference to all China. A king, class A, has an extensive worship; a king, class B, has a less extensive worship; class C, class D, class E get a steadily diminishing share of worship; class L (Sultan of Zanzibar), class P (Sultan of Sulu), and class W (half-king of Samoa), get no worship at all outside their own little patch of sovereignty.

Take the distinguished people along down. Each has his group of homage-payers. In the navy, there are many groups; they start with the Secretary and the Admiral, and go down to the quartermaster—and below; for there will be groups among the sailors, and each of these groups will have a tar who is distinguished for his battles, or his strength, or his daring, or his profanity, and is admired and envied by his group. The same with the army; the same with the literary and journalistic craft; the publishing craft; the cod-fishery craft; Standard Oil; U. S. Steel; the class A hotel—and the rest of the alphabet in that line; the class A prize-fighter—and the rest of the alphabet in his line—clear down to the lowest and obscurest six-boy gang of little gamins, with its one boy that can thrash the rest, and to whom he is king of Samoa, bottom of the royal race, but looked up to with a most ardent admiration and envy.

There is something pathetic, and funny, and pretty, about this human race's fondness for contact with power and distinction, and for the reflected glory it gets out of it. The king, class A, is happy in the state banquet and the military show which the emperor provides for him, and he goes home and gathers the queen and the princelings around him in the privacy of the spare room, and tells them all about it, and says:

"His Imperial Majesty put his hand upon my shoulder in the most friendly way—just as friendly and familiar, oh, you can't imagine it!—and everybody *seeing* him do it; charming, perfectly charming!"

The king, class G, is happy in the cold collation and the police parade provided for him by the king, class B, and goes home and tells the family all about it, and says:

"And His Majesty took me into his own private cabinet for a smoke and a chat, and there we sat just as sociable, and talking away and laughing and chatting, just the same as if we had been born in the same bunk; and all the servants in the anteroom could see us doing it! Oh, it was too lovely for anything!"

The king, class Q, is happy in the modest entertainment furnished him by the king, class M, and goes home and tells the household about it, and is as grateful and joyful over it as were his predecessors in the gaudier attentions that had fallen to their larger lot.

Emperors, kings, artisans, peasants, big people, little people—at the bottom we are all alike and all the same; all just alike on the inside, and when our clothes are off, nobody can tell which of us is which. We are unanimous in the pride we take in good and genuine compliments paid us, and distinctions conferred upon us, in attentions shown. There is not one of us, from the emperor down, but is made like that. Do I mean attentions shown us by the guest? No, I mean simply flattering attentions, let them come whence they may. We despise no source that can pay us a pleasing attention—there is no source that is humble enough for that. You have heard a dear little girl say to a frowzy and disreputable dog: "He came right to me and let me pat him on the head, and he wouldn't let the others touch him!" and you have seen her eyes dance with pride in that high distinction. You have often seen that. If the child were a princess, would that random dog be able to confer the like glory upon her with his pretty compliment? Yes; and even in her mature life and seated upon a throne, she would still remember it, still recall it, still speak of it with frank satisfaction. That charming and lovable German princess and poet, Carmen Sylva, Queen of Roumania, remembers yet that the flowers of the woods and fields "talked to her" when she was a girl, and she sets it down in her latest book; and that the squirrels conferred upon her and her father the valued compliment of not being afraid of them; and "once one of them, holding a nut between its sharp little teeth, ran right up against my father"—it has the very note of "He came right to me and let me pat him on the head"—"and when it saw itself reflected in his boot it was very much surprised, and stopped for a long time to contemplate itself in the polished leather"—then it went its way. And the birds! she still remembers with pride that "they came boldly into my room," when she had neglected her "duty" and put no food on the window-sill for them; she knew all the wild birds, and forgets the royal crown on her head to remember with pride that they knew her; also that the wasp and the bee were personal friends of hers, and never forgot that gracious relationship to her injury: "never have I been stung by a wasp or a bee." And here is that proud note again that sings in that little child's elation in being singled out, among all the company of children, for the random dog's honor-conferring attentions. "Even in the very worst summer for wasps, when, in lunching out of doors, our table was covered with them and every one else was stung, they never hurt me."

When a queen whose qualities of mind and heart and character are able to add distinction to so distinguished a place as a throne, remembers with grateful exultation, after thirty years, honors and distinctions conferred upon her by the humble, wild creatures of the forest, we are helped to realize that complimentary attentions, homage, distinctions, are of no caste, but are above all cast—that they are a nobility-conferring power apart.

We all like these things. When the gate-guard at the railway-station passes me through unchallenged and examines other people's tickets, I feel as the king, class A, felt when the emperor put the imperial hand on his shoulder, "everybody seeing him do it"; and as the child felt when the random dog allowed her to pat his head and ostracized the others; and as the princess felt when the wasps spared her and stung the rest; and I felt just so, four years ago in Vienna (and remember it yet), when the helmeted police shut me off, with fifty others, from a street which the Emperor was to pass through, and the captain of the squad turned and saw the situation and said indignantly to that guard:

"Can't you see it is the Herr Mark Twain? Let him through!"

It was four years ago; but it will be four hundred before I forget the wind of self-complacency that rose in me, and strained my buttons when I marked the deference for me evoked in the faces of my fellow-rabble, and noted, mingled with it, a puzzled and resentful expression which said, as plainly as speech could have worded it: "And who in the nation is the Herr Mark Twain *um Gotteswillen*?"

How many times in your life have you heard this boastful remark:

"I stood as close to him as I am to you; I could have put out my hand and touched him."

We have all heard it many and many a time. It was a proud distinction to be able to say those words. It brought envy to the speaker, a kind of glory; and he basked in it and was happy through all his veins. And who was it he stood so close to? The answer would cover all the grades. Sometimes it was a king; sometimes it was a renowned highwayman; sometimes it was an unknown man killed in an extraordinary way and made suddenly famous by it; always it was a person who was for the moment the subject of public interest of a village.

"I was there, and I saw it myself." That is a common and envy-compelling remark. It can refer to a battle; to a handing; to a coronation; to the killing of Jumbo by the railway-train; to the arrival of Jenny Lind at the Battery; to the meeting of the President and Prince Henry; to the chase of a murderous maniac; to the disaster in the tunnel; to the explosion in the subway; to a remarkable dog-fight; to a village church struck by lightning. It will be said, more or less causally, by everybody in America who has seen Prince Henry do anything, or try to. The man who was absent and didn't see him to anything, will scoff. It is his privilege; and he can make capital out of it, too; he will seem, even to himself, to be different from other Americans, and better. As his opinion of his superior Americanism grows, and swells, and concentrates and coagulates, he will go further and try to belittle the distinction of those that saw the Prince do things, and will spoil their pleasure in it if he can. My life has been embittered by that kind of person. If you are able to tell of a special distinction that has fallen to your lot, it gravels them; they cannot bear it; and they try to make believe that the thing you took for a special distinction was nothing of the kind and was meant in quite another way. Once I was received in private audience by an emperor. Last week I was telling a jealous person about it, and I could see him wince under it, see him bite, see him suffer. I revealed the whole episode to him with considerable elaboration and nice attention to detail. When I was through, he asked me what had impressed me most. I said:

"His Majesty's delicacy. They told me to be sure and back out from the presence, and find the door-knob as best I could; it was not allowable to face around. Now the Emperor knew it would be a difficult ordeal for me, because of lack of practice; and so, when it was time to part, he turned, with exceeding delicacy, and pretended to fumble with things on his desk, so I could get out in my own way, without his seeing me."

It went home! It was vitriol! I saw the envy and disgruntlement rise in the man's face; he couldn't keep it down. I saw him try to fix up something in his mind to take the bloom off that distinction. I enjoyed that, for I judged that he had his work cut out for him. He struggled along inwardly for quite a while; then he said, with a manner of a person who has to say something and hasn't anything relevant to say:

"You said he had a handful of special-brand cigars on the table?"

"Yes; *I* never saw anything to match them."

I had him again. He had to fumble around in his mind as much as another minute before he could play; then he said in as mean a way as I ever heard a person say anything:

"He could have been counting the cigars, you know."

I cannot endure a man like that. It is nothing to him how unkind he is, so long as he takes the bloom off. It is all he cares for.

"An Englishman (or other human being) does dearly love a lord," (or other conspicuous person.) It includes us all. We love to be noticed by the conspicuous person; we love to be associated with such, or with a conspicuous event, even in a seventh-rate fashion, even in the forty-seventh, if we cannot do better. This accounts for some of our curious tastes in mementos. It accounts for the large private trade in the Prince of Wales's hair, which chambermaids were able to drive in that article of commerce when the Prince made the tour of the world in the long ago—hair which probably did not always come from his brush, since enough of it was marketed to refurnish a bald comet; it accounts for the fact that the rope which lynches a negro in the presence of ten thousand Christian spectators is salable five minutes later at two dollars an inch; it accounts for the mournful fact that a royal personage does not venture to wear buttons on his coat in public.

We do love a lord—and by that term I mean any person whose situation is higher than our own. The lord of the group, for instance: a group of peers, a group of millionaires, a group of hoodlums, a group of sailors, a group of newsboys, a group of saloon politicians, a group of college girls. No royal person has ever been the object of a more delirious loyalty and slavish adoration than is paid by the vast Tammany herd to its squalid idol in Wantage. There is not a bifurcated animal in that menagerie that would not be proud to appear in a newspaper picture in his company. At the same time, there are some in that organization who would scoff at the people who have been daily pictured in company with Prince Henry, and would say vigorously that *they* would not consent to be photographed with him—a statement which would not be true in any instance. There are hundreds of people in America who would frankly say to you that they would not be proud to be photographed in a group with the Prince, if invited; and some of these unthinking people would believe it when they said it; yet in no instance would it be true. We have a large population, but we have not a large enough one, by several millions, to furnish that man. He has not yet been begotten, and in fact he is not begettable.

You may take any of the printed groups, and there isn't a person in the dim background who isn't visibly trying to be vivid; if it is a crowd of ten thousand—ten thousand proud, untamed democrats, horny-handed sons of toil and of politics, and fliers of the eagle—there isn't one who is trying to keep out of range, there isn't one who isn't plainly meditating a purchase of the paper in the morning, with the intention of hunting himself out in the picture and of framing and keeping it if he shall find so much of his person in it as his starboard ear.

We all love to get some of the drippings of Conspicuousness, and we will put up with a single, humble drip, if we can't get any more. We may pretend otherwise, in conversation; but we can't pretend it to ourselves privately—and we don't. We do confess in public that we are the noblest work of God, being moved to it by long habit, and teaching, and superstition; but deep down in the secret places of our souls we recognize that, if we *are* the noblest work, the less said about it the better.

We of the North poke fun at the South for its fondness of titles—a fondness for titles pure and simple, regardless of whether they are genuine or pinchbeck. We forget that whatever a Southerner likes the rest of the human race likes, and that there is no law of predilection lodged in one people that is absent from another people. There is no variety in the human race. We are all children, all children of the one Adam, and we love toys. We can soon acquire that Southern disease if some one will give it a start. It already has a start, in fact. I have been personally acquainted with over eighty-four thousand persons who, at one time or another in their lives, have served for a year or two on the staffs of our multitudinous governors, and through that fatality have been generals temporarily, and colonels temporarily, and judge-advocates temporarily; but I have known only nine among them who could be hired to let the title go when it ceased to be legitimate. I know thousands and thousands of governors who ceased to be governors away back in the last century; but I am acquainted with only three who would answer your letter if you failed to call them "Governor" in it. I know acres and acres of men who have done time in a legislature in prehistoric days, but among them is not half an acre whose resentment you would not raise if you addressed them as "Mr." instead of "Hon." The first thing a legislature does is to convene in an impressive legislative attitude, and get itself photographed. Each member frames his copy and takes it to the woods and hangs it up in the most aggressively conspicuous place in his house; and if you visit the house and fail to inquire what that accumulation is, the conversation will be brought around to it by that aforetime legislator, and he will show you a figure in it which in the course of years he has almost obliterated with the smut of his finger-marks, and say with a solemn joy, "It's me!"

Have you ever seen a country Congressman enter the hotel breakfast-room in Washington with his letters?—and sit at his table and let on to read them?—and wrinkle his brows and frown statesman-like?—keeping a furtive watch-out over his glasses all the while to see if he is being observed and admired?—those same old letters which he fetches in every morning? Have you seen it? Have you seen him show off? It is *the* sight of the national capital. Except one; a pathetic one. That is the ex-Congressman: the poor fellow whose life has been ruined by a two-year taste of glory and of fictitious consequence; who has been superseded, and ought to take his heartbreak home and hide it, but cannot tear himself away from the scene of his lost little grandeur; and so he lingers, and still lingers, year after year, unconsidered, sometimes snubbed, ashamed of his fallen estate, and valiantly trying to look otherwise; dreary and depressed, but counterfeiting breeziness and gaiety, hailing with chummy familiarity, which is not always welcomed, the more-fortunes who are still in place and were once his mates. Have you seen him? He clings piteously to the one little shred that is left of his departed distinction—the "privilege of the floor"; and works it hard and gets what he can out of it. That is the saddest figure I know of.

Yes, we do so love our little distinctions! And then we loftily scoff at a Prince for enjoying his larger ones; forgetting that if we only had his chance—ah! "Senator" is not a legitimate title. A Senator has no more right to be addressed by it than have you or I; but, in the several state capitals and in Washington, there are five thousand Senators who take very kindly to that fiction, and who purr gratefully when you call them by it—which you may do quite unrebuked. Then those same Senators smile at the self-constructed majors and generals and judges of the South!

Indeed, we do love our distinctions, get them how we may. And we work them for all they are worth. In prayer we call ourselves "worms of the dust," but it is only on a sort of tacit understanding that the remark shall not be taken at par. *We*—worms of the dust! Oh, no, we are not that. Except in fact; and we do not deal much in fact when we are contemplating ourselves.

As a race, we do certainly love a lord—let him be Croker, or a duke, or a prize-fighter, or whatever other personage shall chance to be the head of our group. Many years ago, I saw a greasy youth in overalls standing by the *Herald* office, with an expectant look in his face. Soon a large man passed out, and gave him a pat on the shoulder. That was what the boy was waiting for—the large man's notice. The pat made him proud and happy, and the exultation inside of him shone out through his eyes; and his mates were there to see the pat and envy it and wish they could have that glory. The boy belonged down cellar in the press-room, the large man was king of the upper floors, foreman of the composing-room. The light in the boy's face was worship, the foreman was his lord, head of his group. The pat was an accolade. It was as precious to the boy as it would have been if he had been an aristocrat's son and the accolade had been delivered by his sovereign with a sword. The quintessence of the honor was all there; there was no difference in values; in truth there was no difference present except an artificial one—clothes.

All the human race loves a lord—that is, loves to look upon or be noticed by the possessor of Power or Conspicuousness; and sometimes animals, born to better things and higher ideals, descend to man's level in this matter. In the Jardin des Plantes I have seen a cat that was so vain of being the personal friend of an elephant that I was ashamed of her.

# EXTRACTS FROM ADAM'S DIARY

*Monday.*—This new creature with the long hair is a good deal in the way. It is always hanging around and following me about. I don't like this; I am not used to company. I wish it would stay with the other animals. . . . Cloudy today, wind in the east; think we shall have rain. . . . *We?* Where did I get that word—the new creature uses it.

*Tuesday.*—Been examining the great waterfall. It is the finest thing on the estate, I think. The new creature calls it Niagara Falls—why, I am sure I do not know. Says it *looks* like Niagara Falls. That is not a reason, it is mere waywardness and imbecility. I get no chance to name anything myself. The new creature names everything that comes along, before I can get in a protest. And always that same pretext is offered—it *looks* like the thing. There is a dodo, for instance. Says the moment one looks at it one sees at a glance that it "looks like a dodo." It will have to keep that name, no doubt. It wearies me to fret about it, and it does no good, anyway. Dodo! It looks no more like a dodo than I do.

*Wednesday.*—Built me a shelter against the rain, but could not have it to myself in peace. The new creature intruded. When I tried to put it out it shed water out of the holes it looks with, and wiped it away with the back of its paws, and made a noise such as some of the other animals make when they are in distress. I wish it would not talk; it is always talking. That sounds like a cheap fling at the poor creature, a slur; but I do not mean it so. I have never heard the human voice before, and any new and strange sound intruding itself here upon the solemn hush of these dreaming solitudes offends my ear and seems a false note. And this new sound is so close to me; it is right at my shoulder, right at my ear, first on one side and then on the other, and I am used only to sounds that are more or less distant from me.

*Friday.* The naming goes recklessly on, in spite of anything I can do. I had a very good name for the estate, and it was musical and pretty—*Garden of Eden.*

Privately, I continue to call it that, but not any longer publicly. The new creature says it is all woods and rocks and scenery, and therefore has no resemblance to a garden. Says it *looks* like a park, and does not look like anything *but* a park. Consequently, without consulting me, it has been new-named *Niagara Falls Park*. This is sufficiently high-handed, it seems to me. And already there is a sign up:

KEEP OFF THE GRASS

My life is not as happy as it was.

*Saturday.*—The new creature eats too much fruit. We are going to run short, most likely. "We" again—that is *its* word; mine, too, now, from hearing it so much. Good deal of fog this morning. I do not go out in the fog myself. This new creature does. It goes out in all weathers, and stumps right in with its muddy feet. And talks. It used to be so pleasant and quiet here.

*Sunday.*—Pulled through. This day is getting to be more and more trying. It was selected and set apart last November as a day of rest. I had already six of them per week before. This morning found the new creature trying to clod apples out of that forbidden tree.

*Monday.*—The new creature says its name is Eve. That is all right, I have no objections. Says it is to call it by, when I want it to come. I said it was superfluous, then. The word evidently raised me in its respect; and indeed it is a large, good word and will bear repetition. It says it is not an It, it is a She. This is probably doubtful; yet it is all one to me; what she is were nothing to me if she would but go by herself and not talk.

*Tuesday.*—She has littered the whole estate with execrable names and offensive signs:

This way to the Whirlpool

This way to Goat Island

Cave of the Winds this way

She says this park would make a tidy summer resort if there was any custom for it. Summer resort—another invention of hers—just words, without any meaning. What is a summer resort? But it is best not to ask her, she has such a rage for explaining.

*Friday.*—She has taken to beseeching me to stop going over the Falls. What harm does it do? Says it makes her shudder. I wonder why; I have always done it—always liked the plunge, and coolness. I supposed it was what the Falls were for. They have no other use that I can see, and they must have been made for something. She says they were only made for scenery—like the rhinoceros and the mastodon.

I went over the Falls in a barrel—not satisfactory to her. Went over in a tub—still not satisfactory. Swam the Whirlpool and the Rapids in a fig-leaf suit. It got much damaged. Hence, tedious complaints about my extravagance. I am too much hampered here. What I need is a change of scene.

*Saturday.*—I escaped last Tuesday night, and traveled two days, and built me another shelter in a secluded place, and obliterated my tracks as well as I could, but she hunted me out by means of a beast which she has tamed and calls a wolf, and came making that pitiful noise again, and shedding that water out of the places she looks with. I was obliged to return with her, but will presently emigrate again when occasion offers. She engages herself in many foolish things; among others; to study out why the animals called lions and tigers live on grass and flowers, when, as she says, the sort of teeth they wear would indicate that they were intended to eat each other. This is foolish, because to do that would be to kill each other, and that would introduce what, as I understand, is called "death"; and death, as I have been told, has not yet entered the Park. Which is a pity, on some accounts.

*Sunday.*—Pulled through.

*Monday.*—I believe I see what the week is for: it is to give time to rest up from the weariness of Sunday. It seems a good idea. . . . She has been climbing that tree again. Clodded her out of it. She said nobody was looking. Seems to consider that a sufficient justification for chancing any dangerous thing. Told her that. The word justification moved her admiration—and envy, too, I thought. It is a good word.

*Tuesday.*—She told me she was made out of a rib taken from my body. This is at least doubtful, if not more than that. I have not missed any rib. . . . She is in much trouble about the buzzard; says grass does not agree with it; is afraid she can't raise it; thinks it was intended to live on decayed flesh. The buzzard must get along the best it can with what is provided. We cannot overturn the whole scheme to accommodate the buzzard.

*Saturday.*—She fell in the pond yesterday when she was looking at herself in it, which she is always doing. She nearly strangled, and said it was most uncomfortable. This made her sorry for the creatures which live in there, which she calls fish, for she continues to fasten names on to things that don't need them and don't come when they are called by them, which is a matter of no consequence to her, she is such a numbskull, anyway; so she got a lot of them out and brought them in last night and put them in my bed to keep warm, but I have noticed them now and then all day and I don't see that they are any happier there then they were before, only quieter. When night comes I shall throw them outdoors. I will not sleep with them again, for I find them clammy and unpleasant to lie among when a person hasn't anything on.

*Sunday.*—Pulled through.

*Tuesday.*—She has taken up with a snake now. The other animals are glad, for she was always experimenting with them and bothering them; and I am glad because the snake talks, and this enables me to get a rest.

*Friday.*—She says the snake advises her to try the fruit of the tree, and says the result will be a great and fine and noble education. I told her there would be another result, too—it would introduce death into the world. That was a mistake—it had been better to keep the remark to myself; it only gave her an idea—she could save the sick buzzard, and furnish fresh meat to the despondent lions and tigers. I advised her to keep away from the tree. She said she wouldn't. I foresee trouble. Will emigrate.

*Wednesday.*—I have had a variegated time. I escaped last night, and rode a horse all night as fast as he could go, hoping to get clear of the Park and hide in some other country before the trouble should begin; but it was not to be. About an hour after sun-up, as I was riding through a flowery plain where thousands of animals were grazing, slumbering, or playing with each other, according to their wont, all of a sudden they broke into a tempest of frightful noises, and in one moment the plain was a frantic commotion and every beast was destroying its neighbor. I knew what it meant—Eve had eaten that fruit, and death was come into the world. . . . The tigers ate my house, paying no attention when I ordered them to desist, and they would have eaten me if I had stayed—which I didn't, but went away in much haste. . . . I found this place, outside the Park, and was fairly comfortable for a few days, but she has found me out. Found me out, and has named the place Tonawanda—says it *looks* like that. In fact I was not sorry she came, for there are but meager pickings here, and she brought some of those apples. I was obliged to eat them, I was so hungry. It was against my principles, but I find that principles have no real force except when one is well fed. . . . She came curtained in boughs and bunches of leaves, and when I asked her what she meant by such nonsense, and snatched them away and threw them down, she tittered and blushed. I had never seen a person titter and blush before, and to me it seemed unbecoming and idiotic. She said I would soon know how it was myself. This was correct. Hungry as I was, I laid down the apple half-eaten—certainly the best one I ever saw, considering the lateness of the season—and arrayed myself in the discarded boughs and branches, and then spoke to her with some severity and ordered her to go and get some more and not make a spectacle or herself. She did it, and after this we crept down to where the wild-beast battle had been, and collected some skins, and I made her patch together a couple of suits proper for public occasions. They are uncomfortable, it is true, but stylish, and that is the main point about clothes. . . . I find she is a good deal of a companion. I see I should be lonesome and depressed without her, now that I have lost my property. Another thing, she says it is ordered that we work for our living hereafter. She will be useful. I will superintend.

*Ten Days Later.*—She accuses ME of being the cause of our disaster! She says, with apparent sincerity and truth, that the Serpent assured her that the forbidden fruit was not apples, it was chestnuts. I said I was innocent, then, for I had not eaten any chestnuts. She said the Serpent informed her that "chestnut" was a figurative term meaning an aged and moldy joke. I turned pale at that, for I have made many jokes to pass the weary time, and some of them could have been of that sort, though I had honestly supposed that they were new when I made them. She asked me if I had made one just at the time of the catastrophe. I was obliged to admit that I had made one to myself, though not aloud. It was this. I was thinking about the Falls, and I said to myself, "How wonderful it is to see that vast body of water tumble down there!" Then in an instant a bright thought flashed into my head, and I let it fly, saying, "It would be a deal more wonderful to see it tumble *up* there!"—and I was just about to kill myself with laughing at it when all nature broke loose in war and death and I had to flee for my life. "There," she said, with triumph, "that is just it; the Serpent mentioned that very jest, and called it the First Chestnut, and said it was coeval with the creation." Alas, I am indeed to blame. Would that I were not witty; oh, that I had never had that radiant thought!

*Next Year.*—We have named it Cain. She caught it while I was up country trapping on the North Shore of the Erie; caught it in the timber a couple of miles from our dug-out—or it might have been four, she isn't certain which. It resembles us in some ways, and may be a relation. That is what she thinks, but this is an error, in my judgment. The difference in size warrants the conclusion that it is a different and new kind of animal—a fish, perhaps, though when I put it in the water to see, it sank, and she plunged in and snatched it out before there was opportunity for the experiment to determine the matter. I still think it is a fish, but she is indifferent about what it is, and will not let me have it to try. I do not understand this. The coming of the creature seems to have changed her whole nature and made her unreasonable about experiments. She thinks more of it than she does of any of the other animals, but is not able to explain why. Her mind is disordered—everything shows it. Sometimes she carries the fish in her arms half the night when it complains and wants to get to the water. At such times the water comes out of the places in her face that she looks out of, and she pats the fish on the back and makes soft sounds with her mouth to soothe it, and betrays sorrow and solicitude in a hundred ways. I have never seen her do like this with any other fish, and it troubles me greatly. She used to carry the young tigers around so, and play with them, before we lost our property, but it was only play; she never took on about them like this when their dinner disagreed with them.

*Sunday.*—She doesn't work, Sundays, but lies around all tired out, and likes to have the fish wallow over her; and she makes fool noises to amuse it, and pretends to chew its paws, and that makes it laugh. I have not seen a fish before that could laugh. This makes me doubt. . . . I have come to like Sunday myself. Superintending all the week tires a body so. There ought to be more Sundays. In the old days they were tough, but now they come handy.

*Wednesday.*—It isn't a fish. I cannot quite make out what it is. It makes curious devilish noises when not satisfied, and says "goo-goo" when it is. It is not one of us, for it doesn't walk; it is not a bird, for it doesn't fly; it is not a frog, for it doesn't hop; it is not a snake, for it doesn't crawl; I feel sure it is not a fish, though I cannot get a chance to find out whether it can swim or not. It merely lies around, and mostly on its back, with its feet up. I have not seen any other animal do that before. I said I believed it was an enigma; but she only admired the word without understanding it. In my judgment it is either an enigma or some kind of a bug. If it dies, I will take it apart and see what its arrangements are. I never had a thing perplex me so.

*Three Months Later.*—The perplexity augments instead of diminishing. I sleep but little. It has ceased from lying around, and goes about on its four legs now. Yet it differs from the other four legged animals, in that its front legs are unusually short, consequently this causes the main part of its person to stick up uncomfortably high in the air, and this is not attractive. It is built much as we are, but its method of traveling shows that it is not of our breed. The short front legs and long hind ones indicate that it is of the kangaroo family, but it is a marked variation of that species, since the true kangaroo hops, whereas this one never does. Still it is a curious and interesting variety, and has not been catalogued before. As I discovered it, I have felt justified in securing the credit of the discovery by attaching my name to it, and hence have called it *Kangaroorum Adamiensis*. . . . It must have been a young one when it came, for it has grown exceedingly since. It must be five times as big, now, as it was then, and when discontented it is able to make from twenty-two to thirty-eight times the noise it made at first. Coercion does not modify this, but has the contrary effect. For this reason I discontinued the system. She reconciles it by persuasion, and by giving it things which she had previously told me she wouldn't give it. As already observed, I was not at home when it first came, and she told me she found it in the woods. It seems odd that it should be the only one, yet it must be so, for I have worn myself out these many weeks trying to find another one to add to my collection, and for this to play with; for surely then it would be quieter and we could tame it more easily. But I find none, nor any vestige of any; and strangest of all, no tracks. It has to live on the ground, it cannot help itself; therefore, how does it get about without leaving a track? I have set a dozen traps, but they do no good. I catch all small animals except that one; animals that merely go into the trap out of curiosity, I think, to see what the milk is there for. They never drink it.

*Three Months Later.*—The Kangaroo still continues to grow, which is very strange and perplexing. I never knew one to be so long getting its growth. It has fur on its head now; not like kangaroo fur, but exactly like our hair except that it is much finer and softer, and instead of being black is red. I am like to lose my mind over the capricious and harassing developments of this unclassifiable zoological freak. If I could catch another one—but that is hopeless; it is a new variety, and the only sample; this is plain. But I caught a true kangaroo and brought it in, thinking that this one, being lonesome, would rather have that for company than have no kin at all, or any animal it could feel a nearness to or get sympathy from in its forlorn condition here among strangers who do not know its ways or habits, or what to do to make it feel that it is among friends; but it was a mistake—it went into such fits at the sight of the kangaroo that I was convinced it had never seen one before. I pity the poor noisy little animal, but there is nothing I can do to make it happy. If I could tame it—but that is out of the question; the more I try the worse I seem to make it. It grieves me to the heart to see it in its little storms of sorrow and passion. I wanted to let it go, but she wouldn't hear of it. That seemed cruel and not like her; and yet she may be right. It might be lonelier than ever; for since I cannot find another one, how could *it*?

*Five Months Later.*—It is not a kangaroo. No, for it supports itself by holding to her finger, and thus goes a few steps on its hind legs, and then falls down. It is probably some kind of a bear; and yet it has no tail—as yet—and no fur, except upon its head. It still keeps on growing—that is a curious circumstance, for bears get their growth earlier than this. Bears are dangerous—since our catastrophe—and I shall not be satisfied to have this one prowling about the place much longer without a muzzle on. I have offered to get her a kangaroo if she would let this one go, but it did no good—she is determined to run us into all sorts of foolish risks, I think. She was not like this before she lost her mind.

*A Fortnight Later.*—I examined its mouth. There is no danger yet: it has only one tooth. It has no tail yet. It makes more noise now than it ever did before—and mainly at night. I have moved out. But I shall go over, mornings, to breakfast, and see if it has more teeth. If it gets a mouthful of teeth it will be time for it to go, tail or no tail, for a bear does not need a tail in order to be dangerous.

*Four Months Later.*—I have been off hunting and fishing a month, up in the region that she calls Buffalo; I don't know why, unless it is because there are not any buffaloes there. Meantime the bear has learned to paddle around all by itself on its hind legs, and says "poppa" and "momma." It is certainly a new species. This resemblance to words may be purely accidental, of course, and may have no purpose or meaning; but even in that case it is still extraordinary, and is a thing which no other bear can do. This imitation of speech, taken together with general absence of fur and entire absence of tail, sufficiently indicates that this is a new kind of bear. The further study of it will be exceedingly interesting. Meantime I will go off on a far expedition among the forests of the north and make an exhaustive search. There must certainly be another one somewhere, and this one will be less dangerous when it has company of its own species. I will go straightway; but I will muzzle this one first.

*Three Months Later.*—It has been a weary, weary hunt, yet I have had no success. In the mean time, without stirring from the home estate, she has caught another one! I never saw such luck. I might have hunted these woods a hundred years, I never would have run across that thing.

*Next Day.*—I have been comparing the new one with the old one, and it is perfectly plain that they are of the same breed. I was going to stuff one of them for my collection, but she is prejudiced against it for some reason or other; so I have relinquished the idea, though I think it is a mistake. It would be an irreparable loss to science if they should get away. The old one is tamer than it was and can laugh and talk like a parrot, having learned this, no doubt, from being with the parrot so much, and having the imitative faculty in a high developed degree. I shall be astonished if it turns out to be a new kind of parrot; and yet I ought not to be astonished, for it has already been everything else it could think of since those first days when it was a fish. The new one is as ugly as the old one was at first; has the same sulphur-and-raw-meat complexion and the same singular head without any fur on it. She calls it Abel.

*Ten Years Later.*—They are *boys*; we found it out long ago. It was their coming in that small immature shape that puzzled us; we were not used to it. There are some girls now. Abel is a good boy, but if Cain had stayed a bear it would have improved him. After all these years, I see that I was mistaken about Eve in the beginning; it is better to live outside the Garden with her than inside it without her. At first I thought she talked too much; but now I should be sorry to have that voice fall silent and pass out of my life. Blessed be the chestnut that brought us near together and taught me to know the goodness of her heart and the sweetness of her spirit!

# EVE'S DIARY

Translated from the Original

*Saturday.*—I am almost a whole day old, now. I arrived yesterday. That is as it seems to me. And it must be so, for if there was a day-before-yesterday I was not there when it happened, or I should remember it. It could be, of course, that it did happen, and that I was not noticing. Very well; I will be very watchful now, and if any day-before-yesterdays happen I will make a note of it. It will be best to start right and not let the record get confused, for some instinct tells me that these details are going to be important to the historian some day. For I feel like an experiment, I feel exactly like an experiment; it would be impossible for a person to feel more like an experiment than I do, and so I am coming to feel convinced that that is what I *am*—an experiment; just an experiment, and nothing more.

Then if I am an experiment, am I the whole of it? No, I think not; I think the rest of it is part of it. I am the main part of it, but I think the rest of it has its share in the matter. Is my position assured, or do I have to watch it and take care of it? The latter, perhaps. Some instinct tells me that eternal vigilance is the price of supremacy. (That is a good phrase, I think, for one so young.)

Everything looks better today than it did yesterday. In the rush of finishing up yesterday, the mountains were left in a ragged condition, and some of the plains were so cluttered with rubbish and remnants that the aspects were quite distressing. Noble and beautiful works of art should not be subjected to haste; and this majestic new world is indeed a most noble and beautiful work. And certainly marvelously near to being perfect, notwithstanding the shortness of the time. There are too many stars in some places and not enough in others, but that can be remedied presently, no doubt. The moon got loose last night, and slid down and fell out of the scheme—a very great loss; it breaks my heart to think of it. There isn't another thing among the ornaments and decorations that is comparable to it for beauty and finish. It should have been fastened better. If we can only get it back again—

But of course there is no telling where it went to. And besides, whoever gets it will hide it; I know it because I would do it myself. I believe I can be honest in all other matters, but I already begin to realize that the core and center of my nature is love of the beautiful, a passion for the beautiful, and that it would not be safe to trust me with a moon that belonged to another person and that person didn't know I had it. I could give up a moon that I found in the daytime, because I should be afraid some one was looking; but if I found it in the dark, I am sure I should find some kind of an excuse for not saying anything about it. For I do love moons, they are so pretty and so romantic. I wish we had five or six; I would never go to bed; I should never get tired lying on the moss-bank and looking up at them.

Stars are good, too. I wish I could get some to put in my hair. But I suppose I never can. You would be surprised to find how far off they are, for they do not look it. When they first showed, last night, I tried to knock some down with a pole, but it didn't reach, which astonished me; then I tried clods till I was all tired out, but I never got one. It was because I am left-handed and cannot throw good. Even when I aimed at the one I wasn't after I couldn't hit the other one, though I did make some close shots, for I saw the black blot of the clod sail right into the midst of the golden clusters forty or fifty times, just barely missing them, and if I could have held out a little longer maybe I could have got one.

So I cried a little, which was natural, I suppose, for one of my age, and after I was rested I got a basket and started for a place on the extreme rim of the circle, where the stars were close to the ground and I could get them with my hands, which would be better, anyway, because I could gather them tenderly then, and not break them. But it was farther than I thought, and at last I had to give it up; I was so tired I couldn't drag my feet another step; and besides, they were sore and hurt me very much.

I couldn't get back home; it was too far and turning cold; but I found some tigers and nestled in among them and was most adorably comfortable, and their breath was sweet and pleasant, because they live on strawberries. I had never seen a tiger before, but I knew them in a minute by the stripes. If I could have one of those skins, it would make a lovely gown.

Today I am getting better ideas about distances. I was so eager to get hold of every pretty thing that I giddily grabbed for it, sometimes when it was too far off, and sometimes when it was but six inches away but seemed a foot— alas, with thorns between! I learned a lesson; also I made an axiom, all out of my own head—my very first one; *The scratched Experiment shuns the thorn.* I think it is a very good one for one so young.

I followed the other Experiment around, yesterday afternoon, at a distance, to see what it might be for, if I could. But I was not able to make out. I think it is a man. I had never seen a man, but it looked like one, and I feel sure that that is what it is. I realize that I feel more curiosity about it than about any of the other reptiles. If it is a reptile, and I suppose it is; for it has frowzy hair and blue eyes, and looks like a reptile. It has no hips; it tapers like a carrot; when it stands, it spreads itself apart like a derrick; so I think it is a reptile, though it may be architecture.

I was afraid of it at first, and started to run every time it turned around, for I thought it was going to chase me; but by and by I found it was only trying to get away, so after that I was not timid any more, but tracked it along, several hours, about twenty yards behind, which made it nervous and unhappy. At last it was a good deal worried, and climbed a tree. I waited a good while, then gave it up and went home.

Today the same thing over. I've got it up the tree again.

*Sunday.*—It is up there yet. Resting, apparently. But that is a subterfuge: Sunday isn't the day of rest; Saturday is appointed for that. It looks to me like a creature that is more interested in resting than it anything else. It would tire me to rest so much. It tires me just to sit around and watch the tree. I do wonder what it is for; I never see it do anything.

They returned the moon last night, and I was *so* happy! I think it is very honest of them. It slid down and fell off again, but I was not distressed; there is no need to worry when one has that kind of neighbors; they will fetch it back. I wish I could do something to show my appreciation. I would like to send them some stars, for we have more than we can use. I mean I, not we, for I can see that the reptile cares nothing for such things.

It has low tastes, and is not kind. When I went there yesterday evening in the gloaming it had crept down and was trying to catch the little speckled fishes that play in the pool, and I had to clod it to make it go up the tree again and let them alone. I wonder if *that* is what it is for? Hasn't it any heart? Hasn't it any compassion for those little creature? Can it be that it was designed and manufactured for such ungentle work? It has the look of it. One of the clods took it back of the ear, and it used language. It gave me a thrill, for it was the first time I had ever heard speech, except my own. I did not understand the words, but they seemed expressive.

When I found it could talk I felt a new interest in it, for I love to talk; I talk, all day, and in my sleep, too, and I am very interesting, but if I had another to talk to I could be twice as interesting, and would never stop, if desired.

If this reptile is a man, it isn't an *it*, is it? That wouldn't be grammatical, would it? I think it would be *he*. I think so. In that case one would parse it thus: nominative, *he*; dative, *him*; possessive, *his'n*. Well, I will consider it a man and call it he until it turns out to be something else. This will be handier than having so many uncertainties.

*Next Week Sunday.*—All the week I tagged around after him and tried to get acquainted. I had to do the talking, because he was shy, but I didn't mind it. He seemed pleased to have me around, and I used the sociable "we" a good deal, because it seemed to flatter him to be included.

*Wednesday.*—We are getting along very well indeed, now, and getting better and better acquainted. He does not try to avoid me any more, which is a good sign, and shows that he likes to have me with him. That pleases me, and I study to be useful to him in every way I can, so as to increase his regard. During the last day or two I have taken all the work of naming things off his hands, and this has been a great relief to him, for he has no gift in that line, and is evidently very grateful. He can't think of a rational name to save him, but I do not let him see that I am aware of his defect. Whenever a new creature comes along I name it before he has time to expose himself by an awkward silence. In this way I have saved him many embarrassments. I have no defect like this. The minute I set eyes on an animal I know what it is. I don't have to reflect a moment; the right name comes out instantly, just as if it were an inspiration, as no doubt it is, for I am sure it wasn't in me half a minute before. I seem to know just by the shape of the creature and the way it acts what animal it is.

When the dodo came along he thought it was a wildcat—I saw it in his eye. But I saved him. And I was careful not to do it in a way that could hurt his pride. I just spoke up in a quite natural way of pleasing surprise, and not as if I was dreaming of conveying information, and said, "Well, I do declare, if there isn't the dodo!" I explained—without seeming to be explaining—how I know it for a dodo, and although I thought maybe he was a little piqued that I knew the creature when he didn't, it was quite evident that he admired me. That was very agreeable, and I thought of it more than once with gratification before I slept. How little a thing can make us happy when we feel that we have earned it!

*Thursday.*—my first sorrow. Yesterday he avoided me and seemed to wish I would not talk to him. I could not believe it, and thought there was some mistake, for I loved to be with him, and loved to hear him talk, and so how could it be that he could feel unkind toward me when I had not done anything? But at last it seemed true, so I went away and sat lonely in the place where I first saw him the morning that we were made and I did not know what he was and was indifferent about him; but now it was a mournful place, and every little thing spoke of him, and my heart was very sore. I did not know why very clearly, for it was a new feeling; I had not experienced it before, and it was all a mystery, and I could not make it out.

But when night came I could not bear the lonesomeness, and went to the new shelter which he has built, to ask him what I had done that was wrong and how I could mend it and get back his kindness again; but he put me out in the rain, and it was my first sorrow.

*Sunday.*—It is pleasant again, now, and I am happy; but those were heavy days; I do not think of them when I can help it.

I tried to get him some of those apples, but I cannot learn to throw straight. I failed, but I think the good intention pleased him. They are forbidden, and he says I shall come to harm; but so I come to harm through pleasing him, why shall I care for that harm?

*Monday.*—This morning I told him my name, hoping it would interest him. But he did not care for it. It is strange. If he should tell me his name, I would care. I think it would be pleasanter in my ears than any other sound.

He talks very little. Perhaps it is because he is not bright, and is sensitive about it and wishes to conceal it. It is such a pity that he should feel so, for brightness is nothing; it is in the heart that the values lie. I wish I could make him understand that a loving good heart is riches, and riches enough, and that without it intellect is poverty.

Although he talks so little, he has quite a considerable vocabulary. This morning he used a surprisingly good word. He evidently recognized, himself, that it was a good one, for he worked it in twice afterward, casually. It was good casual art, still it showed that he possesses a certain quality of perception. Without a doubt that seed can be made to grow, if cultivated.

Where did he get that word? I do not think I have ever used it.

No, he took no interest in my name. I tried to hide my disappointment, but I suppose I did not succeed. I went away and sat on the moss-bank with my feet in the water. It is where I go when I hunger for companionship, some one to look at, some one to talk to. It is not enough—that lovely white body painted there in the pool—but it is something, and something is better than utter loneliness. It talks when I talk; it is sad when I am sad; it comforts me with its sympathy; it says, "Do not be downhearted, you poor friendless girl; I will be your friend." It *is* a good friend to me, and my only one; it is my sister.

That first time that she forsook me! ah, I shall never forget that—never, never. My heart was lead in my body! I said, "She was all I had, and now she is gone!" In my despair I said, "Break, my heart; I cannot bear my life any more!" and hid my face in my hands, and there was no solace for me. And when I took them away, after a little, there she was again, white and shining and beautiful, and I sprang into her arms!

That was perfect happiness; I had known happiness before, but it was not like this, which was ecstasy. I never doubted her afterward. Sometimes she stayed away—maybe an hour, maybe almost the whole day, but I waited and did not doubt; I said, "She is busy, or she is gone on a journey, but she will come." And it was so: she always did. At night she would not come if it was dark, for she was a timid little thing; but if there was a moon she would come. I am not afraid of the dark, but she is younger than I am; she was born after I was. Many and many are the visits I have paid her; she is my comfort and my refuge when my life is hard—and it is mainly that.

*Tuesday.*—All the morning I was at work improving the estate; and I purposely kept away from him in the hope that he would get lonely and come. But he did not.

At noon I stopped for the day and took my recreation by flitting all about with the bees and the butterflies and reveling in the flowers, those beautiful creatures that catch the smile of God out of the sky and preserve it! I gathered them, and made them into wreaths and garlands and clothed myself in them while I ate my luncheon—apples, of course; then I sat in the shade and wished and waited. But he did not come.

But no matter. Nothing would have come of it, for he does not care for flowers. He called them rubbish, and cannot tell one from another, and thinks it is superior to feel like that. He does not care for me, he does not care for flowers, he does not care for the painted sky at eventide—is there anything he does care for, except building shacks to coop himself up in from the good clean rain, and thumping the melons, and sampling the grapes, and fingering the fruit on the trees, to see how those properties are coming along?

I laid a dry stick on the ground and tried to bore a hole in it with another one, in order to carry out a scheme that I had, and soon I got an awful fright. A thin, transparent bluish film rose out of the hole, and I dropped everything and ran! I thought it was a spirit, and I *was* so frightened! But I looked back, and it was not coming; so I leaned against a rock and rested and panted, and let my limbs go on trembling until they got steady again; then I crept warily back, alert, watching, and ready to fly if there was occasion; and when I was come near, I parted the branches of a rose-bush and peeped through—wishing the man was about, I was looking so cunning and pretty—but the sprite was gone. I went there, and there was a pinch of delicate pink dust in the hole. I put my finger in, to feel it, and said *ouch!* and took it out again. It was a cruel pain. I put my finger in my mouth; and by standing first on one foot and then the other, and grunting, I presently eased my misery; then I was full of interest, and began to examine.

I was curious to know what the pink dust was. Suddenly the name of it occurred to me, though I had never heard of it before. It was *fire!* I was as certain of it as a person could be of anything in the world. So without hesitation I named it that—fire.

I had created something that didn't exist before; I had added a new thing to the world's uncountable properties; I realized this, and was proud of my achievement, and was going to run and find him and tell him about it, thinking to raise myself in his esteem—but I reflected, and did not do it. No—he would not care for it. He would ask what it was good for, and what could I answer? for if it was not *good* for something, but only beautiful, merely beautiful— So I sighed, and did not go. For it wasn't good for anything; it could not build a shack, it could not improve melons, it could not hurry a fruit crop; it was useless, it was a foolishness and a vanity; he would despise it and say cutting words. But to me it was not despicable; I said, "Oh, you fire, I love you, you dainty pink creature, for you are *beautiful*—and that is enough!" and was going to gather it to my breast. But refrained. Then I made another maxim out of my head, though it was so nearly like the first one that I was afraid it was only a plagiarism: "*The burnt Experiment shuns the fire.*"

I wrought again; and when I had made a good deal of fire-dust I emptied it into a handful of dry brown grass, intending to carry it home and keep it always and play with it; but the wind struck it and it sprayed up and spat out at me fiercely, and I dropped it and ran. When I looked back the blue spirit was towering up and stretching and rolling away like a cloud, and instantly I thought of the name of it—*smoke!*—though, upon my word, I had never heard of smoke before.

Soon brilliant yellow and red flares shot up through the smoke, and I named them in an instant—*flames*—and I was right, too, though these were the very first flames that had ever been in the world. They climbed the trees, then flashed splendidly in and out of the vast and increasing volume of tumbling smoke, and I had to clap my hands and laugh and dance in my rapture, it was so new and strange and so wonderful and so beautiful!

He came running, and stopped and gazed, and said not a word for many minutes. Then he asked what it was. Ah, it was too bad that he should ask such a direct question. I had to answer it, of course, and I did. I said it was fire. If it annoyed him that I should know and he must ask; that was not my fault; I had no desire to annoy him. After a pause he asked:

"How did it come?"

Another direct question, and it also had to have a direct answer.

"I made it."

The fire was traveling farther and farther off. He went to the edge of the burned place and stood looking down, and said:

"What are these?"

"Fire-coals."

He picked up one to examine it, but changed his mind and put it down again. Then he went away. *Nothing* interests him.

But I was interested. There were ashes, gray and soft and delicate and pretty—I knew what they were at once. And the embers; I knew the embers, too. I found my apples, and raked them out, and was glad; for I am very young and my appetite is active. But I was disappointed; they were all burst open and spoiled. Spoiled apparently; but it was not so; they were better than raw ones. Fire is beautiful; some day it will be useful, I think.

*Friday.*—I saw him again, for a moment, last Monday at nightfall, but only for a moment. I was hoping he would praise me for trying to improve the estate, for I had meant well and had worked hard. But he was not pleased, and turned away and left me. He was also displeased on another account: I tried once more to persuade him to stop going over the Falls. That was because the fire had revealed to me a new passion—quite new, and distinctly different from love, grief, and those others which I had already discovered—*fear*. And it is horrible!—I wish I had never discovered it; it gives me dark moments, it spoils my happiness, it makes me shiver and tremble and shudder. But I could not persuade him, for he has not discovered fear yet, and so he could not understand me.

# EXTRACT FROM ADAM'S DIARY

Perhaps I ought to remember that she is very young, a mere girl and make allowances. She is all interest, eagerness, vivacity, the world is to her a charm, a wonder, a mystery, a joy; she can't speak for delight when she finds a new flower, she must pet it and caress it and smell it and talk to it, and pour out endearing names upon it. And she is color-mad: brown rocks, yellow sand, gray moss, green foliage, blue sky; the pearl of the dawn, the purple shadows on the mountains, the golden islands floating in crimson seas at sunset, the pallid moon sailing through the shredded cloud-rack, the star-jewels glittering in the wastes of space—none of them is of any practical value, so far as I can see, but because they have color and majesty, that is enough for her, and she loses her mind over them. If she could quiet down and keep still a couple minutes at a time, it would be a reposeful spectacle. In that case I think I could enjoy looking at her; indeed I am sure I could, for I am coming to realize that she is a quite remarkably comely creature—lithe, slender, trim, rounded, shapely, nimble, graceful; and once when she was standing marble-white and sun-drenched on a boulder, with her young head tilted back and her hand shading her eyes, watching the flight of a bird in the sky, I recognized that she was beautiful.

*Monday Noon.*—If there is anything on the planet that she is not interested in it is not in my list. There are animals that I am indifferent to, but it is not so with her. She has no discrimination, she takes to all of them, she thinks they are all treasures, every new one is welcome.

When the mighty brontosaurus came striding into camp, she regarded it as an acquisition, I considered it a calamity; that is a good sample of the lack of harmony that prevails in our views of things. She wanted to domesticate it, I wanted to make it a present of the homestead and move out. She believed it could be tamed by kind treatment and would be a good pet; I said a pet twenty-one feet high and eighty-four feet long would be no proper thing to have about the place, because, even with the best intentions and without meaning any harm, it could sit down on the house and mash it, for any one could see by the look of its eye that it was absent-minded.

Still, her heart was set upon having that monster, and she couldn't give it up. She thought we could start a dairy with it, and wanted me to help milk it; but I wouldn't; it was too risky. The sex wasn't right, and we hadn't any ladder anyway. Then she wanted to ride it, and look at the scenery. Thirty or forty feet of its tail was lying on the ground, like a fallen tree, and she thought she could climb it, but she was mistaken; when she got to the steep place it was too slick and down she came, and would have hurt herself but for me.

Was she satisfied now? No. Nothing ever satisfies her but demonstration; untested theories are not in her line, and she won't have them. It is the right spirit, I concede it; it attracts me; I feel the influence of it; if I were with her more I think I should take it up myself. Well, she had one theory remaining about this colossus: she thought that if we could tame it and make him friendly we could stand in the river and use him for a bridge. It turned out that he was already plenty tame enough—at least as far as she was concerned—so she tried her theory, but it failed: every time she got him properly placed in the river and went ashore to cross over him, he came out and followed her around like a pet mountain. Like the other animals. They all do that.

*Friday.*—Tuesday—Wednesday—Thursday—and today: all without seeing him. It is a long time to be alone; still, it is better to be alone than unwelcome.

I *had* to have company—I was made for it, I think—so I made friends with the animals. They are just charming, and they have the kindest disposition and the politest ways; they never look sour, they never let you feel that you are intruding, they smile at you and wag their tail, if they've got one, and they are always ready for a romp or an excursion or anything you want to propose. I think they are perfect gentlemen. All these days we have had such good times, and it hasn't been lonesome for me, ever. Lonesome! No, I should say not. Why, there's always a swarm of them around—sometimes as much as four or five acres—you can't count them; and when you stand on a rock in the midst and look out over the furry expanse it is so mottled and splashed and gay with color and frisking sheen and sun-flash, and so rippled with stripes, that you might think it was a lake, only you know it isn't; and there's storms of sociable birds, and hurricanes of whirring wings; and when the sun strikes all that feathery commotion, you have a blazing up of all the colors you can think of, enough to put your eyes out.

We have made long excursions, and I have seen a great deal of the world; almost all of it, I think; and so I am the first traveler, and the only one. When we are on the march, it is an imposing sight—there's nothing like it anywhere. For comfort I ride a tiger or a leopard, because it is soft and has a round back that fits me, and because they are such pretty animals; but for long distance or for scenery I ride the elephant. He hoists me up with his trunk, but I can get off myself; when we are ready to camp, he sits and I slide down the back way.

The birds and animals are all friendly to each other, and there are no disputes about anything. They all talk, and they all talk to me, but it must be a foreign language, for I cannot make out a word they say; yet they often understand me when I talk back, particularly the dog and the elephant. It makes me ashamed. It shows that they are brighter than I am, for I want to be the principal Experiment myself—and I intend to be, too.

I have learned a number of things, and am educated, now, but I wasn't at first. I was ignorant at first. At first it used to vex me because, with all my watching, I was never smart enough to be around when the water was running uphill; but now I do not mind it. I have experimented and experimented until now I know it never does run uphill, except in the dark. I know it does in the dark, because the pool never goes dry, which it would, of course, if the water didn't come back in the night. It is best to prove things by actual experiment; then you *know*; whereas if you depend on guessing and supposing and conjecturing, you never get educated.

Some things you *can't* find out; but you will never know you can't by guessing and supposing: no, you have to be patient and go on experimenting until you find out that you can't find out. And it is delightful to have it that way, it makes the world so interesting. If there wasn't anything to find out, it would be dull. Even trying to find out and not finding out is just as interesting as trying to find out and finding out, and I don't know but more so. The secret of the water was a treasure until I *got* it; then the excitement all went away, and I recognized a sense of loss.

By experiment I know that wood swims, and dry leaves, and feathers, and plenty of other things; therefore by all that cumulative evidence you know that a rock will swim; but you have to put up with simply knowing it, for there isn't any way to prove it—up to now. But I shall find a way—then *that* excitement will go. Such things make me sad; because by and by when I have found out everything there won't be any more excitements, and I do love excitements so! The other night I couldn't sleep for thinking about it.

At first I couldn't make out what I was made for, but now I think it was to search out the secrets of this wonderful world and be happy and thank the Giver of it all for devising it. I think there are many things to learn yet—I hope so; and by economizing and not hurrying too fast I think they will last weeks and weeks. I hope so. When you cast up a feather it sails away on the air and goes out of sight; then you throw up a clod and it doesn't. It comes down, every time. I have tried it and tried it, and it is always so. I wonder why it is? Of course it *doesn't* come down, but why should it *seem* to? I suppose it is an optical illusion. I mean, one of them is. I don't know which one. It may be the feather, it may be the clod; I can't prove which it is, I can only demonstrate that one or the other is a fake, and let a person take his choice.

By watching, I know that the stars are not going to last. I have seen some of the best ones melt and run down the sky. Since one can melt, they can all melt; since they can all melt, they can all melt the same night. That sorrow will come—I know it. I mean to sit up every night and look at them as long as I can keep awake; and I will impress those sparkling fields on my memory, so that by and by when they are taken away I can by my fancy restore those lovely myriads to the black sky and make them sparkle again, and double them by the blur of my tears.

*After the Fall*

When I look back, the Garden is a dream to me. It was beautiful, surpassingly beautiful, enchantingly beautiful; and now it is lost, and I shall not see it any more.

The Garden is lost, but I have found *him*, and am content. He loves me as well as he can; I love him with all the strength of my passionate nature, and this, I think, is proper to my youth and sex. If I ask myself why I love him, I find I do not know, and do not really much care to know; so I suppose that this kind of love is not a product of reasoning and statistics, like one's love for other reptiles and animals. I think that this must be so. I love certain birds because of their song; but I do not love Adam on account of his singing—no, it is not that; the more he sings the more I do not get reconciled to it. Yet I ask him to sing, because I wish to learn to like everything he is interested in. I am sure I can learn, because at first I could not stand it, but now I can. It sours the milk, but it doesn't matter; I can get used to that kind of milk.

It is not on account of his brightness that I love him—no, it is not that. He is not to blame for his brightness, such as it is, for he did not make it himself; he is as God make him, and that is sufficient. There was a wise purpose in it, *that* I know. In time it will develop, though I think it will not be sudden; and besides, there is no hurry; he is well enough just as he is.

It is not on account of his gracious and considerate ways and his delicacy that I love him. No, he has lacks in this regard, but he is well enough just so, and is improving.

It is not on account of his industry that I love him—no, it is not that. I think he has it in him, and I do not know why he conceals it from me. It is my only pain. Otherwise he is frank and open with me, now. I am sure he keeps nothing from me but this. It grieves me that he should have a secret from me, and sometimes it spoils my sleep, thinking of it, but I will put it out of my mind; it shall not trouble my happiness, which is otherwise full to overflowing.

It is not on account of his education that I love him—no, it is not that. He is self-educated, and does really know a multitude of things, but they are not so.

It is not on account of his chivalry that I love him—no, it is not that. He told on me, but I do not blame him; it is a peculiarity of sex, I think, and he did not make his sex. Of course I would not have told on him, I would have perished first; but that is a peculiarity of sex, too, and I do not take credit for it, for I did not make my sex.

Then why is it that I love him? *Merely because he is masculine*, I think.

At bottom he is good, and I love him for that, but I could love him without it. If he should beat me and abuse me, I should go on loving him. I know it. It is a matter of sex, I think.

He is strong and handsome, and I love him for that, and I admire him and am proud of him, but I could love him without those qualities. If he were plain, I should love him; if he were a wreck, I should love him; and I would work for him, and slave over him, and pray for him, and watch by his bedside until I died.

Yes, I think I love him merely because he is *mine* and is *masculine*. There is no other reason, I suppose. And so I think it is as I first said: that this kind of love is not a product of reasonings and statistics. It just *comes*—none knows whence—and cannot explain itself. And doesn't need to.

It is what I think. But I am only a girl, the first that has examined this matter, and it may turn out that in my ignorance and inexperience I have not got it right.

*Forty Years Later*

It is my prayer, it is my longing, that we may pass from this life together—a longing which shall never perish from the earth, but shall have place in the heart of every wife that loves, until the end of time; and it shall be called by my name.

But if one of us must go first, it is my prayer that it shall be I; for he is strong, I am weak, I am not so necessary to him as he is to me—life without him would not be life; now could I endure it? This prayer is also immortal, and will not cease from being offered up while my race continues. I am the first wife; and in the last wife I shall be repeated.

At Eve's Grave

Adam: Wheresoever she was, there was Eden.


The End

Visit us on the Web

## Piccadilly Books, Ltd.
www.piccadillybooks.com

CPSIA information can be obtained
at www.ICGtesting.com
Printed in the USA
LVHW012004220920
666820LV00006B/276